RHYANNON BYRD
EDGE *of* DANGER

HQN™

Recycling programs
for this product may
not exist in your area.

ISBN-13: 978-0-373-77399-2
ISBN-10:   0-373-77399-4

EDGE OF DANGER

www.HQNBooks.com

Printed in U.S.A.

Dear Reader,

I'm thrilled to present *Edge of Danger,* the second book in my new PRIMAL INSTINCT series with HQN Books. Set within a world where paranormal creatures live hidden among an unknowing humanity, this provocative trilogy continues with the story of Saige Buchanan and the dark, devastatingly sexy shape-shifter who steals her heart.

Michael Quinn is a hero who refuses to forget his past…or to risk his future. And yet the instant he sets eyes on Saige in a crowded Brazilian bar, he wants her with a relentless hunger that's impossible to deny. But Saige has fears of her own. To get what he wants, Quinn must conquer not only his own demons, but those of the wary, tempestuous Buchanan, as well.

I'm so excited to be sharing Quinn and Saige's wickedly seductive romance with you, and I hope it will be one that truly touches your heart!

All the best,

Rhyannon

To my amazing editor, Ann Leslie Tuttle, without whom none of this would have been possible. Endless thanks for the wonderful guidance, support and insight.
You're helping me to grow so much as an author and I'm so incredibly lucky to be working with you!

EDGE *of* DANGER

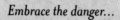

Embrace the danger...

CHAPTER ONE

Embrace the danger....

Thursday evening
The Amazon

IF THE WOMAN was trying to blend in, she wasn't very good at it. It'd taken Michael Quinn no more than five seconds to pick her out in the dim, crowded interior of *O Diablo Dos Ángels,* a rickety roadside *barra* in the bustling market town of Coroza, Brazil. He'd been traveling for two days now, working his way through the stifling, humid depths of the Amazonian rain forest, and it showed in his haggard appearance. Two days that felt more like weeks, each passing hour grating against his nerves like a rusty nail, until he was in what could only be classified as a category-five, off-the-Richter-scale, completely uncharacteristic foul mood.

Not that he was usually cheery. Normally Quinn just...existed. It'd been years since anything, or anyone, had managed to touch him or throw him off his firm, even keel—and now this. He couldn't explain it, but from the moment he'd been given Saige

Buchanan's photograph, his cool, steady calm had begun to fade, slipping away from him like water spiraling slowly down a drain. And in its wake, he'd been left with this seething intensity…this gripping tension.

What made it even worse was the fact that Quinn hadn't even wanted the assignment—had, in fact, been adamant in his refusal. And yet, here he was, with his damp shirt sticking to his skin, the heavy scent of tobacco and sweat making his head hurt, while something piercing and uncomfortably sharp slithered through his system at the sight of his prey.

Huh. So this is little Saige, he thought, moving along the wall, away from the door, careful to avoid her line of sight as she sat at a small table on the far side of the room, a bottle of water held in one delicate hand. At her side sat a young man who couldn't have been more than nineteen, his dark skin, hair and eyes attesting to his Brazilian heritage. The boy's lips were moving, and though Quinn's hearing was far better than a human's, he couldn't make out the words over the raucous cacophony of sound coming from the crowd.

It seemed a strange setting for an American woman and her young companion, and yet, no one bothered them. Not even the drunks. Was she a regular, then? Under the owner's protection? Or was there some other reason the locals kept their distance?

Whatever the answer, it couldn't be from lack of notice. Saige Buchanan stood out among the weathered patrons like a neon sign in the midnight pitch of night, glittering and bright.

Quinn rubbed his palm against the scratchy growth of stubble that came from going several days without a shave, then slowly shook his head, already revising his analogy. No, the reportedly brilliant anthropologist wasn't brash or bold, like neon. As bright as she shone, there was a soft, almost tender aura about her, which probably made her stick out even more than that angelic face, lush body or unusual shade of hair. Neither red nor brown, it hovered somewhere in between, picking up the soft, hazy glow of light that spilled down from above, struggling against the lengthening evening shadows.

A heavy wooden door suddenly slammed behind the bar and Quinn locked his jaw, marveling that the ramshackle structure didn't crumble down around them in a pile of mortar and bricks. Flicking a quick glance upward, he was surprised the stained ceiling actually managed to remain in place, even with the various thick support beams wedged between it and the sawdust-covered floor. Without a doubt, this place made him uncomfortable. He didn't like being closed in, confined, preferring the outdoors and the endless freedom of the sky.

And why don't you stop moaning and just get on with it? The sooner you get your hands on her, the sooner you can get out of here.

Sound words, and yet, now that he'd found her, the last thing on earth Quinn wanted to do was touch her—to get his hands on her. Not that he was concerned he couldn't handle her if she decided to be difficult. Saige Buchanan may have been *more* than an average human female, but then he was hardly an average man. He could scent that her Merrick had yet to fully awaken—and until it did, he would be able to retain the upper hand when it came to physical strength.

Later, *after* her awakening…well, he'd never gone head-to-head with a Merrick female before, but he sure as hell hoped she wouldn't be able to kick his ass. If that ever happened, his friends back at the compound would never let him live it down.

As a member of the Watchmen, an organization of shape-shifters whose duty it was to watch over the remaining bloodlines of the original ancient clans, Quinn had been taught a little about the Merrick, once one of the most powerful nonhuman species to walk the earth. And since the crap that had recently gone down with Saige's older brother, Ian Buchanan, he now knew even more. But Saige was…different. Unlike her brother, who experienced certain physical changes when the Merrick blood in his veins rose to the surface of his body, it was believed that Merrick females, while gaining in strength and agility and heightened senses, didn't change in appearance. She wouldn't sport talons on the tips of her delicate fingers. Wouldn't bulk up with thick, massive muscles. And her nose wouldn't alter its dainty, feminine shape.

But you're forgetting the fangs.

Ahh, right. Evidently, that was one of the changes the Merrick women *did* experience, in order to feed the primitive parts of their nature. Lifting his hand, Quinn rubbed at an odd tingle on the side of his neck, as if he could already feel the pleasure-pain of Saige

Buchanan sinking her pearly whites into his flesh,
taking the hot wash of his blood into her mouth, at the
same time she took him deep into her body.

Whoa...

Scowling, he lowered his hand, fingers curling into
a tight fist, and wondered what was wrong with him.
Had the heat gone to his head? Had going without sex
addled his brain? Or was he truly losing his mind?

Leaning his elbow against the small counter built
into the side wall of the bar, Quinn shook off the irritating thoughts and signaled a stout, middle-aged
woman who roamed the room with a tray, delivering
drinks while she chatted with the customers. As she
stepped closer, he could read the name *Inez* embroi-
dered onto her apron, and despite the friendly way
she'd handled the crowd, she leveled a cold, chilling
look at him. Her dark eyes were wary now, and as they
slowly inspected him from his scarred boots, up over
his dirt-streaked jeans and damp black T-shirt, he said,
"Uma cerveja, por favor."

"Tell me," she replied in heavily accented English,
the corners of her wide mouth pinched with suspicion. "Why do you watch our Saige like you are
hungry?"

Quinn locked his jaw, angry that he'd revealed the
focus of his attention to those watching him.

"Well?" she persisted with an air of command that
made him suspect she was more than a barmaid.

"No idea what you're talking about," he countered
in a low, graveled voice, returning her hard stare.
When it was obvious he wasn't going to back down,

she muttered under her breath and turned around, making her way back to the bar.

Mentally kicking himself in the ass, Quinn purposefully withdrew his attention from the American and looked around the *barra*. In a strange way, he felt as though he'd walked onto a movie set. It was that surreal, complete with braying donkey outside the front door, the veil of smoke from cigarettes and cigars so thick you could all but slice it with a knife. The only thing that made it bearable was Saige. Her scent wrapped around him like a soft, clinging vine, enticing and warm and sweetly addictive. It was like…like a rain shower, refreshing and clean, washing away the suffocating grime. It even eased the tension he felt at being in such a crowded, noisy, closed-in space. With a conscious effort, Quinn focused on that mouthwatering scent, drawing more of it into his lungs, desperate to block out the rest of his surroundings.

Unable to help himself, his gaze slid back to Saige, greedily soaking up the visual details, hungry for the data. For the way her wavy hair fell around the delicate angles of her face. That impish sprinkle of freckles and the lush shape of her provocative mouth as she spoke with the young Brazilian.

Even without the photograph tucked into his back pocket, Quinn knew he'd have recognized her the second he set eyes on her. Though her coloring was fairer than her brothers', her feminine frame slight compared to their brawny strength, she still bore the marks of the Buchanan bloodline. Despite the thick smoke that filled the room, he could see the dark, deep

blue of her eyes as if he were sitting at her side. And
there was something about the angle of her jaw that
attested to the Buchanan stubbornness he'd dealt with
on a firsthand basis since meeting her siblings.

The small, tight T-shirt she wore fit her body like a
glove, hugging a pair of lush breasts that were surprising on a frame as slight as hers, and his mouth almost
curved with an appreciative male grin. Just because he
didn't plan to touch, didn't mean he couldn't appreciate the view. The frayed khaki shorts and flannel shirt
tied around her waist did nothing to disguise the
womanly curve of her hips, and Quinn found himself
wondering if her ass would be as enticing as the rest
of her. He guessed her height to be somewhere around
five-six, and though that wasn't overly tall, she looked
smaller, somehow fragile. Still, her muscles were
toned beneath the peaches-and-cream complexion,
testament to the fact that she lived a physical life. She
probably spent her time crawling in and out of archae-
ological digs, climbing up the treacherous sides of
mountains, traipsing through the rain forest—all
places where a fey little creature like herself didn't
belong.

The corner of Quinn's mouth twitched as he pondered her reaction to that chauvinistic observation.
The impudent set of her chin told him that Saige
Buchanan was the kind of woman who went where she
wanted, when she wanted, her safety and the opinion
of others be damned.

The boy said something, smiling at her, and she
reached out, ruffling his thick black hair with an easy

camaraderie that spoke of friendship. Of closeness. Quinn's eyes narrowed, and he about jumped out of his skin when the serving woman, Inez, came up behind him, smacking his beer bottle down on the counter. She muttered under her breath some more as she stomped away, and he grabbed the bottle, taking a long swallow of the lukewarm beer, while silently lecturing himself.

Wiping the back of his wrist over his mouth, he grimaced, thinking it was impossible that he could be jealous of a kid. It was moronic to think he could be jealous at all. Jealousy stank of possession, and he gritted his teeth, unwilling to go down *that* particular road.

Still, Saige was his responsibility until he delivered her safely to Ravenswing, a Watchman compound in Colorado and Quinn's home, where her two brothers were waiting for her. He knew the Buchanans hadn't wanted one of the Watchmen alone with their baby sister, just as he knew Kierland Scott, his best friend and unofficial leader of their unit, would have assured the Merrick that they had nothing to fear from him. From the others, yeah—but not from Quinn. His bed partners, when he needed sex, were always ones he was never likely to run into again, which meant soon-to-be housemates were off-limits.

Rolling his shoulder in a hard, irritated gesture, Quinn focused his thoughts back on the task that lay ahead of him. He needed to get her home, in one piece, and it wouldn't be easy. A Merrick female was going to be considered easy pickings by those who were hunting her. He and the Watchmen had hoped that

Riley Buchanan, the middle son, would awaken before his sister, but now that he'd set eyes on Saige, Quinn knew that wasn't going to be the case. He could scent the coming change in her, the awakening of her ancient bloodline, and though she hadn't fully awakened *yet*, it was on its way.

Which meant that a newly liberated Casus was most likely already onto her, and Quinn's job had just gone from dangerous…to deadly. Though there was still so much they didn't understand, it was firmly believed that the Merrick awakenings were triggered by the presence of the Casus, a race of preternatural monsters who preyed upon the Merrick, feeding from their flesh for power, as well as revenge. The immortal Casus, who'd been imprisoned for centuries for their indiscriminate killing sprees, had finally discovered a way to escape from their holding ground back to this realm. And though their numbers were still small, Quinn and his fellow Watchmen feared what was to come.

Taking another long swallow of beer, he watched Saige from beneath hooded eyes, wondering how much she knew. What was she doing in South America? Did she know the Casus were hunting her? And where the hell was Paul Templeton?

Templeton was the Watchman who'd been assigned to Saige for the past several months, but when they'd put in the call for him to bring her back to America, there'd been no response. Either Templeton had gone AWOL, which no one believed, or he was already a casualty of what was set to become a war of deadly proportions.

Circumstances being what they were—which was

about a mile deep in shit and sinking fast—Quinn knew he didn't have any choice but to move as quickly as possible. He needed to act. Now. But something kept him back. Kept his ass planted against the rickety counter, his body vibing with a hot, angry restlessness.

When someone accidentally knocked over a chair, Saige turned toward the sound, angling her head to the side, revealing the vulnerable length of her throat. It was at that moment that hungers too long restrained stretched to awareness within Quinn, the animal side of his nature blinking its eyes open to a lazy, danger-ous, smoldering fire. He didn't take blood in the way that a Merrick did, but he still longed to clamp his teeth onto that tender, provocative part of her, while sending himself as deep into her as he could get.

As if she felt the press of his stare on that pale, feminine curve of flesh, she lifted her hand to the side of her neck. Then she suddenly twisted in her chair, scanning the room, and Quinn quickly turned toward the wall, giving her his back. His fingers clenched around the bottle, nearly shattering the glass in his grip.

Had he gone out of his mind? All hell was about to break loose, and here he was nursing a warm beer, with a raging case of lust that could only land him in trouble. He didn't have time for this crap.

Stop stalling, damn it, and get on with it.

Turning purposefully back toward the room, he watched as she said something to the boy and stood up, making her way to the bar. She was talking to the short, smiling man behind the counter as Quinn moved to her side, draining the last of his beer. The second she turned and caught him in that deep, dark blue stare, the color as fascinating as the luminous perfection of her skin, he knew he'd been marked.

Quinn set his empty beer bottle down on the counter, preparing to introduce himself, when she reached for it. He wondered what she was doing as her fingers closed around the thick green glass, her expression instantly shifting from wary unease to full-blown panic. Then, before he could even guess her intention, she suddenly hurled the bottle at his head. The glass cracked against the edge of his right eyebrow, splitting the skin, the hot wash of blood flooding his vision.

Son of a bitch.

She immediately started running, shouting something in Portuguese to the boy, who took off past Quinn, out the front door. Moving in the opposite direction, Saige hefted the backpack she'd grabbed from the table onto her shoulder and pushed her way out the back exit, disappearing into what Quinn knew was the jungle.

Swearing, he tossed a wad of bills on the counter and set off after her, hoping to God he could catch her before the fool woman managed to get herself killed.

As he ran out of the bar, into the humid warmth of the evening, the air thick and damp against his skin, the last watery threads of sunlight began fading beneath the heavy weight of night. Quinn followed her scent, dodging the clinging vines of the jungle, his long legs making good time against her shorter strides, but she was fast.

Too fast, he realized in the next moment, as a

strong, noxious odor reached his nose, coming from the same direction Saige was moving.

We're out of time, he thought, gripping his T-shirt and pulling it over his head as he allowed the change to flow over him.

Hell was already there, and she was running straight into its deadly grasp.

CHAPTER TWO

MOVE IT…MOVE IT…MOVE IT.

Saige Buchanan chanted the choppy refrain within her mind again…and again, forcing her legs to keep going, even after the cramping had set in, demanding she stop. Though she'd done her best to sit at the table and act as if nothing was wrong, reality couldn't have been further from the truth. Exhaustion weighed heavily on her shoulders, her nerves so frayed, she felt as if she were unraveling at the seams. Despite the fact she felt safe at the local *barra* that was owned by Inez and her husband, Rubens, who were good friends of hers, Saige knew she shouldn't have risked meeting with Javier Ruiz in such a public place. But she'd needed to go back for the valuable maps she'd stored in Inez's safe before she left for America, and it had been her last chance to see her young employee. In the time he'd worked for her and the other members of the research team at their dig site, Saige had come to think of the cheerful Brazilian as a younger brother, and she hadn't wanted to just disappear without telling him goodbye.

The plan had been so simple. Say her farewells to

her friends, grab the maps, then put herself in plain sight as she headed for the airport in the nearby town of São Vicente. Instead, she'd run without the maps, and for all she knew she might have gotten Javier marked as a target by the dark-haired stranger who'd been watching her with that sharp, penetrating stare. Saige couldn't be certain of who or what the man was, or even what he was after, and she hated the fact that she might have exposed Javier to danger.

Face it, chica. *You screwed up. Big-time.*

A low, choked stream of curses slipped from her lips at the frustrating thought while she shoved the dense jungle foliage out of her way, jumping in mid-stride to avoid a thick tangle of roots, but it was too late to go back and undo her actions. She'd made a mistake, and she was paying the price for it, perhaps even running for her life.

Was the man giving chase a new threat, or was he somehow involved with whatever had been tracking her every move for the past few days, stalking her like a shadow? Saige had felt its malevolent presence almost every hour she'd worked in the jungle, like a low-frequency wave of evil that made her skin crawl. Even now she could have sworn its noxious scent lingered on the evening air, slipping into her pores like a sickness.

Knowing what she did of the gypsy legend that foretold the time when the Casus would escape their holding ground and make their way back to this realm, prompting the awakening of the ancient Merrick bloodlines, Saige couldn't deny the growing veil of terror creeping over her, binding her in its cold, slimy grasp. *Had* the Casus escaped? Had the moment she'd always feared, since hearing the first hazy fragments of the legend from her mother, finally arrived? Fragments that Elaina Buchanan had nearly driven herself insane to uncover, as her obsession with the Merrick had reached a point that even Saige had known was unhealthy—but in her own way, had understood. Fragments Saige herself had spent her life working to piece together. To fully understand.

Or…was the threat merely a mortal one? Had she already become a target of the Collective Army? Saige had no doubt that, once aware of the awakenings, the ruthless human mercenaries devoted to obliterating all preternatural life from the world would do everything they could to destroy the Merrick. All of which meant that until she actually came face-to-face with her enemy, she would be left guessing as to which one had found her first—supernatural monster…or human zealot?

"And where exactly does the guy from the bar fit in?" she grunted under her breath as she hoisted her backpack higher onto her shoulder, her fingers biting into the strap so hard they'd gone numb. Was he after the powerful cross she'd unearthed in the depths of the jungle…or her life? Either scenario seemed likely, and yet, it wasn't ancient weapons or murder she'd seen when she'd touched that empty beer bottle. It had been *sex.* Hard, grinding, explicit images of the two of them together, his mouthwatering body covering her, thrusting savagely between her spread thighs, while he growled her name and she sank a heavy pair of fangs into the side of his strong, corded throat. Her body had writhed beneath his dark, beautiful form, consumed by searing waves of pleasure, and she nearly stumbled as she pressed her left hand low on her belly, against the strange, provocative sense of heaviness that filled her. It was almost as if he were actually a part of her—as if he were, in that moment, driving that thick, heavy part of him deep inside her, igniting a fire that threatened to consume her—and she bit her bottom lip to keep from moaning at the breathtaking sensation. Her temperature spiked, a stinging in her gums unlike anything she'd ever experienced before, the painful cadence of her heart more from the hard, demanding rise of hunger than from fear.

Which means that you've gone stark barking mad! You don't feed from the enemy, you idiot. And that guy sure as hell wasn't your buddy.

Frustrated that she had so little control over the violent, visceral cravings of her Merrick, Saige ground her teeth and focused instead on keeping her body moving as quickly as possible, her speed so much greater than a human's, despite the fact that her awakening had only recently begun. She still looked the same…still sounded the same, but inside…inside she was becoming something so much more than what she'd been. Her senses were sharper, the vivid, breathtaking details of the surrounding jungle swarming her mind with a brilliant, chaotic flood of information. Colors exploded with electrifying focus, her hearing so precise she could detect the nocturnal animals scurrying for shelter in the underbrush.

Certain that she could sense the stranger closing in behind her, Saige pumped her legs with greater force, ignoring the sharp burn of pain in her muscles as she shoved at the thick, damp leaves that crowded in on her. The small, silver compass that she wore around her neck thumped repeatedly against her pounding heart, beneath her sweat-damp shirt, and for a moment she wished that it was the cross, which could supposedly be used as a source of protection for anyone who wore it.

Wincing as the jungle flora scratched against her arms and legs, Saige figured a little protection would have come in handy right about then, but the cross was already gone. After finally uncovering the second Marker's resting place that very morning in the stifling, humid depths of the rain forest, Saige had secretly sent the cross to Colorado in the care of a fellow colleague named Jamison Haley, then purposefully remained behind as a decoy. It'd been a risky move, but she was banking on the expectation that if they *were* out there watching her, the last thing in the world the Casus would expect her to do, after discovering one of the Markers, was separate herself from the powerful talisman.

Which apparently wasn't the smartest move, now was it?

Obviously not. She might have managed to throw them off Jamison's trail, but at the expense of throwing herself into what looked to be one heck of a fire.

"But it's not like you had any choice," she muttered to herself, casting a quick glance over her shoulder before narrowing her gaze back on the darkening forest. Untold dangers lurked in its shadowed depths, her Merrick blood altering her vision, allowing her to see far better than her human eyes had ever done—and yet, she still couldn't say what lay ahead in the coming flood of night. She only knew it was there….

Enemies are coming who will take me from you.

When she'd laid hands upon the mysterious weapon, those were the words its voice had whispered through her mind, eerie and ancient and soft, so unlike the "voices" or "images" she usually picked up. But then her strange little talent for reading physical objects was most often a lark…a fluke. Only in her work did it tend to give her something meaningful. An object unearthed from hundreds of years ago, if not more, revealing its secrets to her as Saige first touched her fingers to its surface.

It was when it came to everyday life that the excitement faded. She would pick up a ketchup bottle in a restaurant and find herself privy to the internal thoughts of the last person who'd held it. *Did I turn the iron off? Are these calories going straight to my thighs? Should I have the ice cream for dessert…or the apple pie?* Hardly earth-shattering revelations, and she'd gotten good at shuffling the mundane facts in and out of her mind, like a revolving door, giving them little notice. Only when touching something from the past did she pay attention—focus and search for more.

Like when she'd found the first elaborately carved

cross—or Dark Marker, as Saige had learned they were called—in Italy last year, and it had told her of its power: that it was one of the ancient weapons meant to destroy her enemies, as well as a source of protection. Saige had been awed by its warmth against her skin, by the beauty of its intricate design, and she'd vowed to search for the others with the use of the maps she'd found wrapped in an oilcloth, buried beside it. Worried that her discovery of the Marker was a portent of things to come, she'd wanted her mother to have the cross's protection, and so she'd left the talisman with Elaina Buchanan while on a trip home to South Carolina. Now that her mother was gone, Saige only hoped the right decision had been made in passing the Marker on to her eldest brother, Ian. Her mother had written a letter asking that the cross be left in Ian's possession, and Saige had found it impossible to ignore Elaina's last wish. Knowing how much Ian had always despised any talk of the Merrick, all she could do was pray that the first Marker wasn't lost…or thrown out, because there was no doubt they were going to need it. Especially now that she knew there were others who wanted the powerful, mysterious weapons.

After hearing the second Marker's chilling words of warning, Saige had known she had to do everything she could to protect it. With the rest of the international research team having headed back to their various home countries the week before, she and Jamison, an archaeologist from London, had been the last remaining members to stay behind, continuing on with her

private search. Over the course of the past year and a
half, Saige had come to know Jamison well, and he
was one of the few of her colleagues she actually considered a friend. Young and studious, the freckle-faced
Brit wasn't exactly a warrior, but what he lacked in
brute strength he more than made up for with brains,
and Saige trusted him implicitly—which was why
she'd entrusted him with her precious find. She would
meet up with him on Tuesday afternoon in Denver, and
then once reunited with the cross, her plan was to
track down her brother Riley and force him to take the
Marker whether he wanted it or not, knowing he could
protect it better than she ever could.

It would have been nice to think that Riley, a county
sheriff in the Rocky Mountains, would invite her to
stay with him, so that they could go through this nightmare together, but Saige had no illusions. She knew
her brothers had loved her in their own way, but her
and Elaina's obsession with the Merrick had driven a
painful wedge between them, a rift that had only
widened as they'd grown older. She hadn't talked to
Ian in years, and even though she still saw Riley from
time to time, their relationship continued to suffer.
They hadn't spoken since Elaina's funeral, nearly six
months ago, but the wounds from their argument were
still fresh in her mind, seeping and raw. He'd called
her obsession with the Merrick a ridiculous waste of
her life, criticizing the dangers she kept subjecting
herself to, traipsing all over the world in search of
answers to a past that they had sure as hell better hope
never touched their lives. Though Saige knew there

was a part of him that believed the stories they'd been raised on, Riley was hardly willing to accept the truth about their bloodline with an open heart. He believed, but he wasn't happy about it, harboring a bitterness that Saige had never shared…nor completely understood. A bitterness that had made his last words to her the most painful of all, as well as ones she wouldn't ever forget…or forgive.

And above all, he'd made it clear that she was in this alone.

Which you should be damn used to by now.

Saige scowled at the silently sighed words, refusing to waste time feeling sorry for herself, no matter how scared she was. And there was no denying her fear, the sickly emotion coating her skin in a slick, clammy film. After spending her entire adult life in preparation for this moment, now that the time of the awakening had finally begun, terror consumed her. She wanted nothing more than to crawl into a safe pair of arms and seek comfort…solace. If not from her family, then from someone who at least cared about her. Who would wrap her in his arms and hold her tight, sheltering her in his strong, possessive embrace, even if only for a few stolen hours of peace.

Dream on, Saige—because in case you didn't notice, this isn't a fairy tale.

Other than her mother, the closest she'd ever come to having anyone take an interest in what happened to her was the Watchmen, but even they'd abandoned her now. There'd been a moment back at the bar when she'd thought there was a chance the gorgeous stranger was another of the mysterious "watchers," like the man who'd disappeared earlier that week, but it was a benchmark of their organization that they always kept their distance, never getting as close as he had. Saige figured she should know, considering she and her brothers had been under surveillance for years, if not their entire lives, by the shape-shifters whose job it was to watch over the ancient bloodlines. The suddenly absent Watchman had simply been the latest in a long line of men and women whose responsibility it had been to keep an eye on her, waiting for the day when she was no longer human.

Saige had always done her best to ignore them. After all, they never interfered in her life. They were just there, like the birthmark on her hip, constant and predictable. And in a strange way...oddly comforting.

But there'd been something alarmingly different about the breathtaking stranger back at the bar. Instead of easing her mind, he'd completely overwhelmed her senses. When she'd touched his empty beer bottle, the vision that had roared through her brain had been shocking in its force, completely stunning her. Saige normally didn't read objects that strongly. Nor did she pick up on such powerful, visceral emotions, and she'd panicked...running straight into the comforting arms of the jungle. A place where she'd always felt at home, despite its inherent dangers. The forest wasn't an enemy, and it wasn't simply a place. It was her companion and she trusted it, knew what to expect from it, unlike people.

People were unpredictable, but nature always fol-

owed its course. Yes, it could be merciless and unfor-
giving, but it could also be generous in spirit, sharing
its beauty…its splendor, asking for nothing in return
but respect. Saige had always felt at peace in its
embrace, but tonight, she drew no comfort from her
lush surroundings. The shadows were closing in on
her, panic tripping her feet, thickening in her lungs,
burning in her muscles. Scents that had once been
clean and fresh now slithered against her skin, sinking
into her pores, wet and dank and meaty. Her sanctuary was being transformed, stolen from her, replaced
by terror and fear, and she wanted to get her hands on
the one responsible and make him pay.

*Which would be a heck of a lot easier to do if you'd
taken what your body wants…and found someone to
feed from. And the cross would have helped, as well.*

Hating that she'd become such a bloody whiner,
Saige gritted her teeth and ran faster, pushing her body
to its limit, when a stark, demonic howl suddenly
broke through the night, directly ahead of her. She
stumbled, almost falling, but turned to her right and
kept running, painfully aware of the shock jolting
through her system. She went hot…then cold, her eyes
wide as she struggled to wrap her mind around it.
Though she'd been a believer for so long, it was still
a brutal assault on her system to find that she'd
actually been right.

Oh God, she thought, followed swiftly by a choked,
breathless outburst of "Shit!" and "Hell!" and "Not
now, damn it!"

Struggling to keep hold of her backpack, Saige

managed to lean down and grab hold of the small knife that she carried in the top of her right boot, clutching it within her damp grasp. The terrifying, sickening howl came a second time, right in her direct path again, and a sharp, choking sound of panic broke from her throat. Not knowing what to do, she cut left this time, feeling as if she were being herded…hunted…stalked. Which she was.

Think, damn it. Think!

Her Merrick grew more restless, seething within her body, eager to break free and confront the coming threat—but until she nourished that savage, primitive part of her soul, the ancient creature would be unable to fully break its way out of her, no matter how much danger she found herself in.

Which means that you are so freaking screwed, she thought, just seconds before the dark-haired stranger called out her name, his deep, resonating shouts coming from just behind her, full of guttural fury and concern.

"Saige! Goddamn it, stop running. The Casus is closing in. You're going to get your crazy little ass killed!"

Not if I can help it, I'm not.

She panted, her chest heaving as she cut to her right for a second time, completely clueless as to where she was going. Was she running in circles? Running right toward it? Another scraping howl came from ahead of her again, as if the monster was playing with her—taunting her—and she struggled against a strange, instinctive urge to suddenly turn around and run back toward that rough, compelling voice still shouting for her to stop. It was the sexiest thing she'd ever heard, even when cut with the savage edge of rage, fitting the mouthwatering male to perfection.

Don't get dotty now, woman. You don't know him. And don't forget what made you run in the first place. He was thinking about having sex with you, not saving your life.

Right, right. She wasn't thinking clearly. God, she wasn't thinking at all, operating on nothing but pure adrenaline and fear at this point.

The man was gaining on her, getting closer, and she could have sworn she could draw in his intoxicating scent. The bar had been too smoky for her to pick him out right away, until the power of his stare had touched her like a physical caress. Still, it wasn't until she'd stood beside him that she'd gotten the full effect of that rich, woodsy, masculine smell—so different from the vile odor that filled the jungle ahead of her, coming from the Casus.

She slowed, her face damp with the salty sting of tears, and had no idea in which direction she should turn. Some soldier she was.

Suddenly, the stranger roared with fury, and in the next moment, the creature Saige had spent a lifetime envisioning burst out of the thick foliage, about thirty feet in front of her. She stumbled, screaming, eyes glued to the sight of its massive, grotesque body and beastly mouth of fangs, the muzzled shape curling in a cruel, sadistic smile as it zeroed in on her. Its grayish skin stretched tight over heavy, bulking muscles, body hunched from the ridges that marked its curved spine. A faint clacking noise came from its hands, where it clinked its razor-sharp claws together, the deepening shades of twilight casting a silvery glow on their sinister length.

"Merrick," it growled, and the smile spread in an expression of pure, unadulterated evil.

Terror clawed at Saige's throat, and she could read in its pale blue eyes its anticipation as it lurched toward her at an awkward, loping run. She flinched, knowing she was going to die, the knife held tight in her fist. She was prepared to go down fighting, when a great swooping rush of air brushed against her back.

In the next instant, the night went black.

One second she was standing her ground, facing certain death...then Saige Buchanan was flying.

CHAPTER THREE

Despite the furious, keening howls of the Casus, Saige could hear the stranger's graveled voice snarling a visceral string of curses near her ear. She twisted and kicked, struggling to break free…to see what was happening, but he'd thrown something soft and damp over her head, pitching her into an infuriating darkness. She couldn't even punch or scratch at him, her arms pinned tight in a hard, unbreakable hold, the backpack smashed uncomfortably against her chest.

"Fuck," he grunted, clutching her tighter, while his body burned like a fever against her back. Another sinister, bellowing scrape of sound came from below, just seconds before something cruelly sharp, like a claw, grazed her left calf. Saige flinched from the searing pain, a soblike noise tearing from her throat as the knife slipped out of her stunned grasp, falling to the ground below.

She hated not being able to see, the terrified landscape of her mind providing one vivid, grossly detailed scenario after another. Was the monster leaping for her again, its gruesome jaws gaping? Reaching out for her with extended claws? And how exactly was she…*flying?* What in God's name was happening to her?

She wanted to demand an explanation from the beautiful stranger who had his strong, muscular arms banded about her torso, holding her tight, but couldn't stop screaming long enough to form the words. For long minutes, he carried her through the sweltering twilight, over the dense jungle that she could scent just beneath them, until her screams finally died, her sickening fear slowly replaced by a mounting fury.

"Put me down!" she seethed, the enraged sound muffled beneath the cloth. "Goddamn it! Put me down or you're going to be sorry!"

"And let you become its next meal?" he growled, his own anger giving his words a biting, guttural edge. "I don't think so."

He was obviously pissed that she'd run from him— and the fact that she'd tried to brain him with that bottle probably hadn't helped.

Refusing to feel guilty for what she'd done, she continued to rant at him, though it was another five minutes before he finally lowered their elevation, the flapping rush of what sounded strangely like powerful wings becoming softer as they whopped against the forest's upper canopy. An embarrassing, completely girly squeal of sound jerked out of her when his hold began to ease, though he didn't completely release her until her feet touched the ground. Her forward momentum made her stumble for a few steps, so that by the time she managed to drop her backpack, peel what looked to be his shirt off her head and get turned around, she caught only a glimpse of massive ink-black wings from the corner of her eye. In the next instant, they disappeared behind him, the movement so smooth, it was as if he'd absorbed them into his body.

Gasping at the stunning sight, Saige stumbled back a step, then another, while he stalked toward her, his powerful muscles coiling and flexing beneath the bronzed sheen of his skin. His mouth was set in a hard, uncompromising line, his dark, angry eyes burning like a midnight stretch of star-studded sky, pulling her in, making it impossible to look away. She was trapped, held in place by the sheer power of his presence, and Saige knew she'd have been terrified by the smoldering force of his fury, if she weren't so bloody angry herself.

"*What* are you?" she demanded, holding her ground as he came a step closer. She'd deliberately put the emphasis on *what* instead of *who,* his species a heck of a lot more important to her than his name.

Instead of answering, he stopped a few yards away and crossed his strong arms over what was assuredly the most mouthwatering chest Saige had ever seen, either in the flesh or on the silver screen. Solid, powerful slabs of muscle were packed beneath smooth, burnished skin that gleamed like satin, begging for the touch of a woman's hands. For the soft, sensual press of her lips, inviting her to lose herself in his warm, masculine flavor. She didn't need any proof to know it would be dangerously tempting. Didn't need to taste him to tell he would be perfect and spiced and wildly addictive. It was there in that earthy, evocative scent, reinforcing the unsettling fact that she was hungry—*starving*—for something that she instinctively knew this man, this stranger, could give her. Something that the awakening creature within her wanted...*badly*.

And I've apparently lost my freaking mind, she thought, wondering how she could be caught up in such an urgent, violent clutch of lust when she'd only just escaped death by a wing and a prayer. Literally.

"Do you belong to the Collective?"

The dark slash of his brows lifted. "How many shifters do you know in the Collective Army?"

So he was a smart-ass even when he was pissed off. Great. "Then who the hell are you?"

"Name's Michael Quinn," he replied in that deep, husky voice that was the perfect complement to those devastating looks. There was even a bit of twang to the words, hinting at a long-forgotten accent. He took his time looking her up and down, and with a wry drawl rounding out the edges of his speech, he said, "I'd ask if you're Saige Buchanan, but I think that's fairly obvious."

He must have read her intention to turn and run again, because his eyes narrowed as he quietly added, "I caught you once, lady. Don't think I won't be able to do it again."

"Are you kidnapping me, then?"

"I'm just stating a simple fact," he rasped, his tone saying that he definitely thought she was crazy. "If I tell you not to run, then you had damn well better stay where you are."

"And just where do you get off telling me what to do?" she objected through her clenched teeth, mustering what was left of her bravado, hoping it didn't land her in more trouble than she could handle. And considering she'd managed to drop her only weapon, it didn't look as if she could handle much at the moment. At least not from him. He had a racehorse-lean physique that was nothing but sleek, solid muscles and beautiful lines—the perfect personification of a dangerous predator. No doubt the man was built for power and speed, as well as other things she had no business thinking about, considering she didn't know him from Adam. And she was alone with him in the jungle.

"One would think you'd be a bit more grateful, considering I saved your life," he pointed out in one of those cool, utterly male voices of reason that always made her want to stamp her foot in a childish display of temper. Thankfully she squelched the ridiculous impulse and straightened her spine instead, determined to stand her ground. With her shoulders pulled back, Saige lifted her chin and wished for the thousandth time that she'd grown a few more inches at some point in her life. She'd always hated arguing with someone who towered over her, and she suddenly had a vision of herself facing him down while strapped into a pair of four-inch stilettos, then nearly snorted at the absurdity of it. Not exactly jungle-wear, but at least she could have used the heel as a weapon.

Through the thick weight of his lashes, he watched the chaotic shift of emotions flash across her face, her thoughts scattering like so much confetti being tossed in a violent breeze. She shifted uncomfortably, her skin too sensitive, her breath short, and could have sworn there was a soft, hazy spark of humor easing the sharp edges of that piercing gaze, which just pissed her off even more. Here she was shaking in her boots and the arrogant jerk thought it was funny.

Before she could think better of it, she opened her mouth and gave voice to the snide retort perched on the tip of her tongue. "Let's get one thing straight here, birdbrain. You may have been handy back there, but I did *not* ask for your help."

He'd started to move closer, but halted midstep, his dark, onyx-colored eyes narrowed to menacing slits. "Did you honestly just call me *birdbrain?*"

Saige lifted her chin a notch higher at his outraged tone, almost giving herself a crick in the neck. "You're damn right I did," she muttered, figuring she had no choice now but to brazen out her loss of sanity.

He shook his head, clearly at a loss as to what to make of her. "I'm starting to think you'd rather I'd left you back there to become its next plaything. Is that it, Saige?" His tone was more graveled now, his jaw hard as he stalked closer. "Or do you not know what Casus do to women before they kill them?"

She shivered and wrapped her arms around her middle, chilled despite the stifling heat of the evening. Now that the terror of that blind flight was over, her mind spun with dizzying speed, centering on one undeniable fact. After all the worrying…and wondering, she now knew, without any doubt whatsoever, that the Casus *were* real—that they were the ones after her. A bloody monster who could rip her apart with its bare hands as if she were nothing more than a troublesome insect, and in that moment, Saige finally realized that there'd been a silent, frightened part of her that'd been wishing…*hoping*…that maybe, just maybe the legend was wrong. After all her planning and research and the crazy things she'd done to make sure she protected the Dark Markers, she'd been hoping it wasn't real—the monsters and murder and mayhem. And now that she knew the truth, there was no going back. Ever.

"I know what the Casus are—what they're capable of," she whispered, hating the way her throat shook and her eyes burned. Hating that she couldn't hide it from him—from this beautiful stranger whose presence completely screwed with her body and her mind. "I don't need details."

"Maybe you do." His tone was equally soft, but hard, his mesmerizing eyes still narrowed with frustration. "Especially if you think you can traipse off through the jungle like a stupid little idiot when you have a sadistic killer on your tail."

"Excuse me for panicking," she ground out, caught in that dizzying, explosive state between fury and fear, "but I wasn't thinking about monsters when I ran. I was too busy trying to get away from you and your perverted mental sex show!"

The second the words left her mouth, his expression turned livid. "Just what the hell does that mean?"

Saige glared at him, while in a far corner of her mind she accepted the fact that this was by far the strangest conversation she'd ever had—and God only knew she'd had a few. She hadn't meant to blurt that little tidbit out, but terror had apparently seized her ability to self-edit.

Clearing her throat, she tried for a calmer tone. "I…I know what you were thinking about back at the *barra*."

His gaze sharpened with suspicion, the sharp ridges of his cheekbones flushed a dull shade of red that she could clearly see in the thickening lavender twilight. For a moment it looked as if he was going to demand *how* she knew, but then he scraped his hands back through his short black hair, the raised position of his arms accentuating the predatory power of his muscles, making him look like some kind of carnal god come down to tempt her with the savage beauty of his body. Pressing one hand to her pounding heart, Saige could have sworn that a nearly silent, gritty burst of laughter rumbled deep in his chest, though the seductive sound never quite reached her ears.

"Do you read minds, then?" he asked.

Unwilling to reveal the truth, she hedged, saying, "I'm not blind, Mr. Quinn. It wasn't hard to read your thoughts with that look you had on your face."

She couldn't believe it, but his blush actually deepened. "Christ, you Buchanans are all the same, aren't you?" He pushed his hands into the front pockets of his jeans, staring at her with a searing intensity that made her feel hot and cold all at once.

Taking a deep breath, Saige searched his expression…and found herself mesmerized by the shifting heat and shadows in his dark, beautiful eyes. Was he after the Marker? Or was it something else he wanted?

"What do you know about the Buchanans? What exactly do you know about *me?*" *Other than the fact that you know I want to bite you,* she silently groaned, thinking uncomfortably of the vision. It was madness, how much the idea of sinking her teeth into him excited her. The heaviness and stinging heat in her gums was growing worse, signaling the release of the Merrick's fangs.

It won't be long now, she thought. Like a match set to a fuse, there was something about the tantalizing Michael Quinn that had her primal blood surging, pulling her awakening closer to the surface…urging it on.

Which meant that her hunger would grow stronger, demanding to be fed.

He watched her with that hard, silent gaze, making her feel as if he were listening in on her private thoughts, which she seriously hoped wasn't the case. Finally, after what seemed like a long, painful forever, he answered her question in a low rumble of words. "I know enough to believe that you understand what's going on here. I also know about your family, your mother, even the cross you found in Italy. And I'm also pretty damn sure that you'll know exactly what I mean when I say that I'm a Watchman." He paused, as if waiting for her to deny it, but she simply stood there, dazed, wondering what in God's name she was going to do. Being a Watchman meant that he was one of the good guys, which should have been a relief…and yet, Saige couldn't deny that she felt more restless than ever.

"You can trust me, Saige. If we're going to make it out of here alive, you *have* to trust me."

"Trust you?" She stared, thinking he was unlike anything or anyone she'd ever imagined as a Watchman—and yet the truth burned in that dark, smoldering gaze. She believed him. But if he was what he claimed, then he was clearly breaking every one of the Watchmen's rules. "I know how this is supposed to work," she murmured, unable to disguise her suspicion. "You're meant to *watch* me, to keep your distance. Not walk right up to me in the middle of a crowd…while thinking about…about what you were thinking," she finished lamely.

"You know what they say about desperate times calling for desperate measures? Well, this is one of them." He pulled a photo of her out of his back pocket, and held it up for her to see. "I have orders to get your troublesome little ass back to Colorado, to your family. Your brother Riley gave me this to help me find you."

Saige looked at the picture taken of her two years ago, when she and Riley had spent Christmas at home with Elaina, then back at the man who called himself Quinn. "Why would Riley send you after me? And what was all that about back at the bar?" she demanded, only to immediately wish that she hadn't, too aware of the fact that the more she thought about that explicit image, the warmer she got, until it felt as if she were melting from the inside out, and her stomach actually gave an embarrassing growl.

Cool it, Saige. You need to stay sharp…not starving.

Unfortunately, the primal creature awakening within her had other ideas.

Quinn rolled one of those broad, bronzed shoulders

in a casual gesture, as though the situation was no big deal and she'd overreacted. "Yeah, I was thinking about having sex with you—but that doesn't mean that I'll do it. Doesn't even mean that I want to."

Huh. She didn't know whether to be relieved, insulted or strangely disappointed. "Well, gee, thanks."

"Look, my temporary case of lust, or insanity, or whatever you want to call it has been cured," he added with an impatient scowl, probing meaningfully at the nasty gash at the edge of his eyebrow. "So let's just get the hell out of here before that thing tracks us down."

He returned her picture to his back pocket, then reached down and picked his T-shirt up from where she'd dropped it on the ground, his muscles bunching across his chest and arms with each movement of his beautiful body. Saige blinked, wondering what kind of gene pool a guy had to come from to look *that* good, the dusky, vibrant glow of twilight only accentuating his raw masculinity, as if he were some dark, sylvan creature escaped from a primeval forest—and she seriously hoped there wasn't an embarrassing stream of drool slipping from the corner of her mouth.

"What was up with the blindfold, anyway?" she asked, her voice oddly husky as she watched him pull the shirt over his head, the soft black cotton tight against his powerful build, hard biceps stretching the seams at the sleeves.

Despite his lingering anger, he slanted her a laughing look. "Your brothers mentioned your fear of flying."

"So you thought not being able to see would make

it better?" She shook her head, her tone dry as she rubbed her palms on the front of her shorts. "And for the record, I'm not afraid of flying. I'm just a firm believer that if the gods had meant for us to take to the skies, they would have given us wings."

He didn't say anything, just arched one midnight brow in her direction, and she pressed her lips together, fighting the ridiculous urge to grin. Since the second she'd first set eyes on this man, she'd felt like a hormonal wreck, going from one extreme to the other in a dizzying maelstrom of emotions that were wreaking havoc on her sanity. Prickly. Frustrated. On edge and uncomfortably agitated—while at the same time filled with some odd, inexplicable sense of security. She felt sheltered and threatened all at once, aware of him in a way that she'd never experienced before, the disquieting sensation flowing through her with piercing intensity. In the past, Saige had always been at ease around men, working among them as an equal…just another one of the guys. She didn't usually take notice of them as sexual creatures, not even the blatantly beautiful ones—and never in the way that she was "noticing" Michael Quinn.

And her "fascination," for lack of a better word, was officially freaking her out.

Not knowing much about how Watchmen shifted into the shapes of their beasts, she wanted to ask him where the breathtaking black wings had gone, but bit back the oddly personal question, feeling as if it breached some intimate barrier that she couldn't cross. Not when he was staring at her as if he couldn't stop. "Hand me the photo," she said instead, holding out one hand.

"Why?" His tone was odd…almost wary as he held her stare. For such a testosterone-oozing male, she couldn't help but notice that he had the most amazing eyelashes, ones that actually cast shadows on his sharp cheekbones.

"Just hand me the photo," she repeated, snapping her fingers like some kind of commando she-bitch. God only knew she wasn't making much of a first impression, but she chalked it up to circumstance, seeing as how it'd been a bitch of a night—one that was only just getting started.

Saige took the picture from his grasp when he offered it to her, and the second her fingers touched the paper, she knew he was telling her the truth. Riley *had* given it to him. Damn it. She hated having to apologize, but knew it was the right thing to do.

Still, the words were tight in her throat as she said, "I'm sorry about what happened back there." She ended the apology with a pointed look toward his injured brow and tried not to wince.

Instead of accepting, he made a rude, utterly male sound in the back of his throat. "You threw a goddamn bottle at my head, Saige. I don't think some lame-ass *sorry*'s gonna cut it."

She bit her tongue to keep from mouthing off, wanting information more than she wanted to argue—but Quinn had questions of his own. "What can you tell me about Paul Templeton?" he grunted, taking the picture from her and slipping it back into his pocket again.

Saige didn't recognize the name. "I don't know anyone named Templeton."

"He's the Watchman who was assigned to you," he explained with a grim expression, rubbing one hand against his shadowed jaw. "And I'll bet money you knew Paul was trailing you. You must have some idea of what happened to him."

She shrugged, while a sour feeling slid through her insides. "I honestly don't know. He just seemed to disappear a few days ago."

"Christ," he muttered under his breath, and she wondered if the missing Watchman had been a friend of Quinn's.

It was ironic, how she'd always taken the Watchmen's surveillance for granted, never really appreciating it, until this man he called Templeton had vanished. Suddenly, she'd been alone and afraid, reminding her of how she'd felt as a child, when all the men in her life had turned away from her, one by one. After her dad had run out on them, her brothers had been her world, until they, too, had drifted away from her. Ian had run away from home, unable to handle Elaina's obsession with the family bloodline, and God only knew what had happened to make Riley so resentful. He'd changed after Ian had left, and they'd never been close again.

Turning her attention back to Quinn and the missing Paul Templeton, she said, "I got worried when I could no longer sense him watching me. I've been…more cautious than usual the past few days, unsure of what to expect."

Liar.

Am not, she silently growled back. Maybe that wasn't the complete truth…but it was a version.

A skinny one that isn't going to do him a damn bit of good. You need to tell him about the Marker!

From the way he watched her, she wasn't even sure he was buying it, but when he spoke, he simply said, "We can talk this out later. Right now we need to get on the move. I have a room in São Vicente where we can spend the night."

"You still haven't explained what you're doing here," she murmured. All the photo had told her was that Riley *had* asked him to bring her to Colorado, but it'd said nothing about why.

"Like I said, I'm here to get you back. Preferably in one piece." His tone bristled with impatience, and there was an undercurrent of energy buzzing about him that told her he was completely in tune with the surrounding jungle, reading the signs and aware of any coming danger. "After seeing what happened when they came after your brother, I have no doubt that bastard is going to be gunning for you hard and fast."

Her stomach dropped, and she wet her mouth, not liking the sound of that. She took a sudden step forward, the distance between them no more than a foot now, bringing the details of his gorgeous face into sharper focus. "What do you mean *when* they went after my brother?"

Around them, the forest fell silent and still, as if waiting with her in breathless suspense as Quinn quietly said, "He's already gone through his awakening."

Saige hadn't expected the sharp stab of fear that twisted through her middle, along with something that felt uncomfortably like guilt. For a moment all she could do was hold that dark gaze, trying to find some kind of reassurance in it, and then she finally found her voice. "Is Riley okay? What happened? Was he prepared? Please tell me that Ian didn't throw out the Marker."

"Riley's fine," he told her, watching her closely. "But he wasn't the one."

She blinked. "Ian?" she said, her hoarse tone thick with surprise. "Jesus, it was *Ian?*"

"Yeah, but he's all right. A little lost at first, but we found him in time to give him the information he needed."

There was a note of censure in his graveled voice that cut her deeper than she'd have thought possible. After all, it wasn't that she hadn't *tried* to share what she knew with her brothers. Well, maybe not with Ian, but damn it, she'd tried to warn Riley. Not that she'd known then as much as she did now. She'd learned so much since she'd last seen him at their mother's funeral—things that she'd planned on sharing when she made it back to America, whether he wanted to listen or not.

But time had run out…more swiftly for Ian than it had for her, if what this man claimed was true.

"Of course Ian's all right," she said, her voice soft, while her mind churned it over…and over, trying to grasp it. She should have figured it out before. If she hadn't been so scared, she'd have realized that Riley wouldn't have had any involvement with the Watch-men, giving Quinn her picture and asking him to come after her, unless something had *already* happened. And she could just imagine how furious Ian must have been to discover he was the first, considering how he'd always detested any talk about the Merrick. "According to Riley, Ian's like a cat. He must have nine lives."

"I imagine he lost a couple during the past few weeks," Quinn commented dryly. "The thing hunted him down, Saige, targeting some of the women he'd dated. They're making it personal, striking where it hurts."

Stunned, she barely managed to scrape out her words. "Are you telling me that it killed *human* women?"

"*Killed* is putting it too lightly. It tortured them, and made it a slow, grueling process, just to mess with your brother's mind."

"But I thought they would come after *us*—after the Merrick." She wrapped her arms around her middle again, somehow trying to hold herself together. "We're the ones they're supposed to want. The ones they need."

"Oh, they'll come after you," he rasped, the husky notes of his dark-velvet voice stroking her senses, despite her horror with the situation. "And they'll do everything they can to screw with your life until they've got you." He shifted closer, making her want to retreat from his intensity...from that piercing gaze and his devastating beauty. "That's where I come in."

Her breath caught so hard that her chest ached. "Meaning?"

"Meaning you're my responsibility now. Wherever you go, I go. I'm not letting you out of my sight, so you might as well get used to it."

Saige could tell from his tone that he was hardly thrilled by the circumstances. "I didn't ask for this."

"Yeah?" he drawled. "Go ahead and ask me how much that matters."

She was angrier at fate at the moment than with him—but fate wasn't there to hear her complaints. "Are you always this aggravating?" she demanded, giving him her best glare.

For a split second, a funny expression crossed his chiseled features, and he lifted those mouthwatering shoulders in a wry shrug. "Believe it or not, I'm usually the most easygoing guy around. I guess you just bring out the worst in me."

"The worst in you, huh?" Lowering her brows, she wondered what she must have done in a past life to have earned such cosmically crappy luck. "Funny how I always seem to have that effect on people."

"Aggravating or not, I intend to keep you alive, and that thing back there is programmed on to you." Saige knew what he meant. She'd heard about a Casus's ability to lock on to a Merrick, as though she were some kind of metaphysical beacon for its hunger. "That's why we need to get to the safety of Ravenswing, the Watchmen compound in Colorado, as soon as possible."

Saige shook her head, a new fear quickly taking

form, twisting through her like a physical pain as she reached down and grabbed hold of her backpack, hooking it over her right shoulder. "I'm not going anywhere until I've checked on Javier."

Dark brows drew together over darker eyes. "Who?"

"The boy I was with tonight," she explained, adjusting her hold on the heavy pack. "He lives in Coroza with his brothers, not far from the bar."

Quinn frowned. "You know he'd be better off if you just stay away from him."

"But you said yourself that the Casus went after some of the women Ian knew," she argued. "I need to make sure that Javier made it home okay. Give him enough money to get out of town for a while."

"Then call him," he said flatly.

"He and his brothers don't have a phone," she explained with a heavy dose of frustration.

He studied her posture, his hard, hypnotic gaze lingering on her face...her eyes, noting her determination. "It isn't safe for you to go near him, Saige. If they've marked him, you'll be putting yourself in danger again. Just going back into Coroza is a hell of a risk."

She was going to have to go back into Coroza one way or another, anyway, considering she still had to retrieve the maps from Inez's safe—but she wasn't going to explain any of that to Quinn. And at the moment, her only concern was Javier. "You can try to stop me," she said, "but I'm giving you fair warning. If you do, I'll stab you in the heart the second you let your guard down, then come back without you."

She'd expected him to shout at her, but it was quickly becoming apparent that Michael Quinn wasn't an easy man to predict. Instead of reacting with anger, he actually grinned at her quietly spoken threat, the devilish curve of that hard mouth making her toes curl inside her hiking boots, though she struggled not to show it. "You're not afraid of me at all, are you?"

She was *almost* grinning back at him as she said, "Just don't forget it."

"I'm not likely to," he murmured, the heavy look in his eyes making her shiver with awareness. In that moment, she was distinctly aware of their differences. Of his rugged maleness compared to her softer femininity. And yet, she still didn't feel threatened. Not by Quinn.

No, for some unfathomable reason, she felt *safe*.

A gentle breeze blew her hair across her face, and she lifted one hand, tucking the wayward strands behind her ear. "I understand the risk, Quinn. But I *have* to do this. I couldn't live with myself if I didn't."

He held her in his dark gaze as the seconds stretched out like a body being tortured on the rack. Just when she was ready to start arguing in earnest, he blew out a rough breath, and quietly said, "How's the leg?"

Her leg? Glancing down, Saige noticed the bloodied scratches the Casus had left on her calf. She knew it was a sign of her nerves that the wound wasn't bothering her. Looking back at Quinn, she said, "It'll be fine."

He arched his brows. "Then are we walking or flying?"

Relief hit like a physical blow to her chest, though she tried to hide it. Thinking over his question, Saige listened to the night. She could tell from the distant sound of church bells that the terrifying flight had kept them close to the outskirts of the city, rather than taking them deeper into the jungle. "We're not far from Coroza," she murmured. "You can't very well go flying into town."

He shrugged, though there was an odd light in his eyes, as if he were teasing her. Not knowing what to make of him, Saige looked to the evening sky for her bearings, then headed west, acutely aware of the man named Michael Quinn following closely beside her…every step of the way. It was an odd, overwhelming sensation, having him so near. And one she wished she didn't like nearly as much as she did.

Pressing one hand to her stomach, she struggled to push away the unwanted sensations, and reminded herself that her life had just been turned upside down…and would never be normal again.

Not that you did normal all that well anyway, she thought with a frown.

She didn't know him, and she sure as hell didn't trust him with her secrets, but as they walked through the verdant beauty of the jungle, Saige couldn't deny that she was utterly…unusually…and unequivocally fascinated by the dark, intoxicating stranger who'd just landed in her life.

She only wished she had a clue what to do about him.

CHAPTER FOUR

SENSING THE ARRIVAL of a dominant predator, startled wildlife scurried back into the underbrush as Gregory DeKreznick stepped from the thick, humid veil of jungle. Wearing a feral smile, he stalked toward the center of the clearing nestled beside a meandering offshoot of the river, the darkening summer sky shot with fading, violent streaks of purple and pink. A lone wooden hut sat at the north end of the small, cleared patch of dense tropical foliage, a fisherman's weathered boat propped against its side, testament to the trade of the man who'd lived there, until Gregory had killed him earlier that week. Mere miles from the site where Saige Buchanan had been searching for another of the lost Dark Markers, the meager dwelling had been an ideal location for him and his fellow Casus and so they'd claimed it as their own.

Tonight, the small cabin huddled silent and dark in the moonlight, telling him that at least for the moment, he had the clearing to himself.

Throwing back his wolf-shaped head, the monstrous creature stared up at the infinite, cloud-scarred stretch of night, and allowed his true shape to melt away, pulling back into the body of his human host. Rolling his broad shoulders, Gregory cracked his head to the side with a popping burst of sound, then slicked his chin-length, sun-streaked hair back from his chiseled face, the spattering of blood from the evening's kills still warm against his skin. Scratching lazily at his chest, he savored the thick, meaty taste of his most recent victims against his tongue, running the tip across the smooth surface of his straight white teeth.

He could have taken Javier Ruiz and used him as bait to draw out his prey, but there'd been no need to go through the hassle when killing him had proven so much more effective. Gregory had gotten what he needed, and as a whole, the Ruiz brothers had been fairly satisfying—though not nearly as sweet as when he feasted on warm, womanly flesh. Men were filling, but females gave him so much more…pleasure, like savoring a fine wine after years of nothing but tepid water.

That was the difference between him and Royce. A team player to the very end, Royce Friesen had been told not to feed from the humans, and so he'd obeyed, drinking the water while Gregory savored the succulent feast. And what a feast it was. He'd hungered for too long while trapped in the holding ground they'd named Meridian. While locked away from the things that made him whole…that made him complete, and no matter what Calder and his followers had told him before his release, Gregory had no intention of obeying their asinine rules.

Friesen, however, lived the servile existence of a good little soldier, only dining on the local livestock. He'd even been warned not to feed from the Merrick bitch until she'd fully awakened—and though it went against everything that the Casus were, the idiot obeyed, following his orders to a T. Even knowing that Gregory grew stronger every day, Royce remained committed to his decision to comply with Calder's ridiculous dictates, and today it had nearly cost him. They'd trailed Saige Buchanan for hours, expecting her to leave the country once she'd found the second Marker and that milksop of an archaeologist had skipped out, but she'd spent the afternoon scurrying all over town instead. By the time she'd headed toward *O Diablo Dos Ángels* late in the day, Royce had already gone too long without one of his meager feedings and was growing weak. He'd been forced to travel into the jungle in search of animal prey, leaving Gregory to watch over their target while she visited with her friends at the rustic *barra*.

Enjoying having her all to himself, without Royce's irritating presence, Gregory had watched her from afar, biding his time like a shark slowly circling in for the kill, and it had almost paid off. When she'd run into the jungle, he'd thought she'd finally be his…only to have her snatched from his grasp. But he didn't intend to let it stand.

With a sharp smile of anticipation for the moment he knew would eventually be his, Gregory stretched his arms over his head, aware of the muscles flexing beneath his skin, along with the hard ridges of bone and ropey sinew. For a human, the body he'd taken wasn't half-bad. Over six foot, with a muscular build, it was better than he'd expected from something that was no better than mere prey, even if the man did have a speck of Casus blood flowing through his veins. When the shades of Gregory's kind were freed from Meridian, they were required to seek out a human who carried the ancient blood of their ancestors in order to retake a corporeal form. Once taken, the human's soul was forced from its body. The Casus, however, retained the host's memories, which enabled them to function in these unusual modern times—and they were thankfully capable of shifting into their true form when needed.

Gregory wondered if Malcolm, his only blood brother and the first to be sent back from Meridian, had enjoyed his freedom this much, then quickly beat down the destructive thought, locking it away with his hatred, where it belonged. It hurt too much to think of Malcolm—of what that eldest Buchanan bastard had taken from him. That was why Gregory wanted his hands on Saige so badly—to show that prick what it felt like to have something taken away, ripped from your life, knowing that you could never get it back.

She might have been "meant" for Royce, but Gregory had no intention of letting the other Casus have her. She'd gotten away from him tonight—but it wouldn't happen again. No matter what Friesen decided to do next, Gregory had a plan, one that he intended to execute with or without his fellow Casus.

While Royce and the others concerned themselves

with securing the crosses and building up their strength in order to bring more of their kind back from Meridian, Gregory cared only for Buchanan blood. After all, it was the Merrick who had trapped the Casus so many years ago, cursing them to a fate worse than death. Because of their immortality, they could not die, and so they'd simply wasted away to mere shades of the powerful beings they'd once been, forced to dwell within human bodies once they'd regained this realm. But it was the eldest Buchanan sibling who had used the first Dark Marker to destroy his brother's soul, condemning Malcolm to the pits of hell for all eternity. For that, as well as the incarceration of his species, Gregory had vowed to make them pay. The ability to love might not be a common trait for the Casus, but they understood loyalty to family like no other. In a world as vicious as theirs, sometimes it was the only way to survive.

"And Watchman or not," he rasped with a hard smile, remembering the moment when he'd licked the blood from her leg off his claws, "I'm going to enjoy taking little Saige Buchanan to pieces."

Rumbling a dark burst of laughter under his breath, he started to step toward the cabin, when a sound to his left snagged his attention, and he tensed, listening…completely alert to his surroundings as readiness spread through his muscles like a sharp, piercing pain. Pulling back his shoulders, he'd just taken a deep pull on the humid air when a solid bulk of muscle and bone rammed into him, slamming him to the damp, moss-covered floor of the clearing. "You wanna explain what happened tonight?" the Casus roared in his face, pinning his forearms to the ground. "I can smell her on you!"

Knowing it would only infuriate Royce further if he remained calm, Gregory casually related the evening's events, and his comrade took the news as badly as he'd hoped. Concealing the enjoyment he got from seeing Royce so furious, he finally concluded with a solicitous drawl, "You *did* tell me to keep an eye on her."

"You incompetent idiot," Royce seethed, his rage glittering like so many shards of ice in his pale blue gaze. "I told you not to lose her—not to reveal yourself. What did you think you were doing?"

"Exactly what I was bred to do," he replied with a sharp smile.

Royce's eyes narrowed with fury. "Don't push me, Gregory. In future, you stay away from her. If you don't, I'll make sure you pay."

"As fun as this is, get the hell off me, Royce. We both know you can't kill me."

The beast lowered its snout, going nose-to-nose with him. "Is that what you think?" it asked silkily, the sinister words warbled within the muzzled shape of its wolflike head. "The only reason Calder allowed you to come through with me was because he considered you too much of a liability back in Meridian and he wanted you gone. And the only reason I agreed to bring you along was because I wanted out of there, and no one else would take responsibility for you. But you lay a finger on Saige Buchanan again, and I'll kill you myself."

"And face Calder's wrath?" Gregory mocked, clucking his tongue.

Royce's words shook with his anger. "After the screwup Malcolm made of his assignment, don't think for one second that Calder gives a shit about what happens to you."

Gregory laughed. "And you think Calder cares any more about you, Royce? The truth is that he doesn't give a shit about either one of us."

Shifting back on his haunches, Royce released his hold on Gregory's arms, eyeing him with a cold, hard stare. "He's a good leader," he ground out.

"Just not a very trusting one." Gregory snorted, hoisting himself up onto his elbows. "Has he told you how he learned to send us across? Hell, he hasn't even told you how many Markers we're after, or exactly why we need them."

Royce moved to his feet in a fluid ripple of powerful muscle, allowing his true form to gracefully slip away, easing back into the shape of his human host. "He has his reasons," he muttered.

"Sure he does," Gregory drawled, rolling his eyes. "And at any rate, tonight wasn't my fault. This was the best chance we've had to grab her since she found the Marker. Would you have rather I just let her slip on by?"

"We were only going to grab her if we ran the risk of losing her. Otherwise, we were told to wait until she's fully awakened."

"And the Marker?"

"The Marker we could have stolen from her," Royce

growled, his lip curled with disgust. "But now, because of your little stunt, she knows we're after her, which means she's going to be guarding it as well as she can."

"She already knew," Gregory countered, his brows arched as he stared up from his place on the warm, damp ground. "Why else do you think she's always looking over her goddamn shoulder? She knows we're watching her."

Royce's mouth tightened, the muscles across his chest flexing with each of his hard, heavy breaths. "Knowing and suspecting are two different things. That Watchman bastard isn't going to let her out of his sight now. And if he flew, chances are that he's a bloody Raptor." Royce glared down at him, his lip curled in an arrogant expression that made Gregory want to tear into him, as slowly and painfully as possible. "So now, thanks to you, we've lost her *and* the Marker."

"Not exactly," he offered in a soft rumble of words as he moved to his feet.

Royce paused in the act of turning away, his brow drawn in a deep frown. "What the hell does that mean?"

"It means that I don't think she has it. At least not on her."

At his sides, Royce's big fists clenched tighter, the veins sticking out in sharp relief beneath the golden sheen of his skin. "What are you talking about?"

"I was able to cut her tonight," he explained, rolling his shoulder, "which means she wasn't wearing it."

"Then she must have hidden it," Royce murmured, raking one hand back through the thick, chocolate strands of his hair. Despite the fact that their human hosts—American brothers who had owned a tourist fishing boat in Rio—were almost identical in appearance, Friesen's hair was not only shorter, but several shades darker.

"If she did," Gregory drawled, "then she's an idiot for not keeping hold of the only thing that can protect her." Calder had told them that they would be unable to kill her so long as she wore one of the ancient Markers, the power of the crosses protecting her from their fangs and claws.

"Either that, or she's very clever. Somehow she must have figured out that we're after the Markers, as well. I told you before, you're underestimating her."

"Am I?" Gregory asked with a laugh as he scraped a palm over his rough jaw. "She ran tonight, just like a pathetic woman."

Royce sent him an impatient look. "And since you said yourself she was running *away* from the Watchman, I think we can safely assume that had nothing to do with you at that point."

"You're giving her too much credit," he muttered, shaking his head. "I keep telling you that she's nothing more than food."

"It doesn't matter what you think of her, Gregory, because she's *my* food. As soon as you know where your Merrick is, do as you like—but until then, stay away from mine."

Gregory held up his hands in a sign of surrender.

"Come on, man. There's no need to be so suspicious. I was going to bring her to you," he murmured, enjoying the potent force of Friesen's frustration as it blasted against him like a hot wind.

Royce jerked his chin and snorted. "Do you honestly expect me to believe that?"

"Still don't trust me?" he asked lightly, wearing a ghost of a smile.

A bitter laugh fell from Royce's lips. "Try 'will *never* trust you.'"

"And yet," Gregory said softly, his gaze hard and steady, "you need me."

"I need that Marker…and then I need the woman. You, I have no use for."

"Hmm, well, I suppose I would be lying if I didn't say that the feeling is mutual," he offered with a low, throaty chuckle. "And, like you said, I have my own waiting for me, so you can have her flesh." It was a lie, but as much as he enjoyed taunting his comrade, he knew better than to push too far. Not yet, when they now had a Watchman to contend with.

And Gregory knew how touchy Royce was about the little Merrick bitch's life.

According to legend, each time a Casus shade escaped from Meridian, one Merrick would awaken, in keeping with nature's need for balance. In an effort to promote order among the newly escaped Casus, it'd been decided that since only a fully awakened Merrick could provide their kind with the "ultimate" feeding, each escaped Casus would be allowed exclusive rights to the Merrick their return to this realm had caused to awaken. It was an important rule, as only a Merrick could provide the power charge needed for the Casus to "pull" another one of his kind back from Meridian, bringing them across the divide. Seeing as how the desire to build their numbers so that they might rule as they once did was the driving force that motivated so many of his kinsmen, the awakened Merrick were going to become a hot commodity.

Gregory, however, couldn't have cared less about his species' power base.

The only power that concerned him was his own, and for that reason alone, he planned to eventually find his Merrick and kill it. But first, he'd deal with the Buchanans.

"Until you can focus," Royce drawled, "you know damn well that you're never going to find your own Merrick."

"Oh, I'll find mine," he murmured, scratching lazily at his blood-spattered chest. He knew the full extent of Royce's anger from the simple fact that the uptight bastard had failed to notice he was covered in blood. "But for now, our problem is Saige Buchanan. You can't blame me for tonight. If you had been there, you wouldn't have been able to resist any more than I did."

"I've resisted so far, haven't I?" Royce said over his shoulder as he headed toward the cabin. Though the moonlight somewhat softened its defects, it still seemed a marvel that the structure remained standing, its sad-looking roof sloping on the right side, as if it would eventually just slide its way into the dark, murky waters of the river.

"At least I didn't come home empty-handed," Gregory commented with casual indifference, following after him.

"Do I even want to know?" Royce asked with a hard sigh as he opened the front door.

Stepping inside the ramshackle structure, Gregory headed toward the lone sink and began running water in its stained basin. His reflection stared back at him in the dingy panes of the window before him, providing a hazy view of the moon and the wine-dark water that snaked its way through the jungle like a serpent. "I paid a visit to her little helper on my way back here."

From the corner of his eye, he watched as Royce's hands fisted angrily at his sides for the second time that night, but knew the bastard didn't have the guts to take a swing at him. Not when Gregory was vibing with the hard, thick power of his recent kills. "You bloody idiot," Royce growled through his clenched teeth, his rage echoing through the room like a physical force, nearly shaking the shadows from the cobwebbed corners. "Why in the hell would you do that?"

"I wanted to know more about the Marker," he calmly explained, splashing water onto his face and chest. After losing Saige, he'd wanted to hit her where it hurt. And he had.

"And?" Royce growled, taking a step closer.

"The boy claimed to know nothing about where she's keeping the cross, but he did say that he thinks they're keeping some kind of papers for her at the bar."

Turning, he caught Royce's pale, interested gaze. "If Calder's right about her having the maps, that could be them."

They had been told there was a good chance that Saige Buchanan had found a set of maps that led to the location of the Dark Markers. The maps, according to Calder, were a closely guarded secret that not even the Watchmen knew about, and an invaluable resource to the ones who possessed them. Which meant that he wanted them—badly.

"You were thorough?" Royce asked, his voice deceptively soft.

Gregory lifted his brows. "Trust me," he purred. "The boy told me everything he knows."

"It doesn't matter." Royce sighed. "If the maps were there, she probably got them tonight."

Grabbing a towel from the counter, Gregory wiped at his damp face, then hooked the cloth behind his neck. "She didn't. He said she got scared away before she could get them."

Royce slid him a thick look of frustration. "And did it ever occur to you that he could have been lying?"

Gregory rolled his eyes. "I had my claws dug into his groin, Royce. The kid would have told me where I could find his mother if that's what I'd wanted."

Pushing one hand back through his short hair, Royce stared through the open front door, obviously thinking over his options. It was a waste of time, but Gregory let him have his illusion of command. When the moment was right, he'd show the bastard exactly who was the dominant Casus.

"She'll have to go back for them," Royce finally rumbled. "When she does, we have no choice but to go ahead and take her—but it won't be easy."

Gregory shook his head, understanding why Calder put so much trust in Royce Friesen. Calder obviously knew a follower when he saw one. The first Casus since the start of their captivity to succeed in organizing his kinsmen into a cohesive force, bringing rule to the anarchy, Calder was the one who'd finally offered them hope…a chance of escape. Like an angel surrounded by devils, he'd promised to deliver them into salvation—and yet, Gregory didn't trust him.

And he had good reason to be wary, seeing as how Calder had been less than honest with his brother. Not only had Malcolm been denied certain information, but he'd been led to believe that it would take some time before Calder and his followers would be strong enough to send more Casus across. And yet, no sooner had they learned that Malcolm had safely made the transition, than they sent through two more. Two Casus who would hunt down their own Merrick, and then go after the Marker that Malcolm had hoped to secure for himself. Not to please Calder, but because his brother had planned to use the cross to barter for Gregory's release, in the event he wasn't able to "pull" him across himself. Malcolm hadn't expected to have competition for the crosses so soon, and Gregory knew he must have been furious when he discovered that Calder had sent through others right after him.

Still, it was a long, strenuous process—one that was already taking its toll on Calder and his followers, which was why it was so important for the released Casus to contribute to the effort and "pull" back as many as they could using their own power. To date, there had been three Merrick kills: one in Canada, one in Germany and the last made in Australia. In all three cases, the Casus had been able to bring another across after feeding off the Merrick, and now they, too, would join the search for the Markers, doing everything they could to get their hands on the ancient crosses that Calder was so desperate to possess. They would also continue to hunt, seeking out any Merrick who managed to send a Casus back to Meridian. Without the power of a Dark Marker, the Merrick were unable to destroy the Casus's soul in the way that Ian Buchanan had done to Malcolm, but they could still kill the host body, in which case the Casus shade was instantly sucked back into the holding ground, where it would wait to be released again.

As their numbers grew, Gregory knew that Calder's hope of keeping peace among the escaped Casus wouldn't work. As much as his kinsmen wanted their species to return to power, they would simply tear each other apart in a bloodthirsty battle for the ancient crosses, seeing as how Calder had promised to significantly reward those who found a Marker and delivered it safely into Ross Westmore's possession. Westmore was another mystery in Calder's scheme—one they knew next to nothing about. All he and Royce had been told before coming across was that the mysterious Westmore—whose species was unknown—would be their contact man once they made it into this realm, and was to be entrusted with any Markers that they obtained. Though they'd had brief contact with a few of Westmore's men, they'd yet to meet the man himself, and Gregory couldn't deny that his curiosity had been piqued. After all, Westmore was not only helping to orchestrate their return to power, but had also managed to infiltrate one of the most secretive organizations in history, using their money to fund the Casus hunts.

As far as Gregory was concerned, the guy was either a genius…or completely insane.

Leaning against the counter, he crossed his arms over his chest, wondering if this mysterious Westmore would agree with Royce's prediction that catching Saige wouldn't be easy. "You know, I was always told that you held too much respect for the Merrick."

Friesen snorted. "I don't respect them, but I know better than to underestimate them."

"You shouldn't waste your time. It's obvious that they're no match for us."

Lifting his right hand, Royce rubbed at the back of his neck. "It's thinking like that, Gregory, that makes you a liability. Among other things," he muttered. Turning away from the doorway, he paced toward the threadbare sofa slumped against one wall, then back again, past the single archway that led to the bedroom, where a stained mattress lay on the floor.

"You actually think we'll have trouble taking her?" Gregory asked, snuffling a dry laugh under his breath. "A woman? You've got to be kidding."

"She's not exactly alone anymore, is she? Raptors

are some of the most bloodthirsty breeds there's ever been."

Gregory curled his lip. "Don't embarrass yourself by actually sounding afraid of him."

"The problem with men like you," Royce warned, slanting him a disgusted glare, "is that you always fail to realize the difference between fear and intelligence."

"You're starting to sound cranky, Royce." Taking the towel from around his neck, Gregory tossed it into the sink and slicked his hair back from his face, then bound it into a ponytail with the elastic band he kept around his wrist.

Tired of wasting his time on the obstinate ass, Gregory turned to leave, only to be caught short when Royce grabbed hold of his shoulder. "Where do you think you're going?"

Shrugging off Royce's hold, he flashed him a sharp smile. "All this chatting has worked up my appetite." The words were meant to incite, but there was an undeniable truth to them. His cock was already hardening at the thought of satisfying his hunger, anticipation thickening like a feral syrup in his veins.

"Don't you think you've had enough for tonight?"

"They were just a snack," he drawled, his mouth kicking up at the corner with a cocky grin as he headed toward the door. "Now I'm ready for the main course."

"We need to get back to the bar and keep an eye out for her. And if you don't stop picking off the locals," Royce called out, "we're going to have an angry mob on our hands."

With one last glance over his shoulder, Gregory could see just how badly Royce wanted a go at him, and his grin spilled into a slow, satisfied smile. "Then I guess it'll be just like old times."

CHAPTER FIVE

North Coroza

IT TOOK ALMOST an hour for Saige and Quinn to reach the crowded neighborhood where Javier Ruiz lived with his brothers. Night had spilled over the jungle in a warm, heavy pour of darkness, the last streaming shades of color finally fading from the bruise-colored heavens. Despite her continued assurances that the Casus couldn't possibly attack them in such a populated area, Quinn kept a vigilant eye on the narrow, winding streets, as if expecting the obscene creature to suddenly emerge from the thickening shadows.

Watching him from the corner of her eye as they made their way down the weathered, cobbled road, Saige could sense that he had questions about what she was doing in Brazil. But Quinn was biding his time, his focus for the moment centered more on their surroundings than anything else. Not nearly as patient herself, Saige plagued him with questions about her brother's awakening, and learned that Ian had used the cross she'd found in Italy to kill the Casus who'd been hunting him. Her mother, who had kept her maiden

name of Buchanan for herself and her children, had
heard the term "Arm of Fire" from her grandmother,
but it wasn't until Quinn explained how the cross had
literally transformed Ian's arm into a fiery weapon
that Saige had understood what the term meant. She
also learned that her brother had somehow soaked in
the creature's thoughts at the time of its death. He'd
not only "seen" that more of the Casus had already
escaped from their holding ground, but that they were
also after the Markers themselves.

Saige absorbed the information with a sinking sensation in the pit of her stomach, thinking of the warning the second Marker had given her just that morning.

Enemies are coming who will take me from you.

Throughout the day, her conscience had plagued
her for involving Jamison Haley in her problems, and
knowing that it was the Casus who were seeking the
Markers only increased her sense of guilt. If the
monsters discovered she no longer had the ancient
talisman, they could very well conclude that she'd
given it to the young archaeologist—which meant that
she'd put his life in extreme danger.

Damn you, Haley. You should have just told me no.

Any other person would no doubt have done just
that, if asked for a favor as bizarre as the one she'd
begged from Jamison. But the endearing Brit was one
of those rare few who actually believed that sometimes
things really *did* go bump in the night—things that
humanity was better off not knowing about. As such,
he'd believed her when she'd gone to him for help.

He also had a problem saying no to females who

asked him for favors, which she'd ruthlessly used to her advantage.

And yet, as horrible as Saige felt for exploiting Jamison's soft side, there was still a tiny voice in her head arguing that she'd done the right thing by sending him to Colorado with the cross. If Ian was right, and the Casus *were* after the Markers, then protecting the cross was the only thing that really mattered, regardless of the risk to herself and the people she cared about—and she knew that if Quinn were aware of what she'd discovered, he'd feel the same way.

The intense Watchman definitely seemed like the type of man who put his job above all else. Even though she obviously frustrated the hell out of him, he remained intent on keeping her alive…keeping her safe. As they headed through the ramshackle town, his dark gaze constantly scanned the narrow alleyways and high buildings, alert to any danger, the tension in his tall body evident in the rigid set of his broad shoulders and the subtle flexing of his strong, powerful hands. It was clear that he didn't care for the tight, closed-in walkways of the crowded neighborhood.

"How much farther do we have to go?" he rumbled in that sexy drawl that made her pulse quicken each and every time he spoke. Saige shivered in reaction, somehow feeling that evocative sound in the center of her body, penetrating and warm, as if she'd swallowed a hot, smoldering ball of fire.

"Just a few more blocks," she said, wishing the skies would unleash a frigid rain to cool the simmering heat beneath her skin. She was uncomfortably aware of the Merrick's agitation growing worse with each moment that she spent with him. It prowled within her body like a panther pacing its cage, taking a primal, feral interest in the man walking at her side. Struggling to remain calm, she crossed her arms over her chest and drew in a deep breath that filled her senses with the pulse of the ethnic neighborhood, and more important, with that hot, mouthwatering scent she'd already come to recognize as pure, intoxicating Quinn.

"Have you ever been to South America before, Mr. Quinn?" she asked, surprised by the huskiness of her voice.

"Just Quinn." The brackets etched around his mouth deepened as he added, "This is my first time down here."

"I thought so," she murmured, a small grin playing softly at the corner of her lips. The roughened surface of the road crunched beneath their booted feet, but Saige hardly noticed the grating sound, too fascinated by the hard play of muscle beneath his burnished skin as he lifted one hand, pushing it through the dark scrub of his hair. The cut would have looked severe on any other man, but it simply emphasized Quinn's outrageously good looks. Despite his "in your face" male ruggedness, his features were impossibly perfect, like something that'd been sculpted from marble, his sharp cheekbones only accentuating the strong, masculine angles.

Clearing her throat, she went on to say, "You look as if you don't quite know what to make of this place."

Seemingly oblivious to the fact that she was practically drooling over him, the tension around his mouth eased a little as he slanted her a lopsided smile. "Is it that obvious?" he asked, his smile widening as he rubbed his left hand over the tanned length of his right forearm. "I was hoping the tan might help me blend in."

A shaky laugh vibrated in her throat, and she inwardly rolled her eyes at herself, unable to believe that she, Saige Buchanan, the most independent woman she knew, had gone gaga over a breathtakingly gorgeous stranger like some teeny-bopping airhead. "You just seem preoccupied with the neighborhood," she replied, forcing her attention back to the shadowed street. On either side of the narrow road, windows flickered with the soft glow of light, reminding her of blinking, watchful eyes, and she tightened the flannel shirt around her waist, then hefted her backpack higher onto her right shoulder, seeking comfort in the mundane tasks. "I guess all this probably takes some getting used to," she added, stepping around a frenzied group of chickens that were pecking at some scraps outside an open doorway. "Especially if you're accustomed to the wide-open spaces of the mountains."

"I guess so," he drawled with a deep, decadent rumble of laughter that sounded so purely male, her temperature spiked higher. It was an almost dizzying sensation, that wild, steady rise of her Merrick within her body, the primal creature shifting sinuously beneath her skin as it raised its head and sniffed delicately at the air. She choked back a low, sensual purr, the carnal sound vibrating softly on her tongue, and could have sworn that she could taste the rich, sumptuous flavor of her need. The Merrick was *hungry* with bloodlust, its craving for nourishment more intense than it'd ever been before, and Saige suspected she knew why.

It was Quinn. Her growing fascination with the dark, mysterious Watchman had easily bled past the woman and into the powerful creature living within her. Even though her awakening of that ancient blood had only just begun, she could feel the building heat in her gums, the fiery burn in her veins…and knew it was coming closer. Mounting. Growing stronger. She was driven by a primal instinct to touch…and taste…and possess—the visceral, sexual urges so potent, she felt almost drunk on their power.

Desperately in need of a distraction, she searched her mind for a topic that was guaranteed to get her mind off sex and back on track. "So we, um…obviously know that the Casus are after me, but what about the Collective?"

Saige watched his expression harden, and could tell from his tone that he held no more love for the ruthless organization than she did. "What about them?"

"Are they already hunting us? Me and my brothers?"

"We've had some scouts show up in Henning, where your brothers live…or lived," he explained. "Ian is at the compound now, and we're still trying to convince Riley to move up, as well. We're worried about him being down in town on his own, but so far the scouts haven't done anything more than sniff around."

"That seems odd," she murmured. "Do you think they know Ian is at Ravenswing?"

He lifted one rugged, beautiful hand, and rubbed at the back of his neck, his powerful bicep straining the sleeve of his T-shirt. "If they do, I'm sure we'll know soon enough, seeing as how Collective soldiers aren't ones to employ patience. But for the time being, our biggest problems are the Casus and the Consortium."

Saige sent him a startled look of surprise. "But I thought you were a part of the Consortium."

"You know about the council?" he asked, his own surprise evident in the softly spoken words. Turning right at the next corner, they continued deeper into the aged neighborhood, the winding road taking a slight incline up the mountainside, back toward the jungle, while the succulent scents of home-cooked meals thickened on the air.

"From what I understand," she told him, "the Consortium governs all the ancient clans, like some kind of preternatural United Nations."

And as far as Saige knew, it was the Consortium who had helped the Merrick imprison the Casus over a thousand years ago, after the Casus's relentless killing of humans threatened to expose the existence of the nonhuman races. The council had fashioned the Dark Markers to destroy the immortal killers, only to be murdered by the newly created Collective Army before they could complete the task. Years later, the Consortium had finally been formed again, but by then its original archives had been lost...all traces of the Markers supposedly destroyed during the Collective's bloodthirsty raids, which nearly led to the destruction of the clans. By the time the Consortium was back in power, no one knew where the Markers were, or how to find them...or even if they had ever truly existed. The new Consortium had supposedly been searching for the original archives for centuries, as had the Collective, hoping the lost records would lead to some answers, but as far as Saige knew, neither group had ever found them.

"You actually report to the Consortium, don't you?" she asked, wondering if Quinn was even aware of the maps' existence.

"Yeah," he rasped, slanting her an odd look.

"What?"

Quinn rolled his broad shoulders with only a fraction of movement, finally shoving his restless hands into his pockets. "I guess I'm just surprised that with as much as you know about everything—which seems to be a hell of a lot—you never tried to warn your brothers about what you'd learned. It would have been nice if they'd known what was coming."

Instead of getting defensive, Saige responded with a small, bitter smile. "Who says I didn't?"

She could read the questions in his dark eyes as he cut her a slow, interested look.

Wrapping her hands around the frayed strap of her backpack, she explained. "The last time I saw Riley, I tried to warn him...to tell him that I feared I'd found the cross in Italy for a reason. That I was afraid it could be a sign, one that meant the legendary awakenings the gypsies had foretold were actually coming.

And do you know what he told me?" she asked, barging ahead without waiting for a response. "He said we'd be monsters if the things I believed ever turned out to be true, same as the Casus, and that we'd be better off dead. Then he said that if I ever mentioned the Merrick to him again, I could forget he was my brother."

Quinn frowned, turning his attention back to the encroaching shadows. "I don't know what Riley's problem was," he said, "but I might as well go ahead and warn you now, Saige. Both of your brothers are going to be furious when they learn that your awakening has already started and you didn't come to them for help. They really are worried about you."

"I doubt that," she offered with a soft laugh. She had no idea how to deal with such a bizarre thought…and couldn't help but doubt its truth, no matter how much Quinn believed it.

He slanted her a curious look, studying her from beneath those heavy lashes, and Saige had the strangest feeling that he could see right through her, into all the embarrassing longing and churning doubts that plagued her. "You just might be in for a surprise when we get to Colorado."

"Look, I don't know what impression my brothers have given you, but we're not exactly close," she said, her gaze sliding away from those dark eyes that made her feel too exposed…too bare. "It's been that way since Ian started getting older. Everything began to change after that. My mother's preoccupation with the family bloodline drove a wedge between me and my brothers, until not talking about the Merrick became the axiom of our twisted little family."

"If that's true, then I guess it would help explain why Riley never mentioned your warnings to Ian."

"To be honest, I'm not surprised that he didn't," she offered quietly, her mind taking her back to the past. "Something happened when Riley was in his teens, after Ian had already run away, but he's never told me what it was. All I know is that he never talked about the Merrick again from that point on." She drew in a deep breath, staring for a moment up at the peaceful beauty of the clear, star-studded sky. "Whatever it was, it still haunts him. When things started happening to Ian, Riley probably did everything he could to convince himself there was an explanation, logical or otherwise, that didn't involve the Casus and the Merrick. I can imagine how he reacted when he was finally forced to face the truth."

Another low rumble of laughter vibrated in his chest, the wry sound confirming what she'd already guessed. "He definitely didn't take it well when my unit contacted him, but once we explained exactly what Ian was going up against, he came with us to help. And after he saw what the Casus was capable of, it drove him crazy that he didn't have any way of contacting you. He was ready to come after you himself when we couldn't get in touch with Templeton, but Kierland Scott, who heads up our unit, refused to tell him where you were. Said Riley was only going to run off and get himself killed, when he needed to be at Ravenswing, learning how to prepare for his own awakening."

"But he's still refusing to stay at the compound, right?"

He nodded. "Says he needs to be in Henning, protecting the townspeople who trust him to do just that."

"That sounds like Riley." Saige tilted her face toward the slow-blowing breeze, seeking relief from the thick evening heat and her own burning frustration. "But maybe he's doing the right thing, keeping an eye on everyone. I was so certain the Casus would only target the Merrick, without wasting their time on humans, and look how wrong I was."

"Even with as much as you've managed to learn, Saige, you still can't expect to know everything. Until this started, none of us knew what to expect," he offered in a low tone, almost as if he were trying to put her at ease. "Hell, we're still piecing it all together...still trying to figure it out. Why do they want the Markers? What are they really after? How are they escaping from the holding ground and why now, after all this time?"

A brittle laugh jerked from her throat. "It's maddening, when you think about it. Every answer only leads to more questions...and more frustration."

Lifting his hand, he rubbed at the back of his neck again, making her wonder how much stress he'd been carrying. "That's why my unit broke with our code and made contact with your brother."

"And that's why you're in trouble with the Consortium?" she asked, surprised by how curious she was about him. Not just about the events that had led him to South America, but Quinn, the man, and as they hiked together up the rustic road, there were instances where she actually left reality behind, and found herself simply soaking in the compelling patterns of his speech and the way he moved, the way he breathed...even how he laughed.

There was a wry edge to his words as he answered her question. "Our involvement with the Merrick awakenings hasn't exactly been sanctioned by our superiors. But we all decided that it was time to do more than simply watch from the sidelines."

"Speaking of watching, how did you miss the discovery of the Marker in Italy? You said before that it was Ian who told you about it, after you'd made contact with him and taken him to Ravenswing. But wasn't there already a Watchman keeping tabs on me?"

Quinn gave another low, rugged laugh. "Kellan Scott was watching you at the time. He's the younger brother of my best friend, Kierland, and a good kid, but he still has a lot to learn. Seems he was a little too easily distracted by the local female population when he should have been working, keeping an eye on what you were up to."

Snuffling a soft chuckle under her breath, she accidentally brushed against him as she sidestepped a rusty bicycle lying in the street. Her breath caught at the feel of hard muscle and hot male skin...making her wonder if he'd be that hard and hot everywhere.

Ripping her mind away from the dangerous territory of that particular thought, she cleared her throat, saying, "I bet you guys were pretty pissed when you realized what he'd missed."

He nodded, his tone gruff as he said, "Yeah, but we

were already ticked at him for not doing his job and watching you the way he was meant to."

She lowered her gaze, thinking of the last Watchman who'd been assigned to her. "Do you think Templeton is dead?"

With his hard jaw and grooved brow, Quinn's expression revealed his worry and frustration. "He would have contacted us by now if he was still alive. It's a sobering thought, considering Templeton wouldn't have been an easy man to take down, even for a Casus."

"I hope it was quick," she said softly, the words thick in her throat. "I hate the thought of it torturing him the way you said the Casus tortured those poor women who Ian knew."

"If it makes you feel any better," he rasped, "Ian used the Marker to make that bastard pay. It made one hell of a weapon."

"I don't suppose you brought it with you?"

He shook his head. "We figured it was too risky, seeing as how we're so far away from the compound. What exactly are you doing down here, anyway?"

"Didn't Templeton tell you?"

"He said in his last report that he had his suspicions." His tone was casual, but Saige could sense the keen edge of his curiosity. "To be honest, I'd rather hear it from you."

Wondering how much to reveal—and how much she should keep to herself, at least until she knew more about him—Saige collected her thoughts for a moment as they made their way past a group of teenage boys sprawled on the front steps of a noisy building, the open windows allowing the layered, raucous sounds of music and voices to drift down from above. "I'm sure you already know," she began, "that unlike my brothers, I chose not to run from what's inside us. I've always been a believer, and I've spent my life researching the Merrick. I guess you could say that the pieces of the puzzle finally pulled me here."

Quinn arched one brow. "Meaning?"

Wetting her lips, she ignored the annoying twinge of guilt in the pit of her stomach. Until she knew him better, there was only so much Saige was willing to share. "Meaning that I have reason to believe a Marker might be buried here. I got lucky and was able to join up with a local dig that was already in process, and I've been secretly working toward finding it ever since."

"We wondered if you were searching for another one," he murmured, looking as if he didn't know quite what to make of her. "Most humans wouldn't be so daring."

A reluctant grin curled the corner of her mouth. "But we Buchanans aren't exactly human, are we?"

"No, you're not," he agreed, rubbing his hand over the shadowed angle of his jaw, the ink-black stubble only accentuating the wicked sensuality of his looks. "You're also hell on a guy's ego."

"Why's that?" she asked, finding it difficult to believe that anything could dent his masculine pride.

"I'm just spit-balling here, but it could have some-thing to do with how you tried to brain me with that beer bottle," he offered dryly.

"And here I thought the Watchmen were supposed

to be so tough," she snorted, eyeing his wounded temple. "It isn't even bleeding anymore."

"It's not so much the blood that irritates me as the fact that you had no reason to attack me."

The corner of her mouth twitched at his put-out expression. "Would it make you feel better if I let you hit me back?"

Saige had never actually watched a man's lip curl before, and was fascinated by the sight. "I don't hit women."

"Just because I'm a woman," she lectured him, "doesn't mean I can't hold my own. I grew up with two older brothers, which means I learned how to fight dirty early on."

"Don't worry," he responded under his breath, turning his attention back to the shadowed street. "I don't think you're weak, Saige. I just think you're crazy."

Unsure if he was teasing or actually serious, she opted to remain silent until they reached the next corner. "Javier's apartment is at the end of this block."

"Just make it quick," he murmured, looking over the area. It was difficult to tell where one building ended and its neighbor began, the various balconies and awnings giving the three- and four-story structures a look of crooked imbalance. They'd always reminded Saige of building blocks stacked by a child, on the verge of teetering over if the wind blew too hard. "I don't like it here. We're not that far from the jungle, and there are too many places to hide."

"This will only take a minute," she assured him, hiking her backpack higher on her shoulder. Stepping up onto the raised front porch of the ground-floor apartment, Saige lifted her hand to knock, every sound coming from the nearby buildings making her flinch. Obviously her nerves were still raw from her recent brush with death, as well as her worry for her friends.

Blowing her hair out of her eyes, she knocked once…and waited. Then knocked again. Frowning, Saige started to reach for the door handle, when Quinn drew in a deep breath and grunted, suddenly grabbing hold of her hand and securing it in his steely grip.

"What are you doing?" she whispered, flicking him a startled glance. Like waves of heat, she could feel a strange energy pouring through the touch of his skin against hers, and her anxiety cranked higher.

"You can't go in there," he told her in a low, almost soundless growl.

Her eyes went wide. "No one in Javier's family would hurt me. They're my friends."

"It's too late," he grunted, his expression one of grim resignation. "Come on."

"What?" Saige pulled at his grip with her fingers and dug in her heels. "What are you talking about?"

"Casus," he growled.

"Cas…" The word trailed off as she suddenly registered the strange, thick odor seeping beneath the door, and her stomach roiled.

Oh God, no. No. No. No.

"Javier!" she gasped, lurching for the handle, but Quinn held her in place. Banding his left arm around her waist, he pulled her away from the door and down the wooden steps of the porch.

"Trust me, Saige. You don't want to go in there." The words were hard…bitten, and yet somehow compellingly gentle as he scanned the street from side to side. The narrow road, for the moment, was empty, this section of the neighborhood quiet but for the bustling din of families sharing their evening meal, the clattering sounds of crockery spilling from open windows and doorways that had been left open to help alleviate the humid evening heat.

The breeze surged, bringing the combined scents of food and blood and what smelled like charred flesh into sharper focus. "I can't…I can't—" she choked out, painfully aware that she had to know what had happened. She couldn't just run—not when there was a chance that Javier was in there, broken and bleeding…but alive.

Twisting suddenly out of Quinn's grip, Saige turned and ran back up the steps, her backpack falling to the porch as she lunged for the handle. When it wouldn't budge, she threw her shoulder against the door, instantly breaking it open. In the back of her mind, she acknowledged the fact that she shouldn't have been strong enough to take down a door on her own, no matter how old it was, but the thought faded as she rushed into the ground-floor apartment. Her feet hit something wet and slick…and the next thing she knew, she was on her hands and knees in a thick, sickening pool of blood. It spread out around her like a crimson sea of hell, and her stomach heaved. Bile rose in her throat, and she lifted her head, too choked to scream as she took in the sight before her.

"Ohmygod," she whispered, her lips so numb from the shock, the words felt strangely foreign in her mouth as she sluggishly stumbled to her feet. She was only distantly aware of Quinn's strong, rough hands steadying her, of the sharp, virulent curse he scraped out, her entire attention focused on the mangled corpses of the Ruiz brothers.

Four bodies, all dead, sat with their backs propped against the far wall of the small sitting room, their long legs stretched out before them on the floor, while their heads lolled to the side like lifeless rag dolls. Gruesome, animal-like slashes and bite marks faded as their flesh continued to shrivel and char, huge pieces missing in some places, as if they'd been…eaten. What remained of their bodies smoldered, but without fire and flames, as if their skin was simply incinerating of its own volition—their eyes left open, mouths slack as blood continued to pool around them in a slow, sluggish pour.

A hysterical scream suddenly crawled up from the deepest part of her body, and she scraped her blood-stained hands into her hair, her body bent forward, as if the pain were pulling her in on herself. She teetered on the rim of a dark, deep chasm that was endless and black as pitch, a breath away from plunging forward, headfirst into that bottomless, suffocating pit. The horror was viciously destructive, like a poison rushing through her veins as she thought of Javier's close-knit family. The brothers had had nothing but each other, and yet, they'd been the most giving people she'd ever known. And now they were dead—slaughtered—because of her.

The Casus, she thought. *It had to have been the Casus.*

Fighting the nauseating waves of heartache, she gulped in a huge, desperate gasp of air, and the pain transformed from one second to the next, the rise of fury—of murderous, red-tinged, gnashing rage—building up from the soles of her feet. It spilled through her body like something ugly and thick, slithering beneath her skin, and Saige realized in that moment that the primal passion of her Merrick was being distorted by hatred and anger. As she lifted her head and turned to stare at Quinn, his eyes went hooded. His body tensed. Saige knew he could feel it. Knew he could sense the rise of her beast, and acceptance settled across his stoic expression.

He was prepared to deal with whatever she needed to throw at him. To deal with *her.*

Giving in to the visceral, animalistic burn of rage, she made a deep, guttural sound in the back of her throat, then rushed at him, battering him with her fists, her blows landing heavily on his shoulders and chest. She wanted him to fight back, to lash out at her, justifying her attack, but he only held her, weathering the brunt of her assault, while doing his best to keep her from hurting herself. It made her angrier…made her want to hate him…to hurt him. Saige screamed again, louder, deeper, until the sound bled into a raw, sobbing cry and her violent fury crashed down into another shuddering, heaving storm of tears.

Unable to face him, she turned away, curling back in on herself, and found herself staring once again at the charred bodies positioned with such sadistic care against the far wall. Blinking, she was riveted by a familiar silver bracelet on the blackened corpse that sat at the far right. The bracelet had been a gift to Javier on his sixteenth birthday from his parents, who'd both died a month later in a fire at the factory where they worked.

With wide, horrified eyes, she suddenly noticed that the fingers of his right hand had been bitten off at different lengths, as if taken one by one. Bile rose again in her throat while the tears ran unchecked down her hot, burning face. Oh God. Had the monster tortured him? And if so…why? Javier hadn't known anything about the Marker. Not that she hadn't trusted him—she just hadn't wanted to put him at risk.

Huh. Looks like you screwed up again.

She'd thought she was protecting him, sending him away when she'd seen Quinn at the bar, and instead, she'd sent the young man right into her enemy's arms. "How…how could it do this?" she whispered in an unrecognizable croak.

Placing one strong, warm hand on her shoulder, Quinn moved closer, until she felt his oddly comforting heat at her back. "I don't know what's going on, but this wasn't Casus. At least not all of it."

Saige shook her head, trying to make sense of what he'd said. "I don't…I don't understand."

"The bodies. Someone's covering up the fact that they were butchered, and they could still be nearby. We need to get out of here."

She nodded numbly, swaying slightly as the room seemed to roll away from her. Quinn cursed something hot and gritty under his breath, then lifted her into his arms, carrying her out of the apartment. Saige buried her face in the side of his throat, her hands clutching at his broad shoulders. She didn't know where he was taking her, and she didn't care.

"Shh," he whispered as she quietly sobbed, his warm lips tender against her temple, the bristles of his beard soft against her skin. "I've got you."

She shivered, holding him tighter, and curled against his chest like a child, willing to let him take her out into the night. He could have taken her to the ends of the earth at that moment, and she wouldn't have argued...wouldn't have fought him. Saige breathed in the rich warmth of his skin, finding sweat and salt and clean male musk, and wanted nothing more than to drown herself in that intoxicating blend of the jungle and the sun and the man. Like a balm for her soul, she needed it to wash away that horrific odor of death that would no doubt haunt her forever.

"We need to get to São Vicente," he told her, his voice soft as he reached down to grab her backpack from the ground, then set off down the dark, uneven street with a swift, determined stride. "We'll stay in my room tonight, then head out in the morning."

"You should do the smart thing and just get away from me, Quinn." She squeezed her eyes tighter, wanting to force out the horrific memory, but it was right there, playing on the backs of her eyes, burning its way into her brain like a scar. "You were right, about everything. They're going to come after me," she explained in a thick voice, shifting so that she could stare up at him through the hot wash of tears. "They won't stop. Not if they were willing to do something like that."

His expression hardened as he kept his eyes on the road. "That's why I'm here. This isn't something you have to go through alone."

"I won't have your blood on my hands, as well," she whispered, the words wrecked by emotion.

"You won't." He shifted his hold, pulling her tighter against his chest. "I'm a big boy, Saige. I can take care of myself. Right now the only thing we have to worry about is getting you to Colorado."

She swallowed, knowing what she would have to do, as soon as she had the strength, and rested her head on his shoulder. It was strange, how the intimate embrace felt like the most natural place in the world for her to be. "How far are we from the hotel?"

"About half an hour. I'm going to find us a cab," he rasped, and she nodded, struggling to get control of her tears. She was broken and raw and bleeding inside from the heartbreak…from the horror she'd seen, and no matter how hard she tried, she couldn't turn it off. Couldn't shut it down.

And yet, in that moment, Saige felt utterly safe, protected by nothing more than a stranger's strong, possessive embrace.

CHAPTER SIX

São Vicente

QUINN COULD HEAR her crying in the shower.

Pacing from one side of the gaudy, crimson-and-gilt-covered hotel room to the other, he struggled to throw off the tension knotting his muscles, climbing like some insidious parasite through the back of his shoulders and neck. Despite the droning buzz of the air conditioner perched beneath the lone window, his skin was slicked with sweat, burning with heat, his muscles coiled hard and tight with the need to take action, but there was nothing he could do. No way to make things right. Instead, he was stuck in this hellish suite, listening to Saige fall apart…unable to do a goddamn thing to stop it.

Christ, just ease up with the tears, he silently growled, relishing the thought of how good it would feel to get his hands on the bastard responsible for murdering the Ruiz brothers. Saige was a wreck over the loss of her friend, and though he tried to suck it up and shrug it off, he could *not* get it together. He was too wound up, too on edge to do anything but pace the tacky carpet, wishing he could just undo the last few hours and start things over.

God, if he could, he'd undo the last five years of his life and take himself back to a time when his insides didn't get twisted up whenever a woman drew his interest.

Not that she's like any woman you've ever known.

Quinn paused in his pacing and rubbed at the bristled angle of his jaw, raging against the simple truth of that particular statement. Muttering a sharp curse under his breath, he slanted a dark look toward the bathroom door, the sound of her crying punching at him like a physical blow. After Janelle's emotional meltdowns, which his ex-fiancée had often suffered toward the end of their relationship, Quinn had thought he was immune to the sound of a woman's tears, but he'd been wrong. Listening to Saige's grief was like a thousand tiny razor blades slicing at his gut, each one cutting him just that little bit deeper, stripping away an extra layer of his already shredded control.

Pivoting on his right foot, he continued to eye the bathroom door as he stalked past the massive king-size bed with its blinding gold satin bedspread, wondering how much longer she was going to stay in there. He doubted this place had an endless supply of hot water, and he didn't want her standing in there freezing her ass off.

After they'd made it to the hotel, Quinn had immediately shuffled her into the bathroom, ordering her into the shower—and for once, the stubborn-headed woman hadn't argued. While she'd leaned against the tiled bathroom wall, staring sightlessly at the linoleum floor, he'd started the water for her, hoping it would help calm her down if she could wash off the dark smears of blood that'd dried on her hands and knees. She'd nodded when he'd asked if she'd be okay on her own, and so he'd closed the door behind him, waiting until he heard the rustle of the plastic curtain before walking away.

Once he'd attached a few of Kellan's latest techno gadgets—dime-size, ultrasensitive motion detectors— to the door and window, Quinn grabbed his cell phone from the duffel he'd left in the room and keyed in a brief text that would feed into the main computer system back at Ravenswing. As he'd explained to Saige during their earlier trek through the jungle, the Watchmen never used phone lines in high-security situations like these. Instead, he coded a brief line of text, letting his friends know that he had Saige and would be heading back with her in the morning. He didn't mention Javier or the boy's brothers, not wanting to worry them until he had a better understanding of what he was dealing with. The kills had looked like the work of the Casus...and yet, the charring of the bodies was standard operating procedure for the Collective Army, which didn't make any friggin' sense at all.

Collective soldiers employed a military-grade biochemical agent to destroy the evidence of their kills— whether they'd beheaded a vampire or gutted a lycanthrope—but Quinn had never seen the flesh-eating corrosive used on human corpses. On the rare occasions when the fanatical soldiers were the first to discover victims who'd been killed by a nonhuman species, he'd always heard that the deceased were given a secret, ceremonial burial.

So then what had happened in that apartment? Had the Collective found the murder victims, and then been unable to remove the bodies for burial, using the corrosive as a last resort to disguise how the young men had died? Or had they somehow orchestrated the murders to look like Casus kills, and then charred them? And if so, what the hell was their motive?

Turning to stalk back across the garish room, Quinn threw off that last idea with a frustrated roll of his shoulders, knowing damn well that it was an unlikely scenario. The Collective had no qualms about butchering those they considered "impure"—but they didn't kill humans. That wasn't the way they operated, no matter how whacked in the head they were. The purity of humanity was the very thing they vowed to protect. It made no sense for them to murder a human family— and yet, his gut told him the militant fanatics *had* somehow been involved with the killings.

Slanting another narrow look toward the bathroom door, Quinn knew this latest development meant more trouble for him and his charge. No matter how it played out, there were too many psychopathic players in this little nightmare for it to have anything but a chilling ending. And it was, in every sense of the word, a nightmare. He was thousands of miles from the safety of the compound, had an emotionally distraught woman on his hands, as well as a seriously ill-timed bout of lust, with not only a Casus on their trail, but also what could very well prove to be the unlimited resources of the Collective Army.

Hell, at this point, saying he was screwed was just putting a good spin on things.

And if you were smart, you'd have told Kierland to shove it when he gave you this assignment.

True, but his gut cramped at the thought. Aiden Shrader would have been more than happy to come if Kierland had allowed it, and Quinn knew damn good and well how things would be playing out if his friend were standing there in his place. Smug bastard would be *in* that shower with her, offering his own brand of comfort.

The irreverent Watchman would have taken one look at Saige Buchanan, and he'd have wanted her. It wasn't a guess on Quinn's part—it was a given. She was too vibrant and soft and tender not to draw a man's notice.

And yet, as delicate and feminine as she was, her strength was an innate part of her, making her look completely at home there in the lush, primordial wilds of the jungle. It was as if she were some primal, earthy being that held hidden, secret wells of power—which she did. Quinn had heard that Merrick females were fascinating creatures, and after meeting Saige, he couldn't help but agree.

Face it, man. You're ready to lie down and let her wipe the floor with you.

Scraping his hands back through his short hair, he blew out a rough breath, wishing he had a clue what he was doing. None of this had gone the way he'd planned, and he sure as hell hadn't been expecting to find himself this affected by her. It was madness, considering she'd been nothing but a total pain in the ass.

Cursing a foul streak, he ground his palms into his eye sockets, but no matter how hard he tried, he could *not* get rid of the constantly revolving images slowly stripping away his sanity. They played over and over, pushing him…knotting his insides…grinding him down until he was raw.

Saige sitting in the bar, drawing his eye as she lifted one delicate-boned hand and pushed her long, wavy hair behind her ear.

Saige running through the jungle, looking wild and primeval, the most breathtaking thing he'd ever set eyes on.

Saige crying in his arms, so warm and womanly and soft, holding on to him as though she'd never let him go.

And where exactly are you going with all this?

Christ, he had no idea what was going on in his head. Either the humidity was messing with his mind, or there was something far more dangerous at work. Quinn didn't even know her, but he wanted to, in every sense of the word, and it terrified him. He'd been so sure that he'd frozen out that hungry, curious part of his soul after Janelle, but now he couldn't help but wonder if he'd been wrong.

If it'd just been sex, he wouldn't have liked it, but he could have dealt with it. He'd always had a healthy sex drive, but then his kind generally did. You couldn't have an aggressive animal nature without sharing its more predatory desires. Still, Quinn wasn't a man to be ruled by his physical needs. He'd been down that path once before, and he still carried the scars as a vicious reminder of his stupidity.

Yeah, he wanted to take Saige under his body, losing himself in a dark, destructive pleasure that he knew would be unlike anything he'd ever experienced—but there was more to it than that. And it was the *more* that had him twisted up inside.

Poor Quinn. Maybe Saige was right, and you really are brainless.

A low, self-deprecating rumble of laughter surged up from his throat, and he'd just turned to pace his way back across the hideous crimson carpet, his hands locked behind his head, when a dull thump came from the bathroom. Frowning, he lowered his arms as he walked to the door, pressing his ear against the wood. "Saige?"

When she didn't reply, he called her name again, but there was still no answer.

"Either you let me know that you're okay," he growled, lust and frustration thickening his words, "or I'm coming in."

Again, Quinn waited, only to hear nothing but the rushing surge of the water through the pipes. Gritting his teeth, he twisted the knob, a damp blast of heat hitting him in the face as he opened the door. A thick mist covered the mirror over the sink, obscuring his reflection, the gold-and-red shower curtain still pulled closed. "Saige? Come on and talk to me, honey."

He waited another handful of seconds, and then, knowing he was going to live to regret it, Quinn finally grabbed hold of the edge of the curtain.

With a deep breath, he yanked it back.

And there she was.

Saige sat slouched in a corner of the tub, slender arms wrapped around her bent knees, her face turned toward the wall, profile obscured by wet skeins of hair that fanned out across her pale shoulders like burgundy strands of silk. She didn't even flinch at the sound of his voice as he said her name, her chest rising and falling with the soft, silent pattern of her hitching breaths.

Bending down, Quinn crouched at the side of the tub, thankful that she still wore her panties and a thin white tank top. He knew what it was going to cost him to touch her, but there was no help for it. He couldn't just leave her there, no matter how badly he wanted to.

Yeah, right, that familiar smart-ass snickered in his head, and he ground his jaw, painfully aware that walking away from her was the last thing in the world he wanted to do.

Welcome to hell, Quinn. Might as well do your best to get comfortable. You won't be leaving anytime soon.

"Saige, look at me." She gasped at the light touch of his hand on her arm, and finally lifted her face, turning toward him with glistening, tear-drenched eyes. The paleness of her skin only accentuated the deep, storm-dark blue of her eyes, the faint smudges beneath giving her a hollow, fragile look that made something in his chest feel like it'd been smashed with a hammer.

"Come on," he forced himself to say through his gritted teeth, disgusted with himself for being jacked up with lust when she was in such a vulnerable state. He didn't have any right to be near her, and yet, he seemed destined to play her white knight.

Turning off the water, he reached for the towel that hung from the rack on his right, and reminded himself to be gentle, even if it killed him. "Let's get you out of there," he murmured, and as she turned toward him, lifting her arms like a child waiting to be held and kissed all better, he used everything he had to hold his ground.

Just chill and get a grip. There's no reason to panic, because you know better than to let your guard down.

It was true. He *did* know better.

But as she reached for him, Quinn wondered if this woman wouldn't prove to be the death of him, after all.

SAIGE STRUGGLED to focus on the hard, impossibly gorgeous face that loomed before her, her vision blurred by the shivering combination of lukewarm water and hot tears. In a distant corner of her mind, she knew she should have been mortified by the situation, but she couldn't find the energy to care that she was all but naked, her drenched clothing doing little to conceal what was beneath.

Not that it mattered. Quinn was obviously too experienced to ogle her half-naked body like a teenage boy in the throes of lust. And yet, Saige knew he wasn't unaffected. She could sense his sexual awareness on the hot, thick air as if it were a living, breathing entity rising between them, slick and heavy against her skin.

But there isn't a chance in hell he's going to acknowledge it, she thought as he carefully pulled her to her feet, lifting her out of the tub before wrapping a soft towel around her body. Glancing up at his dark face, she blinked as she noticed that his bottom lip had been busted. Between his stubble-roughened cheeks, his mouth was a hard, sensual line, the corner of his lower lip swollen and bruised. "I did that, didn't I?" she asked in a husky rasp, vaguely recalling how she'd punched at him in Javier's apartment. Blood still stained his temple, as well, from where she'd bashed him with the beer bottle at the bar.

"Don't worry about it," he rumbled, shrugging it off. "I get worse than this sparring with Kierland back at the compound."

"For what it's worth, I'm sorry." The tears in her throat garbled the throaty confession, but she fought them back, doing her best not to fall apart on him all over again. After everything he'd done, the guy didn't deserve a sopping emotional freak on his hands. She could save the rest of her meltdown for later, when she was on her own.

"Nothing to be sorry about," he murmured, his tone somehow both firm and gentle at the same time, and she couldn't help but remember the heroic way in which he'd carried her out of that nightmarish scene, cradling her in his arms. There was a small, needy part of her that wanted to crawl back up into those powerful arms and curl against his chest, but she knew that was too pathetic. Not to mention completely insane.

Get it together, Saige. You. Have. Got. To. Get. It. Together.

There was still so much anger inside her, mixing with the unbearable grief, like a cold, gnawing fury that made it hurt to breathe…to move. But at the same time, there was a strange, unfamiliar warmth. A slick, provocative spill of heat that began to pulse deep inside her, and she stiffened in his hold, dizzy, her throat dry, raw from her crying jag.

Looking away from him, Saige wet her lips, wondering what was happening to her. Awareness flowed over her like a cool, calming mist, reminding her of a Brazilian rain shower, while she burned beneath her skin, prickly and hot. She needed to move, to escape, her senses on high alert, as if she were surrounded by danger.

And in a way, she was, seeing as how she was surrounded by the hard, predatory intensity of Michael Quinn. She didn't fear him physically, but he was definitely dangerous to her peace of mind. Her sense of self. Her control.

She couldn't deny that she wanted to take him. And she wanted to be taken. God, did she want to be taken. She wanted to lose herself…wanted to forget…to wash away the horror…the terror. Like chasing the illusory comfort of a dream or the pillowlike perfection of a cumulus summer cloud, Saige wanted to clutch on to the stunning aura of strength that pulsed from his tall, hard body and fall into it. Wanted to breathe this powerful stranger into her system, soak him up, take from him, greedy and desperate for every part of him she could get.

She wanted so much, so badly, that it overpowered her common sense.

And the next thing she knew, she was lost.

Without any conscious direction from her brain, Saige suddenly found her body pressed against his, her face buried in the side of his throat, and with a thick surge of biting, ravenous hunger, she breathed in the addictive warmth of his skin. She moaned when she found sweat and salt and rich, mouthwatering male musk—when she found the forest and the sun and the man. The heady blend was as intoxicating as it was provocative, making her hungry. It compelled her to tread carefully out to the edge of danger and dip her toes into the churning frenzy of emotion roiling up inside her, battering her mind, her organs, making her feel dizzy and bruised.

He trembled against her, his muscles locked hard and tight, as if he would push her away, but he didn't. Instead, Quinn slowly took hold of her face in his hot, work-roughened palms and tilted it back, staring down into her eyes. His pupils were dilated, the glittering, gleaming black all but swallowing his irises, his nostrils flaring as he breathed her in. A low growl rumbled in his chest, and his lips parted the barest fraction, his breath warm and sweet and delicious, magnifying her need to an unbearable pitch. He had the look of a man trapped between heaven and hell, suspended there on that painful precipice, and then, with a strained, choked sound of angry surrender, he finally lowered his head. One strong, powerful hand fisted in the damp tangle of her hair, holding her still, while the other curved against the side of her throat, his thumb pressed provocatively against her hammering pulse as the heat of his mouth brushed against hers. It was a light, fleeting touch of lips, as if he were afraid of taking too much and alarming her, but she was too far gone for caution.

Moaning deep in her throat, Saige went in for a wild, openmouthed kiss, and nearly died from the warm, honeyed perfection of his taste. Whimpering, she stretched up onto her tiptoes, wanting more. Needing it. Crawling out of her skin for it as the towel slipped from her shoulders to the floor. In all her life, she'd never known anything this urgent and demanding, as though her hunger for him was a living, breathing thing pouring through her body, making her crave…making her desperate. And as Quinn took control, kissing her back with a dark, almost savage mastery, all she could think was that she needed this moment, this kiss. God, did she need it. It was bright and shining and pure, bringing a measure of tenderness and ease to the raw, aching wounds that had been cut into her soul.

Tonight had been such a nightmare, and now she felt like a shipwreck survivor being pulled from the icy, thrashing torment of the sea to be delivered into safety, wrapped in waves of smoldering, luxurious warmth. The blissful sensation was dappled and soft, like falling into hot, bubbling honey, and she wanted to writhe in it. The provocative heat invaded every cell, every fragment of her mind, until she just wanted to sink into it, burrowing deeper, and stay there forever.

She could hide there, lost in that lush, lavish haven, and never have to face reality again.

Hold on to it, Saige. Whatever you do, don't let it go.

Making a rough, sexy sound that slipped deliciously into her mouth, Quinn curved his big hands down the sides of her spine, over the curve of her backside, the tips of those long, wicked fingers pressing intimately between her shaking thighs, stroking the damp cotton of her panties. Breathing a harsh, guttural curse against her mouth, he slipped one finger beneath the elasticized band, touching the screamingly hot, sensitive mouth of her sex, where she was melting, coming undone for him.

Saige cried out, trying to crawl her way up his body.

"More. Oh God. *More,*" she groaned, rubbing against that softly seeking finger, wanting it to do things she had no business wanting from a man she barely knew.

But Michael Quinn didn't feel like a stranger. He felt like the one place in the world where she belonged. Saige knew it was a dangerous, insane kind of thought— one that could no doubt land her in some serious trouble—but at that moment, she just didn't give a damn.

"Christ," he breathed in her ear, the hard, masculine sound edged with a savage, visceral need that told her just how much he wanted her—until his next words slammed her back to a cold, cruel sense of reality. "We can't do this, sweetheart. Not like this."

Blinking, she struggled to make sense of the words, terrified of the awful tension she could feel taking hold of his body. He shuddered against her, tenderly stroking the tight, drenched entrance of her sex, then carefully pulled his hand from between her legs. His breathing sounded as if he were in pain as he placed his hands on her shoulders.

With her heart sinking, Saige shook her head as he pressed her back, away from his heat...his hardness. "Quinn?" she rasped, unable to keep her bottom lip from trembling.

"No." She flinched at the harshness of that single word, his voice little more than a graveled scrape of sound as he held her in a hard, blistering stare. "Not. Like. This."

"Yes," she argued, her voice rising. "Now!"

Before she lost this feeling. Before she lost the ability to feel anything at all.

But his fingers bit into her shoulders when she tried to press closer, holding her back. "Touching you right now puts me in first-class dickhead territory, no matter how badly I want it. I can't do that."

She blinked more rapidly against the hot, mounting rush of tears, mentally slipping back to that god-awful room in Coroza, maddened by the senseless loss of her friends. "Oh God," she sobbed, and she could feel the sickening grief and fear overtaking her again, smashing her down into something small and needy. "Please, Quinn. Take this away. Just take it away."

He ground his jaw so hard, she was surprised his teeth didn't crack. "Damn it, Saige. You're not thinking clearly right now, and I—"

"You wanted me at the bar," she interrupted, the words pouring out of her, surging up from some unknown, untapped inner well of desperation. "I know you did. You wanted inside me—you even wanted my teeth in your throat. Wanted me to feed from you."

His eyes darkened with suspicion at the telling words, but he only said, "I want a lot of things that I can't have."

"Look around, Quinn. There's no one here telling you that you can't have me," she whispered, silently begging him just to give her what she needed.

"Stop it, Saige."

"God, what the hell—"

"I'm not trying to be a bastard here," he growled, dropping his hands to his sides as he took a step back, while something wrenching and bleak flickered in those dark, devastating eyes. "I'm just trying to do the right thing."

"Amazing," she said with a low laugh, the sound dry in her throat, choking her. Or maybe that was the tears. *The one time I try to lose myself in some casual sex, and the guy has to go and turn out to be a friggin' saint.* "If you weren't interested, all you had to do was say so."

"Jesus, if you only knew." That hard, smoldering gaze burned a searing trail from her bare feet, up the shivering length of her body, then stalled at her chest, where her nipples pressed thick and dark against the threadbare white cotton. "You could tempt a saint, woman."

Her mouth twisted with a bitter smile. "Just not you, huh?"

His gaze flew back to hers, and a guttural sound ripped from his throat, like a man being tortured, pushed to the edge of his control. "This isn't a simple situation, damn it. There's a lot that you don't know about me."

Pushing her wet hair back from her face, she said, "God, Quinn. It's not like I was asking you to marry me. Strangers have sex all the time."

"It isn't that simple." He crossed his arms over his T-shirt-covered chest, his intense stare hiding so much more than it revealed. "And you're hardly the kind of woman who jumps into the sack with a guy she's only just met."

"We're strangers, remember?" she snapped, reaching down for the towel and holding it against her chest, clutching it like a lifeline. "What makes you think you know what kind of woman I am?"

The brackets around his mouth deepened, the ink-black stubble on his cheeks and jaw giving him a dark, dangerous edge. "I can tell just from looking at you that you're not the kind who sleeps around."

He might have been right, but his words still pissed her off. "Fine. Whatever. At this point, I don't really give a damn," she muttered, brushing past him as she walked out of the bathroom. She found her backpack sitting on the foot of the bed, and quickly pulled out a T-shirt to sleep in, as well as a dry pair of panties.

When she turned back around, she nearly collided with Quinn's broad chest, he was standing so close. "I need to change," she said in a low, tight voice, staring at the strong, burnished length of his throat.

"If it's any consolation," he practically growled, "I'd give anything if this was any other night."

"Yeah, me, too." She wanted to hold on to the safety of her anger, but without the distraction of desire, the grief was too powerful, crowding in on her again, suffocating and thick, stealing the air from her lungs. She groaned at the onslaught, a harsh, animal sound coming from deep inside her, and the next thing she knew, Quinn was pulling her into his arms again, tucking her head into the crook of his shoulder. She squeezed her eyes closed, but the tears kept leaking out, salty and hot, drying in scratchy trails across her face.

When she rubbed her cheek against his cotton-covered chest, it almost felt like nuzzling him, like a child with its parent, seeking comfort and protection. And yet, her feelings for him were anything but platonic.

"I think I'm going to hate you for this," she said in a small voice, humiliation adding a new layer of misery to the night.

His chest shook with a silent, bitter burst of laughter, his heart beating strong and powerful beneath her ear as he stroked one warm hand down her back. "You couldn't possibly hate me as much as I hate myself right now."

Saige started to laugh at his dry confession, then remembered Javier and instantly choked off the light-hearted sound, feeling like a traitor.

"It's okay," he said in a low, velvety rumble.

Thinking it was uncanny, how easily he seemed to read her mind, she pulled out of his hold, saying, "Not tonight, it isn't."

"You shouldn't fight it," he told her. "My mother would always say that laughter is the soul's way of dealing with grief. The two opposites somehow balancing the other."

"Like the Merrick and the Casus," she whispered, staring up at him. "Devils and angels."

His eyes crinkled sexily at the corners, momentarily softening his expression. "There's no doubt the Casus are some evil sons of bitches, but after meeting your brothers, I'm not so sure you can call the Merrick angelic."

Saige shook with a silent bubble of laughter, but it only bled into something sharper…more painful. "I underestimated the Casus." Her voice cracked, and she swiped at a fresh wave of tears with her fingers. It seemed like forever since she'd cried, and now she couldn't seem to stop. Couldn't get control of her dizzying, gut-wrenching emotions. "I should have known better by now, after everything that I've learned. I thought I had it all figured out, that I understood what they wanted, how they worked, but I don't know anything. I made a stupid mistake, staying here in town, and those young men paid for it."

"You can't blame yourself."

She shivered, wrapping her arms around her middle, as if she could somehow hold herself together when everything seemed to be breaking apart. "Who else should I blame?"

"The bastards who are responsible," he muttered, his stride restless as he paced away. "You didn't kill those young men."

She lifted her chin, unwilling to let go of her guilt that easily. "No, but they died because of me."

"Christ," he breathed out, his tone thick with frustration as he shoved his hands back through his hair. "If Kierland were here, I know he'd be able to say it all a hell of a lot better than I can. I'm not—" He broke off, stopping to stare out the window at the dazzling skyline of the city, before hesitantly saying, "I'm not always good with words, but I know what it's like to want to take responsibility for things you can't control." He turned his head, slanting her a dark, haunted look from across the room. "You have to find a way to let it go."

"Did you?" she asked, positive that he carried his own demons. "Find a way to let it go?"

He turned back toward the window, silent and still, but she could feel the frustration in him, that hot, primal wave of tension growing stronger, blasting against her. He looked dangerous, even violent, but she couldn't keep her eyes off him—couldn't stop eating him up like a decadent, visual feast. He was so hard and beautiful with the bright lights of the city flickering across his chiseled profile, a hard, invincible warrior who feared nothing, and yet, there was something lonely and broken about the mysterious Watchman. Something that called to her—that made her want to be the one to walk to him and offer comfort. To get inside his head and learn his secrets.

And that should be your clue to get the hell out of here.

She had no business getting close to him. After what had happened to Javier, she had no business getting close to anybody. The best thing she could do was keep her distance, and leave Michael Quinn in peace.

Clutching the sleep shirt to her chest, she quietly said, "I'll just get changed now," and headed into the bathroom. Shutting the door behind her, Saige did her best to keep her mind blank as she quickly hung up her wet clothes in the shower and slipped on the dry ones. When she opened the door again, she found Quinn exactly where she'd left him.

"Are you hungry?" he asked, turning away from the window.

Pressing one hand to her belly, she shook her head, the idea of food making her suddenly nauseous. "I'd rather just go to bed." He gave a slow nod, obviously doing his best to keep his eyes on her face, and not on her body, her legs bare beneath the hem of her shirt. She pulled in a deep breath, ready to tell him good-night, when Saige suddenly heard herself saying, "Lie down with me?"

The words tumbled out of her in a soft, trembling rush, and yet, they seemed to land between them with the stunning impact of a grenade, jarring and un-bearably loud.

Quinn cleared his throat, looking as if she'd just

asked him to dive into shark-infested waters. "After what happened in the bathroom," he rasped, his deep voice tight with restraint, "I don't think that would be a good idea."

"Please," she whispered, hating that she was begging again. She hadn't planned on asking him for something so intimate, but the idea of what the next day would bring made her want to stay close to him for as long as she could. Made her want to be in the strong circle of his arms, even if they were doing nothing more than sleeping. "I promise I'll keep my hands to myself. No funny stuff. I just—" she swallowed, forcing out the uncharacteristic confession "—I just really feel like being held right now, Quinn."

She wondered if he had any clue how out of character this moment was for her. If he could see just how difficult it was for her to admit that she needed something, *anything,* from another person. Even asking Jamison to help her get the Marker out of Brazil had been easier than this—but then that had been for...for something bigger than her. The greater good. The safety of the friggin' world. But this—this was about nothing but what *she* needed. What *she* wanted.

Her lungs burned as she waited for his response, her heart beating so rapidly, it reminded her of a bird getting ready to take flight from her chest.

After what felt like a quiet forever, Quinn finally lifted one hand, rubbing it against the shadowed angle of his jaw. "No funny stuff, huh? I think that's supposed to be my line," he murmured dryly, and the sudden, stunning surge of relief made her feel almost light-headed.

She couldn't read the dark, shadowed look in his eyes, but there was a wicked, nearly imperceptible curve to the corner of his mouth as he propped his hip against the window ledge and bent forward to pull off his boots. Worried she'd throw herself at him, scaring him off, Saige turned away when he reached behind his head, grabbing a handful of his T-shirt. Sinking her teeth into her lower lip, she quickly pulled back the bedspread and slipped between the cool, crisp sheets. She curled onto her side, aware of her heart beating harder…faster. A moment later, Quinn turned out the bedside light and slipped in behind her, the feel of his denim-covered legs bringing a wry smile to her lips. He'd taken his shirt off, but left on his jeans.

"You always sleep like this?" she asked, burrowing back against him until he completely spooned her. Her head fit perfectly under his chin, her back snuggled up against the hot, hard width of his beautiful chest.

"Just be quiet and lie still," he grunted, his voice strained as she wiggled her hips into a more comfortable position, rubbing against him. One large hand gripped her waist, the heat of his fingers seeping through her T-shirt as he held her in place and inched his groin away from her bottom. "Tomorrow's going to be a helluva day, so sleep while you can."

"And what are you going to do?" she murmured, sleep the furthest thing from her mind as she allowed herself a moment to imagine what it would feel like to have the power of him over her…moving within her.

His breath was warm against her scalp, sending a delicious, dizzying wave of sensation flaring across her skin, and then he quietly said, "I'm going to stay right here, holding on to you. Now go to sleep, Saige."

"Are you sure it's safe?"

"I have alarms on the door and window," he murmured in a low, husky rumble. "No one's coming in without us knowing about it. I'm not going to let anyone hurt you."

She shivered from the dark, possessive quality of his voice, while something thick and warm spilled through her system.

So this is what it feels like to have a man's protection, she thought, a little dazed…and uncertain. It wasn't that she didn't like the feeling. What wasn't to like? It was just…well, it was one of those feelings that you knew, instinctively, were too good to be true. Which made liking it not only stupid, but dangerous.

Michael Quinn might not be a threat to her safety—but something told Saige that he could be hell on a woman's heart. "Just so you know, there won't be any second chances with me. You've blown your one shot," she warned him, partly teasing, but acutely aware of how badly she wanted him to change his mind. Still, as wrecked as she was, Saige wasn't going to beg him again. Her pride might have been lying in shreds back on the bathroom floor, but it was determined to rally to her defense.

"We'll see about that," he countered in a quiet rasp, his voice so low, she couldn't tell if he'd meant for her to hear the graveled words or not.

Despite the strangeness of the situation, exhaustion finally began to creep over her in a thick, heavy pour, but there was one last question that she wanted to ask him. "Before I go to sleep, will you tell me what you are?"

"You already know what I am," he whispered in her ear, and she could almost hear his lopsided grin in that deep, beautiful voice. "Christ, I'm almost starting to think that you know more about the Watchmen than I do."

Nudging him with her elbow, she said, "You know that's not what I meant."

He sighed, and it wasn't until she'd finally closed her eyes, deciding that he wasn't going to answer, that he quietly said, "The wings come from my father, who was a Raptor. Do you know anything about them?"

"I've heard rumors," she said softly.

"A word of advice?"

"What?" she asked, wondering if even half of what she'd heard about the ruthless, sometimes terrifying shape-shifters was true.

Quinn threw his arm over her middle, securing her in place, then pressed closer, until she had no doubt that he was as aroused as she was. A hard, thick ridge burned against her bottom, through his jeans, and she held her breath…waiting. But he didn't whisper erotic intentions in her ear. He didn't whisper at all.

Instead, all he gave her was a simple, graveled warning. "Don't believe everything that you hear." His hold tightened, just enough for her to take notice as he added, "Because most of the time, it's nothing but a lie."

"I know," she whispered, burrowing deeper into the pillow.

And as she drifted into sleep, Saige couldn't help but wonder if his words were self-directed. Had he lied to her? Or did he know, in some way, that she'd lied to him?

CHAPTER SEVEN

Friday morning

WITH THE BRIGHT GLARE of South American sunlight pouring in through the slanted blinds, Saige struggled to pull herself out from under the comforting shadows of the covers. She was alone in the king-size bed, but she hadn't been that way for long. She could still feel the heat of Quinn's body at her back, like a tactile memory that had settled over her skin, unwilling to fade away. He'd kept his word and held her through the long, quiet hours of darkness—making it the first time in twenty-six years that she'd actually spent the night with a man.

And about time, too, you uptight, workaholic stress case.

Groaning at the sad reality of that statement, she rolled to her stomach and pulled the sheet over her head, while her face burned with heat. She wouldn't have believed it was possible, but she'd somehow managed to fall asleep with that big, rugged body wrapped around her. Or maybe it wasn't so surprising, considering she'd been running on pure adrenaline for what seemed like forever, constantly worrying that the next moment might be her last. Despite the fact she barely knew the enigmatic Watchman, there was no denying that she'd felt safe last night in a way that she'd never felt before, and her body had reacted by grabbing at some much-needed rest while it still could.

"I realize it's been a rough week, but you thinking about getting up anytime soon?"

Saige shook her head at the rich, deep rumble of Quinn's voice, thinking the guy should come with a warning label. *Caution: Approach this male at your own risk. Possible dangers include excessive drooling, rapid heart rate...and in some cases, hormone-induced spontaneous combustion.*

Her mouth twitched at the whimsical thought, which was so unlike her. She didn't normally take the time to be silly over guys, too much of her energy devoted to her job and the search for answers about the Merrick—but she understood why it was happening now. An innate sense of self-preservation had her mentally focused on Quinn, instead of the grief that still sat like a sickening weight in her belly, the loss of her friend too painful to think about. She'd do it later, when she could curl up in a dark, quiet place...and slowly fall apart. Somewhere solitary and private, without any interruptions. Somewhere Michael Quinn couldn't come rushing to her rescue—giving her another opportunity to make a fool of herself.

Wincing, she sank deeper into the bedding, wishing there was some way to block out the mortifying memory of those moments in the bathroom. Being turned down by him once was painful enough—Saige had no intention of humiliating herself again.

Thinking it was time to come out and stop hiding, she'd just started to push down the covers when the sound of her name cracked like a cannon blast through the room, making her flinch.

"Saige!"

She jumped at the brusqueness of his tone. "What?" she snapped, her own voice muffled by the sheet.

"Come on, already. We've got to get on the move."

He sounded closer than before, that sexy rasp filling her head...her senses, and she found herself wondering if he'd look as good in the harsh reality of bright morning sunlight as he had last night. Too curious to resist, she cracked one eyelid and peered over the edge of starched white cotton, blinking once, twice...and had to bite back a groan as she realized he looked even better.

Damn. That just isn't fair.

Clearing her throat, she tried for a tone that could pass for normal. "Do we have any coffee?"

His low, husky bark of laughter filled the room, doing that melty thing to her insides again. "If I say yes, will you finally get out of that bed?"

"I'll think about it." Sitting up, she released the death grip she had on the sheet, and threaded her fingers together in her lap, trying to play it off as if this kind of thing happened to her all the time—waking up in a strange hotel room...with a gorgeous shape-shifter who was "sort of" grinning at her from the foot of the bed. Make that a half-naked hunk, with his chest bare, the dark, silky trail of hair circling his belly button drawing her eye like a magnet. She followed it lower…lower, until the sexy line of hair slipped inside the waistband of his jeans, where the top button had been left undone.

For a moment her gaze simply lingered on him with a hazy longing that she was having a hard time disguising, until she noticed the razor in his right hand. "What are you doing?"

Lifting his free hand, he rubbed at the dark, sexy bristles covering his angular jaw. "I was going to give you a minute to wake up while I shave this thing off."

"No!" she burst out, unsurprised when he stared back at her as if she were crazy. "I just… I think… That is, maybe you should leave it. It's probably a good disguise, if the Collective already know what you look like."

His dark brows drew together in a curious frown. "You feeling okay?"

Was he mental? No, she wasn't feeling okay. How could she be feeling okay when it felt as if her body had been taken over by a sex-crazed body snatcher?

If it'd just been last night, in the heat of the moment, then she could have brushed it off and done her best to forget about it. But that wasn't the case. Even now, after being rejected once, Saige wanted to throw herself at him. It felt as if she'd contracted some kind of erotic jungle fever—one that demanded she get down and dirty with Michael Quinn as soon as humanly possible. Or not-so-humanly, considering they were both far from normal.

It was definitely a raging, feral case of lust, the

images so clear in her mind, burning with crisp, breathtaking precision, she almost felt as if she could reach out and touch them. Touch *him*. He'd turned her on in a way that no other man ever had, and now she couldn't get her traitorous body to turn back off. She all but hummed with a low frequency of constant, simmering hunger, itching beneath her skin for his scent and his heat and his taste.

Of all times to turn into a nympho, you sad, sad little woman.

Frowning, Saige could just imagine Quinn's report back to his compound. *Subject prone to embarrassing displays of lust. Recommend all men keep up their guard around her.*

Wow. Wouldn't that make a great impression on her brothers?

She knew, in a way, that her quest for the truth about the Merrick had been a means of proving to Ian and Riley that she and Elaina weren't crazy. She wanted them to see her as a serious researcher. An academic. Coming back into their lives as a man-hungry head case was so not what she'd had in mind.

Watching Quinn from the corner of her eye, she couldn't help but hate how composed he appeared, as if oblivious to the sexual tension skittering on the air between them. "So are we just going to pretend like last night didn't happen, then?"

For a split second he tensed, and she knew she'd surprised him by bringing it up. Hell, she'd surprised herself, the words slipping out again with no conscious direction from her brain. Maybe that terrifying

run through the jungle had jarred something loose in
her head, her words just spilling out now of their own
volition, as if her mouth had a mind of its own.

"I was sent here to protect you, Saige." He turned
away from the bed, heading toward the dresser, where
he put the razor back inside his black duffel bag. "And
to get you back to Colorado in one piece."

She arched one brow, waiting for him to turn back
around and explain what that had to do with their
physical attraction, but he remained silent and still.

"Well then." Her gaze slid away, toward the window, where the city skyline sprawled like an urban
jungle beneath the burning summer sun. She hesitated
for a moment, thinking about what she had to do.
She'd known since last night. Since the second she'd
seen what that bastard Casus had done to her friends.

Quinn's reaction to her question might have cut, but
she couldn't deny that it made her decision just that
little bit easier to accept.

"I have some things here in São Vicente," she
murmured, careful to avoid his gaze as she delivered
the lie. "In a safe at one of the local hotels, where a
friend of mine is a manager. I need to get them before
we head out."

She could feel the weight of his look as Quinn
turned toward her. "If it's something that can be
replaced, leave it."

"I can't," she breathed out, finally looking at him.

He crossed his arms over the black T-shirt he'd just
pulled on, his brows drawn together in a frustrated
frown as he leaned back against the dresser. "You're

going to have to give me more than that, Saige. We need to be on the move. Staying here a minute longer than we have to is just asking for trouble. We're already pushing it as it is."

"Well, this is something we definitely need." She paused, taking a deep breath as she held his dark, deep gaze. "It's all my research, Quinn. All the…notes I've taken. The ones that led me here to search for the Marker."

Uncrossing his arms, he moved away from the dresser and walked toward her, around the foot of the bed, not stopping until he stood at her hip. Pushing his hands into his pockets, he stared down at her with that primal, piercing intensity that made her feel stripped down to the bone. Completely exposed. "You really think it's here?" he asked.

She did her best to keep her expression guarded, giving nothing away. "Absolutely. And when it's safe, I'll have to find a way to come back for it."

Quinn shook his head, while the mesmerizing play of heat and shadows in his dark eyes made her shiver. "I think it'll be better if we send down a team. You'll be able to tell them where to look."

"Well, if I don't get my research, I won't be able to tell anyone anything. The papers can't be left here, Quinn. We can't risk them falling into the wrong hands."

She could see his suspicion. His frustration. It was all there in those dark, hypnotic eyes. But he didn't argue. And he didn't call her a liar.

Instead, he took a step back and jerked his chin

toward the bathroom. "Then get up and move it. We don't have any time to lose."

TWENTY MINUTES LATER, they'd downed two cups of coffee and some pastries and were ready to leave. Quinn had made arrangements to have a rental car waiting for them when they returned, then left his bag with the front desk while they set off on foot toward the Redondo Hotel, which was a short four blocks away.

"This is a stupid idea," he muttered as they made their way down the bustling street, the early-morning South American sun already beating down on their shoulders like a stifling wave of heat, the air so swollen, it was like a thick mist.

"Speaking of stupid, do you really think it's smart to fly out today? Heading straight to the airport? Won't they be expecting that?" Over breakfast, Quinn had shared his concerns about the charring of the Ruiz brothers' bodies. Saige knew that if the Collective was hunting them, as well, her chances of making it to Colorado alive were rapidly diminishing.

Which only cemented her belief that she was doing the right thing. Quinn didn't deserve the job he'd been given. No one deserved to be stuck with her, much less a man who had no emotional stake in her survival.

He lifted his right arm, pushing one big hand back through his hair, the hollows of his cheeks grim beneath the dark stubble that still covered the lower half of his face. "Actually, we'll be taking precautions, driving up to Ros Ablos first, and then taking a short flight from there up to Santina, in Colombia."

"And from there?"

"We'll keep changing things up, until we catch Highway 25 in Mexico. It'll take us through New Mexico, and straight up into Colorado."

Traveling that way would take time, but it was similar to the route Saige had originally planned to use, since it would keep her out of the major travel centers, where the Casus and the Collective could be looking for her. She'd have to revise her plan now and, once she'd managed to ditch him, make sure Quinn couldn't find her.

Not that making the journey with him at her side wouldn't have been wonderful. She'd have loved to have him with her, offering his protection…his companionship. But after what had happened to Templeton, and then Javier, knowing that the Casus were onto her, that they would be following her trail, she simply wasn't willing to take the chance. She'd meant what she said the night before, when she'd told him she wouldn't have his blood on her hands, as well.

"We've got a long trip ahead of us," he added.

"Yeah, I guess we do," she murmured, unable to quiet the irritating voice in her head. The one that kept insisting that it wasn't just her worry for Quinn's safety that had prompted her plan.

And you know exactly what it is.

"Not going there," she muttered under her breath, trying to push the disturbing thought away. But it was there, lingering in the back of her mind like a stain that she couldn't wash out or ignore.

It was an issue of trust.

Not in Quinn. But herself.

She couldn't guarantee that she wouldn't throw herself at him again, and she wasn't up for another round of Humiliation 101. One lesson was enough to last her a lifetime. And there was no doubt that she'd liked being with him, having those hard, strong arms holding her close, far more than she could afford.

No, the smartest thing was to cut her losses while she still could. She always did better on her own, anyway.

"I was just wondering," he rumbled, the deep rasp of his voice pulling her back to the moment.

"About what?"

"Why you believed so easily, right from the start."

"About the Merrick?" she asked.

"Yeah."

Saige sent him a cocky smile. "It's a woman thing. We're more intuitive, you know. We actually manage to think with our hearts, rather than our—"

"Don't say it." He smiled in a way that made his eyes crinkle sexily at the corners, which was just overkill, as far as she was concerned. "I do *not* think with my dick."

"Sheesh, Quinn." She gave him an innocent blink. "I was only going to say your *head*."

He laughed, and she nearly tripped on an uneven bit of sidewalk, unable to take her eyes off his mouth. It was too hard…too beautiful. Perfectly masculine, and impossibly sexy.

"At least you're not still calling me birdbrain," he offered in a wry drawl.

She snuffled a laugh under her breath and flashed

him another smile. "That was pretty ingenious, wasn't it?"

"Just don't mention it to Shrader," he said in a low, suffering tone. "He'll wear it out using it."

"Who's Shrader?" she asked, thankful that she'd pulled her hair back in a ponytail as the humidity seemed to thicken.

"He's one of the Watchmen in my unit back in Colorado."

"And a friend?" she murmured, while they navigated the morning street stalls, where locals sold everything from food to clothing to household items.

"A friend, as well as a total pain in the ass," he answered. "He wanted to be the one to come after you, but your brothers didn't trust him. So I got saddled with the job instead."

"And they thought you were the safer choice?" She snorted, shaking her head while trying to ignore the twinge of hurt that came from knowing he hadn't wanted the job.

He grunted under his breath, and she took mercy on him, asking a question of her own. "When Templeton went missing, why didn't you just have one of the South American compounds come after me?"

"Families are usually assigned to units from their home countries. And the nearest Brazilian unit down here has their hands full with a violent nest of Deschanel vampires at the moment. We do our best to monitor the vamps, but there are still rogue nests that slip under the radar, until they decide to settle into a particular feeding ground. Then we have to do what we can to control the situation until the Consortium makes a ruling."

"Yikes," she murmured, thankful that Quinn and his unit had been willing to break the rules to help her brother. Going back to his earlier question, she said, "As for my family bloodline, it was easy to accept. I knew, early on, that my brothers and I were…different. I saved myself the trouble of trying to fit in and learned to stick with the freaks."

"You're not a freak," he argued, wearing a dark scowl.

"And this from a guy with wings," she teased, sending him a wink.

He laughed again, the low, rich sound melting through her like chocolate, sumptuous and sweet and addictive. "I guess you have a good point."

"I have a few, but don't get your hopes up. I'm really just a pain in the ass, like you said."

"Did I say that?"

"If you didn't—" she sighed "—then I'm sure you were thinking it."

Instead of offering a denial, he simply pushed his hands into his pockets and smiled, his white teeth flashing within the dark, rugged beauty of his face.

"You know, Quinn, you're kinda cute when you smile."

"And like I said before," he drawled, rolling his eyes, "you're hell on a guy's ego."

"What?" She lifted one hand to shield her eyes, trying to tell if he was blushing. "Cute isn't manly enough?"

"Cute," he explained in another deep, suffering tone, "is hardly what I would consider a manly description."

"Well, you don't strike me as the type who needs compliments."

His mouth flattened, as if he'd only just realized he was participating in the playful exchange, and he said, "I'm not."

"I know," she said. "You wear your arrogance like it's a part of you."

He grunted in response again, his dark eyes scanning the street, and she suddenly realized that despite the casual flow of their conversation, he was still in full protector mode, completely focused on their surroundings. It made her look at the people crowding the streets with a different eye, wondering if they were what they seemed.

Or something more.

Something deadly.

"They could be anyone, couldn't they?" she said, her voice low…soft. "I mean, they take over a human body when they make it back to this realm. So who's to say where they are? Or who?"

"When they're in the shape of their human host, they'll look like everyone else. I don't think they even give off a scent when in human form," he said in a graveled voice, moving closer to her side on the crowded sidewalk. "The only distinctive feature anyone noticed on the Casus Ian fought was its eyes. According to your brother, they burned a cold, ice-blue no matter which form he was in, just like the one that came after you last night. So it could be that that's something we can use to our advantage."

"Well, at least it's something," she whispered,

knowing she'd be obsessively checking the eye color of every person she came into contact with. "I wonder why I never heard anything like that before."

"I wouldn't complain," he said, his tone unmistakably wry. "You already seem to know more than any of us. How exactly did you manage that, anyway?"

Her shoulders lifted. "Just luck really. A lot of it came from Elaina, things that had been passed down in our family, generation after generation. And then I've managed to pick up pieces along the way, especially from some of the gypsy families I've made friends with in Europe." She paused for a moment, and then asked the question that had been burning in the back of her mind for months. Years. "What exactly will happen to me, Quinn?"

WATCHING SAIGE FROM the corner of his eye, Quinn thought it was crazy, how good she could look after such a hellish night. Not to mention one of the worst crying jags he'd ever seen.

Thinking about her question, he knew why she'd asked. He could feel it building in her this morning, the need to feed…to change—but he couldn't hide his surprise that she didn't already understand everything there was about being a female Merrick. "You don't know?"

A small shrug lifted her shoulders. "My mother didn't really have much information about our female ancestors."

"I'm afraid we don't know much, either," he told her, wishing like hell that they were anywhere but on a crowded city street. He wanted her somewhere safe. Somewhere he wouldn't have to worry about her with each second that went by. "But from what little has been written about the Merrick, it's believed that you won't *change* in the same way that your brother does."

The corner of her mouth twitched into a small smile. "I guess that's a relief. I really wasn't looking all that forward to going Hulk."

A gruff laugh jerked out of his throat, surprising him. It was strange, how easily he laughed with her. He hadn't enjoyed himself so much with a woman since…

No. Not going there.

But he couldn't ignore the fact that for all her attitude, he liked being around Saige Buchanan. She was…infectious, her energy crackling, charging him up. Her temper was quick, but so was her laughter. Which was amazing, considering she hadn't had much to laugh about since he'd met her.

And last night, he hadn't dreamed.

Quinn couldn't explain it, but for the first time in years, his dreams hadn't tortured him in the quiet hours of the night.

"What's being done about the other Markers?" she asked, already moving on to a new topic as she pulled him out of his internal thoughts.

"To be honest," he rasped, "not a hell of a lot. We were hoping you would be able to shed some light on the subject for us. Until Ian showed us the cross you discovered in Italy, we had no way of knowing if the Markers even existed, or if they were just part of the folklore that surrounds the Merrick and the Casus. It was a hell of a shock to realize that they were not only real, but that one had been found."

"Do you have any idea how many there are?"

He shook his head. "Not a clue. But they're going to be invaluable in the coming war. I've talked with Kierland, and we both believe it's going to become a cutthroat race to find the others. Not only are the Casus after them, but as soon as word gets out that we're in possession of a Marker at Ravenswing, every awakening Merrick is going to want to get their hands on it, knowing it's the only way to truly destroy the bastards hunting them. We could very well end up going head-to-head with the good guys, as well as the bad."

"I wonder what the Casus want them for. If they can't be destroyed, then there has to be another reason. Why are they so desperate to get their hands on them?"

"I don't know. But we can't risk it happening. That's why we decided to leave the Marker under close watch back at Ravenswing. And I can guarantee you right now, Kierland is going to want to sit down with you and go over your research with a fine-tooth comb, until he understands exactly how you found the first one, and what makes you think the second one is buried here in Brazil."

"Don't you want to know how I found it?" she asked.

"Once we're back at Ravenswing, you can bet your ass that I'm going to want an explanation. But right now, the only thing that matters is getting you back in one piece."

She was quiet for a moment, and then she said, "The Marker is far more important than my life, Quinn."

"That's a hell of a thing to say," he grunted, the harsh words cut with something dark and edgy and primal. Some unnamed emotion that roiled through him, twisting him up inside, until he felt like one wrong move could make him snap. Send him crashing through some internal barrier that helped keep him closed off, shut down. "They're important, yeah. But they're not worth dying for."

She looked away from him, pulling the backpack higher onto her slim shoulder. "I guess that depends on your viewpoint," she said in a low voice.

"It depends on nothing," he growled, grabbing hold of her arm and pulling her to a stop. They stood in the center of the bustling sidewalk, but he didn't care. "There's no object on earth worth risking your life over, Saige. And if your brothers were here, they'd tell you the same thing."

Without looking at him, she jerked her chin to the side, toward the four-story building that stood to their right. "This is the hotel. I think it will be better if I go in by myself."

He reached out and grasped her chin, forcing her to meet his eyes. "Why?"

She blinked, looking too pale, too fragile. "Some of the archaeologists I was working with were staying here and we became friends with the manager. He's very protective," she told him, pulling her lower lip through her teeth. "This will go a lot faster if I don't have to answer twenty questions about you."

"I don't like it."

"Like it or not," she said, "it's going to save us time."

HE STARED DOWN at her, hard, and Saige watched his nostrils flare as he pulled in a slow, deep breath. "Your Merrick's getting closer," he said in a low, husky slide of words.

"How can you tell?"

"It's in your scent…in your eyes." He took in another deep, searching breath, and glared at the quaint hotel. "For anyone who isn't human, the signs are there. You're not very strong yet, but it's obvious that there's something inside you."

Though he didn't mean the words in a sexual sense, her body apparently didn't care, something low in her abdomen clenching with a soft glow of awareness. Before she gave herself time to think about what she was doing, Saige reached up and caught him about the neck, pulling his head down so that she could touch her mouth to his. She'd wanted to have one last taste of him before she walked away, but he ripped the control right out of her hands and turned the kiss into something that was *more*.

With his hands clutching her waist, Quinn kissed her back. Harder. Deeper. Tasting every part of her mouth, leaving no part of her unexplored…unclaimed. His mouth moved in a way that was utterly male, inherently primal, dazzling her with its sexuality. Her body went hot…wet…swelling with heat that had nothing to do with the thick, humid air that pressed in on them, heavy and damp. He moved closer, pressing against her, his blatant hardness against her softer curves, and his tongue swept her mouth like a challenge, wiping away all resistance.

Saige recognized it for what it was, though she'd never encountered anything like it before. Not once, in her entire life. Like a brand, he'd placed his ownership over her, one whose possessive nature snaked through her system, heating her from the inside out.

Breathless, and not a little panicked, she broke away, stumbling back. He stared down at her with a quiet, raging intensity, his dark eyes glittering and hot. She opened her mouth, shaking her head when nothing came out, her wits scrambled. That thing he'd done with his tongue was... She struggled for the words that would do it justice. It was like sex. Like being penetrated, hot and wet and darkly possessive. She'd tasted his hunger—*his need*—and it'd fueled her own.

"Be quick." His voice was hard, gritty.

She wet her lips, tasting him there, torn between wanting to stay there with him—and knowing that he didn't deserve it.

Get away from him, Saige. Now, while you still can.

Gritting her teeth, she turned, forcing herself to walk away. She reached the entrance to the hotel and grasped the handle, barely registering the hot burn of the metal against her hand. Looking over her shoulder, she gave him a wan smile. "For what it's worth, Quinn, I wanted to tell you thanks."

He didn't ask for what. He just gave her one of

those dark, silent looks that somehow seemed to say so much more than words. Then with a deep, trembling breath, Saige turned and headed into the hotel.

CHAPTER EIGHT

WHY DID THE RIGHT THING have to feel so wrong?

That was the question that had been twisting its way through Saige's mind since the second she'd walked, or rather run, away from Michael Quinn. She felt sick, her insides cramping with a churning blend of guilt, adrenaline and the cold, cruel burn of fear.

Isn't this where you start acting like one of those too-stupid-to-live women in the movies, running toward the big, scary house where the axe murderer is hiding, instead of away from it?

"Shut up," she growled, far too aware of just how well that scenario fit the facts.

Face it, lady. You're mental.

Probably. But at this point, crazy seemed to be working for her.

Ditching Quinn had been surprisingly easy, but then, he hadn't been expecting her to do something so foolish as to run off on her own. Once she'd made her way inside the hotel, it'd been a simple matter of writing him a quick note, which she'd left at the front desk, before slipping out a back exit. She didn't know how long Quinn had waited before giving chase—or if he'd even bothered to come running after her—but the crowds on the streets had worked in her favor. She'd done her best to make sure that if she was being followed, either by the Casus or the Collective, that she'd ditched anyone who might be on her trail. Now, as she neared the entrance to *O Diablo Dos Ángels,* she pressed her hand to her chest, willing her breathing to return to normal.

You're nervous.

Well, yeah, she thought. The Casus could be any-where. Anyone.

Relax. This is the last place they'd expect you to come back to. You're safe here.

Maybe. At least as safe as she was going to get.

Unless you were with Quinn.

Stifling a groan, Saige walked inside the dimly lit *barra.* Too early for most customers, only a few barflies perched themselves on wooden stools, holding court like degenerate royalty. Inez spotted her in-stantly, signaling for her to head back toward the office. Saige worked her way through the tables, fol-lowing the older woman past a swinging door, into a narrow hallway. She didn't like coming back to this place, possibly putting Inez and her husband, Rubens, in danger, but she couldn't leave the maps behind. And after what had happened to Javier, she had to make sure that the couple was at least warned.

It was crazy, the limits she'd gone to in order to protect a piece of metal, but the last damn thing she was going to do was let those bastards get their hands on the cross. She'd rather die. It made no sense, but the Marker had… She struggled for the right word to explain what was simply inexplicable. She'd found it, and that made its safety her responsibility. So here she was, risking her life to get the maps that she hoped like hell would lead her to the rest of them.

Two down. Who knows how many to go.

Gritting her teeth against the throbbing headache building steadily behind her eyes, Saige followed Inez through the last door in the hallway, a faded *Confidencial* stenciled onto its surface in dark red. The instant Inez turned toward her, Saige's throat clogged with tears. "Javier and his brothers are dead," she croaked.

Inez nodded, her red-rimmed eyes revealing her knowledge of the murders. "Where is the American?" she asked in Portuguese.

Saige rolled her shoulder, no longer surprised by Inez's amazing perceptiveness. The woman always seemed to know things she shouldn't, as if she had some sort of sixth sense. "I ditched him."

Inez narrowed her dark eyes, *tsking* under her breath. "If he was protection from the evil that is hunting you, then that was not wise."

"No choice," she mumbled, surprised by her friend's words. Inez was usually as distrustful as she was.

"Hmm," the older woman murmured, and Saige fought the urge to squirm beneath the piercing scrutiny of Inez's stare. "You *care* about him, don't you?"

Color flooded her face that had nothing to do with the stifling heat, the whirring desk fan only circulating the hot, humid air in an ineffective struggle against the elements. "Don't be ridiculous. I hardly know him." She paced from one side of the small, cluttered office to the other, while her friend bent down and began opening the safe. "I haven't even known him for twenty-four hours, Inez."

"And is time really so important, young one? I thought you had learned more than that by now."

She closed her eyes, silently praying that Inez wouldn't slip off into one of her well-intentioned lectures on the universe and destiny.

Pushing back the windblown strands of hair that'd slipped from her ponytail, she watched as Inez pulled the small, oilcloth-wrapped maps from the safe and offered them to her. "It's for the best," Saige said unsteadily, taking the maps and slipping them into her backpack. "He doesn't deserve to be pulled into my nightmare."

Inez shook her head as she moved back to her feet, her dark eyes uncomfortably knowing. "Maybe that was his choice to make, Saige."

"It wasn't." She hefted the backpack onto her shoulder and cleared her throat against the knot of emotion threatening to choke her. "They made him come. I was just a job. One that was no doubt going to get him killed."

"Hmm," Inez murmured for the second time. "I could be wrong, but he didn't seem like the kind of man who could be *made* to do anything he didn't want to."

True, but then Quinn had told her himself that he hadn't wanted the assignment.

"Stop trying to handle this all on your own and go home to your family," Inez told her. "Rubens and I can look after ourselves, but it isn't safe for you here, my friend."

Wise words, but for the fact that Saige knew the danger would follow her. Her only hope was to lose whoever might be following her and keep moving as quickly as possible until she made it to Colorado. Then, once she'd met up with Jamison in Denver, maybe she'd take the Marker and go after that murderous bastard, just like Ian had. After what it'd done to Javier, God only knew she had the motivation.

Putting her arms around her friend, Saige gave Inez a quick, fierce hug. "Thank you. For everything."

Inez took hold of her face in her cool, soft hands. "You do not thank someone when friendship is given freely, Saige. All I want is for you to be careful." Sniffing, the older woman turned away and opened the office door. "Now come with me. Rubens and I will put together a quick snack for you before you go."

"I can't," she said, following Inez down the hallway. "If Quinn decides to come after me, this is the first place he'll probably look. I need to get moving."

Her friend made a frustrated sound in her throat. "You need to be smart, Saige, and go back to him. Before it's too late."

But the instant they walked back into the bar, she knew that it already was.

It was the eyes that gave them away.

The second that Saige followed Inez from the

hallway, she knew the newcomers leaning back against the bar were there for more than a cool drink to ease the stifling morning heat. They were there for *her*.

It was a jarring shock to her system, the fact that they were both beautiful. Tall and dark and muscular. Gorgeous, even. Brothers, she would have guessed, based on the similarities in their build and features.

They might have looked human, but she could see the shadow of truth in their cold, ice-blue eyes.

For a moment, she thought of turning and running, but she couldn't do that. Not with Inez and her husband there. Rubens stood behind the bar, wiping down the counters, oblivious to the danger that stood just feet away, where both men—*both Casus*—watched her with a sharp, predatory intensity.

If she ran, her friends could very well pay the price, and she wasn't going to let that happen. Forcing herself to remain calm, Saige put her hand on Inez's arm and forced a small smile to her lips. "The men at the bar are from the guide company we were using. I need to talk to them about the next expedition that's coming in during the fall, but I can do that on my way to the bus station."

Inez nodded, but Saige could see the questions in the other woman's eyes. "Are you sure they're not trouble?"

Saige leaned in to put a kiss to her cheek. "I'll be fine, I promise. And I'll call as soon as I can."

She could feel Inez's worried gaze burning into her back as she turned and headed toward the human-looking Casus. One would have been bad enough, but two was impossible, and she racked her brain for a way to get out of a situation that she knew she didn't have a chance in hell of escaping from.

As she stepped closer, a slow, decidedly malevolent smile spread across the mouth of the man on the right, his longer hair just brushing the edges of his jaw. "Well, if it isn't little Saige," he rasped in a low, husky drawl.

"What do you want?" she asked, amazed that she'd managed to speak in such a cool, calm tone of voice, considering she knew exactly what it was that they wanted.

Which was her blood. Her flesh. Her *life.*

The man's smile widened, reminding Saige of the Cheshire cat in Alice's strange nightmare, and she wished this was just a bad dream that she could wake up from. But she wasn't going to be that lucky.

The one with the shorter hair, on the left, cut a knowing look toward the place where Inez and Rubens now stood whispering at the far end of the bar. "Shall we take this someplace more private?"

Saige gave a jerky nod, knowing she didn't have any choice. Her heartbeat filled her head like the primal, churning beat of a jungle drum, a surreal haze falling over the moment, as if it wasn't real. As if she could snap her fingers…*and poof*…just make it all go away.

But she knew they weren't going anywhere. Not without her.

Together, they stepped into the bright South American sunshine, each man gesturing for her to walk

between them. Despite her T-shirt and shorts, the heat
was suffocating, covering her in a clammy sheen of
moisture. Or maybe that was simply her fear. Clutching on to the strap of her backpack with both hands,
Saige lowered her gaze, staring at the spidery cracks
that blossomed over the uneven concrete like a star-
burst. Her emotions were just as chaotic, zinging from
one stratosphere to another, and she moved numbly as
they headed down the rustic road, toward the edge of
town. She was distantly aware of a few passing
trucks…a mother walking her four children to the
market…a little boy riding his bike. She drew in a deep
breath, and her pulse started racing, her breath coming
faster…faster. Just when panic took over and she made
a sudden move to turn and run, the man on her right
locked his hand around her bicep, pulling her into his
side so hard she was amazed the bone in her arm didn't
break.

"I don't think you're going anywhere, sweetheart."

"Easy, Gregory," the one with the shorter hair
warned in a low voice. "We're still in town, where too
many eyes could be watching."

"Don't worry, Royce. I won't hurt her." He leaned
closer, whispering his husky words into her ear. *"Not
yet."*

The man named Royce reached out and took hold
of her left hand, holding it in a biting grip, so that she
was trapped between them as they made their way
toward the end of the road, the dense, brilliantly green
jungle looming ahead. "You've put me to a lot of
trouble, Saige," he rumbled in a conversational tone,

as if they were doing nothing more sinister than enjoying a morning stroll. "Still, I can't tell you how convenient you made this for us by coming back to the bar."

The bright glare of morning sunlight scorched her eyes, and she could feel the sickening moisture of sweat gathering against her skin where they gripped her arm and hand. With each step, her options were fading rapidly, her panic rising as she realized she was just waltzing toward her death, doing nothing to stop it.

And from what Quinn had told her, she knew it wouldn't be quick.

"I wasn't aware that you guys hunted in pairs. Are you brothers?" she croaked, silently praying for a miracle. *For Quinn.*

The one holding her arm, Gregory, gave a gritty laugh. "Your bastard brother killed mine. Now I have no brothers."

Saige blinked, trying to absorb the stunning information, realizing on an instinctual level that his hatred held a personal flavor. One that went beyond an ancient feud. One that would make her death, her suffering, that much more important to him.

"The human bodies we've taken were brothers," Royce offered by way of explanation.

"How do you…do this? Take these bodies?"

Keeping a watchful eye on their surroundings, he said, "When we're released, our shades automatically seek out a human host who possesses Casus blood, just as the legend claims. Even now, awakenings are taking place all over the world, our numbers growing greater every day."

"But how?" she whispered, silently counting down the steps that would take them into the cover of the jungle. "How are you escaping from your prison?"

"There is one Casus, a great leader," Royce explained, "who has discovered a way to combine his life force with his followers' and send our shades through the gate."

"But there is another way, as well," Gregory whispered near her ear. "One that's more fun. More satisfying. Wanna know what it is?" Without waiting for her reply, he said, "When we feed from a fully awakened Merrick, we gain enough power to pull one of our kinsmen back from Meridian all on our own."

"Meridian?"

"Our name for the holding ground," Royce said in a low voice.

"Does that mean that you'll keep hunting my brother?" she asked, hoping that Ian was doing everything he could to protect himself.

"Of course, though I hear he's doing a good job of hiding out with his little Watchmen buddies. But the more Merrick we kill, the more Casus we can pull back. And since that bastard killed Malcolm, he's now free game."

"If the legend is true, and a Merrick awakening begins for each Casus that escapes from this…this Meridian, then which one of you caused mine?" she asked, painfully aware that she wouldn't be able to pass on anything that she learned to Quinn and the others. Which was probably why the Casus were willing to tell her. They knew their secrets weren't going anywhere.

"The privilege of feeding from you belongs to me," Royce stated in a soft, rugged rumble of words. "After we've gotten what we came here for, Gregory will go and find his own Merrick."

She could tell that Royce's words irritated his partner, as Gregory's long fingers bit into her bicep so deeply, she knew her arm would be black and blue. Doing her best to ignore the pain, she said, "Dare I ask where we're headed?"

"That's up to you," Royce murmured, casting a quick look over his shoulder, as if to make sure they weren't being followed. "We know you've already found a second Marker, Saige."

"Wh-what Marker?" she whispered, while inside she was screaming...falling apart. Did they know about Jamison? Did they know what she'd done with the cross?

The one named Gregory shifted closer. "I can smell your fear. You're not fooling anyone, bitch. We saw you unearth it in the jungle yesterday morning."

"How long have you been watching me?" she croaked, wincing as both Casus tightened their grips, on the verge of crushing her bones.

"Long enough to know that you're a pain in the ass," Gregory drawled, flashing her a sharp smile.

Saige would have laughed if she hadn't been so terrified. "So I've been told."

She thought of the teasing conversation she'd had

with Quinn that morning, and something hurt in her chest, the ache bleeding into her blood and her bones. God, she'd been so stupid to leave him. Stupid to think she could make it back to America on her own. She hadn't even made it out of Coroza.

They drew nearer to the jungle, and she said, "If you've been here that long, why haven't you already killed me?"

Something low and wicked spilled from Gregory's mouth, too evil to be a laugh. "Because he was waiting for you to ripen up."

"You mean awaken?" she asked, her voice thick.

"That's right." He leaned closer, pressing his nose to her temple as he breathed in her scent, his lips cool against the heat of her skin, making her stomach churn. "Eat you too early, and you won't be anywhere near strong enough to give ol' Royce the kick he needs."

They reached the end of the road and took their first steps into the jungle, the dense foliage seeming to swallow them whole, like a primordial monster. The rain forest was no longer her haven…her sanctuary. Within moments it was as if they were in a different world—one where the predators reigned supreme and evil lurked within the sun-dappled shadows, waiting to strike. "In case neither of you noticed, I'm still not awakened."

"We know," Gregory told her. "But after last night, we couldn't risk you wandering off with your little Watchman."

"You shouldn't have run from the Raptor," Royce added, finally releasing her hand. He remained close to her side as he added, "He was your best chance."

"Quinn will come for me," she whispered, wishing she actually believed it was true.

"Think so?" he responded on a soft thread of laughter, a ghost of a smile playing at the corner of his mouth. "After the way you ditched him?"

"You were watching me in São Vicente?"

Royce shook his head, reaching out to pull a thick tangle of vines out of their way, the damp blades of grass that covered the ground brushing against their calves. "Didn't need to. We knew you would be coming back to the bar, so we've been waiting for you. But it's obvious you ran from your protector. There's no way he would have let you come here on your own."

She bit her tongue, refusing to tell him anything about Quinn or why she'd run, and he said, "And now you're going to take us to the Marker."

"No," she said slowly, lifting her head as a multicolored flock of birds took flight from the treetops, the fluttering of their wings like a thousand tiny feet pattering against a floor. Saige wished she could take flight in just the same way. That, like Quinn, she could carry herself away from the nightmare, knowing her next words could likely be her last. "I don't think I will."

Royce grabbed hold of her left arm, jerking her to a halt. "Do you care about those people back there, Saige?" he rasped, his ice-blue eyes narrowed with hatred…with hunger.

"You wouldn't want them to end up like the boy, now would you?" Gregory murmured before she could respond, and she whipped her head in his direction.

"What did you just say?" Her voice was little more than a breath, gasping and soft, as the haze of terror that had numbed her finally began to fade. In its place, a dark, raging fury began to rise from within her, keeping company with her seething Merrick, throwing everything into jarring, shocking focus. She remembered little Javier and his brothers. Remembered his happiness. His laughter and his smiles.

And most of all she remembered what these bastards had done to him.

"The kid did his best to hold out for you, but in the end, he was helpful enough to let us know you'd left something of value in the safe at the *barra*." Gregory sent a meaningful look toward the backpack still hooked over her shoulder. "We assume you have the maps. It'd be a shame for him to have suffered for no reason."

"You son of a bitch!" she hissed, wanting to tear him apart with her bare hands. She could feel the Merrick's primal rage gathering force inside her—could feel its biting frustration that it couldn't punch its way out and go for the monster's throat.

"That's it, little girl." Gregory stepped closer, sniffing at her like a lion eyeing a tasty piece of meat. "Your Merrick wants to come out and play, but first you have to give it what it needs."

He was right. Her Merrick *did* want to come out—but playing wasn't what it had in mind. It was crawling its way to the surface, desperate for release, but she wasn't strong enough. Until she fed, taking the blood that the Merrick needed for nourishment, the primitive part of her soul would be unable to break free.

But it was there, writhing with rage…with the gnawing need to strike out and cause as much pain as Javier had suffered. "It was you, wasn't it?" she snarled, sickened by the fiery burn of pleasure warming Gregory's icy gaze. "You tortured him! Bit off his fingers! You demon!"

He smiled like a viper preparing to strike. "If you're that upset about his fingers," he drawled, "then you don't want to know what I bit off next."

The instant she registered his meaning, she went crazy. There was no other way to describe it. Shaking with rage, Saige jerked out of Royce's hold and threw herself at Gregory, clawing at his face, kicking and screaming and punching at every part of him that she could reach. He grunted as Royce grabbed her from behind, pulling her off him. Through a red-tinged haze of fury and pain, Saige watched the bastard lift his arm. Then his powerful fist slammed into her jaw, and everything went black. One second she was screaming, kicking, clawing. And then…nothing. Just a dark, blank, empty oblivion.

When she finally came back, she had no idea how much time had passed. Minutes? An hour? Two? Her throat hurt, and she could taste her tears and blood in her mouth, her jaw throbbing with a dull, pulsing ache of pain. Praying that she hadn't been raped while unconscious, she ran her hands over her shirt and shorts, a fresh stream of silent tears slipping from her closed eyes when she found them intact. Cracking her eyelids, Saige saw that she was lying on the ground in the middle of a small clearing. She could hear the flow of the river nearby, the cloudless sky painfully blue against her eyes as she blinked against the blinding light of the sun. Dark, dense jungle surrounded them on three sides, the only building a sad-looking cabin that stood on the north side of the clearing, near the riverbank.

For a breathtaking instant, Saige thought she was alone. Her breath caught, the sharp, stabbing joy of relief making it difficult to breathe.

And then she saw the Casus.

They stood about ten feet away, leaning over a haggard-looking wooden table that stood beneath a towering tree, their intense stares focused intently on the maps that had been spread over the weathered tabletop. Her backpack lay on the ground behind them, tossed aside. Royce was speaking, his low voice cut with biting frustration as he said, "I can't believe the damned things are in code."

"What did you expect? They weren't meant to be easy," Gregory drawled, and then, as if he could feel the press of her stare, he lifted his head and smiled. "The little bitch is awake. Maybe she can shed some light on the situation."

Straightening away from the table, Royce jerked his chin toward the maps. "You're going to show us how to read these."

"Read what?" she muttered, fighting to ignore the pain in her jaw as she shifted to her knees. She'd have stood up, but her head was spinning too badly and she knew she'd have ended up sprawled on her face across the moss-covered ground.

Grabbing one of the maps, Royce stalked toward her, while Gregory followed close on his heels. "Wrong answer," he growled, and Saige could see the sharp points of what looked like a lethal set of fangs resting beneath his upper lip, glinting in the sunlight.

"If you're going to eat me," she challenged, "then get it the hell over with."

"I'll kill you when I'm damn good and ready," he snarled, shoving the map in her face. "But first you're going to tell us how to use these to find the Markers."

"Why do you even care?" she shouted, pushing the map out of her face. "What do you want with them? What good are the Markers going to do the Casus?"

He stared, hard, and there was something in his eyes that gave him away. A brittle, jagged burst of laughter ripped from her throat, and she pressed her hands to her stomach. "Ohmygod. You don't even know, do you?"

"Why we want them is none of your bloody business," he growled. "And if you don't want to die, right now, then you had better start explaining."

Saige lifted her chin, almost hoping that she could make him angry enough to kill her quickly, rather than dragging it out...making it last. "Then you might as well go ahead and do it, because I'll never tell you how to read them!"

Bending his knees, he crouched down in front of her at the same time he reached out, gripping her hair in his free hand, and she cried out from the stinging burn of pain. "You *will* tell me, Saige."

"Even if I wanted to, I can't just tell you how to read

them," she gasped, pulling ineffectually at his thick wrist. "The code is complicated, and it changes from map to map. They're nothing more than a long stream of directions, each one blending into the next. I don't even know for sure how many are listed on those pages, and I probably won't know for years. It took me months just to decipher the one that led me here."

Making a thick sound of disgust in his throat, Royce shoved her away and moved back to his full height. Crawling back on her hands and feet like a crab, Saige stared up at his murderous expression, wondering if he would finally go ahead and take her life.

"What now?" Gregory asked, stepping to Royce's side.

"We keep her alive," he growled through his gritted teeth as he turned, taking the map back to the table, where he placed it with the others. She gasped when she saw that he had a gun tucked into the waistband of his jeans, resting at the small of his back. It seemed a strange weapon for a Casus to carry, and she wondered with an odd sense of detachment if he even knew how to use it.

"Keep her alive?" Gregory repeated, cutting Royce a look of disgusted disbelief as he turned back to face them. "You can't be serious."

"Until we know if anyone else can read them," Royce said, scraping his hands back through the short strands of his hair, "we don't have any choice. And since there's no sense feeding from her until she's fully awakened anyway, I might as well wait."

Stepping closer, Gregory shifted his pale gaze to her

face as he said, "She still hasn't told us what she did with the second Marker. I could *make* her talk."

"No! No, I'll tell you!" she suddenly cried out, moving unsteadily to her feet. "I hid it, at the campsite where I was staying with the research team. I knew I was being watched, and I didn't want to risk the Marker getting stolen."

"You little liar." Royce stalked forward in rapid strides, backhanding her across the face so hard that she nearly fell to the ground again. Dazed, Saige shook her head, the hot, metallic taste of blood in her mouth making the primal creature inside her quicken with awareness.

"We've already turned the campsite upside down, and it isn't there. So I'll give you one more chance, Saige. Tell us where the talisman is, or I'm going to make Gregory a very happy boy and let him have what he's been wanting since he first set eyes on you." His voice lowered, almost as if he were telling her a secret. "It won't kill you, but I can promise that you'll wish it had."

A low, wicked rumble of laughter came from Gregory, his wide smile clearly revealing his intentions. With a quick glance down his tall body, Saige could see that he was already hard, and it was the most difficult thing she'd ever had to do, standing there before them with her spine straight, when she wanted nothing more than to curl up into a hard, tight ball and pray for Quinn.

A bit ironic, don't ya think? Considering you ran away from him.

Royce placed his long fingers beneath her chin, pulling her face back toward him until she met his angry gaze. "Last chance, Saige. Where is it?"

She wet her mouth. "I told you, it's at the—"

The lie died on her lips as the hand holding her face instantly transformed, and a sharp, hissing sound filled her ears as she felt his bones cracking, reshaping, while long, terrifying claws cut through the human tips of his fingers. "Don't think for one second that I won't gut you if you make me any angrier. I want the power from your Merrick, as well as the code to those bloody maps, but piss me off again, and my anger is going to outweigh my wants. You understand me?"

Slanting her gaze to the side, she scrambled to think of a way out of this, while focusing on a distant heap of what looked like rotting garbage at the edge of the clearing, just beneath a tree near the river. At first, Saige wasn't even sure what she was staring at. She only knew it wasn't…right. She narrowed her eyes, unable to tear her gaze away as some horrible, unbearable truth slithered through her brain.

And then she made out the masculine shape of a blood-covered foot protruding from the pile of mud and clothing…and what she now realized was flesh. Revulsion swept through her system, gagging her. Royce pulled his monstrous hand away from her face, and she bent forward, bracing her hands on her knees as she fought a sharp, rising wave of nausea.

"Saige, meet Paul Templeton. Or at least what's left of him," Gregory offered with a cruel laugh.

"Ohmygod," she groaned, careful to keep her gaze

away from what was left of Templeton's mutilated corpse. "Why didn't you just burn him, like you did the others?"

Royce grabbed hold of her arm, jerking her upright. "What the hell are you talking about? What others?"

"Javier's body was charred, same as his brothers. Why couldn't you have just done that to Templeton? Why leave him…like that?"

She watched Royce's pulse throb in his temple as he let go of her and turned toward Gregory. "You know what this means, don't you?"

"It means nothing," the Casus drawled, shrugging his broad shoulders.

Royce took a challenging step toward the other man, vibrating with rage. "It means that after the screwup your brother made of his hunt, Westmore's men are watching us. That they're following you around in town, covering your goddamn tracks!"

"And what if they are?"

"Westmore is Calder's partner, you fucking idiot! Not his servant!"

She wanted to ask who they were talking about, but with their attention completely focused on each other, the opportunity was too good to pass up. Careful not to move too quickly, Saige began inching her way backward into the surrounding jungle.

She hated that she was leaving the maps, promising herself that she would find some way to get them back, and took another step…and then another, ready to turn and start running, when a hot, rough palm suddenly clamped over her mouth, stifling her scream.

Saige drew in a deep, gasping breath through her nose, her eyes going wide as a warm, familiar scent filled her head.

And in the next instant, her body lifted vertically into the air.

CHAPTER NINE

FOR THE SECOND TIME in twenty-four hours, Quinn found himself in the unsavory position of saving Saige Buchanan's crazy, suicidal, infuriating little ass. Either the damn woman had a death wish, or she was certifiably insane. Either way, she was a liar, and he didn't want to waste his time dealing with her. If it weren't for the fact that he knew her brothers would make his life a living hell, he'd already be on his way back home, leaving her to figure a way out of this on her own.

You can keep thinking it, but it isn't gonna make it true.

He silently snarled at the thought, hating how easily she'd slipped under his skin. The piece of paper jammed deep in his right pocket burned with a phantom heat, searing against his pride. *A note.* His lip curled at the thought of it. He couldn't believe she'd had the audacity to leave him a damned note, not only thanking him for his help, but also telling him to go back home, as if he were some lackey she could order about on a whim.

He just couldn't get his head around why she'd

done it. It wasn't as if she was better off without him. She hadn't been on her own for more than a few hours, and had already managed to get herself caught by not one, but *two* Casus. Now he was in a bitch of a situation, being torn between the desire to gut the bastards and the need to get Saige to safety, but then there was really only one choice. No matter how badly he wanted their blood, he knew damn well what his number-one priority was. He'd do whatever it took to keep her safe—whether she wanted his help or not.

And considering how she'd ditched him, Quinn could only assume she wasn't looking for a white knight. It was just as well, seeing as how his mood was now as dark as the rest of him.

She clung to his side as he used a thick, sturdy vine to scale his way up the tree, his boots braced against the rough bark of the trunk. The vegetation was too dense in this part of the jungle for him to fly at this elevation, which meant they needed to go higher. But first he had to get the fool woman onto his back, where she wouldn't be choking him in the death grip she had around his neck.

"Hold on to the tree," he grunted as he swung her toward the next wide branch that he came to.

"Ohmygod," she whispered, her wide-eyed gaze flicking between the distant ground and his face as he braced himself on the branch beside her, trying to find a strong enough vine that could take them all the way to the upper canopy. Even though the air above the river was clear for flight, he couldn't risk being seen by anyone traveling by boat, which meant their only option was to go up, where he could fly just beneath the top cover of the rain forest. "Are you crazy?" she cried out softly when he edged away from her, reaching for another vine to test its strength. "You can't leave me here!"

"I'm not leaving you," he growled, casting a quick look down toward the clearing, where the shifting Casus were fighting, doing their best to beat the living hell out of each other. They'd yet to notice that Saige was missing, but he knew that could change at any moment, which meant they needed to get out of there. "We've gotta go higher, so you're going to have to get on my back."

"Okay," she breathed out, obviously afraid of heights. She blinked, trying to give him a small, shaky smile, her eyes luminous and bright. "God, Quinn. I have to tell you what they said. What I've learned."

"Later," he rasped, his rage mounting as he caught sight of her bruised jaw and busted, bloodied lip. He wanted to shout at her. Wanted to demand what she'd been thinking when she decided to leave him. Wanted to throttle her scrawny little neck for scaring the hell out of him.

Christ, he wanted to spread her out and do things to her that he'd never even thought about doing to another woman. Desire was a raging, biting beast in his gut, demanding its due. He didn't care how he had her. He just wanted her, in every possible way there was, until he'd imprinted himself on her so deeply, she couldn't get rid of him. Until she was marked by his scent...his seed...his soul, to the point that any man coming near her would know exactly who she belonged to.

Which means you've gone out of your ever-loving mind.

One moment Quinn was standing there, snarling at himself for being such a fool. And in the next, he found himself grabbing hold of her arm. He pulled her toward him, slamming her against his body so hard that her breath jerked from her lungs, his other arm twisted in a thick vine for balance. Then he covered her mouth with his own. Covered…and possessed it, penetrating that dark, sweet well with the aggressive sweep of his tongue, showing her just how angry he was with her. The kiss tasted of pain and fury and greed, each emotion distinct and unmistakable, revealing parts of himself he knew were best kept locked away.

He'd expected her to fight him, considering how she'd run away. To punch and scratch and kick, but Saige surprised him yet again by kissing him back, throwing her arms around his body, clutching at him as she tried to crawl her way under his skin. Lost in her taste, Quinn kissed her for as long as he dared, knowing that at any moment the Casus would take note of her absence and come after them for the kill.

Jarred by the recklessness of what he was doing, he pushed her away, shoving her back against the trunk of the tree.

Damn it, he thought, scraping his free hand down his face, while his chest heaved with the ragged cadence of his breaths.

Panting, she reached out and touched the hot, burning skin of his bare chest, his shirt discarded somewhere in the jungle, before he'd released his wings in his mad race to find her. There were so many questions swimming through her eyes, like the swirling colors of a churning sea, but he silenced her with a curt shake of his head.

Or at least he tried to.

"Quinn," she whispered. "I can't believe you came back for—"

Before she could finish, her soft, husky words were drowned out by an earsplitting spray of bullets that unloaded from below, ripping into the nearby branches, and Quinn knew their luck had just run out. Unfurling his wings, he pressed Saige back against the rough bark of the tree and wrapped his body around hers, doing his best to shield her from the powerful rounds as they tore through the thick jungle foliage.

He hadn't expected the bastards to have guns, and now they were trapped, with nowhere to go.

"Whatever happens," he growled against the top of her head, "keep climbing and stay the hell off the ground. It will be harder for them to get you that way."

A heartbeat later, the bullets stopped, which meant he had only seconds before they reloaded. She tried to hold on to him as he pushed back, away from her, but he was too fast. Falling backward, Quinn twisted in midair and soared toward the edge of the clearing, where the two Casus stood, but he wasn't fast enough. Another round of bullets tore into the sky, and pain exploded through his right wing like a burst of liquid fire. Gritting his teeth, he fought against the searing agony and slammed full speed into the first Casus, knocking him into the second. The three of them went down in a hard, crashing slide of bodies, the guns scattering across the moss-covered surface of the clearing.

He could hear Saige screaming for him to be careful as he scrambled to his feet and the Casus did the same, slowly circling him, their muzzled mouths almost smiling as they waited for the moment to strike.

"Didn't anyone ever tell you that bullets are cheating?" he growled, knowing he had to find a way to get their weapons. If he could remove the guns from the equation, he had a good chance of getting back to Saige and then flying her to safety. And while he wanted to rip them apart with his bare hands, staying and fighting wasn't an option. Not when Saige's life was on the line.

"We were just trying to get your attention," the one to his left rasped in a deep, graveled drawl. "Isn't that right, Royce?"

"Don't waste time chatting with him, Gregory," the other one barked. "Just go in for the kill. I told you these bastards are dangerous."

Though each of the Casus briefly sported a human hand, which they'd used to fire the guns, the rest of their bodies were already shifted into the monstrous shapes of their inner beasts, complete with hulking, wolf-shaped heads. As Quinn released his own deadly talons, a sharp, lethal set of claws ripped across his lower back, slicing into his skin. Roaring, Quinn used his uninjured wing to slam the Casus to the ground, then twisted, knocking down the other one with a powerful roundhouse as it lunged toward him with wide, gaping jaws. They both came at him hard and fast after that, and the world became a chaotic blur of strikes and kicks and savage, guttural growls. Quinn tore at their leathery bodies with his razor-sharp talons, while doing everything he could to keep out of reach of their claws and fangs.

No matter how brilliant a fighter he was, there wasn't a chance in hell he should've been able to hold them off, but the need to protect Saige was so strong, he kept standing when he should have gone down. Over and over again, he used his talons to rip at their powerful bodies, a torrent of primal roars tearing from his chest as he spun and twisted and kicked at his opponents. And somehow he found a way to ignore the mind-numbing pain and power his way through, doing his best to stay alive.

Not that the little liar deserves it.

He struggled to hold on to that violent burn of rage he felt toward Saige, but it wasn't as easy as it should have been. Fear over what the Casus would do to her spread coldly through his veins, spurring him on. He pivoted on the ball of his left foot, bringing his right leg back around and cracking it against Royce's jaw. Bone crunched with sickening force, but the Casus refused to go down. It parried with a deadly swipe of its vicious claws, and he ducked, dropping just in time to avoid the fatal blow. Kicking out with his left leg, Quinn knocked the other one's legs out from under its great, hulking body, taking him to the ground as Royce came at him again.

Time to end this, he thought, raking his talons across the bastard's throat. The Casus fell instantly to the ground, clutching at the savage wound with his blood-covered hands.

Snarling, the one named Gregory pulled himself back to his feet and charged, his gruesome jaws gaping, dripping with saliva. Quinn used his powerful wings to lift his body off the ground, then twisted in midair, driving his right foot into the creature's temple. The Casus slumped to the ground, dazed. The crushing blow would have no doubt killed a human, but he knew the Casus would survive. Even now, it was beginning to stir, and a quick look to his left showed the other one, Royce, trying to gain his feet, even though his hands were still pressed to his bleeding throat. Knowing he needed to escape while he still could, Quinn quickly retracted his talons and grabbed the guns. Reaching behind him, he tucked them into the waistband of his jeans, then wiped his bleeding mouth on his shoulder.

If it was just him, he'd have stayed and taken his chances against the sadistic monsters, but Saige's worried screams from above won out over his blood-thirsty rage. Biting back a choking groan of pain, he quickly made his way up another vine, climbing up to where he'd left her. The instant his feet were braced against the wide branch, she was touching him with trembling hands, a soft, husky tumble of words flowing from her lips as she took note of his injuries.

"God, you're hurt," she said in a low voice, eyeing his blood-covered right wing as he drew in a deep breath and finished absorbing his wings into his body. She made a thick sound in her throat, running her dark gaze over his wounds. "They've cut you. *Everywhere*."

"I'll be fine," he grunted, knowing that by the time they returned to town, most of the pain would have faded, his body mending more quickly than a human's. The bullet hole through the bone in his wing was the only injury that worried him, and would take the longest to heal.

It was also going to make it hard as hell to fly.

Turning around, he told Saige to climb onto his back, and sent up a silent prayer of thanks when she didn't argue. Instead, she pressed against his spine, wrapping her arms around his shoulders, her legs around his waist, and he began climbing, hand over hand, his muscles screaming from the strain. "Whatever you do," he growled, "don't look down."

"I won't," she whispered, holding him tighter. He took them up nearly another seventy feet, before stopping at one of the highest branches. Bracing his feet, Quinn helped Saige slip around to his front, then held her against his chest as he ran off the end of the branch and unfurled his wings, catching the wind. Vines and branches caught at his arms and legs, but be ignored the pain, flying as fast as he could, powering them through the humid jungle air. Still, despite his determination, he could only travel so far before the pain in his right wing finally took him down.

The second their feet safely touched the grass-covered ground, Quinn released his hold on her and quickly stepped back, locking his jaw as he forced his wings back into his body. "Can you walk?" he grunted, raking his gaze down her body, looking for any injuries.

As if she didn't even hear him, she stepped forward, her voice tender and soft as she said, "What you did back there. My God, Quinn, it was amazing. I've never seen anyone fight like that in my entire life."

"Can. You. Walk?" he growled, hating that she'd seen that side of him. It was one he'd always hidden from Janelle, once he'd realized how she felt about his more mercenary talents. But Saige wasn't staring at him with a terrified look of horror on her beautiful, battered face. In fact, she looked…hungry, as if she were burning with the same violent energy tearing through him.

She nodded in answer to his question, and he turned his back on her, setting off toward Coroza. "We need to move fast and get the hell out of the jungle."

"Quinn," she panted, practically jogging to keep up with his hurried pace. "You just saved my life back there. Again. I don't know how to—"

"Don't," he growled, not interested in anything she had to say. "If I were you, Saige, I'd just stay quiet, because anything that comes out of your mouth right now is probably just going to piss me off."

"Will your wing be okay?" she asked, obviously ignoring his warning. "Will it keep bleeding?"

"Yeah, it'll keep bleeding until I take care of it," he muttered, using his hands to push the dense tangle of leaves out of their way. "Now shut up and keep moving."

"But I want… *Oomph.*"

He rounded on her so quickly, she collided with his chest, her soft hands cool against the heat of his skin, pressed against the furious pounding of his heart. Gritting his teeth, Quinn pushed against her shoulders, forcing her back, not trusting himself to be that close to her. "You wanna stand around and chat right now?" he barked, glaring down at her. "Then fine. Go ahead. But as soon as those bastards are able to move, they're going to be gunning for us. You really wanna be standing here when that happens, or would you rather get somewhere safe?"

"I just want to explain what happened." Her eyes were painfully blue within the dark fringe of her lashes, her voice thick…breathless. "I had my reasons for leaving, but I know I made a mistake."

"Yeah, I'm betting you figured that out about two seconds after they got their hands on you."

CROSSING HER ARMS over her middle, Saige took a deep breath, determined to find a way to get through to him. She didn't know why it was so important, other than the fact that he'd selflessly saved her life—not once, but twice now. As far as reasons went, there was no doubt that was a compelling one. But it was more than that. If she didn't know better, she'd think that she was actually panicking at the thought of losing him, which was crazy, considering she'd never even had him in the first place.

And never would.

"I thought I was doing the right thing, Quinn. And I can explain, if you'll only give me the chance."

He trembled, as if holding in some dark, devastating emotion. "And you think I'll believe anything you have to say? Hell, Saige. For all I know, every word out of your mouth has been a lie."

"You don't really believe that," she argued, while inside she was cringing, knowing he was going to be even more furious when she told him the truth. About everything.

His dark eyes moved over her face with a fierce intensity, shadowed by a pain that went deeper than his physical injuries, and he slowly shook his head. "To be honest, I don't know what to believe when I look at you."

"Who was it, Quinn?" She could see an uncomfortable truth smoldering there in his violent, angry gaze, and the question just rushed up out of her, the need to know impossible to resist.

"Who was what?" he snapped, while his chest heaved, his breaths jerking out in a hard, angry rhythm.

"The one who hurt you?" she said softly, devastated by the thought of someone, some *woman,* having that kind of power over him. But she knew she was right. Saige could see the demons of his past, *could feel them,* rising up within him. A visceral, primitive fury that'd been reawakened by her actions that morning, ripping something dark and destructive to his surface.

He stepped closer, his voice nothing more than a rough, guttural scrape of sound. "This isn't about me. It's about *you.* And my life is *none* of your goddamn business."

"Isn't it? You know all about me. Isn't it only fair that I get to know your secrets?"

"You ran out on me, and then I nearly died saving

your ass!" he roared, vibrating with rage and frustration. The violent emotions blasted against her like a force of heat, and she hated that she'd hurt him. Hated it, but couldn't deny that she had. As if they had physical substance, she could feel the bruises she'd made on his ego. Hear them in the graveled bark of his voice. See them in the ravaged lines of his expression.

From the moment she'd run, Saige had regretted it, each step away from him cutting her a little bit deeper, as if a raw, bleeding wound had been carved into her flesh. She didn't understand it, but then, that was nothing new for her. Her entire life seemed to be one inexplicable mystery after another. Why should her feelings for the impossibly complicated, outrageously gorgeous Michael Quinn be any different?

She had no illusions about how it would end, but who could say how long she had until the end, anyway? All she knew was that in that moment, the truth became blindingly, painfully clear, as if she'd just opened her eyes to a beautiful, breathtaking revelation.

She wanted him. Not just for a fast grab at pleasure, and not to use as a way of forgetting her grief. But for a stolen moment in time, where she could lose herself in him…soak him in…and have him. All of him.

Shivering with emotion, Saige whispered his name, wanting nothing more than to reach out and touch him…hold him. "Please. Let me explain. I'll tell you the truth, if you'll just give me the chance."

"You can talk when we make it back to town. Until then, I'd keep my mouth shut if I were you. You never know," he muttered. "I might not like what you have to say and decide to leave you here after all."

She hated the cold, empty look that fell over his eyes, a strange kind of panic settling inside her that was somehow worse than when she'd been with the Casus. "I know you're angry with me, but you would never do something like that."

"If that's what you really believe, then I guess you're not so smart after all," he grunted, and, turning his back on her, he set back off through the jungle, toward Coroza.

Following after him, Saige knew that if there'd been a door between them, it'd just been slammed in her face. Finding a way to make this right wasn't going to be easy, but there was no way that she was going to give up.

Somewhere in the past twenty-four hours, the rules had changed on her, and now she found herself wanting to run toward him…rather than away. He'd come after her…risking his life to save hers, proving that he was more than tough enough to handle the Casus. Saige wanted to thank him. Comfort him. Wanted to lose herself in that hot, smoldering warmth that arced between them whenever they were together. Wanted to make him understand why she'd done what she had. See him smile. Hear him laugh. And some-how, in some way, earn his trust again.

But most of all, she wanted to find a way to chase away the shadows of pain from his dark, beautiful eyes.

CHAPTER TEN

CONSIDERING HOW BADLY Quinn's wing was damaged, they had little choice but to find another hotel room where they could lie low for a while, this one buried in the heart of São Vicente. And while it wasn't the Ritz, at least they had a decent place to recover from the harrowing hours in the jungle.

Saige only hoped they didn't end up with the *policías* knocking on their door, demanding an explanation for their injuries.

Though Inez had given Quinn one of Rubens's T-shirts when they'd run into *O Diablo Dos Ángels,* warning the couple to get out of town for a few days, they had still attracted attention throughout the long afternoon. The manager at the hotel where Quinn had left his bag that morning eyed them with suspicion when they rushed in to pick up his things—as did the cashier in the local drugstore, where they'd purchased some medical supplies, toiletries and a few pieces of generic clothing for her to wear, since her backpack had been left behind in the jungle. But no one had looked at them quite so strangely as the manager they'd just dealt with down in the lobby. He'd eyed their bruised, battered bodies with a wary gaze as they'd checked in, politely inquiring if they were in need of medical assistance. Saige had forced a small smile, then lied through her teeth, telling him that they'd been in a car accident just that morning and simply needed a place to lie down and recuperate.

Hopefully he'd bought her story and would leave them in peace.

As she looked around the small room, she noted that the glitz of the hotel they'd stayed in the night before had been replaced by the quaintness of a traditional decor, offering casual comfort—and yet, the mere presence of the enigmatic Michael Quinn gave the staid environment an electrifying edge. The second the door was closed and locked behind them, Saige could feel his need to lash out at her sizzling on the air, though he remained broodingly silent. His simmering rage revealed itself in other ways, pulsing off his large body in hot, smoldering waves, evident in the tightly controlled way that he paced before the sliding-glass door. Its open curtains revealed the first vibrant shades of twilight as the sun slowly began melting into the horizon, the deep slashes of ochre and crimson reminding her of wounds cut into the sky—the ominous imagery the perfect complement to go with what had been a horrific day.

Face it, woman. You screwed up so bad.

She mentally slammed the brakes on that irritating train of thought, and struggled to find a place to begin, wondering how she could make Quinn understand her reasons for lying to him…and leaving him.

Carefully breaching the charged silence, she quietly said, "Are you sure you're going to be okay?"

He rolled his right shoulder with a stiff, jerky movement. "Like I said, I'll live."

"Then…can we talk now?"

Shoving his hands deep into his pockets, he kept his back to her as he stopped to stare out the glass door, his body big and broad against the skyline of the city. "I'm trying real hard to understand why you would run, Saige. But for the life of me, I can't figure it out. What did you think you were doing?"

She took a shaky breath, and finally gave him the truth. "Protecting you."

He snorted, clearly unconvinced as he cut a dark look over his shoulder. "That's your excuse? You wanted to protect me?"

"Yes." She swept her tongue across her bottom lip, her hands twisting together, restless and damp with nerves. "That's part of it. At first I just didn't trust you enough to tell you the truth about everything, but then, after what you told me about Ian…and we found Javier, I couldn't stand putting you in danger. I'd already involved Jamison, and it didn't seem fair to make the same mistake with you, considering I'm nothing more than an assignment—one that you didn't even want to begin with."

She wanted him to disagree, to tell her that she was wrong, but he did neither of those things. Instead, he slowly turned around until he faced her, his strong arms crossed aggressively over his muscular chest. The look on his hard, beautiful face clearly said that he still wasn't buying it, but instead of calling her a liar, he said, "We'll get to the part about telling me the truth in a minute. Right now, I want to know who the hell this Jamison is."

Rubbing at her forehead, she wondered how to explain everything that she needed to tell him. "His name is Jamison Haley, and he's a colleague of mine, as well as a friend."

With his lashes shielding his gaze, it was difficult to tell what he was thinking. "And what does any of this have to do with him?"

Saige did her best to ignore the sharp flare of guilt that twisted through her when she thought of the danger she'd put Jamison in. The fact that she'd lied to him, as well, didn't help. Oh, she'd been completely honest with him about the possible—*probable*—danger, she just hadn't stuck to their plan. Jamison had believed that she was heading back to the States right behind him. They'd decided to avoid the major airports, traveling by other means, such as buses, trains and small commuter flights, which she'd hoped would help keep them both under the radar.

Clearing her throat, Saige sat on the foot of the massive king-size bed and forced herself to begin what she knew was going to be a long, difficult explanation. "I'll tell you everything about Jamison in a minute. But there are a few things that I need to explain first." She pushed her tangled hair back from her face, uncomfortable beneath the intensity of his stare, and forced herself to continue. "I was telling you the truth about my reasons for being in South America. I just didn't tell you…everything. As you've probably guessed, there weren't any research papers back at the Redondo Hotel this morning. I only said that so that I could…get away, and I knew you wouldn't just go back to Colorado if I asked you to. But there *was* something that I needed to get, back in Inez's safe at the bar. That's where I'd stored the set of maps that I found buried with the first Marker in Italy. Maps that showed the locations of the other Dark Markers. Or at least some of them."

"You have maps?" he rasped, his voice so soft, she almost didn't hear him.

"I did. Just…not anymore. They're back in the jungle, with everything else that I was carrying in my backpack when the Casus found me."

Quinn scrubbed his hands down his face, while a low, bitter laugh rumbled in his chest. "So because you didn't trust me, you're telling me that those Casus bastards now have a set of maps that will lead them straight to the other crosses?"

She nodded, feeling sick when she thought about it. "Obviously, we'll need to get them back somehow."

"*We* won't be doing anything. I think you've already done enough," he muttered under his breath.

"It's not as bad as it sounds. I mean, it's bad, but they won't be able to break the codes to read them. At least, I don't think they will."

"The maps are coded?" he grunted, shoving his hands back into his pockets.

She nodded again, and he huffed, "Then how could you read them?"

Saige pressed her fingers to her temples, the beginnings of a raging headache coming on as she struggled to find the best way to explain. "Before we get to that, I need to tell you about the Marker."

"What about it?" he demanded, clearly losing his patience.

Knowing he was going to be furious, she lifted her chin and said, "I found it, Quinn. The second cross. Yesterday morning, I found the place where it had been buried in the jungle."

He pulled in a sharp breath, and she waited, fully expecting him to explode. The seconds ticked by, the tension mounting, pulling tighter…and tighter, but the eruption never came. Instead, he simply stared through that dark, shadowed gaze, until he quietly said, "Where is it?"

"Most of the other members of our research team left last week, but Jamison, an archaeologist, stayed behind with me. He's a good friend and didn't want me to be on my own. After I found the Marker, I…explained the situation to him, and then I asked him to take the talisman to Colorado for me."

Slanting her a sharp look of disgust, he paced away from the sliding-glass door, cursing something dark and ugly under his breath. When he'd made it across the room and back again, he turned back toward her, his voice a hard slash of sound as he sneered. "So you spill this whole ugly story to this guy, and he just believes you?"

"Yes."

"That was pretty loyal of him, don't you think?"

Before she could respond, he angled his head a fraction to the side and said, "Were you screwing him?"

Pressing her hands into the mattress at her sides, Saige narrowed her eyes. "That's none of your business," she said softly.

"Like hell it isn't," he growled, pulling back his shoulders, his hands still shoved deep in his pockets, as if he needed to keep them confined. "You went and got the poor son of a bitch tangled up in this and now he's probably going to end up minced because of you. I need to know how involved you are with him."

"He's my friend," she insisted through her clenched teeth. "As well as my colleague. God, Quinn, do I seem like the kind of woman who sleeps her way through her coworkers?"

Something jealous and cruel slid through his eyes, and she braced, knowing his next words were going to cut like a blade. "You tried to fuck me after we'd only known each other a few hours. What am I supposed to think?"

"You son of a bitch," she hissed, surging up from the bed with her right hand lifted. He caught her wrist as she started to swing, the rage in his eyes unlike anything she'd ever seen before.

"I've been beat up enough today because of you," he muttered in a low, almost silent snarl, glaring down at her. "So don't even think about it."

As if burned by the touch of her skin, Quinn suddenly let go of her wrist and gave her his back, staring out at the crimson smear of twilight through the sliding-glass door. Saige closed her eyes and ran her palms down the front of her stained T-shirt, doing her best to get her chaotic emotions under control.

For a long time there was nothing but the ragged sound of their breathing, and then he finally spoke in a slow, husky drawl. "So you ask this Haley guy to head back to Colorado with the cross, knowing that it could very well be dangerous. I mean, Templeton had already disappeared, and your awakening had already started." A low, gritty slide of laughter rumbled up from his chest. "Christ, I'm almost afraid to hear what you have planned for the poor bastard once he gets there."

"I don't have anything *planned* for him. He's going to meet me in the coffee shop of the Douglas Resort outside of Denver on Tuesday afternoon. Then, once I get the cross back from him, he'll head back home to England."

"If the Casus suspect him, he'll be dead long before you get there. You need to call him. Tell him to get his ass to Riley as soon as possible."

"I can't call him," she explained, moving to his side. While Quinn kept his eyes on the darkening skyline, Saige stared hungrily at the rugged perfection of his profile. The shadowed angle of his jaw made him look hard…dangerous, while the sensual shape of his firm, masculine lips made him achingly beautiful. She remembered how the warm, provocative taste of his mouth had melted her in the jungle, and her voice thickened with lust as she said, "I was worried someone might be able to track Jamison's location through his phone, so I told him to keep it off unless there was an emergency. Of course, my phone was in my backpack, so now he has no way of reaching me."

He made a rude sound in the back of his throat. "Yeah, well, the Casus have probably tossed it by now. The only thing they're going to care about is the maps." Slanting her a hard look of frustration, he said, "What the hell were you thinking?"

Saige wasn't sure if he was asking about Jamison, the phone or the entire situation, but it didn't matter. She didn't have a good explanation for any of them, and she knew it. "I wasn't," she said in a small voice, wishing he'd just reach out and touch her. Hold her. Kiss her and help her forget everything that she'd been through. "I don't think I've thought straight since any of this started."

"Does this guy even have a clue what he's up against?"

"He knows what he's doing. Jamison comes from a long line of occult believers. His maternal grandparents are actually some of Britain's most famous ghost-hunters." This time, she was the one who gave a quiet, bitter laugh. "It's probably why we get along so well. He knows that what he's doing is dangerous, but the Marker told… I mean, I had reason to believe that someone was coming for the cross. At the time, I didn't see any other way to keep it safe but to give it to him."

"And he just left you down here? Knowing you were in danger?"

She shook her head. "Not exactly."

"Let me guess," he rasped, arching one dark, slashing brow. "You lied to him, too?"

"I told him I'd be leaving right after him, just going a slightly different way."

"Do you ever tell the truth?" His voice was rough with emotion, and he shifted position, moving toward her, until she could actually feel the heat of his body, his warm, rugged scent filling her head, awakening her senses.

"I hated lying to him, but I had to do whatever I could to keep the Marker safe. I figured it couldn't hurt to hang around Coroza for the rest of the day and let Jamison get a head start with the Marker, while whoever might want it would be watching me, thinking I still had it. And I think it worked, because the Casus didn't even mention his name to me today."

"So you put the cross above your friend's life. And your own." It wasn't a question, but a simple statement of fact, and she could read the disapproval in his tone.

You shouldn't have done it, Saige. You made a mistake...and Jamison's going to pay for it.

"I didn't have a choice, Quinn. You know what's coming. If the Casus want the Markers, like Ian said, like they told me they did today, then there must be something we don't know, and there's already *too much* we don't know. The crosses are important, and Gregory and Royce didn't even know why they need them so badly. After what the Marker told me, I couldn't think of anything else to do. That doesn't mean I was happy about it. If anything happens to Jamison, I'll never forgive myself."

"*It* told you?" he blurted. "What the hell does that mean, Saige?"

She winced, wondering how he was going to take this next part of her confession. "I'm afraid this is the part where things get even more…complicated."

"I don't care if it's the goddamn theory of relativity," he growled, holding her trapped in his stare. "Just explain it."

She chewed on the corner of her mouth, intensely aware that aside from her mother, Quinn was the only other person she'd ever shared her secret with. "When I was a teenager," she began, struggling to control the tremor in her throat, "I—God, you're going to think this sounds crazy, but I developed a…well, I guess you would call it a power."

He kept staring…waiting, until the words suddenly rushed out of her in a rapid, breathless whisper. "When I touch a physical object, it either tells me or shows me something."

The silence stretched out, slow and sticky, like a thick spill of molasses, his eyes somehow darker, deeper…and then he finally said, "Haven't we had enough of the bullshit?"

"I know it sounds crazy, but it's true."

"You honestly expect me to believe that objects…talk to you? Show you things?"

"Is it any crazier than you sprouting wings?"

He ground his jaw, looking as if he couldn't decide between throttling her…or kissing her, and wanting both with equal measure.

"Hand me something," she whispered. "Something that belongs to you."

"I don't think so," he growled, actually taking a

step away from her. If she hadn't been so nervous, Saige thought she might have grinned at his reaction.

"You want an explanation?" she asked, holding his gaze, trying to tell him with her eyes that he could believe her. "Then you're going to have to trust me, Quinn. I need to touch something that belongs to you. A personal possession."

Wearing a cautious, curious look, he reached into his back pocket and pulled out a sleek, silver cell phone. Her hand trembled as she reached for it, her breath sucking in on a sharp gasp the instant she touched the warm metallic surface. As she held the phone between her palms, a series of images sank into her system with a warm, tingling sensation, vibrating against her skin.

Quinn's jaw went hard. "You want to explain what's going on?"

Filled with regret, Saige wished that she could go back and undo that morning. "You were terrified when you realized I'd run off on my own."

"Don't flatter yourself," he told her, his tone oddly devoid of emotion, as if he'd found some way to bury it all inside.

But she could feel his anger and fear bleeding through the phone, pulsing against her skin, the metal so warm it was like holding a living creature within her hand. "After you got in a fight with the manager at the hotel, you took out this phone and called *O Diablo Dos Ángels.* That's when Inez told you that I'd left with two men." Staring into his eyes, she could barely breathe as she soaked in the dark intensity of his expression. "You were worried that they were Casus, and so you flagged down a taxi and offered the driver triple the rate if he'd get you to the bar as fast as he could, where you knew you could pick up my scent."

"How do you know that?" he snarled, his brow drawn in a deep vee over his suspicious gaze.

Saige gave him a small, tentative smile, her insides glowing with a warm, incandescent glow at the knowledge that he'd been so worried about her. "The phone," she said simply, offering it back to him. He took it, holding it carefully between his thumb and forefinger, as if he didn't want to touch it. "I normally don't get so much information, but I guess…it might have something to do with how upset you were."

"Christ," he growled, quickly shoving the phone back in his pocket. "You're actually serious, aren't you?"

Crossing her arms, Saige turned her head, staring sightlessly out the sliding-glass door. "It started when I was a teenager, but I don't know why. As far as I know, no one else in my family is able to do it, but then we don't share much, so who knows about Ian and Riley. I guess we all have our secrets and by the time I realized my gift, Ian had been gone for years and Riley and I weren't close." She looked back up at Quinn, and found herself trapped in the piercing intensity of his stare. "Elaina was thrilled when she realized what I could do, believing it would help in our search for answers about the Merrick. But for the most part, it's something that I've learned to block out. If I focus, though, then I can usually pick up information."

Shadows darkened his gaze with a thick, sudden pour of fury, and if possible, he looked even larger, looming before her like a great, towering force of frustration. "That's what all that shit was about last night at the bar, wasn't it? You freaked out after touching the beer bottle."

The heat in her chest climbed suspiciously up her throat, blooming over her skin like a flash fire. She nodded, her voice hoarse as she admitted, "I saw what you'd been thinking."

He twisted away from her, back toward the glass door, and lifted one arm, rubbing at the back of his neck again. He stood like that for a breathless span of seconds, and then with a gruff edge to his words, he said, "Inez was hysterical by the time I got to the bar. She'd sent Rubens to follow after you, but he came back saying that he'd lost you in the jungle. When I showed up, all she cared about was making sure you were going to be okay."

"Do you really think they'll leave town for a while, like you told them to?"

"Hopefully," he muttered. "But if there's one thing I've learned, it's that you can't make people do something they don't want to. Even when you know their choices are going to get them hurt."

She shivered, swallowing the lump in her throat, unable to tell if he was talking about her...or someone else. Whatever had happened in his past, her recent actions had brought it back to him, adding to her gut-wrenching guilt.

"So this power," he rumbled a moment later, his dark eyes focused on some distant point on the horizon. "You used it to find the first Marker?"

"In a way. It's a long story," she murmured, "but basically I used the power to follow clues that led me to where the cross was buried in Italy, and discovered the maps buried beside it."

"If the codes are so complicated, how did you figure out how to read them? No, wait, let me guess," he drawled, an unmistakable thread of sarcasm rounding out his words. "The maps *told* you."

"Be snide if you like, Quinn. But that's what happened."

"Then where's the next Marker?" he asked, slanting her a sideways look.

She lifted her shoulders. "I don't know. I was trying to figure that out when things started falling apart. But I think it's going to be somewhere in North America."

"Did your mother know about these maps?" he asked, looking back toward the sunset.

Saige stared at the strong, burnished length of his throat, aware of the seething hunger that, even now, lurked just beneath the surface of her skin. Even when she was upset, the rising needs of her Merrick never left her, always there…always wanting, waiting. "No," she said huskily, clearing her throat. "I didn't tell her about them when I brought her the cross."

"Didn't trust her, either?" he asked, sounding tired as he pushed his hands back into his pockets.

"I didn't know until yesterday morning if they would actually work, and I wasn't about to give her something else to worry about when she was already so ill." She took a deep breath, unable to believe her mother had been gone for nearly six months now, then quietly said, "I'm sorry I didn't tell you all of this yesterday, but you…you were a stranger. And I guess you still are. Only…you don't feel like a stranger anymore, Quinn. Actually, to be honest, I'm not sure that you ever really did. It's…complicated."

He kept his gaze on that distant point on the horizon, and then he finally said, "You told me last night that you didn't know how many there are, or where they're hidden. Was that the truth, or just another lie?"

"It was the truth. I've only decoded the first map, which led me here. The code changed for the second set of directions, and like I just told you, I didn't get the chance to finish it. Since they're all linked together, I'm not sure how many directions are listed, or even if I have all the maps. Who knows how many Markers could be out there, waiting to be found."

"Can't you ask for the information you want?"

She gave another low, bitter laugh. "I wish I could, but it doesn't work that way."

He turned his head to stare back down at her, clearly wondering if she was lying. "I'm telling you the truth, Quinn. Even knowing how to read it, the code isn't easy to decipher. It's almost as if the code evolves with each map, becoming more intricate. I doubt I ever would have been able to crack it, if the maps hadn't shared their secret."

"And the Casus, you said they knew about the maps?"

She swallowed at the sudden rise of grief that came with his question. "They tortured Javier until he told them that I had left some papers in Inez's safe. They assumed it was the maps, and were waiting for me to come back for them."

He shifted his body, propping his shoulder against the glass in an indolent, masculine pose, the powerful muscles in his arms looking long and lean as he kept his hands shoved deep in his pockets. "Do you know how they knew about them?"

"I have no idea. I had never even heard anything about any maps until I found them with the Marker. But it's because of the code that they didn't kill me. Well, that and the fact that I'm not fully awakened." She took a deep breath, trying to remember exactly what they had told her. "They said that there's a powerful leader who has figured out a way to send the Casus shades through the gate. And there's another way, as well. When they feed from a Merrick that's been fully awakened, the power charge is supposedly enough for them to actually pull a shade back from Meridian all on their own."

He scowled. "What the hell's Meridian?"

"The name they've given the holding ground."

Shaking his head, his voice was a low, husky rumble of sound as he said, "So they want the Merrick for more than just a good meal and revenge, then."

"I guess so. And the one named Gregory said that other Casus are already here, and that Merrick awakenings are taking place all over the world."

"Did you learn anything else?"

"Only that the Casus Ian killed was Gregory's brother." She turned her head and stared at the burning golden blur of the sun, knowing her next words were only going to add to his pain. "And you were also right about Templeton. His...body was there. At the clearing."

"Christ," he rasped, rubbing his right hand over the bottom half of his face as he tilted back his head.

"When I asked them why they hadn't burned it, like they did with Javier and his brothers, that was when they began fighting. Royce was furious with Gregory. He said that after the screwup Gregory's brother had made of his hunt, someone named Westmore was now covering their tracks. I don't know who this Westmore is, but Royce said that he was partners with Calder."

"And who the hell is Calder?" he growled.

She lifted her shoulders. "I don't know, and I wasn't going to stick around to ask questions. But he must be someone important."

Shivering at the memory of her fear, she looked back toward Quinn. "So long as I live, I'll never be able to make it up to you for getting me out of there." She dared to step closer to him, and reached out, pressing her hand to the firm, bronzed skin of his arm, the powerful bicep straining the sleeves of the borrowed T-shirt. Blood was smeared over his skin, dry to the touch, but she couldn't find the wounds it'd come from. She was about to ask him how he'd healed so quickly, when he placed his right hand on her shoulder and pushed her away.

"Don't get near me right now, Saige."

"Why not?"

His jaw worked, and he quietly growled, "Because I'm still pissed enough to do something I'll regret."

"And I'm stupid enough to take my chances," she shot back, unwilling to back down.

He gave a low, ragged laugh, studying her through heavy-lidded eyes. "You are one serious head trip, you know that?"

"I did what I did because I wanted to keep you safe, Quinn. I didn't want you getting hurt because of me."

He raised his brow. "And what about you?"

She shrugged and said, "I'm used to looking after myself."

"No wonder you drive your brothers out of their minds," he rumbled. "I've never known a woman who was a bigger pain in the ass."

"Yeah, well, I've heard that a lot lately," she drawled, her tone dry.

He grimaced, but she couldn't tell if it was from anger or from pain. In the next moment, he pushed away from the window and walked toward the dresser, where he'd placed the guns he'd taken from the Casus, along with his duffel bag and the things they'd purchased. Picking up the bag from the drugstore, he dumped out the contents on the dresser's pine surface and grabbed the medical supplies, then headed toward the bathroom. "I'm going to take a shower," he said, slanting her a shuttered look. "If you wanna run, fine. I really don't give a shit. But you leave, and you're on your own. I won't be chasing you down again."

"You'd just let me walk out that door?"

He rolled his shoulder, as if to say he couldn't care less what she did. "If that's what you want."

Saige searched his expression, praying he didn't mean it. "I'm sorry I didn't trust you before, Quinn. But I do now."

"Yeah?" he drawled. "Well, just for the record, I don't trust you worth shit."

The bathroom door shut behind him, and Saige paced the room as she listened to the running water, thinking over everything she'd just shared with him. Despite his attitude and anger, there was a lightness in her chest that she hadn't felt in a long time, one that came from sharing her secrets with someone she trusted. She felt at peace in a way that she hadn't experienced in years, and yet, she was also on edge, a subtle, trembling tension vibrating beneath her skin. It was a searing, growing need, sharp and sweet and dizzying. Impossible to ignore.

The water stopped, and she waited, hoping the stubborn man would ask for her help cleaning his wounds. But as the minutes ticked by, she continued to wear a path into the cheap carpet. When a sharp curse came from the bathroom, she finally walked to the door and slowly pushed it open, peering inside. Just as she'd suspected, Quinn stood in nothing but a pair of jeans, with his back to the mirror, his right wing extended. Beads of sweat dotted his brow, evidence of his pain as he reached over his shoulder with his left hand, trying to clean the ragged bullet wound.

Determined not to let him scare her away, she pushed open the door and walked into a warm, Quinn-scented blast of steam. "It's ridiculous for you to do that when I'm here," she told him, pointing at the closed toilet seat. "Sit down."

"I've got it," he growled under his breath.

Ignoring his anger, she said, "Just sit down, Quinn."

He glared at her reflection in the mirror and snarled, "I don't want your help, Saige."

"Yeah, I noticed that. So it's a good thing I'm telling you what to do, rather than asking. Now be a good boy and *sit down.*"

He made a low, aggravated sound in the back of his throat, but finally did as she told him, tossing the antiseptic pad he'd been using in the bin before turning his back to her and straddling the porcelain seat. With the mirror extending the entire length of the bathroom counter, Saige found herself staring right into his eyes as she stepped behind him. She could have fallen into the dark, intoxicating power of that hard, savage gaze, but she gave herself a firm mental shake and forced her attention onto the items sitting on the counter. Reaching for a fresh antiseptic pad, she ripped open the foil packaging, the small square of medicated cotton cool to her fingertips.

Moving closer to Quinn's back, she took a moment to simply appreciate the unique, otherworldly beauty of his wing. The silken feathers were so dark, they looked almost blue beneath the fluorescent glow of light spilling down from above, identical in color to the short, ink-black strands of his hair. Because of the cramped space, he'd had to bend the powerful wing at the joint, while keeping his left wing inside his body. With the swab in her left hand, Saige lifted her right and gently stroked her fingers over the soft, gleaming feathers, marveling at the mysteries of his body—at how he was able to simply absorb something so strong and beautiful inside him.

The bullet had ripped through the thickest part of the wing's flesh-covered bone, no more than six inches from where it extended from his back. Taking a deep breath, she carefully shifted the feathers aside, wincing as she touched the medicated swab to the wound and he hissed through his teeth. As if he needed something to take his mind off the pain, he rasped, "That was a clever move, Saige. Ditching me at the hotel like that. Too many people around for me to take to the sky, and too much crap in the air for me to follow your scent. I have to give you credit for that. Of course, going back to the *barra* has to be the dumbest thing I've ever heard of."

Careful to keep her touch as gentle as possible, she said, "I meant what I told you before, Quinn. I thought I was doing the right thing." She could feel the press of his eyes on her face in the mirror as she concentrated on her task. "They didn't rape me," she added softly, "in case you were wondering."

"Trust me," he muttered. "I know."

"How?" she asked, meeting his dark stare in the mirror.

"If they had," he retorted, "you wouldn't be walking. Hell, you probably wouldn't even be breathing."

"Be careful," she murmured, "or you might even sound like you care."

He grunted in response to her dry tone, and she grabbed another swab. As she turned back to him, her attention caught on the left side of his back, where a thick, pale mark marred the bronzed perfection of his skin. About eight inches long, it started at the inside edge of his shoulder blade and ran down the left side of his spine, ending at the lower edge of his rib cage.

"Is this a scar?" she asked, trailing her fingertips lightly across the line before lifting her gaze to the mirror. She'd noticed the mark before, whenever he'd had his bare back turned to her, as well as the one to the right of his spine, but had never had the courage to ask about them until now. "Or does it have something to do with your wings?"

His mouth went hard, just like his eyes. "Scar tissue."

Wondering what had happened, she trailed her fingers to the place where his right wing emerged from his back, and felt a portion of the thick ridge there, as if the wing had split it down the middle. "Do they hurt?" she asked, keeping her touch light when she felt him tremble, afraid of causing him pain.

For a moment, she didn't think he would bother to answer, and then he sighed and muttered, "Only when I shift."

"How did you get them?"

"None of your goddamn business," he growled, his guttural tone so vicious, it actually made her flinch.

Shifting her gaze back to the mirror again, she

caught his hard, glittering stare and refused to let him go. "You can be as nasty as you want," she told him in a soft voice. "But it isn't going to scare me away."

"Christ," he barked, his voice thick with frustration. "You're friggin' priceless, Saige. Yesterday, I go out of my way to play nice with you, treat you with respect, protect you, and you react by running. But the minute I get ugly, you act like nothing I can do will run you off. What the hell kind of game are you playing?"

"I told you the truth, Quinn. I'm sorry about what I did. Sorry for lying to you, and for running away. It won't happen again."

"Right," he drawled, his tone as bitter as it was sarcastic.

"It's true," she said huskily, wishing she could find a way to make him believe her. That she could find a way to get through to him. Taking a deep, shaky breath, she leaned down and pressed a soft, tender kiss to the top edge of the scar on his left. The instant her lips touched the warmth of his skin, he jerked to his feet, the sudden movement sending her stumbling back into the bathroom wall. A graveled curse tore from his throat as he spun around and snarled, "Don't ever put your mouth on me again!"

With her heartbeat roaring in her ears, she stared at his dark, furious expression and tried to catch her breath. *"Quinn..."*

His chest heaved as he raked her body with a hot, scalding stare, and then he stalked out of the bathroom. Saige stared after him, not knowing what to do...how to get what she wanted. But she wasn't going to give up. He might be furious with her, but he was still the only man who'd ever made her feel this way, and Saige wanted to lose herself in him. Wanted to give herself over to the dark, searing need for pleasure and gratification rising within her, while somehow protecting her heart in the process.

Keep shoveling on the bullshit, Saige. But you know better. You're already falling hard. And the more time you spend with him, the harder you're going to fall.

Maybe, but did she really care?

Because in the end, wasn't having a broken heart better than no heart at all?

CHAPTER ELEVEN

AT THE SOUND OF the cabin's front door creaking open, Royce Friesen lifted his head from his bloodstained pillow. Blinking his gritty eyes, he struggled to focus through a gnashing veil of pain as he watched Gregory stalk through the bedroom doorway, a terrorized human female held tight against the front of his body. The flickering wash of light from the lone candle that sat on the floor beside his mattress fell short of her trembling form, but his keen vision allowed Royce to see her clearly, despite the thickening shadows of night. Her hands had been tied behind her back, the remnants of what had once been a bloodred sundress hanging in tatters around the lush, womanly shape of her figure. She had an earthy, sensual beauty, with her long legs, heavy breasts and thick, curly hair that tumbled in riotous waves over her quaking shoulders. But it was the stark, unmistakable fear in her sloe-dark eyes that called to him, making his groin pull tight with need.

"What the hell are you doing?" he croaked, his voice scratchy from the deep wounds that were still healing in his throat.

Gregory's smile spread slowly across his human face as he nuzzled the woman's ear. "Consider her a gift to help with your recovery."

Lifting up onto his right elbow, Royce wet his lips, his natural instinct for the kill warring with his knowledge that he couldn't risk letting himself lose control. Though his heart was still beating, he'd lost too much blood from his wounds, and now his hunger was like a raging, feral beast within his body, ravenous for a good, long feeding. He wanted her, badly, but feared that his bloodlust, once sated, would quickly rise again, becoming too strong, too powerful, stripping him of his control—and he'd end up suffering the same fate as Malcolm.

As if reading his indecision, Gregory shook his head, while a low, wicked rumble of laughter slipped from his lips. "Poor Royce. You're trying so hard to be good, but guess what? The devil can act the saint, but it still won't get him into heaven."

"I don't want into heaven," he growled, curling his lip. "I just want to stay out of hell. I don't want to end up like your brother."

"And you don't think that's where you're headed?" Gregory drawled. "If you're too weak when you face our enemies, hell is exactly where they're going to send you."

Royce didn't trust Gregory DeKreznick worth a damn, knowing the Casus just wanted him healthy enough to help find the Buchanan bitch, now that they'd lost her. And once they had her, he had little doubt that Gregory would turn on him, seeing as how he suspected that Gregory planned on taking Saige for himself, regardless of the fact that she belonged to him. But he couldn't argue that the psychotic bastard had a point. As it was, he'd be an easy kill for anyone who tried to take him down, and he couldn't let that happen. Not when he'd finally gained his freedom after so many gnawing, excruciating years of captivity.

Royce understood Calder's rules about feeding, agreeing that indiscriminate human killing would quickly draw them unwanted attention—but it was becoming increasingly clear that if he kept going at this rate, he would eventually destroy himself.

As if sensing his weakening resolve, Gregory lowered his head toward his sobbing captive. With a mischievous glint in his pale eyes, he held Royce's infuriated gaze as he ran his tongue along the quivering column of her throat, making her whimper against the dirty gag that bisected her rouged lips. Mascara ran in dark rivulets of terror beneath her frightened eyes, the black smudges somehow heightening her earthy appeal. And despite the shredded state of her dress, Royce could tell from her scent that Gregory hadn't raped her.

His mouth watered, his gums going heavy from the weight of his fangs at the knowledge that she would be tender and fresh between her thighs, like something soft and innocent. He wanted to sink his teeth into her, as well as his cock, with a hunger that burned in his brain like a flame, but he had no doubt that it was a dangerous game, allowing himself to be seduced by Gregory's offering. Somehow, he had the alarming feeling that they had all underestimated the youngest DeKreznick sibling, and would pay for it in the end.

As insane as he was, there was a ruthless determination in Gregory that could very well come back and slam them all on their asses.

Determined to avoid the trap, Royce started to lie back down, ready to tell him to get her out of there, when Gregory gave him a slow, knowing smile…and ran his hand over the woman's bountiful chest, knotting his fist in the soft cotton of her dress. With a single tug, he pulled the garment from her upper body, exposing a pair of full, rounded breasts encased in provocative black lace, the creamy mounds quivering with her gasping breaths.

Hunger tore through his insides like a jagged blade as Royce imagined sinking his fangs into one of those perfect breasts, her blood warm and thick in his mouth…in his throat. Sweat filmed his skin as he thought of how he'd drink from her like a glutton, hammering his body between her creamy thighs, forcing her to come, despite her fear. It wasn't easy, but he'd done it before, back when he was free to walk the earth, and the savage pleasure had become like an addiction, one that had ripped and clawed at his soul after the Merrick had trapped the Casus in that stinking pit of Meridian. That was when he'd make the kill—at that perfect, breathtaking moment when her flesh clamped down on his. He'd smile into her eyes, make her think there was a chance in hell he'd allow her to live. Savor the carnal scent of her passion…the sweetness of her hope, and then he'd allow his true self to break free.

And with a wide, wide smile, he'd rip her flesh from her body and feed the hungers of his soul.

His heart pounded, punching against his ribs, its rhythm quickening, and Royce knew that no matter how logical his mind, it was no match for the rapacious hungers of his beast.

"So what's it going to be?" Gregory murmured, while his hand rubbed small, intimate circles around the woman's navel, her dress barely hanging on the womanly curve of her hips. "Shall I eat her? Or have you finally come to your senses?"

"Leave her and get out," he said thickly, his fangs already slipping from his gums. And as the craving overtook him, swallowing him like a great, raging wave of violence, he could hear Gregory's maniacal laughter over the woman's hoarse, muffled cries.

WHEN ROYCE EMERGED from the cabin a half hour later, he felt like a new man. Wearing the human shape of his host, he drew in a deep breath of fertile-scented air and made his way toward the dark, flowing waters of the river. Blood covered his face and torso, among other bodily fluids, and he needed to wash. As he waded into the cool water, Gregory propped his shoulder against a nearby tree and asked, "Have a good time?"

Royce grunted in response, and Gregory said, "I've been thinking about the Marker."

"And?" he prompted, splashing water onto his face. His heart beat with a forceful, powering rhythm, the night coming alive to his heightened senses in a way he'd almost forgotten, as if he could absorb its scents and sounds and secrets, breathing them into his system.

"There's only one place it could be. She's sent it back to her brothers, which means we're done here. The Raptor will take her back to Colorado, and we'll be waiting for them when they get there."

"Good," he declared, tilting back his head so that he could stare up at the hazy, silvery glow of the moon. He'd been so sure he'd feel nothing but guilt if he broke the rules and fed from human flesh, but he'd been wrong. "After tonight, I'm more eager than ever to get my hands on her. And by that time, her awakening should be complete."

"If I was a betting man," Gregory added, "I'd put Westmore's money on the fact that she's sent it in the care of that archaeologist who followed her around like a puppy."

He nodded, filled with a power that he hadn't known in so long, it was almost like being reborn. "Contact Westmore again," he murmured, stretching his arms over his head. "If we're lucky, they can pick him up and hold him until we get there."

"And then we can dangle him in front of her like a sweet, tasty piece of bait," Gregory quipped, the white of his teeth flashing in the moonlit darkness. Then he turned around and headed off into the verdant heat of the jungle.

CHAPTER TWELVE

STARING THROUGH the sliding-glass door, Quinn used every control technique he'd ever heard of to keep himself in check, but they weren't working worth a damn. The crimson-splashed evening had finally melted into a suffocating darkness that poured over the horizon like a thick spill of ink, blanketing the light. That same darkness smoldered inside him, raging and violent, wanting to lash out and fight, needing the hard burn of aggression to burn out its energy.

It was crazy that he should be so hurt by Saige's lies, and yet, he couldn't deny the bitter scrape of betrayal in his gut.

If he'd been at Ravenswing, he'd have invited Shrader out for a one-on-one sparring session, where they could beat the hell out of each other until Kierland forced his way between them. It didn't happen often, but over the years, when the nightmares became too much, Shrader had always been there to serve as an outlet for Quinn's demons.

He'd hoped he'd have been able to exorcise them by now, but like the scars on his back, they remained a constant, brutal reminder of his past mistakes.

And from the looks of things, you haven't learned a goddamn thing.

Gritting his teeth, he braced his forearms against the cool pane of glass, thinking it'd been a hell of a day. First Saige had run from him. Then he'd nearly had his ass kicked by those Casus bastards. And to top it all off, she'd played nursemaid, as if she could kiss him all better and he'd forget the past twenty-four hours. What next? Was she going to rip out his heart and offer it up to Satan on a platter?

"Christ," he growled, pressing his forehead to the smooth glass as he closed his eyes, locking his jaw so hard that pain radiated through his skull. He didn't have a clue what he was going to do about her, but if he lived to be a hundred, Quinn knew he would never forget the terror that had gripped him when he'd realized Saige had run from him. It'd been hellish and stark, like a physical pain against which he couldn't defend. Couldn't destroy. After thinking he'd lost her, the feral drive to claim the infuriating woman was now almost too strong to resist, the hunger bleeding into his very bones. It was consuming. Primal. Primitive. He wanted her for hours on end, with no stopping. Wanted to imprint himself on her so deeply, she'd forever be marked by the feel of his body covering hers…driving deep inside her…possessing her with a savage, scorching intensity. Wanted to taste every part of her, assuring himself that she was safe and whole and no longer in danger.

It was insanity that he could care this much, this quickly. He'd known Janelle for months before he'd fallen in love with her, and look where it'd gotten him. He'd spent no more than mere hours with Saige Buchanan, and yet, somehow she'd forced her way into parts of him that no other woman had ever breached.

Even knowing that she'd lied to him from the beginning, he couldn't walk away.

He slowly opened his eyes, and for a moment he actually considered calling Kierland and demanding he send Shrader down to take his place. But no sooner had the thought entered his mind than he realized that he couldn't go through with it.

No, all he could do was stand there and seethe, terrified that he was going to give in to his need for her. And once he did, the nature of his beast would take over…and he'd be marked.

Then there'll be hell to pay. But you already know that, don't you?

After he'd stormed out of the bathroom, she'd closed the door, and a minute later he'd heard the shower running. Quinn had used the time to shoot off another text to Kierland, then done his best not to think about Saige's naked body under the hot spray, but now, as the water stopped, he could see her in his mind as clearly as if he'd been standing in the room with her. His imagination supplied the images that were nothing but pure, devastating torture, and his blood went thick, his body hardening against his will. He could see her stepping out of the shower, reaching for a towel. Could see the luminous glow of her skin; the sensual slide of water droplets slipping across her soft, feminine curves.

A handful of seconds, and then the bathroom door opened. Knowing it was only going to land him in hell, Quinn sent a smoldering look over his shoulder. His heart nearly jerked out of his chest when she came out wearing nothing more than a goddamn towel.

He silently cursed, wondering what kind of vile asshole he must have been in a past life to deserve this kind of torment.

"I've been thinking," she said softly, holding the towel's front knot with one hand while pulling the damp, glistening mass of her hair over her shoulder with the other. She met his searing gaze, then licked her bottom lip, and he nearly lost it. Nearly found himself storming across the room and taking her to the floor then and there, not giving a damn about the consequences.

Not trusting himself, he shoved his hands into his pockets and waited for her to continue.

"Obviously there's got to be something more to the Markers than protection," she said. "More than the fact they can be used as a weapon. Why else would the Casus want them?"

"You don't have time to worry about that now," he muttered, rubbing his eyes as he looked back out the window, wishing there was a way he could blot out the memory of her body wrapped in that tiny scrap of cotton.

"What do you mean?" she asked, sounding suspiciously closer.

"Having one of those monsters after you is bad enough, Saige. Two is going to be living hell. The only thing you need to worry about until we make it to Colorado is staying alive. Then you can sort out your little puzzle."

There was silence for a moment, and then she whispered his name.

"Yeah?"

This time when she spoke, there was no doubt that she stood just behind him. "You let me beat up on you last night, when I was upset. I just... I know that you're still angry, and I wanted you to know that I'm here for you."

Quinn lowered his head, a harsh sound tearing out of his throat that almost sounded like a laugh, but was too bitter, too rough. "I don't want to beat up on you," he growled, forcing the sharp words through his gritted teeth. Sweat dotted his brow, one salty bead slipping into his left eye, while his chest heaved.

"Then what do you want?" she asked, and as he pulled in a deep breath of air, there was nothing but pure, intoxicating Saige.

What did he want? God, if she had any idea, she'd be running as hard and as fast as she could. "Trust me," he rumbled, snuffling a short, graveled burst of laughter under his breath. "You don't want to know."

"Whatever it is," she told him, sounding determined, "I can take it."

DESPITE THE TOWEL wrapped around her body, Saige felt naked...completely exposed, as Quinn looked over his shoulder, slanting her one of those dark, searching looks that always made her feel as if he were peering into her mind like a voyeur. "I mean it," she said huskily, her nerve endings screaming with sensitivity, somehow aching for the press of his body against hers. For his heat…his weight.

The corner of his mouth kicked up in a cocky, knowing smirk, and he shook his head. "You say that now, but I wouldn't be so eager if I were you, honey."

She took a deep breath, and quickly said, "Are you… Is it sex that you want?"

His expression tightened, his dark eyes reminding her of the glittering, endless stretch of a midnight sky as he slowly turned toward her, his hands fisting at his sides, body held hard and tight with tension. "Unless you're offering," he said in a low, whiskey-rough voice, "I'd shut up, Saige."

She flicked a quick glance down his body…and almost swallowed her tongue at the hard, unmistakable proof of his interest. Even bound by the faded denim of his jeans, she could see just how hard and thick he was, and that warm, swirling glow of need in her body settled lower. Humiliation was still a factor, considering he'd turned her down once already—but as she stared at the breathtaking bulge behind his fly, the top button of his jeans left undone, providing a provocative glimpse of dark, hair-dusted skin, she couldn't doubt that tonight, at this moment, he wanted her.

Wetting her lips, she managed to croak, "I'm offering."

His muscles bunched beneath the burnished stretch of his skin, looking ready to burst into motion, held in check by the sheer force of his will. In a gritty, almost silent rasp, he said, "Think hard about what you're getting into here, Saige. I'm not like any of the other men that you've known."

"I know that." She bit her lower lip, unable to stop the soft, breathless confession. "I want you, Quinn. It feels like I've wanted you forever."

"I'm not looking to play nice right now," he growled, studying her through the thick weight of his lashes. "Not looking to offer comfort and take your mind off what you've been through. Whatever the hell you're up to, you're going to find yourself in way over your head."

She swallowed, nervous, knowing he was trying to warn her about something, but too desperate for him to care. "I'm not a child, Quinn. I know that you're dangerous for me. Not physically, but in other…ways. Ways I don't even understand. But I also know that I'm going to regret it for the rest of my life if I don't get close to you." She took a step toward him, hoping— praying—that he didn't move away from her. "I *need* to be close to you."

His eyes burned, dark and black and beautiful, glittering as if lit by an inner fire, his mouth parted the barest fraction for the harsh, rushing cadence of his breaths. He looked like a man caught between heaven and hell, torn between wanting to run and the need to take her…touch her, his brow drawn with tension…with pain.

And then he slowly drew in a deep, shuddering breath of air, and reached for her towel. A heartbeat later, he pulled it open and let it fall to the floor as she closed her eyes.

There was a heavy moment of silence, during which Saige knew he was looking at her body. The harsh, raging beat of her heart filled her head, her chest hurting from the force of her breaths, palms damp with nerves and excitement, and she waited…not knowing what to do, terrified she'd break the spell and lose him. She could feel the press of his dark, smoldering stare on her skin. Feel it lingering at her breasts…her nipples. On the curve of her hips, the indentation of her navel. On the soft curls between her legs. Then he made a low, animal-like sound in the back of his throat, and reached out, touching her, rubbing the backs of his fingers over the damp curls, petting them, and she melted with a fresh wave of heat, barely able to stand.

And inside her body, Saige could feel her Merrick rising, lifting its nose, sniffing delicately at the air, eager for his warm, intoxicating scent. It filled her head like some strangely forgotten memory of something comforting and warm like home—and yet, it was painfully exciting, impossibly seductive.

With her breath held tight in her chest, she opened her eyes and watched his face tighten with a savage, primal expression that made him look hard…dangerous…invincible, though she knew all too well that he could bleed. And then suddenly she was in his arms, against his body, which was exactly where she wanted to be. She didn't know why she needed him so badly—all she knew was that she did. That she *had* to have him. Had to soak him into her system, her senses, her soul, taking him as her own. Like something that belonged to her…*with her.*

If someone had told her two days ago that she could feel this way about a man, much less one she barely knew, she would never have believed them. But it was true.

And in some crazy, unexplainable way, she realized that she *did* know Quinn. Maybe not the details and facts that made up his life, his past, but she knew the man. His scent. His moods. His taste and his temper and the seductive, devastating heat of his mouth.

He claimed her with a deep, ravaging kiss that was like sex itself. With a sexy growl rumbling in his chest, he penetrated her mouth with the hot sweep of his tongue, touching her teeth, the smooth insides of her cheeks, the top of her palate. He drank from her, taking her breath…her panting moans, pulling pleasure up out of her as if he could feed on it. His rough, powerful hands grasped her face, holding her trapped for his ruthless possession, the touch of his callused palms only heightening the wild, primal sensations.

She'd no idea it could be like this. Quinn was a force of nature crashing over her, through her, overwhelming her senses, but she wasn't about to back down now. Greedy for everything that he had, that he was, she ran her hands over the broad, silken breadth of his shoulders, down his hard, bulging biceps, and he groaned deep in his throat.

Instantly, she stopped, lifting her hands away as she remembered the savage way the Casus had clawed at his beautiful body. "God, are you okay?" she gasped. "I didn't mean to hurt you."

QUINN STIFFENED at the concern he could hear in her voice. Like a deaf man suddenly bombarded with sound, he didn't know what to do with it…how to process it, the idea beyond his realm of experience.

He couldn't deny that Saige's concern touched him, and in a way that wasn't altogether comfortable, hinting at a deeper level of connection than he was prepared to deal with. Not that he was going to let it stop him from taking what he wanted…what he needed.

Pulling her against him in a desperate hold, he buried his face against her hair, wanting to breathe her into his system. He wanted to be in her mind, in her senses, in her soul. Christ, he wanted to stay connected to her forever, and it killed a part of him to know that it was never going to happen. No matter how tightly he held her tonight, he couldn't shake the wrenching knowledge that she was going to slip through his fingers….

He shuddered, unable to deal, feeling like a predator, the animal inside him rising up, determined to stake its claim. And suddenly the hunger he'd been struggling to control for the past twenty-four hours was unleashed in a vicious, violent explosion of need.

He made a sound—hard and thick—and burst into action.

With his hands on her waist, Quinn lifted her off the floor, crossed the room in long, rapid strides and quickly laid her down on the bed. Instead of covering her body with his, he knelt between her thighs and forced them apart, spreading her legs wide as he grasped her behind each knee, holding her open. The carnal, explicit position opened the drenched, delicate folds of her sex, and he stared, hard, his mouth watering for the thick juices spilling sweetly from her body. She smelled unlike anything he'd ever known— perfect and warm and...*unique*—and though he'd barely touched her, she was already soaked, the shy, tender folds swollen and slick.

He made a primitive sound deep in his throat, and moved his right hand between her legs, stroking the exquisitely soft pink folds with his fingertips while she shifted restlessly on the bed, her lean muscles quivering with need, hands clutching desperately at his shoulders. She was warm and wet to the touch, and he moved over her, bracing his weight on his left arm, then lifted his glistening fingers to her breast, needing her taste before he went out of his mind. A raw, guttural growl tore from his chest as he used his wet fingers to paint her right nipple with her cream, then leaned over and took the glistening bud into his mouth, sucking on her as hard as he dared. Her back arched, a sharp, keening cry of pleasure breaking out of her though she tried to choke it back. Quinn worked the deliciously thick nipple against the roof of his mouth, and her warm, honeyed taste exploded through his senses. Unable to wait, he pushed his hand back between her legs. She was delicate and small, and he wasn't. He shuddered with the need to rip open his jeans and bury himself inside her, but knew it'd be easier on her if he could make her come first. Panting against her breast, he stroked his fingers across her soft, slippery flesh, then rubbed his damp fingertips against the hard, pulsing knot of her clit. He sucked her nipple in deep, rhythmic pulls that matched the stroking of his fingers, and could feel it building in her, her body writhing as she fought against it.

"Do it, Saige. Come for me," he growled, keeping his thumb against her clit as he slipped two fingers just inside the swollen, delicate mouth of her sex, and the orgasm slammed through her like a stunning jolt of electricity, shocking and sharp. She stiffened beneath him, a harsh, throaty cry spilling from her lips, while the violent, thrashing wave of pleasure swept through her, annihilating his control.

WITH HER BODY STILL pulsing from the deep, rhythmic pulls of a devastating ecstasy, Saige watched through heavy-lidded eyes as Quinn reached for his zipper. Her breath panted in a rapid, excited rhythm, and she lifted her gaze, staring at the dark, rugged beauty of his face. He looked like something primal and wild, his eyes crinkled sexily at the corners, mouth parted for his own soughing breaths, and then she felt the hard, thick weight of his cock burning against the inside of her thigh. Looking down, she licked her bottom lip, and breathed out a shaky, *Mother of God."*

His husky, embarrassed rumble of laughter warmed her insides—but she was still too cold without him, too empty. "I need you inside me, Quinn. I need…I need you to make me hot inside."

He groaned, shuddering, his muscles shaking with a hard, vicious tremor. She wanted to reach down and curl her fingers around the long, broad shaft—to feel its heat and the violent rhythm of his pulse in those thick, distended veins, but he grabbed her wrists, pulling them above her head.

Lifting her gaze, she was ready to beg…to plead, when the heat in her gums turned to a molten flame, and with her next breath, the Merrick's fangs suddenly burst into her mouth, heavy and sharp. Driven by a feral, instinctual need to taste him, she lifted her head and scraped their pointed tips over the strong column of his throat, breaking the skin. The hot, intoxicating taste of his blood slid over her tongue, smooth and delicious, and with her lips against his warm skin, she whispered, "Quinn?"

"Your Merrick," he gasped, his voice nothing more than a hoarse, ragged sound as he shuddered above her. "It needs to feed."

She whimpered, hungry and frightened all at once. Despite everything she knew about the Merrick, it was still a shock to feel her body changing, the powerful, visceral force of the creature's cravings taking her over, too strong to resist.

"It's okay," he assured her with breathless words, bracing himself on his elbows so that he could hold her face in his warm, work-roughened palms. "It's okay, Saige. Don't fight it."

Her mouth trembled, giving Quinn a sensual glimpse of small, white fangs, and the throbbing, urgent ache in his cock doubled, the rigid shaft so hard it was almost more pain than pleasure. He'd never seen anything so primal…nor so beautiful as Saige lying beneath him, her mouth swollen from his kisses, her storm-dark eyes wide with hunger, glowing an unearthly blue, while her Merrick rose up within her, struggling to break free. Smoothing his right hand down her side, he touched that most precious, delicate part of her again, stroking the tender silk of her sex, and thrust two thick fingers inside her, pressing deep. Her body, warm and slick and impossibly small, clutched at him, holding him, the feeling so good he nearly lost it then and there. Needing to stretch her, he pressed deeper…then deeper still.

And nearly died when he suddenly realized why she was so tight.

"No," he choked out in a raw, graveled voice. "That can't be possible."

Staring up into his wide, horrified eyes, Saige felt her body go cold, the Merrick's fangs instantly receding. "What's wrong?"

"You're a virgin," he croaked, moving off the bed so quickly, you'd have thought she was on fire.

Struggling to make her pleasure-wrecked muscles move, she managed to lift up onto one elbow and push her hair out of her face. Quietly, she said, "I didn't…I didn't think you would mind."

He paced back and forth at the foot of the bed, both hands shoved into his hair so hard it looked painful. "Christ, this can't be happening." He slanted her a dark, accusatory look, sounding as if it were some kind of crime. "How the hell can you still be a virgin?"

Moving to her knees in the middle of the mattress, Saige pulled the comforter in front of her naked body and cocked one eyebrow. "Well," she said dryly, "it's pretty simple to explain really. You see, if a woman's never—"

"Damn it," he snarled, cutting her off. "This isn't a joke, Saige."

"Yeah?" she shot back, her own anger beginning to rise as her shock faded. "Well, take a good look at me, Quinn. Do I look like I think this is funny? Confusing, yes. But I'm not laughing!"

"I don't get it," he rasped, raking his gaze over her face, her bare shoulders, before grunting, "How is this even possible?"

"It's not like I planned to hold on to my virginity," she snapped, then forced herself to take a deep breath, struggling to get control of her emotions. "I...I guess I've always had trust issues when it comes to men, and the next thing you know, here I am, a virgin at twenty-six. I should have known better, but for some reason, I obviously thought you were different," she added with a roll of her shoulder, and he growled low in his throat.

"Don't throw this back in my face," he muttered, suddenly reaching down and zipping his jeans.

"Why not? You're the one turning me down. Not the other way around. And that *is* what's happening here, right?"

Bracing his hands on his hips, he continued to pace, snarling, "It was dangerous enough when I thought you were experienced. But this is—"

"Dangerous?" she repeated, cutting him off. "What the hell is so *dangerous* about us having sex? I don't have any diseases. And I went on the pill when I was twenty-two, in case I found a man I wanted to get involved with. So you can't get me pregnant."

He narrowed his eyes, and she shivered, wondering what in God's name was going through his mind. "I'm more *demanding* than most men, Saige."

"Yeah?" She lifted her chin. "Well, maybe I'm more demanding than most women."

A bitter laugh jerked from his throat, and he scrubbed his hands down his face. "God, you have no idea. Having that kind of connection with you—knowing that I'm the only one who's ever... Christ, if I lost you, it would destroy me."

"Lost me?" she murmured. "I thought the plan was to keep me alive, Quinn."

He didn't explain his meaning. Instead, he just ground his jaw and tore his gaze away, muttering, "I don't do virgins. Ever."

Well, here it is. The moment you'd feared was going to happen.

Saige had known she couldn't keep him, but she hadn't realized it was going to hurt so badly. She'd understood that men like Michael Quinn weren't meant to be held forever. Not by women like her. But as long as she could steal a few days with him, she'd been prepared to handle whatever came in the end.

Broken hearts didn't kill you. If they did, she'd have died long ago, when every man she'd ever loved had slipped away from her. Her father. Ian. Then Riley. She'd learned early on that men couldn't be counted on to stay. The lessons of her childhood had carried over into the woman's life, but she wasn't going to explain them to Quinn. She had no desire to spill her veins for him, confessing her secret fears. That she was unlovable. That sooner or later, no matter whom she cared about, she would lose them.

Poor, scared little Saige. Too afraid to ever let a man get close to her heart.

But she wasn't talking about love here, anyway. She was talking about connection and need. Lust and hunger. About giving in to the breathtaking sensations she felt whenever she was near Quinn, and for once in her life, doing something for no other reason than that she wanted it. She'd spent years giving her life to the search for answers about the Merrick, living on her own, relying on no one but herself. And then he'd walked into her life, making her want things she'd never expected…never prepared for, only to turn away from her before she even got a taste of them. It made her so angry she wanted to scream. And it hurt so bad, she wanted to curl up in a ball and cry.

Had she really thought she could handle a broken heart if she fell for him? God, she couldn't even handle a bruised ego.

"So you were okay with another meaningless sexual encounter, but God forbid there be something…what?" she asked. "Meaningful about it? Memorable? You worried about me glomming on to you?"

"You don't know what the hell you're talking about," he said under his breath.

"You're right, I don't. No one knows what deep, dark secrets lurk within Michael Quinn's heart and head. It's one of the unknown mysteries of the universe. Tell me the truth, Quinn. Was all this just a way for you to punish me? Use me? Set me up and then walk away?"

"You don't really believe that," he growled, slanting her a dark look from the corner of his eye.

"I don't know what to believe. So explain it to me."

It sounded as if the words were being torn out of him as he shoved his hands deep in his pockets and said, "When emotions are involved, sex can be…*complicated* for my kind."

"Considering how intimate it is," she said, "I would think sex is always complicated."

His eyes shifted away, his gaze sliding toward the floor, while the tops of his sharp cheekbones seemed to burn with color. "Not always."

Jealousy slid through her insides, painful and raw. "Meaning you only sleep with women you don't care about? And then everything's fine?"

"That's exactly what it means." He held his jaw so hard it looked painful, the strain around his eyes making him look haggard and tired. "I crave…*things*."

"Things you don't want with me?" she whispered, blinking against the rise of emotion in her eyes, burning at the back of her throat.

He made a rude sound and shook his head. "Sleeping with me would get you way more than you bargained for. You have no idea how…*possessive* I can be. I'd demand a hell of a lot more from you than you'd be willing to give, Saige."

"I don't think that's it," she murmured, her tone doubtful. "I think you're afraid. Afraid that if you take my virginity, those possessive instincts are going to kick into high gear, and despite the fact that you want to go to bed with me, you don't want to be stuck with me, do you, Quinn?"

"I don't want to be stuck with any woman, Saige. It has nothing to do with you."

She tried not to flinch, but failed. He'd found the perfect weapon to use against her. Rejection. Painful and stark. "If this is because I ran, I've already told you that I'm sorry."

"There are things you don't understand. Let's just leave it at that." He slanted her a blistering look from the corner of his eye, looking as if he wanted to eat her alive. "You should get dressed," he said, his voice thick.

"I can't believe I actually thought you wanted me," she muttered under her breath, climbing off the bed with the comforter held tight against her naked body. She'd made it two steps before he came up behind her, pressing her against the nearby wall. Saige gasped as the heat and hardness of his body covered her bare back, his breath hot against her ear, ragged and dark and deep.

"This has nothing to do with wanting," he growled, his big hands fisted against the wall either side of her head. "My appetites...they aren't *normal*. Being the man who takes your virginity would only make it worse. For me and you."

She swallowed, sweating, the need for him spreading all the way down to her bones, stripping her raw. "I'm a big girl, Quinn. I may be a virgin, but I'm not a child. Whatever it is you're so afraid of, I'm not going to run and cower."

He trembled, resting his brow against the top of her head, the veins on the backs of his hands thickening as he tightened his fists. "You make it bloody difficult to do the right thing," he rasped, and then he stepped back, away from her body.

Saige turned, immediately dropping her gaze to the thick ridge bulging against his fly, wanting to see the proof that he still wanted her. She wet her lips, and he made a sound, like he was in pain, taking another step back. "If you knew anything about me," he growled, "you'd thank me for this."

She couldn't help but wonder what the hell he was talking about. As far as she knew, Raptors were renowned for being lethal fighters, savagely fierce on the battlefield, but she'd never heard of anything unusual about their sexuality. Like all of the shifters who comprised the Watchmen, they were meant to be some of the most alpha men around, with powerful, primal sex drives reputed to make them unbelievable lovers.

Just the thought made her hot under the skin. Or maybe that was simply Quinn. God only knew she felt like she was burning with fever every time she got near him. She started to take a step forward, but fell back against the wall, her head spinning with a sudden wave of dizziness. Lifting her hand, she pressed her palm against her forehead as she closed her eyes, acutely aware of the Merrick seething beneath her skin, furious at being denied what it needed.

"You feel weak, don't you?" he asked, his voice gritty and low.

"I'm just tired," she whispered, aware of him moving closer.

He blew out a rough breath, then quietly said, "I know now is hardly the time, but your Merrick is ready, Saige. If you don't give it what it needs, it's going to drain you. You need to go ahead and feed."

Opening her eyes, she stared at him with blank astonishment as he went on to say, "Those bastards are going to be coming after you. Not only because of your awakening, but because they'll need you to read those maps. You need to be at full strength."

She shook her head, a brittle burst of laughter ripping from her throat. "And what exactly do you expect me to do, Quinn? I know about Merrick feedings. I don't just need your blood—I need to experience pleasure at the same time. I need blood *and* sex, and you've made your feelings on the subject of sex more than clear tonight."

"Male Merrick need blood and sex," he responded, his expression grim as he shoved his hands into his pockets. "But it's different for a female."

Saige narrowed her eyes. "Different how?"

"So long as I make you come while you're taking my blood, you'll get the full charge that you need."

"Oh God, that's priceless." She stared, hard, unable to tell if she was going to laugh or cry. "Tell me you're not actually serious."

"I can give you my blood," he said in an emotionless voice, "and make you come without taking your virginity."

Another brittle laugh jerked from her throat, and she clutched the comforter tighter against her body. "Ooh, Quinn, be still my heart. You're really the romancer, aren't you?"

"You don't have the luxury of waiting, Saige. You need to feed *now.*"

"Yeah, well, thanks for the swell offer," she drawled, "but I'll pass."

She'd just turned to head toward the bathroom when he said, "Despite what happens between us, we still have to deal with the situation. And we have a hell of a lot of ground to cover before we make it to Colorado."

"I'll deal," she muttered, refusing to look at him as she carefully made her way to the bathroom, using the wall for support. Just before she shut the door, she looked back, holding Quinn's dark gaze as she said, "But I'll do it without you."

CHAPTER THIRTEEN

Monday morning
New Mexico

SEATED AT A SMALL round table in the corner of the trendy coffeehouse, Jamison Haley took a sip of his double cappuccino and did his best to project an image of relaxed confidence, while inside his heart hammered a nervous, frenzied beat. He'd been on his own for five days now, and had finally checked into a local hotel the night before, where he'd slept for a solid eight hours. He needed to be back on the road if he was going to make it to Denver in time to meet Saige tomorrow afternoon, but after the hours he'd spent confined on trains and buses and in small commuter planes, he'd wanted to grab a quick breakfast somewhere that didn't smell of sweat and traveling passengers.

In the front pocket of his chinos, Saige's mysterious cross burned like a phantom heat, a constant reminder of his friend and the danger she'd believed would follow them. He wanted to call and make sure that she was okay, but had promised not to contact her unless it was an emergency. And so far, his trip had been rather uneventful. He'd half expected to find himself dodging monsters, like something out of a horror movie, but the worst he'd had to deal with was a belligerent drunk who'd mistakenly taken his seat on a train in Mexico. He only hoped Saige could say the same. Jamison hadn't liked separating from her, but she'd promised to be careful, begging him to do her this one favor. And while Jamison was generally too self-indulgent to ever risk his life for anyone, she was different.

For Saige, he'd have traveled to the ends of the earth.

Leaning back in his seat, he glanced around the crowded coffeehouse, marveling at the varied clientele, from sleepy-eyed teenagers to frenzied young professionals whose cell phones seemed glued to their ears. But it was the redhead in the black leather miniskirt and boots who caught his attention. Maybe it was because she reminded him of Saige—and he'd always had a secret crush on his colleague—or maybe it was the way that she looked at him, like she wanted to eat him alive. Whatever it was, Jamison couldn't take his eyes off her as she targeted him with a warm, inviting gaze. She was so gorgeous, he felt flushed, the rise of color in his face no doubt embarrassingly obvious.

When her coffee was ready, she sent him another slow smile, then walked out of the shop, onto the sidewalk, and disappeared into the morning crowd. Shaking his head, Jamison blew out an unsteady breath and waited for his body to calm down before he grabbed his own coffee and headed back to the hotel. He needed to pick up his luggage and check out before settling into his rental car for the long drive up to Denver. Once there, he'd find a nice place to lie low, until it was time to meet Saige and hand over the cross. Then he'd fly home to England, and take a much-needed vacation, before heading off to his next destination.

Smiling at the front-desk clerk at the hotel, Jamison made his way into the elevator, rode up to the fifth floor, then used his plastic card key to enter his room. He'd just locked the door behind him and slipped the key into his pocket, beside Saige's cross, when he caught a flash of red at the corner of his eye. Spinning around, he choked back a sharp grunt of surprise at the sight of the gorgeous redhead from the coffee shop sitting on the foot of his bed. Her long, beautiful legs were crossed at the thigh, her slender, feminine hands braced behind her on the mattress, the provocative pose accentuating the shape of her breasts beneath a tight, black cotton T-shirt.

The position was blatantly seductive, as if she'd snuck into his room for nothing more sinister than some sweaty time between the sheets with a stranger. But it was the cold, calculating look in her big green eyes that gave her away.

Well, that and the ominous-looking 9mm lying on the bed beside her.

"How did you find me?" he asked, his voice thick as he sank into the room's lone chair, his legs not quite steady enough to hold him.

"Oh, sweetheart, it was easy," she drawled, silver rings glittering on her fingers as she pushed several gleaming strands of hair back from her heart-shaped face, the sunlight filtering in through the slanted blinds making the auburn strands shimmer like flames, as if they'd be hot to the touch. "You really shouldn't have checked into the hotel under your real name. Even the Watchmen know better than that."

"You c-can't hurt me," he stammered, thinking of the cross that burned in his pocket. "Saige said I would be protected."

"Well, that'd be true," she purred, taking hold of the gun as she shifted to her feet in a slow, sinuous movement. She moved across the short space between them, and Jamison watched with wide eyes as she hiked her miniskirt higher, revealing the mouthwatering patch of black satin between her legs, before straddling his lap. She placed her hands on his shoulders, the heavy weight of the gun nearly making his heart stop as she said, "But there's just one tiny problem."

"What's that?" he rasped, his brow breaking out in a cold, clammy sweat.

She gave a deep, throaty rumble of laughter and trailed her free hand over his chest, pressing her open palm against the hammering, terrified beat of his heart. "Your little talisman isn't going to save you from me, Haley. Because I'm not a Casus."

His brows drew together as he stared into her bright, bottle-green eyes. "If not a Casus, then what are you?"

"Doesn't matter," she crooned, leaning forward and placing a slow, evocative kiss against his lips. Despite his fear, his body thickened…hardening inside his pants, and she ground herself against him, practically purring as she said, "All that matters is what you can do for me and the people I work for."

"You want the cross," he said dully, failure sitting like a dead weight in his gut, keeping company with the terror.

"Oh, we want more than that," she whispered against his mouth, and he could feel the cold metal of her silver rings as she cupped the side of his face with her hand. Shifting back, she stared into his eyes as she added, "And you're going to help us get it."

Swallowing against the thickness in his throat, Jamison struggled for his voice. "Whatever it is you want me to do, you might as well forget it. I won't help you."

She shook her head, the lush curve of her lips reminding him of a poisonous viper, as beautiful as it was deadly. "Don't worry, Haley. You don't have to do a thing."

"Then what do you want from me?" he asked, wondering what kind of sick game she was playing with him. Was she going to put the gun to his temple and blow his brains out? Or keep giving him a lap dance while scaring the hell out of him?

His questions were answered in the next moment when she pressed her hand against the right side of his throat, and he suddenly felt a sharp sting, as if one of her rings had somehow pierced his skin. His mind was already going blurry as he realized she'd injected him with some kind of drug.

"Don't fight it," she murmured, pushing the damp strands of his hair back from his face. "For now, all you need to do is sleep. Then, when the time comes, you'll understand why we need you."

"Whoareyou?" he slurred, his head lolling back against the chair, the muscles in his neck no longer able to support its weight.

"My name's Elizabeth," she told him, climbing off his lap. He struggled to keep his eyes open as she stood there waiting for the drug to take its full effect, her red hair streaming over her shoulders like a thick, luminous wave of silk. "But my friends call me Spark."

Spark, he thought, wondering who she was. He wanted to demand more information—some kind of explanation—but he was already going under, the edges of his vision turning hazy and gray.

Jamison's last thought as he drifted into unconsciousness was for Saige, and what would happen to her now that he'd failed.

CHAPTER FOURTEEN

Tuesday, 5:00 a.m.
New Mexico

As HE'D DONE FOR the past five years of his life, Quinn dreamed. Buried beneath the deep, suffocating layers of an exhausted sleep, visions from the past assaulted his senses, the pain so vivid, so real, it was all he could do not to scream from the agony.

He could feel the jerk and tug as knives sawed through his left wing—feel the hot wash of his blood as it poured from his flesh. After dipping their blades into a specially modified compound that made it nearly impossible for him to heal, the Collective soldiers had carved open his skin and pulled his left wing from his back. But their blades had been unable to slice through the wing itself, and so they'd sawed at the bone with their knives, ripping into thick muscle and tendon, the pain so excruciating, he would black out, only to have icy water thrown in his face before they started in on him all over again. To this day, Quinn still had no idea how long he'd endured their sadistic machinations. Hours? Days? Weeks? He'd been missing for almost an entire month by the time Kierland and the others had found where he was being kept and rescued him, but he couldn't make order out of the chaos that lingered in his mind.

His wings had eventually grown back after several long, pain-filled months, but he still bore the signs of their torture—and yet, the physical scars on his back that Saige had commented on were nothing compared to the wounds he carried inside.

And after all this time, the dreams refused to leave him in peace.

Tossing on the cold, sweat-damp sheets of another hard hotel bed, he struggled to break free of the nightmare, but it was impossible. He gnashed his teeth, unwilling to give the fanatical soldiers the joy of his hoarse, gut-wrenching cries as they hacked through his wing. He'd wanted to claw at their faces, raking away their gloating expressions, but they'd ripped out his talons, one by one, leaving his hands swollen and numb.

When they were finally able to sever his left wing, Quinn threw back his head, the sound tearing out of him the most inhuman thing he'd ever heard, guttural and stark. Agony rolled over him in thick, battering waves, the pain growing, mounting, as if hot coals had been poured into the wound. He'd heaved, but there'd been nothing to expel from his stomach but a vile concoction of blood and bile. One of the soldiers had grasped the back of his head and shoved his face in the rancid fluid, bashing his skull against the cold, concrete floor. Darkness clouded in on the edges of his vision, his body racked with spasms as one of them sliced into the right side of his back, the excruciating torment so intense, he'd just wanted to die as they'd gone on to sever his right wing from his body, as well.

He'd prayed they'd go ahead and kill him then, but there'd been more to come.

As he'd lain there, broken and bleeding, one of the soldiers had dragged Janelle in by her hair. It was clear she'd been raped already, her naked body battered and bruised, her eyes glazed, as if her spirit had already died. Quinn had roared for McConnell, the Collective lieutenant he knew had orchestrated his capture, but McConnell had never come.

Instead, he'd been forced to lie there and watch them kill her—slowly, painfully—while they'd asked again and again if he was ready to tell them where they could find more of his kind. Quinn liked to think that they couldn't have broken him, but the irony was that he didn't even know any other Raptors. His father had been the last of his line, his mother human, and his parents had been killed by Collective soldiers when he was only ten.

Janelle's screams had echoed off the stone walls of the chamber as they'd started in on her, terrified and hoarse, and he'd struggled against the chains that held him braced over the low, narrow wooden bench, unable to break free to help her. Though she'd had nothing more than a trace of panther blood in her, it was enough for the Collective to consider her an animal. As he did each time he relived those horrific moments, Quinn watched as they slowly took her life, wishing he could wake up and find some way to stop the wrenching scene from playing through the damaged landscape of his mind, over and over again. Gritting his teeth, he commanded his body to rip itself from the destructive depths of the dream—only to have it change on him, taking a new twist, one that he'd first experienced on Friday night, after his argument with Saige. He roared, fighting his bonds so violently that the metal cuffs tore at his ankles and wrists, terrified as Janelle's long black hair shifted to a warm, reddish brown. And suddenly, instead of his traitorous fiancée, it was Saige who lay there screaming beneath one of the bastards, the laughing soldier holding a knife to her throat, slowly cutting into her flesh while he violated her body, his friends holding her arms and legs. Quinn could see the fury of her Merrick glowing in her eyes, but she was too weak for it to break free, her body drained by the hunger that she'd refused to feed. Vicious, devastated sounds of rage tore from his throat, until the moment when the soldier finally sliced through her jugular, the crimson wash of her blood staining Quinn's mind with the most gut-wrenching pain he'd ever known. He opened his mouth to a guttural cry of primitive, predatory fury....

And then, from one gasping breath to the next, he was awake.

With his chest heaving, his body sweat-slick and sore from the tension that'd gripped him, Quinn squinted at the rain-dappled shadows painting the ceiling of another cheap hotel room. God only knew he should have been too exhausted to dream after the marathon trek they'd made through Central America and Mexico, only stopping to sleep for a handful of hours at a time, but he hadn't been so lucky. Instead, the nightmares had slipped through his exhaustion and struck with the devastating force of a hammer, the new twist with Saige at the end making him wonder if he were slowly losing his mind.

Thrusting his hands back into his hair, he closed his eyes and silently repeated the lecture that had been playing through his head for the past five years.

They aren't real, you pathetic asshole. Not. Real.

But despite the softly hissed words, the memory of the dream still burned in his mind, painful and cruel. For a long time, he'd thought that if he could just close himself down enough, then he'd be able to block out the nightmares—the horrific visions of blood and pain and betrayal that unfolded across his mind in the darkest hours of the night. But no matter how far he withdrew, he couldn't shake them, reliving the nightmare of his torture at the hands of the Collective more times than he could count.

Scrubbing his hands down his face, he wished he could wipe away the bitter taste of betrayal that flavored his mouth, but it was too ingrained in his senses. He should have taken matters into his own hands and dealt with Seth McConnell a long time ago. Maybe then he wouldn't keep living the most horrific hours of his life over and over, slowly driving himself insane, unable to move on.

And you know just where you'd like to move, don't you?

Shaking his head at his own stupidity, knowing he didn't have a chance in hell of a future with Saige, he forced his mind onto their journey. He didn't know how they'd made it this far without any problems from the Casus. Didn't know if it was just that they'd done a good job of evading them…or if the bastards had reasoned out where they were going and had simply decided to head to Denver, waiting for them to lead the way to Jamison Haley and the Marker.

Whatever the reason, Quinn knew their luck wouldn't last, and those final moments of the dream shuddered through him again, making him curse something ugly and raw under his breath.

"Another bad dream?"

Saige's voice came from the shadowed darkness, and as he lifted his head, he found her cuddled beneath a blanket in one of the chairs by the room's third-story window, the flickering glow of a neon sign painting her face in iridescent slashes of color. Rain pounded in a steady rhythm against the bleary glass, accounting for the cloud-darkened dawn, the distant rumble of thunder echoing the pounding in his head. The irritable grumbling of the storm seemed the perfect complement to his mood, the electricity sizzling on the air like the physical hunger suddenly creeping through his veins, setting him on edge. It was as if all the agonizing emotion of his nightmare had channeled itself into a scalding, powerful lust, and Quinn shuddered from the effort of holding himself back.

"You could say that," he muttered in answer to her question about his dream, wondering if he'd been shouting in his sleep. Pushing himself up, he propped his shoulders against the cool grain of the headboard, unable to take his eyes off her. Despite the lingering effects of the horrific nightmare, there was no doubt that he wanted her. Badly. "You still pissed at me?" he rasped. They'd been at each other's throats since the blowup on Friday night, barely talking as they'd traveled from one town to the next. And while he had no intention of discussing his tormenting dreams with her, he was pathetically grateful to have her talking to him, instead of the chilly silence that had crackled between them.

A soft, almost silent burst of laughter slipped from her lips. "For leaving me hanging on Friday? Why would I be pissed? You've probably done me a favor, Quinn. If you'd taken my virginity, I'd be forced to live with the memory for the rest of my life."

He ground his jaw, struggling to keep a hold on his temper. It was amazing how easily she could rile him, but then, she could also make him smile…make him laugh, easier than anyone he'd ever known, as if his emotions were hers to manipulate at will, like a sculptor molding clay. "I told you my reasons, Saige. My intent was never to hurt you."

Just to protect my heart…my sanity.

She turned to stare back out the window, and lifted the blanket beneath her chin. Though he'd shaved his beard on Saturday, two days' worth of bristle covered the lower half of his face, and he rubbed at his jaw, fighting the urge to slip from the bed and stalk toward her, ripping that blanket from her grip, intensely aware that she wore nothing more than a white cotton tank top and panties. "I'm just trying to save us from getting into something that's going to end badly."

Her voice came as little more than a whisper as she said, "And how do you know how it's going to end without even giving it a chance? Life's about taking risks, Quinn. I don't want to spend however much time I have left wrapped up in a bubble, always running, never letting anything or anyone get close to me. I've done that for long enough, and I'm tired of it."

He grunted in response, unable to come up with anything clever when his brain was fogged by the thick burn of desire. It had to be the hardest thing he'd ever done, staying beneath that sheet, his cock so hard he could have hammered through a wall, when every cell of his body wanted to go to her.

No, the hardest thing you've ever done was pushing her away Friday night, instead of laying claim to everything that you wanted.

"If I take what you're offering," he growled, "I'm going to want to keep it."

She turned her head, holding his gaze across the shadowed room. "And who told you that you can't? Maybe I feel the same way."

He didn't believe her—but he wanted to. God, he wanted to. He could see the dark burn of hunger in her, and he wanted to be the one who fed it—who satisfied it. Wanted to sink his cock into her while she sank those pretty little fangs into his throat—wanted to take from her as she took from him in a primal, carnal exchange of pleasure. The craving was so powerful he felt drugged by it, completely captivated by the way she burned with heat, those storm-dark eyes glowing in the quiet darkness as if backlit by the searing heat of the sun.

"For what it's worth," he rasped, "I wish things could be different. You have no idea what I'd give to be able to change how I am."

SAIGE STARED THROUGH the darkness, marveling at how one man could be such a contradiction, so caring, and yet, so distant. So brave and at the same time, completely controlled by his fears. Her anger and hurt over his rejection still simmered beneath her skin, but she couldn't fault the care he'd taken to protect her. After so many years of looking after herself, it was oddly comforting to know that there was someone who worried about her. And yet, she knew she should be smart and protect her heart.

The Casus had the ability to hurt her body. But Quinn... It was becoming increasingly clear that he held the power to hurt her in ways that were so much deeper. So much more painful.

"You know, for a man with wings, you're awfully bound in place," she murmured, thinking of the nightmares he suffered from each night. Nightmares she believed were a part of why he was so afraid of letting himself get close to her.

His voice came through the watery shadows as a raspy, impossibly sexy slash of sound. "What does that mean?"

"You have more freedom than anyone I've ever

known, and yet, you can't move beyond the past. It's just ironic, when you look at it that way."

His tone was pure, guttural frustration as he blurted, "And what do you know about my past?"

"I know it's like a chain around your neck," she told him, the bitterness of his emotions lashing against her despite the distance that separated them. "One that's pulling tighter each day."

He didn't respond at first. Instead, she watched through the first hazy, shimmering rays of dawn as he threw his legs over the side of the bed, his muscles bunching across his mouthwatering abdomen as he moved to his feet. Wearing nothing but a low-slung pair of black sweatpants, he stalked to the window, bracing one arm up high against the rain-splashed window, the breaking dawn giving him an otherworldly glow. There was so much power in him, so much predatory strength and hunger and passion, you could almost see it pulsing from him in slow, provocative waves, like a heartbeat.

Saige shivered at the erotic cadence of the imagined sound, wondering if she'd always be this affected by him, and somehow knowing that she would.

When he finally spoke, he kept his gaze focused on the rosy burn of the horizon. "And what about you?"

She shifted uncomfortably in the chair. "What about me?"

He made a rude, utterly male sound under his breath, then angled his head to the side as he slanted her a wry look. "You don't think your lifestyle says something about you?"

"What do you think it says, Quinn?"

"That you're running," he muttered, looking back out the window.

"From what?" she asked, feeling as if he could see right into her, reading her like an open book.

"From...everything," he replied in a low, husky rumble of words.

"You know," she said, unable to take her gaze from the hard, sculpted perfection of his profile, "it doesn't seem fair that you know all my secrets, but don't trust me enough to tell me the truth about what happened to you."

His jaw locked, the muscles in his arms and torso bulging with some unnamed emotion. "Nothing happened to me," he insisted.

"Your dreams are very real to you," she argued in a soft voice. "Only powerful memories can have that kind of control over us."

QUINN WANTED TO SAY something snide...something cutting that would make her drop the subject, but all that came out was a hard, gritty laugh that echoed his fears...his pain. He didn't want to face the demons in his head. And he sure as hell didn't want Saige around when he did.

All he wanted was to deliver her to Ravenswing in one piece, and hope like hell that he could keep his hands off her until they got there.

Keep fighting it, jackass, but you know what you have to do.

He stiffened at the thought, wondering where it had come from.

You can give her what she needs.

Suddenly, the last horrifying moments of the dream twisted through his mind again, and he shuddered, remembering how her Merrick had struggled to break out of her while the soldier had effortlessly taken her life. Christ, could he somehow be seeing some kind of version of the future? After the strange things that had happened during her brother's awakening, Quinn was afraid to shrug his dreams off as nothing more than a screwed-up extension of his obsessive fears.

Which meant that one way or another, he had to make sure that she fed, before the Merrick's hunger drained her completely. But…she'd already made it clear what she thought of his offer, the bitter scene on Friday night too fresh in his memory. He knew damn well that she wouldn't let him touch her unless she thought he meant to make love to her.

So make her think you've changed your mind.

He pulled his hand down his face, his stomach churning at the thought, knowing it would make him the biggest asshole around.

True, but you don't have a choice. So stop being so goddamn pathetic and get it done.

She was probably going to hate him for it later, but Quinn knew that voice was right. He couldn't take her into Denver without giving her every possible advantage if things headed south when they met up with Jamison. And considering how his luck had been going lately *that* seemed pretty damned likely.

"What are you thinking about?" she murmured, her tone curious…cautious, and he knew she could see the hunger in his eyes as he turned toward her, shifting closer, until he loomed over her in the darkness.

"Quinn?"

"Please, don't say anything, Saige." Reaching down, he cupped her jaw, rubbing his thumb against the corner of her mouth, imagining her soft pink lips spread around his cock. Imagining the ecstasy of spilling down her throat. He didn't know why he tortured himself with the heart-pounding erotic fantasies, knowing they were things he was never going to have, but he couldn't stop.

"What are you doing?" she whispered, her voice trembling, though there was no fear in her heavy-lidded, storm-dark eyes.

It was easy to give her the words, considering they were true. "I know the right thing is to stay away from you, but I can't keep fighting it."

For a moment he thought she would give him the silence he'd asked for, her breath quickening between her parted lips. But then she pulled her lower lip through her teeth, and suddenly said, "Neither can I. You're all I can think about, Quinn."

He groaned at her words, burying his hands in her hair as he pulled her up to his mouth, needing her taste right then, before he went out of his mind. Starving for her warm, honeyed flavor, he kissed his way into that sweet, warm well with an aggressive, primal intensity that made her cry out, her body arching against his, driving him wild.

Desperate to taste her deeper, he angled her head to the side. Her lips were soft…impossibly sweet, the panting gasps of breath that she stole each time he changed the angle pushing him further and further toward the crumbling edge of his control. His hands were everywhere. Touching. Stroking. Gripping on to her with a greedy, bruising hold that he worried would leave marks.

Tearing her mouth from his, she gasped, "Aren't you worried that your friends will get the wrong idea about us?"

"What do you mean?"

"I'll have your scent on me today," she explained, and the shyness he could hear in her soft words made something in his chest clench with emotion. "They're going to know."

"You let me worry about them," he told her, knowing it wasn't going to be an issue. No one would know, because he wasn't going to be the one who came, but he shoved that painful thought into the back of his mind, where it couldn't wreak so much damage. "I don't want you thinking about anyone but me."

"OKAY," SAIGE WHISPERED, her voice unsteady, her mind a chaotic jumble of fear and desire and exhilaration. Terrified that he was going to change his mind, she slipped her hand into the waistband of his sweatpants and curled her fingers around the hard, shocking power of his cock. "Quinn," she breathed out, measuring him with her grip, sliding her hand up and down the rigid thickness, squeezing the distended veins knotting its surface. He was hot to the touch, burning with heat...with hunger, and she'd never felt more feminine than she did in that moment, when she held the breathtaking proof of his desire for her in the palm of her hand.

"You can't read *that,* can you?" he growled, the husky words softened by a wry drawl of humor as he stared down into her eyes.

A slow smile curled her mouth, and she would have laughed if her chest wasn't clenched in a desperate knot of longing. God, she wanted so much from this man, everything that he had. That dark, compelling taste that made her crave the heat of his mouth…his blood. The rich, heady scent of his skin and the hard, powerful weight of his body.

She didn't know what had changed his mind, and in that moment, she simply didn't care. Even though she knew it was wrong, she couldn't stop it. Her heart was going to pay a hefty price, but if this was all she was going to get from him, then she was going to take it. Take it and wring from it every ounce of pleasure that she could, because she didn't have any other choice. It wasn't lust or hunger that drove her. Wasn't just that he was dark and beautiful and so impossibly sexy, it hurt just to look at him.

It was Quinn.

Something had happened to her, and she couldn't undo it. Couldn't make it go away and deny its existence. It was something that she couldn't fight—something that she didn't even want to.

He lifted her in his arms and laid his long body down on the bed, pulling her over him. She straddled his waist, rubbing against him, while his hands tangled in her hair, holding her still for the dark, devastating demand of his mouth. Pleasure built like a storm brewing on the horizon, the sensations pulling her deeper…and deeper. She felt hypersensitive, the heat of his skin searing against her, damp and hot and so different from hers. The delicious warmth of his mouth drugged her, while the scent of him, hot and wild, like a meal, filled her head. He smelled like something she needed to sink her teeth into. Something she needed to savor.

Breaking away from the kiss, Saige stared down into hungry, smoldering eyes that glowed with a preternatural fire, as if lit by an inner flame. "When you look at me like that," she whispered, "I feel like I've won the lottery."

His eyes darkened with emotion, a wry smile lifting the corner of his mouth. "As far as prizes go," he rasped, pushing her hair back from her face, running his fingertips over her cheek…her temple, "I'm not much to brag about."

"That's not true." She ran her hands over his muscled chest, loving how he felt, so firm and silky and hot, praying that he wasn't going to slip through her fingers again. "You're beautiful, Quinn."

REELING FROM HER WORDS, Quinn struggled to remember his agenda, but Christ, it wasn't easy. He had to tread carefully—get her to take what she needed, without triggering the fierce possessive streak of his animal nature any more than he already had.

Did his deception make him an ass?

Definitely.

But could he go through with this and not touch her…taste her?

Not a chance in hell.

Considering he was already damned, he figured he might as well give himself at least a fraction of paradise. And he'd make her feel good in exchange, while giving her the power that she needed.

Rolling her beneath him, Quinn covered her with his body, crushing her into the sleep-warmed bedding as he slid between her thighs. He put his mouth to the center of her chest, over the frenzied beating of her heart, and pulled in a deep, greedy breath. She was already slick between her legs, soaking his sweatpants, making him harder than he'd ever been before. He thrust against her, wanting to be buried deep inside her. Wanting to get deep enough in her that he could feel the pounding of her heart. The heat of her soul.

Pushing his hand into her cotton panties, he nearly died from the feel of her. Damp. Swollen. Burning with heat.

You could always just take her. Just take what you want.

With the dangerously tempting words whispering through his mind, Quinn ground his jaw, knowing damn well that he'd get up and run if he had half a brain.

Instead, he gave in to one of the primal, carnal hungers that'd been driving him mad since he'd first set eyes on her, and slid lower, shifting to the side of her body. Pushing up her tank top, he pressed a warm, intimate kiss against the smooth, quivering skin just beneath her navel, and ripped down her panties. The second they cleared her toes, he moved back between her thighs, forcing them to spread wide for the breadth of his shoulders.

"Not yet," she moaned, her voice smoky with lust as she tried to hold him back.

"Why not?" he demanded in a gritty rasp, tearing his avid gaze from the sweet, wrenching perfection of her sex as she lifted her head and stared down at him.

She licked her bottom lip, and he followed the sensual movement of her tongue like a predator eyeing its prey. "Because as much as I want your mouth on me," she said hoarsely, "I wanted to do it to you first."

A slow, pained smile curved his mouth, his cock damn near bursting at the thought of those tender, blushing lips wrapped around his shaft. "Later," he rasped, the sound like something soft being dragged across sandpaper. "You can do it to me later."

"Promise?" she whispered, sinking her small white teeth into the lush cushion of her lower lip while that unearthly glow burned behind her eyes, lighting them up like stained glass set against the sun.

"Yeah," he said thickly, "I promise, honey."

She gave him a small, eager smile, and stretched beneath him then, the movement inherently feline and graceful. Wanting her with a hunger that burned through his body like a physical necessity, as if he needed the taste of her pleasure like he needed water and air, Quinn lowered his head and licked her. A primal, guttural growl jerked from his chest, and he greedily opened his mouth over the drenched, damp silk of her folds, needing *more*…needing *all of her*. Her warm, pure scent tore another harsh sound from his throat, but that was nothing compared to what her taste did to him. Eating at her with a tender avidity that he couldn't control, his fingers bit into the pale flesh of her thighs as he held her open, thrusting his tongue into the sweet, delicate opening, wanting to penetrate every part of her. To get so deep into her, he could feel the rhythm of her pulse…see the thoughts in her head. She was growing closer, the pleasure mounting in her…building like heat in the bottom of a pan, and he pressed the flat of his tongue against her swollen clit, rubbing it…suckling…teasing it with his teeth. And she broke. One second she was writhing beneath him, and in the next, the pleasure crashed through her like a shocking, stunning force of nature, powerful and strong and wild, and Quinn kept his mouth against her, desperate for every moment of it.

When the powerful orgasm finally began to ease, he took a deep, ragged breath and slipped his thumb inside her tender, pulsing flesh, his gaze traveling hungrily over the pale, feminine line of her body. Her back was arched, her petal-soft mouth open as sharp, keening cries softened on her lips, and he could see the glistening white of her fangs as they slipped from her gums, signaling the rise of her Merrick.

As if she could feel the intensity of his stare, she lifted her head, sending him a shaky, breathtaking smile. "My turn," she said in a smoky tone that melted down his spine like a warm, thick drop of honey.

Those words, combined with that hungry, inherently innocent look in her eyes, ripped him over the edge, battering through his restraint, and he knew that his time had run out. If she didn't do it now, he was going to take this too far.

Surging up over her, Quinn turned his head to the side and fisted one hand in her hair, pushing her face toward his throat. "Now, Saige. Do it now."

"No," she said thickly, shaking her head.

"Yes," he growled, his body tremoring, shaking the bed as he struggled to hold himself back. "You need the blood, baby. I need you to do it, now, while your body's still warm from coming."

"I'm scared," she whispered, sounding as if she was admitting a sin, and his heart clenched with tenderness.

Looking down at her, he cradled her cheek in his palm, holding her with his stare. "It'll be okay."

"What if I hurt you?" she rasped, her fangs gleaming beneath the lush curve of her upper lip.

"You won't," he panted, his face tightening with pain as he clawed on to his own raging hungers. "You won't hurt me."

"I want you inside me first," she moaned, reaching down between them as she lifted her head, scraping her teeth along the column of his throat.

Quinn caught her wrist, wrenching it up to the pillow, and her eyes tightened with wary surprise as he snarled, "Take the blood *first*."

Something in his expression must have revealed more than he wanted, and her own eyes suddenly went wide with shock. *"Oh. My. God."*

"Saige!" he growled, but she was already scrambling away from him. Or at least trying to, unable to go far considering he still held her wrist.

"Not again!" she sobbed, pushing against his chest as they both moved to their knees, her glittering, glowing eyes wild with fury. "You wouldn't do that to me again! You couldn't!"

"I'm just trying to keep you alive," he grunted through his clenched teeth. "You need this, damn it!"

"AND YOU CALLED ME A LIAR!" Saige screeched, not caring if she woke up the entire hotel. "You bastard!"

"Damn it, you're going to hurt yourself," he grunted as she pounded her fist against him while wrenching at her captured wrist, trying to break free.

"Let go of me, Quinn." It was difficult to talk with her fangs still descended, the gnawing hunger of her Merrick slicing through her body like a knife, the pain so intense, she wanted to curl in on herself. But it was nothing compared to the damage Quinn had caused.

"I thought I knew you," she cried, her voice cracking with a harsh sob, which only made her angrier. "How could you do this?"

"I'm only trying to protect you," he rasped, and she could hear the sincerity in his words, cut by some deeper, harsher emotion.

"You want to protect me?" She blinked, struggling to understand him. "Why, when you don't even trust me?"

"This has nothing to do with trust," he argued, his mouth grim, framed by deep brackets as he finally released his hold on her.

"It has *everything* to do with trust." The words were soft, bitter, and she turned away from him, crawling off the bed and grabbing her new backpack from the top of the dresser.

"This isn't over," he growled, moving to his feet, his hard, powerful body vibrating with frustration.

"You're wrong," she whispered, her head spinning with a dizzying blend of confusion and hurt and anger as she stumbled into the bathroom. With one hand on the door, she looked back and held his dark, shadowed stare. "And once we're at Ravenswing, I want you to stay the hell away from me, Quinn."

"You're making a mistake," he argued, his feet braced wide, big hands fisted at his sides.

Saige swallowed a shivering knot of emotion and worked for her voice. "My only mistake was in trusting you," she finally rasped.

Then she quietly shut the door.

CHAPTER FIFTEEN

Tuesday afternoon
Colorado

THE TRIP BACK TO America had been the longest four
days of Saige's life. Not to mention the most frustrating. After all the time they'd spent together, all the
hours they'd been cramped together on buses and
trains and on small, chartered planes, she was still no
closer to understanding a damn thing about the enigmatic Michael Quinn than she had been the first night
they'd met. All she had to go on were the physical
details that he couldn't hide. His scent…his taste.
What it felt like when his body covered hers. The
husky, animal-like sounds he made when he was
turned on. In a darkened room, she could have picked
him out from hundreds of men, he was that imprinted
on her system. But she knew nothing of his heart, or
his past. He remained a mystery, a puzzle—one she
couldn't leave alone, no matter how badly she wanted
to. Despite her bitterness, she was captivated by his expressions, his body language, the pattern of his breathing. Even the placement of his strong, sun-darkened

hands on the steering wheel held an undeniable fascination.

She thought she'd known what lust was, but nothing she'd ever experienced had prepared her for this. For Quinn. Every time he touched her, it was like sinking into bliss, drowning in it, as if pleasure was a clear, cerulean pool buried in the burning depths of the jungle. One that she could fall into, slipping beneath the dappled surface, the deep waves of pleasure swallowing her whole, penetrating her body. It was the most perfect feeling in the world—until he ripped her from paradise, slamming her back to a cold, harsh reality in which he didn't want to touch her.

Damn it, stop torturing yourself.

She knew it was masochistic, but no matter how hard she tried, she couldn't stop thinking about that morning. Every time she did, she wanted to hurt something. Mainly Quinn.

And what made it even worse was that she still wanted him. Wanted to glom on to him and pull him around her, over her, inside her. Melt him into her system, until she could feel him everywhere. Until he was in the beat of her heart, the rush of her blood. And more than anything, she wanted to claim him as her own.

But it was never going to happen. He was too scarred-up inside, too closed down, looking at everyone around him with a wary, suspicious eye. Whoever had done the job on him, they'd done it well. Saige had no doubt that it was a woman. Only a lover could inflict that kind of pain. The kind that was worse than torture, causing the type of destruction that broke you apart until you didn't even recognize yourself anymore, closing you down so that you didn't feel anything at all.

That was Quinn. He went through the motions well enough. He smiled. He teased. He even sometimes laughed, though his sense of humor was definitely wry. But none of those things ever reached past the moment…never reached inside him. Never reached his eyes—and Saige had always been a firm believer that eyes were the mirror of the soul. She'd believed it, and had lived by it. At times, she'd even trusted her life to it.

Quinn's eyes, though beautiful, were always tortured. Even now, as he climbed back into their rented Expedition after pumping gas, she could see the shadows of his past lingering beneath the midnight beauty of his gaze.

"What's going on?" she asked as he pulled into one of the parking spaces behind the gas station instead of heading back out onto the highway.

He rubbed at the back of his neck, staring out the windshield at the dry, blustery late-summer day. "I just called Kierland. He and Shrader are going to head down and meet up with us just outside of Denver, so that we're not heading into this on our own."

"If the Casus are watching the compound, they could follow them right to us." Not to mention the Collective, she silently added. Though they still didn't understand how Javier and his brothers had been charred by a chemical developed by the Collective,

Saige had a bad feeling they weren't going to like the answers when they found them.

"We have ways of slipping out of Ravenswing without drawing anyone's notice," he explained, bracing his elbow on the driver-side door, his left hand rubbing across his wide, sensual mouth.

"So then what are we waiting for?"

He sighed, turning toward her, his expression etched with raw frustration. "You need to feed before we go any farther."

Saige arched a brow. "You don't honestly want to start this conversation again, do you? I thought you were smarter than that, Quinn."

"We have no way of knowing what to expect," he grunted, "and you're getting weak. I can see it every time I look at you. I'm not letting you walk into this without being at full strength."

"You're not letting?" she repeated, shaking her head. "Since when do you 'let' anything?"

"You should have done it long before now," he argued. "We can't keep putting it off. You *need* the strength it will give you."

He started to reach for her hand, and she snatched it back. "Don't even think about it," she said unsteadily. "You might have saved my life in the jungle, but as far as I'm concerned, you've lost the right to touch me."

He caught her gaze, holding that instead. "I can make you feel good. I've done it before." She opened her mouth, a scathing retort perched on her tongue, but he cut her off, saying, "I'm not trying to sound arrogant. I'm just... I'm scared for you, Saige."

"*Don't,*" she whispered, hating how easily he could tear into her. All it took was a look. His eyes so dark and deep and haunted. A certain husky tremor of that velvety, butterscotch voice, and she practically melted into a syrupy pile of honey. Pathetic. He destroyed her with no effort at all, and she couldn't even get him to sleep with her.

"I know you're angry at me, but this is no time to be stubborn."

"You want to talk about stubborn?" A dry, choked sound that should have been laughter tore from her chest, and she made a grab for the soda he'd been drinking during the drive, knowing damn well he'd stop her before she touched the plastic bottle. Ever since she'd told him about her power, he guarded his physical objects like a dragon protecting his treasure, knowing that she might be able to "see" into that thick head of his if she were to lay her hands on anything he'd touched. "You should take a look in a mirror," she quipped with a bitter note of sarcasm when he grabbed hold of her wrist.

Pulling free from his grip, Saige turned toward the passenger-side window, determined to ignore the way her wrist tingled from the touch of his hand. The view of the surrounding forest wasn't nearly as compelling as staring at Quinn, but she didn't care. Anything was better than facing that dark, wary look of suspicion in his eyes. It was wearing her down, making her raw, and she was already wrecked enough by her worry over Jamison and the maps and the Casus.

Silence settled within the warm cab like a thick,

emotional haze that made it difficult to breathe. Guilt. Anger. Lust. Fear. They were all there, churning into a gut-wrenching poison.

She could feel the press of his eyes on her profile—could almost feel the force of his need, of his own gnawing hunger as his smoldering gaze touched her mouth, her jaw…slipping down the warm line of her throat. Lower, over the T-shirt-covered swell of her chest, her nipples pressing hard and thick against the pale gray cotton. She heard the indrawn rush of his breath and closed her eyes, unable to keep from hoping for words she *knew* were never going to fall from his lips.

The moment stretched out, the tension making her want to scream, and then he finally growled, "Just remember to stay sharp," and put the truck into Reverse, pulling out of the space.

Saige swallowed a dry, husky burst of laughter and forced out a soft, "Whatever you say, Quinn."

As he turned out onto the interstate, she leaned her forehead against the chilled glass and wondered why she always wanted the things she couldn't have.

AFTER MAKING THE two-hour drive in a tense, stifled silence, they finally met up with Quinn's friends and fellow Watchmen in the parking lot of a convenience store that was just down the road from where they'd turned in the Expedition. Quinn made a quick round of introductions, and then everyone piled into an imposing black Avalanche and they headed back out on the road, with the two other Watchmen in front, while she and Quinn sat in the back.

Rubbing his palm against his bristled jaw, Quinn immediately asked, "Where are her brothers?"

"We snuck out while they were in the middle of another argument. They haven't stopped going at it since Riley admitted that Saige had tried to warn him about the awakenings," the one named Aiden Shrader replied in a deep, husky rumble as he shifted sideways in the passenger seat. His caramel-colored hair fell below his chin in windblown waves, his face an arresting composition of beauty and ruggedness that no doubt made him popular with the local female population. Flashing a sharp smile, he said, "We left Kellan there to deal with them."

"You mean they wanted to come?" Saige asked, unable to disguise her surprise. Despite Quinn's assurances that her brothers were worried about her, she still had a hard time buying the concept.

It was Quinn's best friend, Kierland Scott, who answered her while he drove, saying, "When we get back, they'll be ready to kill over the fact that we left them behind." He had deep, auburn-colored hair, his eyes a pale, piercing green, and Saige had inwardly rolled her eyes when she'd gotten her first look at him, wondering if all the Watchmen at Ravenswing were as devastatingly good-looking as these three.

"They'll be pissed, all right," Shrader agreed, the corner of his wide mouth kicking up in a crooked, mischief-made grin as he caught her gaze. "I'm afraid we're not always your brothers' favorite people."

"They never did play well with others," she murmured, and the two men shared a quiet laugh, though there was a grim edge to their humor that couldn't be overlooked. Despite trying to put her at ease, it was obvious they were all on edge, not knowing what they were going to find when they reached the Douglas Resort, where Jamison would be waiting for her.

"At any rate," Kierland remarked, "Molly will keep them in line until we can get back."

Quinn had briefly told her about the woman who had finally managed to melt her hard-nosed brother's heart, and Saige couldn't wait to meet Ian's fiancée. She wanted to ask the two Watchmen for more details about Molly Stratton, but Quinn caught Kierland's gaze in the rearview mirror and said, "Bring me up to speed on what I've missed."

"I wish I had better news," he answered with a hard sigh, "but it looks like all hell is going to break loose around here. Some of the other compounds have started to make contact with the awakening Merrick, explaining the situation to those who don't have a clue what's happening to them. And as we expected, once word went out that Ian took down a Casus with the first Dark Marker, reports started coming in of Merrick who are eager to get their hands on the only weapon that can help them. The Reno compound has opened its doors to any Merrick wishing to seek shelter there, but most of the compounds are still too afraid of pissing off the Consortium, which has just sent us an official notice that we're being put under judicial review."

"And to top it all off," Shrader added, "with only the strongest bloodlines being given Watchman surveillance, there are still too many out there on their own that need to be tracked down. Compounds are trying to make contact, but it's going to take time."

"Time we don't have," muttered Quinn, who went on to brief them in greater detail about what he'd learned in Brazil. He ended with a deeper explanation of Saige's "power," and then touched on the strange use of the Collective chemical on Javier and his brothers.

"So you think there might be some connection between the Casus and the Collective?" Kierland asked, his pale gaze focused on the road.

Scraping one hand back through his hair, Quinn exhaled a rough breath. "I don't know. But something isn't right. Whoever the hell this Westmore guy is that the Casus mentioned in front of Saige, he must have found a way to get his hands on those chemicals."

Turning his hazel gaze toward Kierland, Shrader rolled one brawny shoulder and said, "There's got to be some kind of reasonable explanation. One that actually makes some sense."

"Those bodies were charred, just like Collective kills," Quinn said through his gritted teeth. "I didn't imagine it."

"Now isn't the time to get into it," Kierland responded, obviously the peacemaker of the group. "When we get back to Ravenswing you two can argue all you want, but for now let's stay focused."

A moment of silence settled over the group as Kierland turned onto a winding highway that seemed to be taking them to the outskirts of town, toward the mountains. Saige stared out her window, her anxiety mounting, until she felt the weight of a stare focused in her direction. Looking forward, she found Shrader watching her with a strange, curious expression on his handsome face. "Is something wrong?" she asked, wondering what he seemed to find so fascinating.

"You're still hungry," he stated in a low voice.

Heat bloomed under her skin, burning in her face. "It's that obvious?" she asked unsteadily, aware of Quinn cursing something foul under his breath.

The corner of Shrader's mouth twitched with a knowing smile. "It is to us. Care to explain why you haven't fed?"

"I suppose it wouldn't do much good for me to tell you to mind your own business," she muttered, crossing her arms over her chest, unable to shake the feeling that she was walking around with a neon sign flashing on her forehead.

"Honey, since we stuck our necks out for your family, everything you do is our business," Shrader drawled, his hazel eyes suddenly burning with a warm, amber glow within the thick fringe of his lashes. "So I'll go ahead and tell you that it's stupid, allowing yourself to get this weak. You need to feed."

Saige shook her head, snuffling a dry laugh under her breath. "You have no idea how sick I am of that particular phrase."

Shrader flicked a wry look toward Kierland. "Is it just me, or are you sensing trouble in paradise?"

"I'm sensing that you need to mind your own damn business, Aiden," the Watchman replied, taking the next right-hand turn.

"Well, hell." He sighed, lifting one beautifully tattooed hand to scratch at his chin. "Where's the fun in that?"

"The time for fun is over," Kierland rumbled, and she could see through the front windshield that they'd just turned onto the long driveway that led up to the Douglas Resort. Situated on the outskirts of Denver, the exclusive resort had been built at the edge of a thick pine forest, the majestic beauty of the towering trees the perfect backdrop to the Frank Lloyd Wright style of the buildings. They parked in one of the back lots, near the woods, and filed out of the Avalanche together. Saige's breath quickened, her palms damp with nerves as they walked into the lobby, then quickly headed toward the coffee shop. She told herself to stay calm, silently repeating that everything was going to be okay. She'd meet Jamison, take the Marker after thanking him profusely, and then he could get the hell out of there, going back home, where he'd be safe from danger.

But twenty minutes later, she was practically hyperventilating. Despite a thorough search of the lobby, restaurants and lounges, Jamison was nowhere to be found. Saige's throat tightened with terror as she pressed one hand against her stomach, a million horrifying scenarios rushing through her brain, making her ill.

Sending her a reassuring smile, Aiden said, "I'll go talk to the ladies at the front desk. Maybe he grabbed a room here or left a message for you."

"If he did, they won't give you the information," she said hoarsely, her lips numb.

He winked at her, purring, "They'll give me whatever I ask for, sweetheart."

Blinking, she watched him walk away, then sent Quinn a doubtful look. "I thought you said he doesn't like humans."

"He doesn't," he muttered, staying close to her side while Kierland searched the men's restrooms. "He just likes to screw them."

"Charming," she murmured, crossing her arms over her chest, as if that could hold in the pounding of her heart.

"For some reason, they seem to think so." He sent her one of those long, heavy, soul-searching looks that always made her feel like he was slipping under her skin, picking his way through her mind. "Don't even think about getting mixed up with him."

"Let me guess. He doesn't do virgins, either?" she drawled, her tone heavy with sarcasm.

"If he ever lays a hand on you," he said quietly, turning his gaze back to the people milling about the lobby, "I'll kill him."

Unable to tell if he was joking or not, Saige looked back toward the front desk. Shrader was already heading their way again, his frown all the answer she needed. "Oh God," she whispered, the back of her throat burning with the salty sting of tears.

Kierland joined them a moment later, his search unsuccessful, and Quinn took hold of her arm, saying, "We need to get out of here."

Saige moved numbly as he guided her out of the resort, her eyes damp, while guilt burned through her insides like acid. "This isn't happening," she kept whispering under her breath, as if by somehow saying the words, she could make them true. "It *isn't* happening."

Quinn left her standing beside the Avalanche, then stepped a short distance away, his head bent toward Shrader and Kierland as the three men obviously discussed the situation. She wondered if they blamed her, then realized it was a stupid question, considering she *was* to blame.

Turning away, she tried to decide what to do next, when she felt Quinn come up behind her, instantly recognizing his warm, mouthwatering scent. "You okay?" he asked, his tone low…careful, and she wondered if she looked as brittle as she felt—as if one wrong move could shatter her into a million pieces.

"Where do you think he is?" she practically sobbed, feeling as if the bottom of her stomach had just dropped out as she turned around and stared up at him.

Grim lines of worry etched his dark expression. "I wish I could give you some answers, Saige, but we just don't know. Everyone Shrader and Kierland talked to in there said they hadn't seen anyone who fits Haley's description. I don't think he ever made it here."

"I can't believe he's gone. He was just supposed to hide out until I got here. I never thought…I never thought they would actually—"

"Shh," he suddenly rasped, holding up his hand in a signal for everyone to be silent. He slanted a meaningful look toward Kierland, who lifted his face, sniffing at the air.

"What is it?" she whispered, but no one bothered to respond, their attention focused on the nearby forest, as if expecting something to burst from the thick, shadowed woods.

Breath held tight in her chest, Saige pressed back against the cold side of the Avalanche while the gusting wind whipped her hair across her face. The back lot was empty but for a few scattered cars parked on the far side, the majority of guests having used the front one nearer to the entrance, which meant there was no one else around. She had no idea what to expect. She only knew that whatever it was, it was going to be bad.

"Give her the keys," Quinn grunted, and Kierland handed them over into her shaking hands. Without taking his eyes off the woods, Quinn then said, "I want you to get in the truck, Saige, and if anything happens, you get the hell out of here and head back to the place where we turned in the rental. We'll meet you there as soon as we've handled this."

"Handled what?" she asked, wishing she knew what was going on.

"I'll explain later," he snapped. "Just get in the goddamn truck."

Before she could argue, Shrader said, "It smells human." His upper lip curled over his teeth, revealing a stunning pair of lengthening incisors, and she remembered Quinn telling her that Shrader's inner beast was a tiger. From the looks of his fangs, she could well imagine how deadly the Watchman could be when facing off against his enemies.

"Could be Collective," Kierland murmured, a guttural edge to his words that hadn't been there before. According to Quinn, Kierland Scott was a werewolf, and Saige had no doubt that the lycanthrope could be every bit as lethal as his friends.

"There's only one of them," Quinn grunted, taking a step toward the tree.

"That's good, right?" she breathed out, slipping the keys into the pocket of her jeans.

"Believe it or not," Shrader rumbled, "sometimes one is all it takes. The Collective train their soldiers to be some of the toughest bastards you've ever seen, and then they deck them out in weaponry that makes what the special ops guys use look like child's play." Reaching behind him, under his jacket, the tattooed Watchman pulled a handgun from the waistband of his jeans, then went on to say, "And seeing as how you're one of us now, you'd better learn fast to never underestimate them." He tossed the gun toward Quinn, who caught it in midair, then reached down and pulled a wicked-looking knife from a sheath that hugged his heavy calf muscle.

As soon as Shrader had straightened, Quinn tossed back the gun, jerking his chin toward the blade. "I'll take the knife."

The Watchman frowned, but handed it over, muttering, "You always get to have all the fun."

"Cutting someone up is fun?" she croaked, feeling as if she'd stumbled into some kind of bizarre nightmare.

Shrader shrugged his broad shoulders. "Depends on who you're cutting."

Obviously tired of waiting for whoever was out there to come forward, Quinn stepped to the edge of the forest. "We know you're there," he growled. "Might as well stop hiding and show your face."

Saige could hear her pulse roaring in her ears as they all stared into the woods, her heart hammering inside her chest, hard and painful, and then a tall, rangy man with golden-blond hair, wearing jeans and a white T-shirt, suddenly walked out of the shadowed line of trees, his hands raised in a sign of surrender. "I wasn't hiding," he called back, keeping his dark green eyes focused on Quinn. "It just takes a while to walk through a friggin' forest. And it's damn annoying how you bastards do that whole tracking-a-man's-scent thing."

Before anyone could respond, Quinn roared with fury, and then he was suddenly rushing forward, the wicked blade dropped to the ground as he lifted his fist and slammed it into the blond's jaw, snapping the man's head to the side with a loud, painful crack of sound.

"Goddamn it!" the man grunted, immediately blocking another blow that Quinn aimed for his nose. "Will you just listen to me for a minute? I didn't come here to fight you! I'm not even armed!"

"I don't give a shit why you're here," Quinn snarled, slamming the blond's muscled body into a nearby tree so hard that it jarred a shower of needles from the sturdy branches.

"Who is he?" Saige whispered as Kierland and Shrader moved to her sides, wedging her between them in a blatant show of protection, while the blond continued to do his best to avoid Quinn's vicious, hammering punches.

"The question isn't who," Shrader muttered. "But *what*."

"I don't understand. Will someone please tell me what is going on?"

Before either of the Watchmen could answer, Quinn got his hand around the man's throat, trapping him against the trunk of a massive pine tree. "He's one of them, Saige," he growled, no longer even sounding human.

She studied the tall, tawny-haired stranger with obvious surprise. "But his eyes aren't blue."

A low, hard-edged laugh rumbled in Shrader's chest. "He's not a Casus."

"His name is McConnell," Quinn told her, his voice a deep, guttural sound of fury unlike anything she'd ever heard. "Seth McConnell, lieutenant colonel in the Collective Army."

Her breath sucked in with a hard gasp. "He's a soldier?"

"One of the deadliest they've ever had," Quinn snarled. "Isn't that right, McConnell?"

"I didn't come here to cause any trouble," the blond growled, pulling at Quinn's thick wrist. "Which is the only reason I haven't kicked your ass yet. I came because I need to talk to you. Why else do you think I left my truck back at a campsite and walked through the woods? I'm trying to keep a low profile, but it's still a hell of a risk for me to be here."

"There's nothing you could say that I'm interested

in hearing," Quinn grunted, tightening his grip on the man's throat.

McConnell's dark green gaze shifted in her direction, and he rasped, "I can give you information about the human."

Quinn snorted. "You know damn well she isn't human."

"Not her," McConnell choked out, starting to turn an interesting shade of blue. "The archaeologist."

"Jamison!" she cried, starting forward, only to be caught on either side by Kierland and Shrader, who pulled her back between them. "Where is he? What's happened to him?"

Blowing out a disgusted breath, Quinn loosened his hold, and McConnell pulled some much-needed air into his lungs, his green gaze cutting toward Kierland as he said, "I have it on good authority that the archaeologist ran into a certain redhead before he ever made it to Colorado."

Ali three Watchmen cursed under their breath, sharing dark looks, obviously understanding something that Saige didn't. "What? What's that mean? What's going on?" she demanded, on the verge of screeching. She felt like she was missing vital pieces of the conversation, some kind on nonverbal communication going on that she couldn't understand. "If someone doesn't start talking, right now, I'm going to scream. And I don't care who it brings out here!"

"It means they sent Spark after him," Kierland told her in a low voice.

"Spark? Who's Spark?"

"A total raging bitch, that's who she is," Shrader growled. "One whose specialty is luring men close to her, just before she slashes their throats. Or blows their brains out. I hear she likes to mix it up, keep it interesting."

"An assassin?" she breathed out, feeling dizzy as it sank in. "Why would the Collective send an assassin after a human? That doesn't make any sense!"

"You guys killing humans now, too?" Quinn sneered, tightening his fingers once again.

"If you'd take your damned hand off my throat," McConnell wheezed, "I'll tell you what I know."

"Quinn!" she cried out, knowing if he killed the soldier, they might never find out what had happened to Jamison.

Quinn made a rude sound in the back of his throat and kept squeezing. "Don't let him fool you, Saige. Whatever he's after, it's a setup. McConnell here doesn't care for our kind, and that includes our friends, which means he doesn't give a rat's ass what happens to Haley."

"He's right," Shrader muttered, reaching behind him to slip his gun back into his waistband.

Stepping closer to her side, Kierland kept his voice soft as he said, "McConnell's family was killed by a nest of rogue vampires when he was fifteen. He joined the Collective shortly afterward, and quickly moved through their ranks."

"And it wasn't long before he became one of the most ruthless hunters they ever recruited," Shrader added, curling his lip as he stared at the soldier.

McConnell's piercing green eyes narrowed with frustration. "Think what you will," he gasped, "but I've never killed an innocent being, no matter what species they were."

"No," Quinn muttered, getting right in the man's face, "you just torture them until they *wish* they were dead. Isn't that right, *Colonel?*"

A heavy silence settled between the two adversaries while Quinn's rage crackled on the air like a coming storm, and she could have sworn the shadows darkening McConnell's eyes were born from regret. "I've made mistakes," the soldier finally rasped. "But I have *never* ordered someone's torture."

Quinn growled low in his throat, the muscles in his arm shaking with fury, and then he eased his grip for the second time, allowing the man to pull in some much-needed air. In a stark, fractured voice, he said, "What the hell are you after, McConnell?"

"I came to tell you that as far as I know, the human is still alive. But they *are* keeping him prisoner." He took another deep breath of the pine-scented air, then said, "And, believe it or not, I came here to help you."

"You've gotta be kidding." Quinn sneered.

"Actually, I want *you* to help *me.* There's something wrong in the Collective. I need help from an outside source, before it gets out of control."

Quinn stared, hard, his nostrils flaring as he studied the man's eyes. In a low, guttural voice, he said, "You're lying."

McConnell didn't even flinch. "I wish that was true.

If it was, we wouldn't be in this shit. And I wouldn't be risking my life by coming here."

"We're not in anything with you," Shrader grunted at her side.

"I know you hate me," McConnell said to Quinn, making Saige wonder just what had happened between the two men in the past. Whatever it was, she knew Quinn despised the soldier enough to want to kill him. "But I've learned a lot since the last time we saw each other."

"And just what have you learned?" Quinn snarled, still holding his throat.

"That not all of your kind are evil. And not all Collective soldiers fight with honor, or even toward the same ideals. But that's a conversation best left for another time. I came here today because I have important information."

"Did Jamison tell you we were meeting him here?" she asked, wondering how he'd known where to find them.

"As far as I know, he hasn't told anyone anything. I've had my men watching all the roads out of Henning," McConnell explained. "As soon as they saw Shrader and Scott heading through town, they contacted me, and I followed the Watchmen down, hoping to have an opportunity like this."

Shrader cursed under his breath, then said, "And now you're just going to share with us out of the goodness of your heart?"

"Let him talk," Kierland directed. "We might as well hear what he has to say."

With a disgusted snarl, Quinn released his hold on McConnell, pacing away like a wild, predaceous animal that'd just been denied its next meal. "I don't believe this shit," he muttered, pushing both hands back through his hair.

"Say what you came to, McConnell, and then get the hell out of here," Kierland rumbled in a deep, authoritative voice.

McConnell slumped back against the tree, rubbing at his reddened throat while keeping a wary eye on Quinn. "Like I just told you, there's something wrong in the Collective."

Shrader gave a gruff bark of laughter. "Hell, I could have told you sycophants that a long time ago. You're all screwed in the head."

"I mean within the ranks," McConnell snapped, the sunlight glinting against the windblown strands of his golden hair making him look more like a California surfer than a ruthless Collective soldier. "There's a new branch that's been created—one they're trying to keep secret, but a few of the officers, like myself, were told of its existence."

"Why the secrecy?" Shrader muttered, rubbing one tattooed hand against his jaw. "I thought you were all one big, happy, psychotic family."

"This unit," McConnell explained, "it's not like the others. They're being given special allowances."

"Like working with the enemy?" Kierland asked.

McConnell nodded, a grim cast to his golden features that nearly matched Quinn's.

"The Collective would rather die than buddy up

with those monsters," Quinn growled, his big hands flexing at his sides.

"Not if the monsters have something they want," McConnell said in a low voice.

Quinn's dark expression twisted into a grimace. "What does that mean?"

"It means that anyone can be bought, if the price is right," Kierland murmured. "I think McConnell is talking about an exchange of information."

Shrader made a thick sound of disbelief. "What would the Casus have that the Collective wanted?"

"Not the Casus," McConnell corrected him, "but the man I believe is masterminding their return to this world. Once he has complete possession of the Dark Markers, he's promised to give the Collective the location of every nonhuman clan that ever walked the earth."

"If the Collective get that information," Saige gasped, "they could hunt them down, one by one, and obliterate what's left of every species."

Crossing his massive arms over his chest, Shrader eyed the soldier with a narrow stare. "Who's the prick running the show?"

"His name is Westmore."

Quinn shot her a sharp look, warning her not to say anything, and she struggled to conceal her surprise, while the other two Watchmen obviously did the same.

"What can you tell us about him?" Kierland asked.

McConnell shook his head, his expression one of bitter frustration. "Not much. He just waltzed in one day, promising that he'd give us those locations once he had the Markers, as well as demanding all the money and manpower he might need, in addition to unlimited access to our library."

"And what's so special about your library?" Quinn demanded in a quiet snarl.

Holding Quinn's angry gaze, McConnell said, "The archives apparently contain information that he needed."

A wave of shock slammed through the group, all of them staring at McConnell with the same degree of stark disbelief. "Are you telling us that the Collective have found the lost archives that belonged to the ancient Consortium?" he asked unsteadily.

"We found them last year, and the next thing you know, this Westmore guy comes knocking on our door. Seems the Collective generals were eager for what he promised to deliver, since the archives had turned out to be somewhat of a disappointment for them. While they provided some interesting information about many of the ancient clans, they failed to say where they could be found."

"He'll never be able to deliver," Quinn argued in a husky rasp, still pacing with restless energy.

"He already has," McConnell muttered. "To prove himself, he gave us the location of four vampire nesting grounds in Eastern Europe, all of which have now been destroyed."

"Then he must be a goddamn vamp," Shrader grunted.

McConnell shook his head again. "I thought the same thing, until I met him. But I'd swear the guy's as human as I am."

"Then how did he know where the nesting grounds

were?" Quinn demanded, finally coming to a stop about ten feet away from where McConnell still leaned against the tree.

Lifting his shoulders in a baffled shrug, the soldier gave a hard sigh, saying, "I don't know."

"We'd better find out," Kierland said, pushing at the auburn strands of hair the wind had blown over his brow.

Quinn shoved his hands deep in his pockets. "And just what did Westmore want with the archives?"

"I haven't been granted access," McConnell explained, rubbing at his battered jaw, "so I can't say for sure what they contain. But whatever Westmore found, it enabled him to make contact with the Casus in their holding ground, and now those bastards are coming across. He's set something deadly in motion, and it has to be stopped."

A low, bitter laugh tore from Shrader's chest. "And the Collective generals have no problem with the fact that he used the archives to bring back one of the most dangerous species to ever walk the earth? Considering your line of work," he drawled with a thick note of sarcasm, "it seems strange that you guys would just adopt them into your twisted little family."

"From what I understand, Westmore has convinced them that he's on our side, but that something big is coming in the preternatural world. A rise of violence and aggression among the ancient clans that not even the Consortium will be able to control. He's argued that when the time comes, he'll need the Markers and the Casus to fight against the clans, and then once they've been defeated, he'll use the Markers to destroy the Casus themselves. Personally, I don't trust him, and I'm not buying his story."

"And your superiors aren't upset about the trail of victims the Casus are leaving behind them?" Quinn asked.

"After that first Casus killed those women, Westmore put his own men in the field. As far as I know, they're doing their best to cover the kills. And at this point, the generals are already in too deep to back out. They've convinced themselves that the end will justify the means."

Quinn's eyes darkened, and Saige knew he was thinking about how Javier and his brothers had been charred. Obviously, Westmore was using the Collective's chemical agent to destroy the Casus kills, just as McConnell had said.

"And what was their interest in the archaeologist?" Kierland rasped.

"Westmore was contacted by two Casus who were down in Brazil. They believed Saige gave Haley the Marker and asked Westmore to have him picked up. So he sent Spark after him. As far as I know, they're holding him at Westmore's headquarters, which is supposedly in the mountains, but hell if I can find anyone who will tell me where it is." He looked toward Quinn and added, "Now that the two Casus have arrived in Colorado and Westmore has possession of the maps, he wants to get his hands on the one person he's been told can read them."

Looking toward Quinn, Saige could read the fear

in his eyes, and knew she must look just as frightened. It was bad enough knowing the Casus wanted her, but now they knew that Westmore could put the entire force of the Collective behind finding her, as well.

"And so you just decided to share this with us because you've turned a new leaf?" Shrader drawled with a heavy note of skepticism.

"I told you why I was here," McConnell said with a tired sigh. "If we can find some way to work together, then maybe we can put a stop to this before it becomes too big to control."

"What do you suggest?" Kierland asked.

"For now, our own exchange of information." Walking forward, McConnell stopped just in front of Kierland and took a small piece of paper from his pocket, offering it to the Watchman. "That's my number. I've told you everything that I know. If you learn anything that can help me, I'm hoping you'll return the favor."

He started to turn away then, heading back into the woods, when Saige suddenly reached out, grabbing hold of his arm as she cried, "Wait!"

Quinn's voice cut through the air with the cracking force of a whip, making her flinch as he growled, "Do *not* touch him, Saige!"

Taking her hands off his arm, she held McConnell's dark green gaze and quickly recited the number of the cell phone they'd picked up for her that morning. "Please," she added, "if something happens or you have any new information about Jamison, call me."

He held her worried gaze for one heart-pounding

moment, then gave her a sharp nod and turned away, disappearing into the woods as quickly as he'd appeared.

CHAPTER SIXTEEN

Tuesday evening
Ravenswing

FEELING LIKE A KID hiding out in the dark, Quinn
reached for the beer he'd left sitting on the small table
to his right. He sat on the love seat in Saige's suite at
the compound, the only light that of the fading twilight
spilling in through the far wall of windows. With a
rough sigh, he lifted the bottle, noticing the water ring
left behind on the gleaming antique, but he wasn't surprised. It seemed he had a way of damaging everything
he got close to, like some kind of curse or blight on
humanity.

Tilting back his head, he took a long swallow, the
icy chill of the beer burning his throat until his eyes
watered. With a scowl, he set the bottle back down on
the table, wincing from the cold sensation in his chest,
and pulled back his shoulders, disgusted with himself.

He'd never realized just how much of a coward he
was, until he'd been forced to face his need for Saige.
And now that he knew, he wanted to take all that
churning, destructive rage he'd carried for Seth

McConnell all these years and turn it inward, where it belonged. The pretty-faced soldier might have been responsible for destroying his life with Janelle, but Quinn knew that he alone was to blame for ruining any chance of a future he might have had with Saige.

After McConnell had left them at the resort, he'd climbed into the backseat of the Avalanche beside her, furious that she'd not only touched the bastard, but had given him her phone number. He'd wanted to take her new phone and hurl it out the window, but she'd clipped it to her jeans and hadn't let it out of her sight.

As they'd made their way up the mountain toward the compound, he'd thought over the connection between the Casus and the Collective, still finding it hard to believe. Even after everything they'd heard that day, with so many of the confusing pieces of the puzzle finally beginning to click into place, he still could only shake his head at how this was all playing out. He'd wanted to talk it over with Saige, but she hadn't said another word to him. Aside from answering a few questions that Kierland and Shrader had asked her, she'd sat on the far side of the seat, her slender arms crossed over her chest, and stared out her window, her mind a million miles away.

Quinn knew she blamed herself for what had happened to her friend, and he prayed that they would be able to get him back alive. But he didn't hold much hope. If a deal was offered, he knew what they'd want in exchange for the Brit, and there wasn't a chance in hell he was going to allow Saige to get anywhere near Westmore and his minions.

And Quinn knew he wasn't the only one concerned for her well-being.

Taking another sip of his beer, his throat tightened with emotion as he thought of the scene when Saige had finally been reunited with her brothers. The second she'd stepped through the doorway, into the main hall at Ravenswing, he'd fully expected Ian and Riley to start ranting about how she hadn't called, why she hadn't come to them for help. Instead, they'd taken turns grabbing hold of her and hugging her tight against their brawny chests, as if to assure themselves that she was safe and unharmed. Quinn had watched from the sidelines, feeling like an outsider, which he was. After dinner, she'd gone to share a drink with her brothers and Molly, and it'd been clear that he wasn't welcome. A stupid thing to be bothered about, and one he didn't like admitting, but it was hard to hide from your demons when you were sitting alone in the dark, drinking by yourself like a pathetic jackass.

So why not stop and go after what you want?

Cursing under his breath, he'd just stood up to pace the hardwood floor of her sitting room when Saige opened the door, stepping into the twilight shadows.

"Quinn? What are you doing here?" Her husky tone made it clear that he'd surprised her as she slowly closed the door behind her.

Feeling irritable and on edge, he took a step forward, pinning her with a belligerent stare as she flicked on a small lamp. The soft wash of mellow gold warmed the center of the room without quite reaching the darkened corners, kind of like the way he felt inside. He was only willing to reveal so much, keeping the rest in shadow. But it was that isolated darkness that was suffocating him, choking off his ability to function…to breathe. His past had become a noose around his neck and he didn't know how to shake it loose. He was holding on to the rope with both hands, his feet dangling off the ground…and his only hope was Saige. He needed her, in ways that went beyond the possessive instincts of his beast, to something deeper and endlessly more powerful. Something that had settled into his heart and couldn't be undone.

And it scared the ever-loving hell out of him.

Caught in his stare, she pulled her lower lip through her teeth, looking painfully beautiful in a borrowed green blouse and jeans as she said, "I asked what you're doing here, Quinn."

"What kind of question is that?" he muttered, when what he really wanted to say were things he had no business even thinking, much less voicing out loud.

Why can't I trust you to stay with me?

Why can't you love me?

"I'm not trying to ruffle your feathers," she murmured, the thick silk of her hair falling around her shoulders in a warm, vibrant wave that he wanted to bury his face in, breathing her scent into his system. "I just figured I wouldn't be seeing much of you now that I'm no longer your responsibility."

You'll always be my responsibility, he thought savagely, hating that he couldn't give her the truth. Instead, he simply said, "We need to talk."

She lifted her brows, her expression one of casual

curiosity, but he could see the tension in her hands as she gripped the butter-soft leather of the armchair she stood behind, her knuckles turning white from the strain. "About what?"

He lowered his head, staring at the dark sheen of the floor while he lifted one hand and rubbed at the tension in the back of his neck, then lifted his gaze, snagging her beautiful blue stare…and holding it. "Let's start with Jamison. I've been thinking."

"Why do I get the feeling this is just going to piss me off?" she asked, the corner of her mouth twitching with a pained smile.

Pushing his hands into his pockets, he said, "Have you considered the idea that he might have been playing you? Maybe even keeping an eye on you for the Collective? McConnell could have set the whole thing up."

Her eyes went wide, and then she actually laughed, the soft, throaty sound grating against his pride like a jagged, rusty piece of metal. "Are you serious?"

"You have to be reasonable about this and at least admit that it's a possibility," he muttered, struggling to keep hold of his temper. "Especially after today. How suspicious is it that we go to meet Haley at a prearranged time and end up coming face-to-face with McConnell? You've gotta at least consider the idea, Saige."

She shook her head, sending him a pitying look that made him cringe. "I'm sorry," she said softly, "but I just can't do that."

"Why the hell not?" he growled, the words hard and belligerent in his throat.

"Because sometimes," she said huskily, "you just have to trust people."

"So you have that much faith in Haley," he rasped, trying to lock her to him with the power of his stare, even though he knew it was nothing but an illusion. The harder he tried to hold her, the more she would just slip away and the thought made something tear open inside him, like a wound. "Just not in me, huh?"

Her expression closed, as if a shadow was falling over her face like a veil. "I already told you why I ran from you in São Vicente," she said quietly. "I wanted to protect you, Quinn."

He rolled one shoulder in a hard gesture, doing everything he could to mask his hurt. "Yeah, that's what you said."

Her eyes narrowed with frustration. "And you still don't trust me enough to believe me."

"It just seems so complicated," he growled, his frustration rising, punching against his insides, needing an outlet. "The Markers. The maps. The codes. The Casus and the Collective and Haley, and now McConnell showing up, claiming to have seen the light."

"So do you suspect me, as well?" she asked in a small voice, wrapping her arms over her middle, the feminine position only accentuating the lush swell of her chest. Forcing his gaze higher, Quinn eyed the quiver of her pulse in the base of her throat, then higher, lingering on the pale, luminous texture of her skin, the wild rose color of her mouth. She was so tough…and yet so undeniably fragile and feminine and soft. He wanted to curl himself around her and protect her from the world.

He simply wanted. So much. So badly.

Sending her a dark, tormented look, he wondered where the easygoing, emotionless Quinn had gone, no longer even recognizing the man standing there in the room with her. He looked the same. Sounded the same. But inside he'd become a stranger.

"Of course I don't suspect you," he grunted under his breath.

"So then you don't think I'm a traitor," she murmured. "Just an idiot. One who was stupid enough to send the Marker off in the hands of a Collective operative."

"They can be good at tricking people," he said, aware of the heat rising up beneath his skin, burning in his face. "Trust me, Saige. I know what I'm talking about."

She hardened her jaw, her beautiful face tight with strain as she said, "Jamison is *not* working with the Collective. Believe me, don't believe me. I honestly don't care anymore, Quinn."

"You're angry at me." His tone was flat, masking his emotions. "I get that. But don't let it cloud your judgment."

"I'm frustrated, not furious. There *is* a difference," she told him. "And you're one to talk about clouded judgment."

He blew out a rough breath and stared off to the side, into the shadowed depths of the room, wishing he knew how to make things right. Wishing he wasn't so messed up in the head. Clearing his throat, he said, "Believe it or not, I didn't come here to fight with you.

I just…" He rolled his shoulder again and looked back toward her, wanting so many goddamn things that he was never going to have the chance to tell her. "I don't want it to be this way between us."

"You don't want to get close to me, don't want the burden of my virginity, don't want to trust me. And now you don't want there to be *what?* Tension between us?" she asked unsteadily, shaking her head. "Do you even know what you're saying anymore?"

"You wanna know what I want?" he choked out, taking a step closer to her, almost as if he were pulled there against his will.

"God, Quinn! How can you tell me what you want?" she demanded, smacking her hands against the top of the chair. "*You* don't even know what you want!"

"Like hell I don't," he growled, his voice a visceral scrape of sound, tortured and raw. "I want to take you into that bedroom behind you and not let you up again, Saige. I want to keep you there for days. Longer. Fuck you until you can't even walk straight. Until you feel me in your body even when I'm not there. Until you can't get the feel and taste of me out of your goddamn mind!"

Her chest rose and fell with the soft, rushing cadence of her breath as she stared back at him, her beautiful blue eyes clouded by confusion. "And you can't have that because…?"

"Because once we go that far," he vowed, scraping one hand back through his hair, "there's no going back for me. I'll want you to stay. Here. With me. Forever. I'll want to keep you, own you, in ways you can't even imagine."

"AND THAT SCARES YOU." It wasn't a question. Saige could tell from his tone, from the shadow of fear in his eyes, just how terrified he was.

A low, bitter laugh tore from his chest that sounded hard and painful, and he slowly shook his head. "Christ. *Scared* doesn't even begin to cover it."

She wet her bottom lip, shivering from the inside out, feeling as if she were standing at the edge of a deep, bottomless ravine, where one wrong move could lead to disaster. "Did you ever stop to think that maybe I'm tired of always being on the go, always riding the edge? That maybe I'm ready for more?"

He stared, hard, as if trying to penetrate her with those dark, midnight-colored eyes. "I think you'd say anything right now," he told her in a thick, husky voice, "if you thought it'd get you what you want."

"And I think you're just too scared to believe me," she argued in a soft voice, turning away.

"Is that right?" he growled, rounding the chair and taking hold of her shoulder, twisting her back around with such ease, there was no doubt that he could easily overpower her, Merrick blood or not. Not that her Merrick was in any position to wage a fight. Hunger was grinding her down, the need to take nourishment for the primal creature inside her like a bleeding wound upon her soul, one that just kept draining her, hour by hour, day by day.

Saige could tell that he wanted a fight, but she wasn't up to giving him one. Instead, she took a step back, and then another, until she came up against the wall beside her bedroom door. Fighting back a hot rush of tears, she said, "I'll leave here in a few days. Head up to Reno, to the compound Kierland said is taking in Merrick."

Something that looked like panic brightened his gaze, tearing at her heart. "Why in the hell would you want to do that?"

"I think it'd be best if we put some space between us," she whispered, wanting him to argue, but he didn't. Unfortunately she didn't have the same gift for silence. "And it's better for me to be away from here, anyway. Turns out Riley was right about me, after all. I'm not...safe."

"That's bullshit," he snapped, his big, hard body vibing with tension and anger and frustration.

She smiled wryly. "Come on, Quinn. Take a look around. Javier is dead, and now Jamison is suffering God only knows what at their hands. Riley was right. I'm like a poison."

"None of this is your fault!" he practically shouted.

"Why are you even bothering to argue, when I know you don't want me here?"

He ground his jaw, choking out a husky, "I didn't say that."

"You didn't have to," she said shakily. "And I don't want to be here, either. Not around you. I won't have my every action questioned."

"I wouldn't—"

"You do it when you don't even realize what you're doing," she told him in a hollow voice. She no longer sounded sad or angry or confused. Just...tired. "Despite everything, I wish...I wish good things for you, Quinn."

He stared at her so hard, she felt it like a physical touch, one that made her go hot under the skin. "Damn it, Saige. Why do you have to make everything so bloody difficult?"

"I'm not trying to make it anything," she said quietly, wishing she could reach out and touch the ink-black silk of his hair. Press her lips to the burnished slash of his cheekbones. The hard edge of his jaw. "It is what it is, as Riley used to always say."

"I'm not letting you leave here." His voice was so harsh, it didn't even sound like him. "And you're still going to need to feed. When the hunger becomes too much to fight, come find me. Don't...don't do anything stupid."

Her laughter sounded hollow even to her own ears. "Don't worry. I have no intention of sinking my teeth into anyone around here. You included."

"Damn it," he bellowed. "Hate me if you have to, Saige, but I'm not going to allow you to be stubborn about this."

"You're not going to *allow* me anything, Quinn. What I do or don't do is absolutely no concern of yours."

"I thought you were smarter than this," he muttered, moving closer. He crowded in on her, bringing the hard slabs of his chest into contact with the sensitive, swollen tips of her breasts.

"Yeah, well, I thought you were a lot of things, too." She tilted her head back, staring up at him, as dazed as ever by the raw sexuality of him, so searing and thick and impossibly seductive. "I guess we'd both better get used to disappointment. Because if you want me to take your blood, you're going to have to take me to bed first." Shifting her hips, she could feel the hard, rigid proof of his desire pressing against the worn denim of his jeans. "What is it?" she whispered, wishing she could see into his head...into his soul. Wishing she could break him open and find what hurt, pouring all her energy and will into finding a way to make it better. "Are you afraid that you won't see me, Quinn? That you'll only see her face beneath you, instead of mine?"

He jerked away from her as if he'd been burned, the expression on his dark, beautiful face one of pure, unadulterated pain in the dim, milky glow of light. Without a word, he turned and stalked across the shadowed room, toward the door, reaching for the handle.

But then he stopped and leaned forward, pressing his forehead against the pale grain of the wood, and in a deep, tortured voice, he quietly said, "Her name was Janelle."

It was irrational, but just the sound of the woman's name put a sharp, piercing pain in her chest, and Saige forced herself to stand straight, instead of curling in on herself.

He cleared his throat, the harsh rhythm of his breath filling the quiet, tender spaces that separated them. "We...we were going to get married."

Her lungs seized and she closed her eyes, waiting, not sure she wanted to hear this...but knowing that she needed to. Lifting her lashes, Saige studied his posture, noting the rigid tension in his broad shoulders, in the way he held his hard, powerful body.

He turned slightly to the side, leaning his shoulder against the door, his dark eyes focused on the moonlit sky through the wall of windows that took up the far side of her room. "When McConnell approached her, she took the easy way out. She wasn't strong enough to do any different."

"What happened?" she asked, her own voice thick with emotion.

He rubbed one hand down his face, and in a deep, husky rasp, he said, "She had only a fraction of panther blood in her—not even enough to allow her to fully shift—but she'd always been terrified of the Collective. Her family had been killed when she was a little girl, same as mine, and she'd lived in fear every day since. Then Seth McConnell came up to her one day when she was in Denver shopping, and I guess he made her an offer she couldn't refuse. If she helped the Collective capture me, he promised that she'd be protected from the organization for the rest of her life, and she…she was desperate enough to believe him."

"Because of her fear of the Collective?" she asked, wanting so badly to go to him and hold him. To press her lips against the damp heat of his temple, nuzzle his cheek, the sensitive curve of his strong, corded neck, and simply comfort him, as if she could melt into a warm, healing cloud of tenderness and pour herself over him. Ease him. But she did none of those things, knowing that he would only turn away if she did.

"Janelle was afraid of everything," he muttered, staring at a dark, empty place on the floor, his mind a million miles away, no longer in the room with them, but buried somewhere in a past that had ingrained itself in him so deeply, it'd become a prison. "At first, it was almost like I was her savior, her protector, which was probably what drew me to her to begin with. Kierland would tell you that my desire to fulfill those roles probably came from the fact that my father had been unable to protect my mother from the Collective soldiers who'd killed them. Who knows? Maybe he's right. But in the end, I think I ended up scaring her, too. We'd started arguing in the weeks before McConnell approached her. She claimed that she no longer liked the physical part of our relationship. Thought I was too demanding, too possessive. For my kind, our physical needs are often…excessive. Still, I'd tried to be gentle with her," he explained in a rough, pained voice, "but I guess it wasn't enough. By the time Seth came along with his offer, she was looking for a way out, and she thought he'd given it to her."

"She betrayed you?" she whispered, hating the sharp, wrenching waves of despair she could feel rolling off him, slithering through the room like a sickness. One she had no doubt had been eating away at Quinn's soul for years.

"She set me up, and I was caught." A harsh, bitter sound tore from his throat. "And Seth's promise fell short. By the time Kierland and the others figured out where we were, she'd already been raped and killed by the soldiers who handled my so-called interrogation, if that's what you want to call it. Seems that despite McConnell's promises of protection, his colleagues felt she wasn't worth keeping alive. Later, I

heard he went ape-shit when he found out what they'd
done to her. But hell, Janelle never should have trusted
him in the first place."

"You blame yourself more than you do her, don't
you?" she asked, viewing him in a new light, finally
able to see beneath the shadows that darkened him.
And now that she did, she couldn't imagine the
strength it'd taken for him to go on, somehow putting
the pieces of his life back together.

"I expected too much from her," he muttered,
raking his hand back through his hair. "Didn't see her
clearly. Maybe if I'd been more perceptive, I could
have seen what was coming and saved us both a hell
of a lot of pain."

"You made a mistake in trusting the wrong person," she whispered, daring to take a step closer to
him…and then another. "But does that mean you have
to live with it forever, Quinn?"

He turned his head, holding her tear-filled gaze for
a long, breathless moment, and then shifted his body
away from the door, reaching for the handle as he
rasped, "Sometimes we just don't have a choice."

"And sometimes we do," she argued softly.

But he was already gone.

CHAPTER SEVENTEEN

Wednesday, 2:00 a.m.
Rocky Mountains

WIMP. COWARD. IDIOT.

Self-loathing poured through Jamison Haley's veins like thick, syrupy acid, stripping his insides raw. His cell was cold, his arms aching from where they'd been chained to a rough, concrete wall, not to mention his body, which had been put through more than he'd ever imagined he could endure. He wished he could say he'd handled their interrogation like a hero, but knew that would be nothing short of a lie. While he took pride in the fact that he hadn't told them anything about Saige, the truth was that he'd blubbered like a child as they'd cut him, begging the sadistic monsters to either kill him or leave him alone.

Still, he'd managed to string together a convincing lie about where he was supposed to meet Saige that afternoon. And now he *would* die. He knew that once they returned to the house, it would finally be over. He didn't even understand what they were keeping him for. They had the Marker. What more did they want?

Taking a deep, shuddering breath, he used his shoulder to wipe the cold film of fear from his brow and did his best to think about things that had given him joy in life. His work. His friends. Good food and fast cars.

And Saige.

When a soft scraping sound came suddenly from somewhere outside his cell, he squinted, struggling to see through his swollen right eye, his lashes coated with blood that continued to seep from the deep cut just above his right eyebrow. When the dead bolt on the door began turning, he choked back a groan. Fear burned at the back of his throat, his stomach twisting so sharply, he didn't know how he managed not to throw up.

Pathetic excuse for a man.

The words jarred him, as if he'd been dealt a physical blow. Jamison had heard similar words in his lifetime, but only from his father's tongue, the insults hurled at him like weapons meant to damage and destroy his pride. Never had they been self-directed, and he was surprised by how much more destructive they could be when coming from his own mind.

Struggling to see through the moonlit shadows that spilled from a high, distant window, he watched as a tall, muscular man with chin-length brown hair came into the room. He'd been told the man's name was Gregory, and Jamison instantly recognized him as half of the duo that had handled his torture. And while the two men looked human, Jamison knew damn well that they weren't. It was all he could do not to whimper as he re-membered the way their hands had transformed into terrifying claws that they'd used on his back and thighs, his flesh still shredded and raw, caked with blood.

He supposed it was a miracle that he hadn't bled to death, but the fatalistic thought faded from his mind as Gregory stepped closer and he caught sight of the man's cold, deadly gaze. But even more chilling than the look in those pale blue eyes was what he held in his right hand.

A sharp, silvery pair of pruning shears.

His blood rushed to his head, roaring through his ears, while his heart tried to force its way into his throat. He would have opened his mouth and demanded to know what the bastard intended to do, but he was sure that nothing more than an unintelligible sob would escape.

His father's aristocratic voice boomed in his head, gritty and rough. *A Haley never cowers, never runs. A Haley never needs anyone but himself.*

Jamison figured if any moment in his life proved that he *wasn't* his father's son, it was this one. Because as brave as he wanted to be, he silently begged for deliverance from the nightmare closing in around him.

The Casus stepped closer, and Jamison realized that he didn't need to ask what the man intended. No, the answer was already there in those cold, penetrating eyes. As if he were actually looking forward to Jamison's pain, he said, "Didn't anyone ever tell you that lying is a sin?"

Feeling as though a stranger had suddenly taken control of his body, Jamison heard himself give a low, sarcastic snicker and drawl, "What can I say? I guess I'm just a rebel."

A rusty chuckle rumbled in the man's throat, and he lazily scratched his chest while studying him through his lashes. Finally, he rasped, "I hear you're pretty friendly with my girl."

Jamison ignored the pain throbbing in his forehead and lifted his brows. "Your girl? The other guy told me that Saige was his."

"That's what he thinks, but what he doesn't know won't hurt him." A crooked smile curled his mouth, and he gave another low, husky laugh. "Or in this case, I guess it *will* hurt him. I needed ol' Royce, but soon I won't be needing him anymore."

"Something tells me that he won't take the news very well," Jamison offered dryly, amazed he could still find his sense of humor when death was staring him in the face.

"He won't have a choice," Gregory murmured. "Once Saige comes for you, and I have her in my clutches, it will be Royce's time to go."

"Saige *won't* come," he growled, praying that she was smart enough to stay somewhere safe. "You're never getting your hands on her, you sick son of a bitch."

"On the contrary," Gregory drawled with a slow, sickening smile as he reached for Jamison's fingers. "And it's *your* hands, Haley, that are going to bring her to me."

CHAPTER EIGHTEEN

Wednesday afternoon

THE PAST FEW DAYS had been hell.

But this… This was torture. Perched on the roof of the long, L-shaped garage where the Watchmen housed their eclectic collection of cars and trucks, Quinn had spent the past two hours watching Saige spar with Aiden in the training field below. Though she already had a solid background in self-defense, the Watchman was teaching her some advanced moves, as well as working with her on how to properly use the Dark Marker she'd unearthed in Italy, in the event she ever had to face off against a Casus.

He didn't like the other man being so close to her, and if Aiden put his hands on her hips one more time while pretending to correct her stance, Quinn was personally going to see his wrists turned into stumps. He might not have Aiden's lethal tiger bite, but his talons were more than sharp enough to get the job done.

She was doing well, but he could tell that she was tired…not to mention starved, the Merrick draining her more and more every day. Even from his place on the rooftop, he could see the strain around her eyes, evidence of her exhaustion…as well as her worry over Jamison Haley. There'd been no word from the archaeologist, and their searches last night and that morning had turned up nothing. The others weren't completely convinced that McConnell's story was true, believing that Haley might have simply taken the cross and made a run for it, or even handed it over to the Collective. But Quinn couldn't shake the feeling that Haley had fallen into the wrong hands—and if the Collective had actually gotten their hands on him, he knew the Brit would be begging for death by the time they found him.

"You know, if looks could kill," Kierland murmured, seeming to appear from out of nowhere as he sat down beside him on the slanting roof, "then I think Aiden would be a dead man right about now."

Wishing he smoked, if only to have an outlet for his frustration, Quinn squinted against the late-afternoon sunlight, hating that Kierland could read him so easily. That was the problem with being best friends with a guy for over twenty years. No matter how hard he tried to bury his feelings, Kierland could still read him like an open book. "I don't see the point in any of this," he muttered. "It's not like she's going to face one of those things on her own."

"Isn't she?" the Watchman asked, slanting him an odd, questioning look.

Rubbing his hand over his mouth, he said, "I don't want her involved in this war."

"It's not your choice," Kierland said with a hard

sigh, pulling his windblown hair back from his brow. "She's a Merrick, Quinn. Which means she's a part of this, whether you want her to be or not."

"Damn it, she could get hurt," he growled, the seething emotions lingering just beneath his calm surface beginning to bleed through.

Kierland was silent for a moment, the only sounds that of the gusting wind and the training taking place down below. Despite the distance that separated them, Quinn could smell Saige's warm, mouthwatering scent on the air, and the inevitable rise of desire within his body only cranked his tension higher, making him more fractious and on edge.

After what seemed like forever, Kierland finally blew out a rough breath, his pale gaze focused on Saige as he said, "I know your head is spinning right now, but she isn't Janelle. You can't judge her by your past. Think about it, Quinn. Janelle was easily hurt…easily frightened. Saige isn't either of those things."

He gave a gruff, brittle laugh. "Tell that to my head."

"What's going on?" the Watchman asked, his auburn brows drawn with concern.

"Dreams," he muttered. "Since we were down in South America. Even before we met up with Seth. I see the scene with Janelle, and then—" he swallowed, working for the words "—then it becomes Saige that they're raping…murdering."

Kierland cursed under his breath, a gritty edge to his deep voice as he said, "And you think the dreams mean something?"

"I know they're just nightmares," he rasped, forcing the words past the tightness in his chest, "but after all the psychic shit that went down between Molly and Ian, I'm... Hell, I don't know what to think anymore."

"You know," Kierland rumbled, resting his arms on his knees, "sometimes dreams are just our mind's way of screwing with us. Don't place too much importance on them, Quinn. You're going to lose out on something special if you do."

He cut his friend a sharp look from the corner of his eye, as if to say, *How the hell do you know that?*

Shaking his head, the corner of Kierland's mouth kicked up in a crooked grin. "Come on, man. I have eyes. You didn't watch Janelle with this sort of intensity. There's something going on between you and this woman, and you're a fool if you let her just slip through your fingers." He lowered his voice, adding, "And don't tell anyone, but I think the dreams that Ian and Molly shared had more to do with him than his awakening."

"What do you mean?"

Kierland lifted one shoulder. "It's becoming clear that the Buchanans each have gifts. Ian with those dreams that were actually happening, as well as the instances of precognition. Saige with her ability to read objects. Riley...who knows, but I have no doubt we'll learn soon enough. Ian's awakening might have brought his powers into focus, but I think those dreams are his own special gift, completely different from Saige's abilities." He paused, pushing his hair back again, before jerking his chin toward the field. "Which means that *your* dreams are probably just that. *Dreams.* You can't let them screw up your thinking, and you can't keep comparing Saige to something she isn't. In a lot of ways, Janelle was already broken when you found her, which was why you wanted so badly to take care of her, but Saige is one of the strongest women I've ever met. She's solid. She isn't going to crack under pressure, and she stands up to you. She'll be a good partner in ways that Janelle never could have been."

Because at the end of the day, he thought, Janelle had only ever worried about herself.

"You know what our kind is like," he muttered, looking back toward the training field, wanting so badly to believe. "Our sense of possession, especially for Raptors, is...*intense.* If I lost her, I could end up with more than just a broken heart. I could go completely over the edge."

"Yeah, maybe," Quinn agreed. "On the other hand, you could end up with something damn fine." The Watchman turned, giving him a hearty whack on the shoulder as he said, "There's a difference between learning from the past and letting it control us. And you, my friend, are fighting a battle that's already lost. Only thing to do now is figure out how you're going to surrender."

Lost in thought, Quinn quietly left the man who was like a brother to him sitting atop the garage and made his way back to the main house, the magnificent sloping angle of the roof reminding him of a dark, powerful wing lifted in flight. The house was silent and cool, the scents of wood and something baking in the kitchen easing his soul, and as he climbed his way up to his room, he couldn't stop thinking about the things Kierland had said.

Sitting on the edge of his mattress moments later, Quinn scrubbed his hands down his face, keenly aware of a sharp pain in his chest, as if the hard, callused casing surrounding his heart was finally beginning to crumble. He drew in a slow, shaky breath, amazed as the warm, tender spill of something that felt strangely like hope spread sweetly through his veins.

And for the first time in five years, the chains that'd bound him to his past began to break apart.

Reaching behind him, he pulled the snapshot of Saige from his back pocket. The edges were already worn from the number of times he'd taken it out, just to hold it, stare at it. But as he tenderly ran his thumb over her smiling face, he silently admitted that he couldn't settle for a picture any longer.

No, he wanted the flesh-and-blood woman.

He only hoped to God that he wasn't too late.

As she dried her hair after a long, hot shower that she'd hoped would ease her sore muscles, Saige stared into the steam-shrouded surface of the bathroom mirror, thinking how strange it was that after spending so much time on her own, she now had so many people taking an interest in her safety. She could only thank God for Molly, who had turned out to be a wonderful person to talk to, helping her to stay calm through it all. Ian's fiancée was like bottled sunshine, simmering with warmth, and Saige could easily see what had drawn her brother to the beautiful, vibrant blonde. Saige had especially enjoyed hearing about how Molly and Ian had first met. Amazingly, it had been Elaina's spirit that had been responsible for bringing the two of them together. Like Saige, Molly possessed an unusual gift of her own, and could actually communicate with ghosts in her sleep. Their mother's spirit had begged Molly to go to Colorado and warn Ian about the Casus that was coming after him, and the rest had been history. They'd fallen madly in love, and Ian seemed at peace in a way that Saige would have never thought possible.

When she hadn't been talking with Molly or working on the training field, she'd been in conversation with her brothers and the Watchmen about the Dark Markers, as well as the maps she'd found in Italy. And while Saige had answered their questions as best she could, there was still so much that she couldn't explain. She didn't know how the Markers had been scattered over the earth, or even how the maps had been created…or who had created them. She did, however, believe that the maps were only a few hundred years old, which meant they would have been created centuries after the original archives were lost.

Kierland and the others had asked to look over her research, and so she'd made arrangements to have her notebooks, which she'd stored at a research institute in Virginia before heading to Brazil, mailed to Colorado. If anyone had the patience and determination it would take to search through the reams of notes she'd taken over the years, she figured it was the men at Ravenswing. The more Saige learned about the Watchmen, the more they fascinated her. They were so different from one another, and yet in many ways, so alike. They each had their strengths, as well as their weaknesses, but they were all committed to helping the Merrick defeat the Casus.

And while she'd never believed it would actually happen, Saige was slowly getting to know her brothers again, which was strange and wonderful all at once. Still, there had already been a few moments when she'd found herself wanting to wring Riley's neck— the most provoking occurring when she'd learned that he'd left the first Marker in a freaking storage unit along with their mother's personal possessions. When Molly had told her, she'd nearly died, horrified to think how easily the ancient cross could have been stolen, and she couldn't help but be thankful that they still had it. Despite his determination to fight his destiny, Saige had no doubt that Riley's own awakening would begin any day now, and when the Casus came after him, he was going to *need* that Marker.

Especially now that Westmore and the Casus had the one she'd found in Brazil.

Blowing out a rough breath, she turned off the hair dryer and reached for the moisturizer Molly had given her, painfully aware of the worry twisting through her insides. Though she kept a constant eye on her cell phone, there'd been no calls or messages from Seth McConnell, and she was terrified that Jamison was already dead.

And while thoughts of her friend constantly filled her mind, she did everything in her power to avoid thinking about Quinn. Every time she did, Saige wanted to do something crazy. To completely lose control. To rage and scream and track him down, demanding to know why he couldn't find a way to trust in her.

His friends knew something was up. They'd even had the audacity to ask what she'd done to the poor guy, as if *she* was the one rejecting *him*. Swiping at the tears on her lashes, she sniffed, knowing that she had to be strong. But God, it wasn't easy. She just wanted to curl up into a ball and lick her wounds. Wanted to crawl to him and beg him to find a way to love her. Because while the Merrick wanted his blood with a primal, savage craving, the woman wanted his heart even more.

Stupid, stupid girl.

"You're an idiot," she muttered, opening the door and stepping into her darkened bedroom, the drawn curtains blocking out the vibrant, shimmering shades of twilight.

"I think you're brilliant," a dark, velvety voice rasped from the shadows. "Beautiful, too. And sexy as hell."

With trembling fingers, Saige reached out and flicked on the small lamp that sat on the nearby dressing table, unable to believe her eyes. Set on its dimmest setting, the lamp cast out just enough light for her to locate him in the room.

Quinn was lying on her bed, dressed in nothing but a faded pair of jeans, with one arm bent behind his head, the position accentuating the hard, sculpted musculature of his body, while his left leg dangled over the side of the mattress, his bare foot resting against the floor. It was an indolent, relaxed, mouthwateringly male pose. One of a strong, confident man comfortable in the space he took up, as if he had every right to be there, and she couldn't take her eyes off him.

"What are you doing here?" she whispered, her voice as hoarse as it was unsteady. Saige hadn't seen him since earlier that afternoon, when he'd watched her training from the roof of the garage. He hadn't even come down for dinner, and she'd found herself staring again and again at his empty chair, desperate for the sight of him.

And now, as if by some miracle, he was there. In her room. Looking as if he wanted to eat her alive.

Saige didn't know whether to pinch herself…or drop to her knees and thank God for answering her prayers.

Keeping his hungry gaze locked on hers, he rolled up off the bed in a smooth, animal movement, his muscles coiling and flexing beneath the burnished silk of his skin. She actually went light-headed watching the powerful, intoxicating play of muscle in his abdomen as he moved across the room, his body whipcord-lean and honed down to the hard, sleek lines of a predator. He was so beautiful, it hurt to take it all in, and she almost squinted, as if she were staring at the burning brilliance of the summer sun.

When he stood no more than a handful of inches away, he stopped and quietly said, "I've been such an ass."

"Wh-what?" she breathed out, blinking up at him, feeling as if she'd run headfirst into a brick wall, her brains pathetically scrambled from the blow.

His gaze burned like the dark, glittering brilliance of the midnight sky, his voice a low, provocative scrape of sound as he said, "I've tried to fight it from the moment I set eyes on you. But the thing is, I don't even know why I'm fighting anymore, Saige. So…I'm done."

"You are?" she whispered, the soft words thick with desire. She wanted him so badly she could barely stand there, her hunger for him unlike anything she'd ever known. One that grew more demanding with each moment that passed by, whether she was with him or not.

And one that she feared would never again leave her in peace.

"I just need to be close to you," he rasped, lifting his hand to trail his fingertips over the flushed curve of her cheek, threading them into her hair. "I don't care if I get hurt. I don't care about anything but being close to you." He stared down at her with a wild, primal intensity that stole her breath, his eyes heavy-lidded and hot as he said, "No more games. No more fears. Just yes or no, Saige. That's all you need to tell me. Yes? Or no?"

"I want you, Quinn. You know that I do." She trembled, blinking against the tears gathering in her eyes. "But I can't… I'm afraid to trust you. To believe that you won't walk out on me again."

She'd expected him to argue, but he simply dropped to his knees in front of her.

"Wh-what are you doing?" she stammered, staring with wide eyes as he slid his big hands beneath the hem of her towel, lifting the soft white cotton as he reached higher, taking hold of her hips.

"I'm addressing your fears," he told her in a rich, seductive rumble. Then he lowered his head and pressed the breathtaking heat of his mouth against the smooth inner surface of her thigh. "All of them," he breathed against her skin.

Her knees buckled, and he tightened his hold, helping her to stay upright. "I don't...I don't understand."

Flicking a quick look up at her flushed face, his eyes smoldered with a fierce, primal determination as he said, "I can sit and make promises all day, but in the end, they're only words. I figure the best way to get you to understand is to show you." The corner of his mouth kicked up sexily in a warm, crooked smile, and he murmured, "Don't they say that actions speak louder than words?"

"Who's they?" she gasped, shivering from the inside out, but he couldn't immediately answer. His mouth was too busy, his soft lips brushing against her inner thigh again, higher this time, just before his wicked, carnal tongue lapped hungrily across her sleek, moist folds.

"I don't know who they are," he growled against her screamingly sensitive flesh, "and I don't care. All I know is that I want you. More than I've ever wanted anything or anyone." He took another greedy, lingering lick, and shifted back, snagging her heavy-lidded gaze. "We're just going to have to take a leap of faith, Saige."

"Why do I have the feeling this isn't really happening?" she whispered. "That if I blink, you're going to just disappear on me?"

His mouth tilted at a rakish angle, making him look younger...*almost happy.* "Want me to pinch you?"

She wet her bottom lip, her breath coming faster, rushing past her lips with a soft, panting cadence. Shyness burned beneath the heat of her skin, but the hunger was too urgent to deny, too powerful to resist, compelling her to say things she never would have been brave enough to say before. "Call me shameless," she rasped, "but I can think of about a million better uses for those clever hands of yours."

A low, wicked rumble of laughter brushed against her thigh as he suddenly pressed two big, thick fingers up into her body. Her head shot back, a deep, primal sound of pleasure tearing from her throat. She was tight, but desire had already made her swollen and soft, the long, hot digits working past her resistance, and she lowered her head again as she gripped on to his shoulders, watching him with a greedy, avid gaze. Her body thrummed from the slow, sweet pulse of pleasure he created, as if a hot, liquid glow of bliss was burning in her belly.

"I want you inside me," she moaned, keenly aware of the sharp burn in her gums, knowing her fangs were preparing to descend. In the next instant, he surged to his feet and swept her into his arms, his breath heavy as he moved quickly toward the bed. Before her head had even settled against the pillow, the towel was pulled from her body and his hands were between her legs, his broad shoulders spreading her thighs. A low, guttural, animal sound vibrated in his chest as he opened her with his thumbs, and Saige knew he could see all of her. Everything. Every shockingly intimate pink detail. But she wasn't embarrassed. It felt…*right,* the explicit position magnifying her pleasure, simply because she could sense how much he loved it.

She felt his hot breath against her folds as he lowered his head, and then he pushed his tongue into her, kissing her slowly, hungrily, as if she were the most delicious thing he'd ever tasted. She wanted to hold on to it, make it last, stretch it out, but the instant his lips closed over the throbbing heat of her clit, she crashed. Hard. Her body arched, while wild cries broke from her throat that sounded like pain, a strange, hoarse mixture of curses and screams, the pleasure so intense she could feel her human self slipping away as the powerful Merrick rose up within her.

And he didn't ease up. He just kept pushing her into the pleasure, deeper…and deeper, until it'd swallowed her whole, completely destroying her. Saige wanted to hate how good he was, knowing it came from years of experience, but it felt too insanely wonderful to complain. He knew when to be greedy and relentless, and when to be soft, just resting the heat of his tongue against the tender entrance of her body…rubbing in soft, caressing strokes that made her shiver and melt. She floated, weightless, in that warm, thick pool of pleasure, feeling it pour through her system, soaking her in sensation…and when she came in another long, wrenching orgasm, swept up in a rushing, thrashing maelstrom of ecstasy, he growled, drinking her in until she lay there in the tangled sheets, her limbs sprawled, hands curled above her head in a boneless state of surrender. She felt him smile, and her eyes went hot with a warm rush of tears. It made him happy to take her apart…to destroy her, and his pleasure magnified her own, until Saige didn't know how she held it all inside, marveling that it didn't shoot out like glowing beams of light from her fingers and her toes.

He lifted over her then—a dark, savage god of a man—and braced himself on his fists, while she ran her hands up the sinewy strength of his forearms, over the bulging power of his biceps, then spread them over his hard, mouthwatering pecs. "God, I love your chest," she breathed out softly, thinking he had to be the most perfect man ever created.

He gave a low, sexy laugh, leaning down to take a hungry lick of one hard, candy-pink nipple as he rumbled, "You can't love it nearly as much as I love yours."

Trailing her right hand lower, Saige explored the hard, rugged strength of his body, until she reached his jeans. Watching him from beneath her lashes, she pulled her lower lip through her teeth and popped his top button open, then carefully slid down the zipper before slipping her hand inside—and unlike the night in the hotel, this time he didn't stop her. He wasn't wearing underwear, and the instant she touched his cock, he went completely still, not even breathing.

Biting her lip, Saige quickly pushed his jeans past his hips, then curled her hand around the heavy shape of him, loving how he felt. He was pulsing and hot in her hand, so big she knew she should be worried, but there was nothing but the sharp, searing burn of anticipation in her blood as she squeezed his thick, rigid length.

"The mighty Quinn, eh?" she murmured, not even recognizing the throaty purr that was her voice.

He snorted a purely wry, male sound, and she watched the rise of color spread over the beautiful arc of his cheekbones.

Tilting her head to the side, she grinned as she released him and placed her hands on his warm cheeks. "Are you blushing?"

"Men don't blush," he grunted, even as the color in his face flared hotter, making her giggle.

GOD, BUT IT FELT GOOD to hear her laugh again. Until that moment, Quinn hadn't realized how much he'd missed it. Seeing her smile, seeing her happy…it did something to him. Marked him in some strange, mystifying, wonderful way.

Bracing himself on one elbow, he lifted his other hand and pushed the warm, tender silk of her hair back from her face. "I have to be honest with you," he rasped, unable to disguise the gritty, husky thread of emotion in his words. "If we do this, Saige, it's more than sex."

She stared up at him through the thick weight of her lashes, her deep blue gaze luminous and tender and bright. "What do you mean?"

"I mean it's more than *now*. More than this moment. More than tonight."

Her mouth trembled, and he could read the fear in her eyes…the shadows of her own demons trying to take hold, but she didn't run as he'd feared. And as a shy, yielding smile spread across her soft mouth, something inside him eased.

Rubbing his mouth against hers, Quinn reached between them and gently thrust a finger inside the tight, swollen entrance of her body, then added another, slowly working them in and out, doing his best to prepare her.

"Wh-what are you waiting for?" she gasped, while he reached deeper, pulling a low, shivery moan from her throat.

"I'm getting you ready for me," he said through his teeth. She gripped his fingers so tightly, Quinn knew it was going to kill him when he felt all that drenched, cushiony silk clutching his cock. When her virginal body finally gave way to him and took him in.

"Trust me," she gasped, her voice hitching. "I'm ready. In fact, if you don't hurry, I'm going to get there without you."

His rich, velvety rumble of laughter made Saige smile, and he pulled his hand away, rubbing against her, letting her get used to the heat of him…the hardness. "Once I start, it's going to be a hard night. Are you sure this is what you want, Saige?"

She narrowed her eyes. "If you leave me now, I'll have to hunt you down and kill you. Understood?"

Without another word, he locked his smoky gaze with hers as he pushed against the natural resistance of her body. Breathing deeply, she ran her hands down the hard, tensed muscles of his back, enthralled by the power of him…by the primal, breathtaking beauty. With a small, wicked smile, she slipped her fingers across his sensitive flanks, loving the way his breath hissed through his teeth. His brow gleamed and she watched as a bead of sweat trailed from his dark hair, catching at the tip of his ebony brow.

"So tight," he choked out, his voice graveled by pleasure and brutal, grinding restraint as he carefully rocked into her. He was trying so hard not to hurt her, reining himself in, when Saige knew he wanted to thrust, driving that massive thickness inside her until she'd taken every inch of him. She'd hoped he'd go in easily, but her inexperience, as well as his size, made that impossible.

"Too small?" she panted, sinking her teeth into her lower lip as she clutched onto his broad, gleaming shoulders.

He gave her a tender smile, pushing her hair back from her face, before leaning down to press a heated kiss against the corner of her eye. "You're perfect. I love the way you're squeezing me, holding me so tightly. It feels incredible."

"It isn't…easy," she whispered.

The slow, crooked smile that spread across his firm mouth was the sexiest thing she'd ever seen. "We've never done anything easy, Saige. Did you really expect this to be any different?"

"I just… I'd hoped…"

Rolling his hips, he pressed in another hard, impossibly thick inch, and even though there was the expected pain, the feel of him inside her, penetrating her, was more amazing than anything she could have ever imagined. "Stop worrying," he rasped, rubbing his mouth against hers.

"THEN STOP CONTROLLING it and let go," she murmured against his lips, her breath sweet and warm and delicious, like her taste. "I just want you inside me. I want you to give me everything you've got, Quinn. All of it."

It was the soft, urgent pleading in her voice, in the feminine arch of her body beneath his, that completely undid him. With a groan, Quinn took her at her word and drove into her, burying himself deep, until he was surrounded by that lush, drenched heat. The tight, silken feel of her was so good his eyes damn near rolled back in his head, his muscles clenched, the pleasure so intense it was almost pain. With one arm braced beside her head, he ran his other hand down her side, over the delicate curve of her waist. Ravaging her mouth, he rubbed his tongue against hers, tasting every part of her, while his body just kept pushing deeper…and deeper. Her petal-soft lips were warm, the flavor of her mouth drugging his mind, while her body drove him wild. He curled his hand around her hip, sliding lower, along her thigh, catching her behind the knee. Lifting it higher, he worked himself into the damp, tender silk of her body with a powering, desperate rhythm, each slick, hammering thrust somehow better than the last. Every time he drove into her, she pulled him deeper, the provocative friction of his body moving in hers making slick, wet sounds against the sensual cadence of the storm that had blown in, raging beyond the windows.

"When you come," he growled, slamming into her so hard that she gasped, "take what you need, Saige. You won't hurt me."

"Now," she moaned against his throat as she gripped his head in her small, shaking hands, her orgasm crashing through her, stunning him with its power. *"I need you now."*

In the next instant, she sank her fangs deep into his flesh, her low, hungry growl vibrating against his skin, and Quinn erupted in the most violent release he'd ever known. It scraped down his nerve endings, pulling animal sounds from his throat as the ecstasy pounded its way through his body with grinding, explosive force, nearly turning him inside out as it went on…and on in a relentless, mind-shattering assault. It was like being torn apart with pleasure, and then put back together in a way that was wonderful and right and new.

And in the end, all he could do was hold on, determined to never let go.

THEY CLUNG TO EACH OTHER afterward like shipwreck victims washed up on shore, panting and boneless in a melted sprawl of pleasure. After what seemed like a timeless forever, he climbed from the bed, stepped out of his jeans and turned off the lamp. Then he walked to the window and pulled open the curtains. With his body bathed in the ethereal, milky glow of moonlight, Saige watched as he moved across the floor, toward the bathroom, all those long, mouthwatering muscles shifting beneath the burnished beauty of his skin. He came back moments later with a hot washcloth, then spread her out on the sex-warm sheets, arranging her as if she was his to do with as he pleased, his touch gentle as he stroked the soft cotton over her body. When he was finished, he tossed the washcloth aside and leaned over her in the moonlit darkness, fastening his wickedly sinful mouth over one nipple…then the other. It pulled an almost frightened sound from her throat, her mind stunned at how quickly he could reawaken her hungers…her desires. A look. A breath. A touch. His taste sat on her tongue like the most perfect treasure, succulent and warm and delicious, the Merrick satisfied and full. And yet, she wanted to feel his big, beautiful body penetrating her again. Claiming her. Driving her wild.

Slipping his fingers between her legs, he pressed his open mouth against the pounding beat of her heart and asked, "Can you take me again?"

"Always," she whispered, already desperate for him as he moved over her, pushing back into her with a thick, possessive stroke.

And later, in the quiet darkness, he finally told her about the torture he'd suffered at the hands of the Collective. About how they'd hacked his wings from his body, leaving the scars that lined his back, as well as the horror of watching them murder Janelle. Saige wrapped her arms around him, wishing she could take away the pain, hating that they'd both been put through such hell. Whatever Janelle's sins, the woman hadn't deserved to die the way that she had.

"I'm sorry I've been such a bastard," he admitted, holding her against his chest. "I never meant to hurt you, Saige. I've just—"

"Shh," she whispered, shifting over him to press a tender, seeking kiss against his lips. "I understand. I'm just thankful to have you here with me now."

He growled low in his throat and quickly rolled her to her back, pushing his way between her legs as if it was where he belonged. Holding her face in his hot, callused hands, he deepened the kiss, pulling the pleasure up out of her until she was clinging to him, somehow even more desperate for his possession than she'd been before.

"I can't believe you and your thick skull finally gave in," she panted, giving him a shy, teasing smile.

"Lucky for you," he murmured, settling deeper between her thighs, "my skull isn't the only thing that's thick."

She was still smiling when he thrust back inside her, shoving deep…deeper, so hard and thick and hot that it stole her breath. He was big enough that he would never slide in easily, but she didn't care. She loved the way he had to work at getting into her, putting his strength and skill behind the task, and her back arched, the sensation of fullness unlike anything she could have ever imagined. Perfect. Blissful. She felt connected. She felt…right, as if this was how she was meant to exist, with Quinn inside her, a part of her, making her whole. The quiet hours of darkness, the circle of her arms, even the hollows of her palms. He filled all the empty spaces in her life. Even in her body and her heart and her soul.

In the silent hours of the night, he took her again and again, proving just how demanding...how hungry he could be. Against the headboard. On her hands and her knees with his teeth clamped posses-sively onto the tender juncture between her neck and shoulder. At one point they even tumbled off the foot of the bed, and he took her on the floor, powering his hard, beautiful body into hers until husky, feral screams of pleasure were tearing from her throat. She didn't know how he did it, but each time was somehow better than the last, as if the bone-melting pleasure just kept growing...becom-ing sharper, deeper. He left no part of her un-touched...unclaimed, and despite the soreness in her body, she reveled in the visceral, carnal power of his possession. He didn't scare her. How could he, when he was everything that she'd ever wanted? Ever needed.

"You know," she whispered when they were once again cuddling in each other's arms, spent from passion, "according to my mother's stories about my ancestors, I'm meant to find a Merrick male to protect me now that I've awakened."

His voice was a deep, gritty rumble of sound in the darkness as he held her tighter, saying, "Well, that's too damn bad, because you've got me."

The sheer, breathtaking possessiveness of his words made her smile, but as she closed her eyes, Saige couldn't help but wonder how long it would last.

CHAPTER NINETEEN

Thursday, 5:00 a.m.

WITH HER PASSION-WRECKED BODY still thrumming with a slow, lingering pulse of pleasure, Saige pulled the soft afghan tighter around her T-shirt-covered shoulders. Walking to the wall of windows in the sitting room of her suite, she stared out at the early streaks of dawn cutting through the storm-dark sky. The cold of the Colorado morning matched her mood. She was freezing without Quinn's heat, but restlessness had sent her from the comfort of his arms.

The night had been nothing short of amazing, her worry over Jamison's safety the only thing marring its perfection. She couldn't stop wondering where he was, her sense of guilt growing worse with each moment that went by. Here she'd spent the most wonderful hours of her life with a man she'd fallen helplessly in love with, and her friend was somewhere out there, suffering God only knew what.

She'd brought her new cell phone out of the bedroom with her, wanting to make a quick call to check in with Inez and Rubens, just to make sure they were okay. She was ready to key in the international calling code for Brazil when the phone suddenly vibrated in her hand. Quickly hitting the talk button, her heart hammered in her chest as she lifted the phone to her ear.

"Hello," she whispered, holding the small phone so tightly, she was amazed it didn't crack.

"It's Seth," rasped a deep, familiar voice. "We have a problem."

Saige sank down onto the edge of the love seat, sick with fear. "What do you mean?"

"They know I talked," he grunted, and then, before she could comment, he said, "Did Haley wear a signet ring?"

Visions of Javier's mangled hands slithered through her mind, and she bit back a throaty cry. "Yes," she answered in a soft voice. "On his left hand. His family crest. A lion with a bow and arrow."

"That's how I know I've been made," he muttered. "When I opened the door of my motel room a few minutes ago, I found a package they'd left for me. The ring was inside."

As well as Jamison's finger, she thought, unable to hold back the hot rush of tears. "I don't believe this," she groaned, squeezing her eyes tight as if she could block out the horrific images filling her head, but they were unstoppable.

"Saige." She could tell from his tone that she hadn't heard the worst of it. "There's a note with the...ring. They said if I want the rest of him, I have to bring them the first Marker, as well as you."

"Oh, Christ," she breathed out, opening her eyes as she pushed her hair back from her forehead. "Where are they keeping him?"

"I still don't know. The note tells me where to meet them here in town, once I have what they want. You need to convince Quinn to talk to me. I still have some men from my team who are loyal—ones who don't like the way this is playing out any more than I do. Maybe together we can combine forces and search the mountains. If we're lucky, we might be able to find him in time."

"And if you aren't," she shot back, "they'll end up butchering him."

"If I knew where he was, I'd go on after him," he said, his voice thick with frustration. "But they could be anywhere in these mountains. If you want him back, you're going to have to convince the Watchmen to work with me."

Chewing on the corner of her mouth, she tried to decide what to do. "Why would you risk your life for someone you don't even know, McConnell?" she asked, hoping like crazy that she wasn't making a mistake in trusting this man.

"Think what you like," he grunted, "but I'm not an indiscriminate killer."

"You've hunted people like me almost your entire life," she quietly argued.

"I'm not going to stand here and justify my work to you," he countered in a raw, gritty slide of words. "All I can say is that sometimes it's not as easy to let go of the past as we'd like."

Pressing her hand to her watery eyes, Saige snuffled a soft thread of laughter under her breath.

"Did I say something funny?" he snapped.

She shook her head, looking toward the half-open bedroom door. She could see Quinn's long body sprawled across the bed, only half-covered by the tangled sheet, and a smile touched the corner of her mouth as she said, "It's just that you remind me of Quinn. I wonder if you two know just how alike you are."

There was a moment of silence, and then he finally said, "I regret what happened to him. If I had known in time, I would have put a stop to it."

"So you didn't know what they had planned?" she asked, reaching for a tissue and scrunching it under her nose.

"I don't condone torture or rape, and I only kill those who deserve it," he replied with a tired sigh. "Quinn…he's not what I thought he was."

"No, he's not," she murmured, thinking of all he had suffered at the hands of the Collective, and knowing in that moment what she had to do.

She looked back toward the bedroom, understanding damn well that he might never forgive her. Odds were that he wouldn't even understand. She racked her brain for a way to do it differently, but there was nothing. Jamison was in this mess because of her, and there wasn't a chance in hell she was going to put Quinn in danger, as well. Not after everything he'd already suffered at the hands of the Collective. And not when she knew they would kill him if they ever got their hands on him again.

"Quinn will never agree to work with you," she

said, moving to her feet as she slipped the afghan off her shoulders, then looked around for the jeans she'd borrowed from Molly. "And by the time the two of you are done arguing, Jamison will be dead. I have another idea. But you're going to need to pick me up. I'll meet you in half an hour where the road that leads up to Ravenswing turns off the highway. You do know where it is, don't you?"

"What are you talking about?" he rasped.

"The road," she repeated, finally spotting the jeans. "Do you know where it is?"

"Yeah, I know," he muttered. "But exactly what are you planning?"

"I'm going to make my way down to meet you. Alone."

"Are you crazy?" he grunted. "Quinn will never agree to it."

"I don't want Quinn to know," she whispered, "which is why I'll be sneaking out before everyone around here wakes up."

"You *are* crazy!" he snarled.

"Just make sure you bring the ring with you," she told him, grabbing a clean pair of socks from the backpack she'd left on the chair. "I need to see it."

He gave a harsh, guttural grunt, and she could just imagine the look on his face. "There isn't anything on it that's going to help you," he muttered. "You already know exactly what it looks like."

Sitting down to slip on her boots, Saige said, "You're just going to have to trust me, McConnell."

A heavy silence fell over the line again, and then

he quietly said, "Why do I get the feeling there's something you're not telling me?"

"There's a lot I'm not telling you," she replied, careful to keep her voice low. "But you're just going to have to deal with it if you're set on helping me get Jamison back."

"And what are you going to do after you see the ring?" he asked, the resignation in his deep voice telling her that she'd won.

It depended on what the ring told her, but she wasn't going to waste time explaining it all to McConnell. Instead, she simply said, "Hopefully I'm going to know where he is, and then I'm going after him, with or without your help."

A low, strained rumble of laughter echoed through the connection, and she fought down her temper, knowing that she didn't have time for it.

"You need to let Quinn know what you're up to," he told her.

She looked back into the other room, where Quinn lay sprawled like a dark god across the snowy-white linens, so beautiful that it made her chest hurt just to look at him. "I can't."

"Because you know there isn't a chance in hell that he'd let you go through with this," he said with a hard, heavy dose of impatience.

"This is *my* mess," she argued, wedging the phone between her ear and her shoulder as she twisted her hair into a ponytail. "And one that I don't expect him to risk his life over. So just get your ass up the mountain and come get me."

He cursed something foul under his breath, then muttered, "This isn't going to get Quinn on my side."

Saige rolled her eyes as she reached behind her head to unhook the silver chain she wore around her neck, its small, silver compass shimmering in the early-morning light. "I hate to break it to you," she drawled, "but you weren't exactly getting him on your side anyway."

He sighed. "It was worth a shot."

"Yeah, well, I'm afraid Quinn clings on to the past as much as you do."

"Maybe," he murmured. "But I got the impression that he was finally starting to look to the future."

She swallowed, unable to scrape out a response, and was about to disconnect the call when he suddenly said, "Saige."

"Yeah?"

"You're not anything like Janelle," he said. "I just... I hope Quinn realizes that."

"Me, too," she whispered.

But as she disconnected the call and crept quietly back to the bed, staring down at the twin pale scars on Quinn's back, Saige knew she could very well be throwing away whatever chance at happiness she had with the dark, breathtaking Watchman. She closed her eyes, giving him a silent, tear-filled goodbye, and placed her necklace on his pillow.

Then she grabbed a sweater and quietly slipped away.

WAITING IN THE THICK forest that surrounded the large, isolated timber-framed house, Quinn struggled to stay calm…focused. The others probably thought he'd finally gone out of his mind, but he didn't care. He knew this was the right thing to do, just as he knew that he'd fallen helplessly, head-over-heels in love with Saige Buchanan.

And she was in that goddamn house with the monsters.

Just stay in control. Wait for the signal. And then you can go in there and rip those bastards to pieces.

After searching every corner of Ravenswing for her that morning, Quinn had finally called the others together, telling them that she'd left the compound…and taken the first Dark Marker with her. As everyone had started to argue, he'd felt fractured, like something had broken inside him. They'd shown her how to work the alarm, so they knew *how* she'd managed to slip out undetected. What they couldn't understand was *why* she'd done it, and the arguments had raged.

"How much do we really know about her?"

"If she's in trouble, it doesn't make sense that she wouldn't ask for help."

"We know they need her for the maps. Maybe they made her an offer she couldn't refuse, like they did with Janelle. Her own life for the Marker and the codes."

"Hell, she could lay our security out for them. They might even already be on their way here."

While Kierland had sat there silently taking it all in, the Buchanans had argued with Shrader and Kellan, until Quinn had finally just told them all to shut up. With the silver compass and chain she'd left on his pillow clutched in his hard fist, he'd walked to one of the tall kitchen windows and stared out at the cloud-scarred stretch of sky, the rain falling in a heavy, pounding rhythm. Crossing his arms, he'd thought over the hours Saige had spent with him, beneath him, giving of her body so sweetly…so freely. He remembered the way she'd so beautifully surrendered to the dark aggression of his physical hungers, never shying away from him, no matter what he'd asked of her. Remembered how she'd fed so provocatively from his blood, feeding the Merrick part of her nature. And as he'd held her in his arms, she'd told him the story of the delicate silver compass, explaining how Elaina had given it to her as a gift on her sixteenth birthday. It was meant to always help her find her way home, to the place where her heart belonged, and as he squeezed his palm tighter around the necklace, he finally understood why she'd left it for him. She was telling him something significant with that small, simple gesture, and in that moment, he found the faith to believe in her.

Once he got past his initial anger that she had run from him yet again and was thinking clearly, it hadn't been hard to figure out that McConnell had called her cell phone. If she'd been offered the opportunity to help Jamison, Quinn knew she'd have done everything in her power to rescue her friend. Her sense of honor was too strong to allow her to do any differently.

He could live with that. Hell, he could even live with her determination to put the Marker above everything else in her life, just so long as he could live with *her.*

If he lost her… No, he couldn't think about that. If

he did, he was going to lose control and go charging in like a madman, and he couldn't risk it when her life hung in the balance.

Cutting a dark look toward McConnell, who had taken up a position to his left within the thick cover of the forest, the soldier's dark green gaze focused intently on the house, Quinn struggled to hold on to his rage. It was the bastard's fault that Saige was in this mess. But then, the only way he'd been able to find this place—which they believed was Westmore's temporary headquarters—was because McConnell had called the cell phone that Saige had left back at Ravenswing and told him where she was. Quinn had slipped the phone into his pocket when he found it sitting on the dresser in her bedroom, and McConnell's call had come in while he'd been standing there at the kitchen window holding her necklace. With the heavy rains that had only recently stopped completely washing away her scent, there wasn't a chance he'd have been able to track her to this remote location, which meant Quinn owed the guy one hell of a thank-you. Of course, he also wanted to kill him with his bare hands for getting her caught up in this nightmare to begin with.

According to McConnell, Saige had told him where they could find Jamison after she'd touched the ring that had been left at his motel, along with three of the archaeologist's fingers. And while McConnell hadn't understood how she'd done it, he'd followed her directions, which had taken them to this house. But while he and his men had surveyed the area, she'd slipped away from them. When he couldn't track her down, he'd finally made the call to her cell phone, hoping to get through to someone at Ravenswing. Then he and his men had pulled back and waited for Quinn and the others to arrive.

Quinn had no doubt that Saige had snuck inside the house to find Jamison. But the fact she hadn't made it back out meant she'd been caught.

No, don't think about it. She's going to be okay. She's tough.

"I don't have time to sit here waiting for your men to make their move," he snarled under his breath, glaring at McConnell. "Saige is in there with those bastards."

"Okay, then," Shrader drawled from just behind him. "All those in favor of storming the castle gates now, say aye."

"Shut up," he growled, looking over his shoulder to scowl at the smirking Watchman who wore a shirt with the picture of a squirrel and two giant acorns, the caption reading My Nuts Are Bigger Than Yours. "I'm in no mood to deal with your shit today, Aiden."

"You say that now," the Watchman murmured, "but after the fight, I'll be golden and you'll be kissing my ass."

"You help us get my sister out of there alive," Ian rasped, shooting Aiden a sharp smile, his dark blue eyes glowing with the fury of his fully awakened Merrick, "and I'll kiss any goddamn thing you want."

Shrader's tawny brows rose high on his forehead. "Was that actually a joke?"

"Don't pay any attention to him," Riley muttered,

looking as grim as Quinn. "The stress has gone to his head."

"I'll move in closer and see what the holdup is," McConnell grunted, staying within the cover of the forest as he slipped silently toward the back of the house, where his men were supposed to be setting up a diversion that would allow them to sneak inside.

Kierland shifted closer to Quinn's side, his voice low as he said, "You doing okay?"

He was doing as well as he could be, considering he was terrified out of his ever-loving mind.

"I'm a bastard," he growled, wondering where she was in the house. What she was doing. If she was scared. Hurt. Afraid. "I never even told her how I feel about her."

"Yeah? Well, if I were you," his best friend said, "I'd remedy that the second we get her back."

Blowing out a rough breath, he slanted the auburn-haired Watchman a tense look. "Thanks for backing me up at the compound," he rasped, thinking of how Kierland had stood with him when he'd announced that he was coming after her.

"I've known you long enough to trust your instincts," Kierland told him, his light green eyes glowing with a cold, deadly fire as he looked toward the house. "And Shrader and Kellan feel the same way. They just don't want to see you get hurt."

"The only thing that will hurt me is losing her," he said through his clenched teeth, and no sooner had the last word left his mouth, than a huge fireball exploded in the woods behind the house, the brilliant orange flames billowing toward the sky like a dragon's fiery breath. It took only seconds for Westmore's men to respond, and the instant they heard Seth's unit returning gunfire, Quinn looked over his shoulder. "You all know the drill," he grunted.

"Gut the bad guys and save the day," Shrader drawled, a gleaming 9mm held tight in his right hand, while the white tips of his lethal tiger fangs gleamed beneath the curve of his upper lip.

"I don't give a damn about the day," Quinn growled. "Just find Haley, the maps and the second Marker, and then get the hell out of there. I'll get Saige."

Without another word, the Watchmen and Buchanans went in motion, knowing exactly what they had to do. It took only seconds for Quinn to slip into the sprawling, two-story house from a side entrance, and he instantly found himself battling two of Westmore's men. The soldiers fought hard, but the fury of his beast was in full possession, and he quickly disarmed them, before ripping his talons across their throats. While the others searched the main level and climbed the stairs to the upper floor, Quinn caught a faint trace of Saige's mouthwatering scent and headed toward the basement, where he ran into another massive, bulky guard. Wasting no time, he quickly dealt with the bastard, then began a frantic search of the dark, dirty chambers that lined the long hallway. When he broke open the last cell at the end of the corridor and caught a glimpse of dark, reddish-brown hair, his heart almost stopped. Saige was huddled in the corner, and as he rushed toward her, retracting his deadly talons, she lifted her head, staring up at him as if in shock.

"Quinn!" she sobbed, breaking instantly into tears.

"Are you okay? Did they hurt you?" he asked, his deep voice ravaged by emotion, and she shook her head while he helped her to her feet, running his big hands over her body, looking for any sign of serious injury.

"No…I'm fine," she said huskily, the tears streaming down her face, her hands clutching at his shoulders. "I still have the Marker on me, and believe it or not, I haven't even seen Westmore or the Casus yet. Where's Jamison? Is he okay? Is he still alive? The soldiers who put me in here wouldn't tell me anything!"

"The others are getting him." He eyed the red, swollen scratches gouged into her delicate cheeks, and growled, "If you have the Marker, how the hell did they cut your face?"

She winced, her tone dry as she said, "The talisman only protects against the Casus. After I got inside, I managed to sneak past Westmore's men, but then I ran into their redheaded little she-devil." She indicated the small, dank cell with a jerk of her chin, adding, "And that's how I ended up in here."

"Christ," he rasped unsteadily, pushing her hair back from her face, his own eyes feeling suspiciously hot and damp. She hadn't been there long, but he knew they'd been lucky as hell that she'd been left alone. It was frightening enough just thinking of her going up against such a deadly assassin. "Do you have any idea how easily Spark could have killed you?"

"Don't worry," she told him with a small, watery smile. "I didn't go down without a fight. With my Merrick fully charged, I was able to hold my own against her. And I'd have won, too, if Westmore's men hadn't shown up and thrown me in here."

A hoarse, pained laugh jerked from his chest. "You are something else, Buchanan."

"That's good to know, considering I feel like hell right now." The sounds of distant gunfire echoed through the house, reminding them that they were still in danger. He was getting ready to lift her in his arms and get her out of there when she asked, "What are you doing here, Quinn? How did you find me?"

"McConnell was smart enough to call me as soon as he realized you'd slipped away from him," he growled, his relief at finding her alive slowly giving way to his anger and frustration. "What the hell were you thinking?"

SAIGE RAN HER TONGUE across her bottom lip, unable to believe that he was actually there with her, then quietly said, "I wasn't planning on doing it this way, but when we got here, it was obvious that Seth and his men were outnumbered. While they were discussing the best way to get in, a guy in fatigues walked out of the house. He left the back door open and started working on one of their Jeeps. I know it was probably stupid, but I thought that if I could sneak in quietly on my own, then maybe I could find Jamison before anyone knew I was there." She stared up at him, hoping he could understand. "I didn't have any choice but to try, Quinn. I *had* to help Jamison."

Holding her jaw, he rubbed his thumb against the corner of her bruised mouth in a tender, caring gesture. "And so you just decided to handle everything on your own? You couldn't have asked me for help?"

"I did the only thing I could think of," she told him, her stomach pulling tight as she thought of the horror he'd endured during his torture. "I didn't want you to be a part of this—didn't want you anywhere near the Collective. You've already suffered enough at their hands, and if I have my way, you'll never get anywhere near them again for as long as we live."

"What about the others?" he grunted. "I wasn't the only one who could have helped you."

Shaking her head, she tightened her grip on his shoulders, unwilling to let go of him, as if afraid he might slip away from her…or that she would wake up, finding that this had all been an illusion, a dream. "I knew if I asked Kierland or my brothers for help, they'd only end up telling you. And making sure you stayed out of this was more important to me than—"

"Your own life?" he growled, cutting her off. "Christ, Saige. Do you have any idea how lucky we are that you haven't been killed already? If it wasn't for the fact that Westmore needs you to read the maps, you'd already be dead and there would have been nothing I could do to save you."

She took a deep breath, then forced herself to ask, "So did the other Watchmen convince you to come after me, then?"

His jaw worked, and she could see him struggling to control his temper. "Actually," he finally rasped, arching one of his dark, silky brows, "it was the other way around."

Her eyes widened, the sound of her pulse rushing through her ears like the crashing fury of an ocean surf as she said, "You mean…you didn't…you didn't think the worst?"

"That you had run off to make a deal for your life or for Jamison's, the way Janelle did?"

She nodded, and something shifted through his eyes, like a burst of light smoldering behind the midnight beauty of his gaze. "Maybe for five seconds," he confessed, the corner of his mouth kicking up in a sexy, devilish grin, "but then I realized there wasn't a chance in hell that you're not madly in love with me."

The laugh that burst from her chest caught her by surprise, and she lifted her hand, pressing it against her lips. "Is that right?"

"You damn sure better be after what you put me through," he muttered in a low rumble, slipping one big, warm hand beneath her sweater to rest against her lower back.

"I admit it was stupid, Quinn, but I didn't do it to hurt you," she told him, wishing there was some way to show him how much he meant to her. "I was only trying to keep you safe."

The light in his eyes flared, rising into a warm, fiery glow as he said, "And you think dying on me is going to keep me safe? Do you have any idea what it would do to me to lose you?" He took her face in his big hands, rubbing his thumbs in the salty heat of her tears, and she could have sworn she could feel him trembling. "You're going to be the death of me, woman. And the instant we get home, I'm turning you over my knee for putting me through this."

Despite the tightness in her chest, she gave another soft, husky laugh. "You're welcome to try, but don't get too cocky. Now that my Merrick has fed, I can be pretty vicious when I need to be."

He gave her an arrogant grin, and Saige could see the rise of a primal, breathtaking desire tightening his expression. "I'm still bigger," he murmured in a devastatingly sexy voice, "and a hell of a lot meaner."

"And yet, I know you'd rather die than ever hurt me," she said with a soft smile.

"You scared the hell out of me, Saige," he rasped, the stark words sounding as if they'd been torn out of him. He slipped his hands under the heavy weight of her hair, holding her trapped as he lowered his head and gently, hungrily kissed his way into her mouth. "But I wouldn't change a single thing about you," he breathed against her lips. "You're the bravest woman I've ever known."

Tears flooded her eyes, spilling in a hot, endless rush that she couldn't control. "I thought you were going to hate me," she whispered. "God, I was so afraid, Quinn."

"I'll always come for you, honey, and you aren't ever going to lose me." He pulled her against his body, pressing a kiss to her temple as he said, "And after this, I hope there's no way in hell you'll ever doubt how much I trust you. But it would be nice if you could find it in your heart to give me a little trust, too. It would add years to my life if you didn't go rushing into these things on your own anymore."

"I'm sorry," she whispered against his chest. "I was just... I didn't want anything to happen to you."

With his thumbs under her chin, he tilted up her face, a tender, masculine smile curving his beautiful mouth as he said, "I'm a grown man, Saige, and although I don't like to brag, I can be a real badass when I need to be. So you don't have to keep trying to protect me."

She swallowed the tears burning in her throat and quietly said, "After what they did to you, how can you think I'd ever ask you to get anywhere near them?"

"Saige, listen. Being by your side and what happened to me with Janelle are two completely different things," he rumbled, rubbing his thumbs against the tender edges of her jaw. "You'd never turn against me, never set me up. No matter what happens, they won't ever get their claws into me again."

"Oh, I wouldn't be so sure about that," a deep, husky voice drawled from the doorway, and Saige stiffened with fear, realizing their time had just run out.

CHAPTER TWENTY

TWISTING AROUND, Quinn growled low in his throat at the sight of Gregory and Royce stalking into the cell in their human forms. "Is it just me, or does it feel like Christmas this morning?" Royce quipped with a wide, gloating grin as he settled his pale, ice-blue gaze on Saige. "And here's my juicy little present."

Gregory lifted his nose, sniffing the air. "Mmm," he murmured. "Somebody smells...*different.*" He flashed Saige a hard smile and stepped farther into the room. "I knew the wimp's fingers would do the trick, bringing you right to us. I would have bitten them off, the same way I did with the little Brazilian's, but Westmore wanted to keep him alive, and I couldn't guarantee that I wouldn't finish the job once I got the taste of him in my mouth." Rolling his shoulder in a cocky gesture, his smile widened as he said, "So I cut them off with a pair of pruning shears instead."

"You son of a bitch," she screeched, and Quinn moved in front of her, praying like hell that her Merrick was going to be able to help him when things got ugly. Which he'd have been willing to bet was going to be any second now.

"You can't kill her," he growled, keeping a careful eye on both men as they came closer. "Westmore still needs her to read the maps."

"But ol' Westmore isn't here, now is he?" Gregory murmured, his eyes burning with a cold, hate-filled fire. "Seems he was called away on some urgent business this morning. Left orders for all of us to clear this place and bring little Saige here to his new head-quarters. A place where no one is ever going to be able to find her."

"It's a hell of a journey, and that means we'll be free to have our fun with her, so long as she's still breath-ing when we get her there," Royce added, wiping his wrist over his damp, smiling lips. "Though, to be honest, at the moment I don't really give a damn what Westmore wants. I'm starting to think he can figure those bloody maps out on his own," he rasped, his pale eyes glazed as he leered at Saige with a sicken-ing look of lust, and Quinn's talons surged through the tips of his fingers with a hissing burn of pain. He could feel his rage building, could feel the primal power of his fury pumping through his system, urging him to tear out their throats. With the heightened senses of his beast, he could feel the heat of their bodies…smell the scent of their blood. He knew they were a threat to his woman, and Quinn had never felt a more visceral, primitive need to destroy as he did in that moment.

Keeping his voice low, he said, "Whatever you do, Saige, don't let them take you out of here."

He wanted to tell her more, but Gregory suddenly came at him in a blur of speed, and they crashed to the hard, concrete floor. It felt like he'd been hit with a truck, and he struggled to pull air into his lungs as he shoved up with the heel of his right hand, connecting with Gregory's nose. Blood spurted, and the Casus threw back his head, revealing a long, lethal-looking set of fangs.

From the corner of his eye, he watched as Royce moved toward Saige. He couldn't hear what the bastard said, but Saige reacted by snarling at him, and Quinn roared her name as the son of a bitch back-handed her across the face with a powerful blow that cracked her head to the side.

WITH THE METALLIC TASTE of her blood filling her mouth, Saige heard Quinn give a savage shout of outrage, at the same time she felt the darkness inside her spread itself open, like a flower unfurling beneath the golden, pulsing rays of the sun, burning red against the backs of her eyelids.

Lifting her lashes, she stared at the Casus who'd struck her. "You're going to be sorry for that," she rasped, lifting her hand to wipe her bloodied lip.

"After all the trouble you've put me through, you're the one who's gonna be sorry, you mouthy little bitch."

"Not when I'm sending your ass back to hell, I'm not," she drawled, giving him a sharp smile.

"You know, it's gonna be fun breaking you of that smart mouth. If you last that long." He lifted his hand, bracing it against the base of her throat, where her pulse beat out a wild, reckless rhythm. His lips curled as he squeezed, waiting for her to scream with fear, but Saige wasn't about to give him the satisfaction.

Tilting his head to the side, he pondered her with a curious expression. "Should I use my claws, then?"

"You can try," she whispered, "but they won't do you much good."

"Is that right?" he snorted, withdrawing his hand as he took a step forward. He was so close that she had to tilt back her head to stare up at him, the thick scent of his body making her stomach churn. "Westmore already took the second Marker from your little friend, and Spark said you didn't bring the first one with you."

"Well, I guess that'll teach you to listen to pretty little morons, then, won't it?" She laughed, stepping back as she reached down and pulled the Marker from the inside of her right boot, where she'd kept it hidden. Looping its black velvet cord around her wrist, she straightened as she said, "Oops, looks like she was wrong. Imagine that."

"You wouldn't be stupid enough to bring the real Marker with you," he snarled, staring at the ornate cross with narrowed eyes. "Not after you've already lost the other one."

Softly, she said, "Actually, it seemed like a pretty good idea, since I'm planning on killing you with it."

"You're lying," Royce huffed in a low voice. "There's no way that's a real Marker."

Sensing his uneasiness, Saige stared into his pale eyes and slowly smiled. "You don't really believe that. I can see the fear in your eyes. I'd be willing to bet you can feel its power as easily as I can," she murmured, suddenly striking the Casus against his chest with a powerful side kick. Though her body didn't experience the same transformation that Ian's did, she was still much stronger than a human female. Strong enough, in fact, to send Royce crashing back on his ass with her kick.

Holding the cross in her hand, she said, "And you're going to find out just how real this is any second now."

THOUGH HE HAD HIS hands full dodging Gregory's lethal claws and deadly fangs, Quinn couldn't take his eyes off Saige as she took hold of the cross just like Ian had shown her, holding it pressed against the palm of her right hand. She gasped, and he knew the Marker was hurting her, melting into her flesh as it began to transform her arm into a deadly weapon that could destroy the Casus.

The blood she'd taken from him in the night had done its job, giving her the power she needed in order for her Merrick to fully rise up within her. She glowed, primal and wild, her eyes bright, her body moving like a sleek, predatory cat slinking through the jungle.

As she stalked toward Royce, the Casus crawled back on his hands and knees, his ice-blue eyes now wide with fear. "Help me kill her!" he shouted at Gregory, but the other Casus had started to back away from Quinn, one claw-tipped hand holding his bleeding side, while he took a single step toward the door...and then another.

"What are you doing?" Royce growled. "Don't you dare run out on me!"

"I was going to kill you myself," Gregory muttered, eyeing Saige's glowing arm with a bitter, scornful look, "so I might as well let the little bitch do it for me. And unlike my brother, it seems I know when to pick my fights, and when to wait for another day." His lip curled as he lifted his furious gaze to Saige's face. "Better watch your back, Merrick. I'm not finished with you yet."

And then he turned, stalking out of the room. Quinn took a step forward, wanting to go after the bastard and drag him back, but then he looked back at Royce, who was moving to his feet, his powerful body beginning to contort, ripping the seams of his clothing as he shifted into his monstrous Casus form.

"Don't get too close to him!" Quinn shouted, suddenly taking hold of Saige's arm. It was burning to the touch, as if he'd placed his hand in the melting heat of a flame, and he instantly let go, grunting from the pain.

Keeping her glowing gaze on Royce, she said, "You have to trust me, Quinn. I'm not weak. I can handle this asshole."

"I know that," he growled, his deep voice full of anger and fear, as well as an unmistakable thread of pride. "But that doesn't mean you have to do it alone."

He expected her to argue, but she surprised him with a quick, hard smile. "Then whaddya say we take this guy together?"

"Just…be careful," he grunted, terrified for her safety as he moved to his right, helping her to corner the growling Casus.

"You, too," Saige whispered, and then they moved in together. It all happened so fast, it was difficult to keep track of the monster's slashing claws and sharp, snapping jaws. Royce fought hard to hold them off, striking at Saige again and again, but the power of the Marker protected her flesh, his claws simply sliding off her body, unable to penetrate her skin. Though she did her best to help him, Quinn did the majority of the fighting, ripping his shirt off and using his massive wings to block the Casus's strikes. It took her breath away, the powerful, predatory way that Quinn moved his big, muscular body. With his dangerous-looking talons, he clawed at the Casus's thick, gray skin, again and again, carefully avoiding Royce's lethal bite, which she knew could so easily kill him. She was desperate to end the battle as quickly as possible, hating that while she was protected by the cross, Quinn could still be harmed.

The Marker burned against her palm like holy hell, melting her skin, and she struggled to work through the pain, trying to help, while mostly feeling as if she should just stay out of Quinn's way, considering he was such a brilliant fighter. Though she hadn't been able to watch him fight Gregory, since her attention had been focused on Royce, it was clear to her now why the Raptors were considered such a vicious breed of shifter.

Letting out an unearthly howl, the Casus suddenly lunged for Quinn's throat, but he was too fast, easily avoiding the attack. "Get ready!" he shouted, and in the next instant, he used a roundhouse kick to smash his booted foot into the side of Royce's muzzled snout, driving the Casus face-first against the wall. Quickly pinning the monster's body against the rough concrete surface, he growled, "Now!" and Saige rushed forward, slamming the Marker against the base of Royce's thick, muscular neck, just like Ian had told her to do. Fire instantly engulfed her arm, the searing pain excruciating and sharp, making her scream. The creature's body convulsed against the wall, jerking with violent spasms as it dropped back its head and roared a stark, choking sound of fury. She was terrified he would throw her off and escape, but then Quinn moved behind her, laying his arm against hers. He wrapped his big hand around her fist, and with a deep, guttural snarl, he helped her drive the fiery Marker deep into the Casus's body.

Golden flames covered their arms, while Royce's body began to burn with a sizzling, molten glow, as if he were catching fire from the inside out. Gruesome, bubbling blisters spread over the surface of his skin, his body growing brighter, hurting her eyes, the thick, revolting stench of his burning flesh making her gag. Raw, seething cries tore from the Casus's open mouth, echoing off the walls, and just before he was consumed in a massive, stunning explosion, Quinn wrapped his wings around her, protecting her from the scorching heat of the flames. The force of the blast knocked them both against the opposite, concrete wall, their bodies slumping to the floor, barely conscious. Saige had no idea how much time had passed when she slowly opened her eyes, the gentle sound of Quinn's voice filling her ear as he said, "Come on, baby. We gotta get the hell out of here."

Dazed, they slowly pulled themselves to their feet, and Saige sluggishly stumbled a few steps forward. A pile of molten ash still sizzled where the Casus's body had stood, and she frowned, rubbing at her palm. "Damn it," she moaned, blowing her hair out of her eyes.

"What's wrong?" Quinn asked, his voice sharp with concern. "Are you hurt?"

"I'm just pissed that I didn't see anything when he died," she muttered, "the way that Ian did. I feel cheated!"

Coming up behind her, Quinn wrapped his arms around her body, resting his chin against the top of her head. "Do you really?" he murmured, hugging her against him. "Because I feel pretty damn lucky to be standing here holding you in my arms."

"I feel pretty damn lucky, too," she whispered, tilting her head to the side so that she could send him a crooked smile.

Turning her in his arms, he lifted his hand and tenderly touched her cheek. "The Marker definitely did its thing. Not only did it fry his ass, but your cuts are already healed." He glanced down at his arm, and there was a wealth of awe in his deep voice as he said, "Hell, my arm isn't even burned."

Grinning, she lifted the Marker and slipped it over her head. "Thank God Spark was too stupid to look for this in my boot. Though, to be honest," she added with a soft laugh, "she *was* pretty upset at the time, seeing as I'd knocked her front teeth out."

"Where to now?" he asked, and she watched with dazzled eyes as he reabsorbed his massive, beautiful black wings back into his body. "Should I go after Westmore and get the second Marker? If I'm quick, I could probably follow his men and track them to his new headquarters."

Scowling, she said, "What in God's name makes you think I'd send you after Westmore?"

He stared down at her with a strange, wondering look on his face. "I thought the Markers were the most important things to you," he explained, his voice husky and low.

"Don't be ridiculous," she muttered, hating that he could think she'd put the Markers above his life. Placing her hand against the strong, powerful beat of his heart, she said, "*You're* the most important thing to me. And right now you need some downtime before we go rushing off to face any more bad guys."

"In that case," he told her, his eyes shining in a way that she'd never seen before, melting her heart, "why don't we go find the others and get the hell out of here."

AS THEY MADE THEIR WAY up from the basement, it was clear that Westmore's men had already run from the fight. Focused on getting Saige to safety, Quinn silently took note of the strange fact that none of the bodies he'd downed on his way to her cell were where they'd fallen, as if they'd been removed…or had just gotten up and walked away. They ran into Riley and Ian on the ground floor, as the brothers were heading back into the house to search for them. The Buchanans quickly explained that Westmore's men had set the upper floors on fire, the smoke that was now billowing down the stairwells making it difficult to breathe. Together, the four of them headed for the safety of the woods, and Quinn asked the brothers if they'd seen Gregory.

"The Casus?" Ian grunted, his blue eyes still glowing with an unearthly fire, though his body had returned to its human shape. Quinn nodded, and the eldest Buchanan shook his head. "Haven't seen him. He must have snuck out the same way as the others, because we had the exits covered."

They spotted Shrader waiting just inside the surrounding line of trees, and in the next instant, the second-story windows shattered from the heat of the flames, engulfing the house in a roaring inferno.

"Is everyone out?" Quinn asked, hoping like hell that the answer was yes. The Watchman nodded, and he said, "Any trouble?"

"That's the weird thing," Shrader said, shaking his head. "I think Westmore and his men must have already been planning to ditch this place."

"According to the Casus, they were moving to a new headquarters. Seems Westmore wanted to get Saige out of Colorado, taking her someplace where we couldn't find her." He shuddered at the thought that if they'd been just a handful of minutes later, it might have been too late.

"They sure didn't put up much of a fight," Riley muttered, slipping his gun back into his shoulder holster.

"Riley's right," Ian agreed. "I think most of them took off not long after we got here."

"Westmore wasn't even here," Quinn told them, explaining how the Casus had said that he'd been called away.

Looking round at the group, Saige suddenly gripped on to his arm as she said, "Where's Jamison and the Scott brothers?"

BOTH IAN AND RILEY looked away from her, while Shrader's expression turned grim, and Saige knew something was wrong. "Oh God, what happened?"

"By the time we found him," the Watchman explained, lifting one hand to rub at the back of his neck, "he was dying. But…uh, he's going to be okay now."

"I don't understand," she whispered. "Did Kierland and Kellan take him to a hospital?"

Shrader shook his head. "No need."

"But I thought you said he was dying?" she practically screeched, wondering what in God's name the guy wasn't telling her.

"Kierland didn't have a choice," he grunted, looking uncomfortable as hell. "Not if he was going to keep the kid alive."

"A choice about what?" she demanded.

"Are you saying what I think you're saying?" Quinn rasped at her side, his dark eyes going wide with surprise.

Taking a deep breath, she said, "For the last time, will someone please tell me what is going on!"

"Kierland bit him!" Aiden and her brothers suddenly shouted in a chorus of deep male voices.

"You mean he…" Her voice trailed off, the dawning realization pouring through her system shocking her speechless. She could tell from their expressions that Kierland's "wolf" bite must have the power to change another.

She covered her face with her hands, her shoulders silently shook from the jarring force of her relief, and before she could say anything, Shrader growled, "Damn it, woman, we thought you didn't want him to die."

Swiping at the tears under her eyes, she sent the scowling Watchman a wobbly, watery smile. "I'm not upset, Aiden. I think this is…well, it's wonderful."

"It is?" Quinn grunted, eyeing her closely, as if wondering whether or not her head had been injured when Royce's body had exploded and they'd slammed into the wall.

She lifted her shoulders in a small shrug. "Jamison has always been fascinated by shape-shifter lore. Considering the alternative, I think he's going to be thrilled to find that he's now a…werewolf."

Scraping his caramel-colored hair back from his face, Shrader gave a low, ragged rumble of laughter and rolled his eyes. "He seemed pretty excited, but I figured he was just in shock."

"Did anyone find the maps or the Marker?" Ian asked, scratching his whiskered jaw as he looked round the haggard-looking group. "I know Kierland

and Kellan didn't have them when they headed back to Ravenswing with Jamison."

Everyone shook their heads, and Quinn pulled her closer to his side, saying, "We'll track down Westmore, and when we do, we'll get the Marker *and* the maps back."

"No need on the maps," McConnell suddenly uttered from behind them. As they turned around, Saige saw that Seth was offering them what looked like her old backpack.

"What the hell is this?" Quinn demanded, taking hold of the dirty pack.

"The maps," McConnell told him. "I'd like to say I was clever, but the truth is I just got lucky and took them off of one of Westmore's men as he was trying to escape. Seems he'd been working to decipher them, but I don't think he'd had any luck at it."

"Ohmygod, I can't believe you found them!" she gasped, quickly taking the bag from Quinn to make sure the maps were all inside, and nearly sagging with relief when she found that they were.

Looking uneasy, Seth rubbed at the back of his neck. "I figured it was the least I could do, after what happened today."

"This wasn't your fault," Saige told him, moving the backpack to her shoulder as she sent the soldier a soft smile. "If you hadn't called me, we never would have been able to get Jamison out of there."

"Your men okay?" Shrader asked, eyeing the Collective officer with a wary look of respect.

McConnell nodded. "Yeah, they made it out okay.

We tried to stop the fire upstairs, hoping there might be something in the house that could give us some information about Westmore, but it spread too fast. Once you guys head out, I'll put in a call to the fire department before this thing gets out of control."

"There's something that's not right," Quinn rasped. "I don't know about the rest of you, but some of the bodies I took down on my way to Saige weren't there when we came back out of the house. Whatever the hell Westmore and his men are, I'm fairly certain that it isn't human."

Scratching lazily at his chest, Shrader said, "We saw the same thing."

"I have a really bad feeling about this," Ian muttered, pushing his hands into his pockets.

"Well, whatever he is, until he's taken down, I'm going to be a wanted man," McConnell grunted. "But I'll do my best to see what else I can learn about him."

"Watch your back," Quinn said in a graveled voice, "and let us know what you find." Saige noticed that he looked a little green around the gills, but he managed to add, "And we'll do the same. Who knows, maybe we'll be able to piece this thing together."

The man who had once been their mortal enemy nodded, and Shrader rolled his eyes again. "Great," he drawled. "So are we all going to hug now or get the hell out of here?"

McConnell snickered under his breath and sent Quinn a sympathetic look. "How the hell do you live with him?"

"I don't have a choice—" Quinn sighed "—considering I can't kill him."

They were still laughing as they said goodbye to Seth and headed home, sharing their stories, while Quinn told them about how Saige had used the Marker to kill Royce. Of course, she'd then told them about how he'd helped her, unwilling to take all the credit. So much had happened, and Saige knew the next day would undoubtedly be filled with endless hours of talking and planning while they sorted through everything they had learned. There was the strange fact that Westmore's men seemed to have just gotten up and walked out of that house, when they should have been dead or seriously wounded. Then there was the worrisome fact that Gregory was still out there, eager for Buchanan blood, as well as Westmore's strange prediction of anarchy among the clans, which they still didn't understand. Had it been a lie he'd used on the Collective…or another element to this bizarre, often terrifying nightmare closing in around them? And last but not least was the issue of the second map that she needed to finish deciphering, and what they would do once they knew where to find the third Marker.

It would be a long, tiresome day, but after what they'd been through, Saige was just happy to be alive. The moment they reached Ravenswing, she checked in with Kierland, who assured her that Jamison was going to be fine. He even believed that Jamison's missing fingers would regenerate the first time he made a complete shift into the new shape of his wolf, though Kierland didn't think that would happen for at least a few weeks. In the meantime, he told her that Jamison had been sedated and just needed to rest.

By the time she and Quinn reached his rooms, Saige knew they should have been too exhausted to do anything but collapse into bed together. And yet, the instant they were alone, they stumbled into a hot, steaming shower. With glistening drops of water clinging to his dark, thick lashes, he pressed her against the warm tiles, his big hands bold and possessive as they roamed her body, leaving no part of her untouched.

"God, Saige, we're so lucky," he rasped, the thick, hot weight of his cock grinding against her belly as he threaded his hands through her damp hair, holding her face up to his. "Things could have gone so differently today," he groaned, rubbing his thumbs across the heat in her cheeks. "Promise me you won't ever put me through that kind of hell again."

"I promise," she whispered, reaching down to wrap her hands around him. He growled against her lips, then took her mouth, ravaging her with the wild, provocative demands of his kiss, until her trembling limbs could no longer hold her upright. And moments later, they tumbled into his massive bed.

THERE WAS A SOFT, hazy glow in Saige's dark blue eyes as she stared up at him—one that called to his inner beast, making Quinn want to claim her in every possible way, marking her as his own. "I don't want to scare you," he told her, "but I'm not sure how much control I have tonight."

"I like it when you lose control," she whispered, the shy, tender grin curving her siren's mouth so beautiful, it made his chest hurt. "No matter what happens, Quinn, you aren't ever going to scare me away."

He could see the primal power of her Merrick burning in her eyes, and knew it was true. She would be able to meet his dark, powerful demands, and would then make ones of her own, and he trembled at the thought. She was his perfect match, in every way, and he had no doubt that he'd spend the rest of his life wondering what he'd done to deserve her.

Needing to get his explanations out while he still could, he struggled to find his voice as he said, "I'll try to control myself, even though I know it won't be easy. When I become too much, just tell me, and I'll try harder. But you'll never have any doubt of how much I want you. Never have to doubt how I feel. You'll be the most cherished woman in the world, Saige, and I'll spend every day of my life doing everything that I can to make you happy."

"What more could I ask for?" she murmured, giving him a soft, dazzling smile.

Swallowing at the emotion in his throat, he managed to say, "Whatever you can think of, I'll do my best to give it to you."

"Speaking of giving me things, you do realize that when we have kids, they're going to be hell on wheels, don't you? Or maybe I should say *wings*," she drawled, running her hands down his back.

He snuffled a soft burst of laughter and pressed his lips to hers. "I'll give you babies, Saige. As many as you want." The idea of children had never been one he'd allowed himself to think about, and his heart almost burst with the excitement of it…with the pure, exhilarating joy of having a family of his own. "God, you make me so happy, woman."

Before she could respond, he thrust into her, too hard, too soon, but she melted around him, taking him in, and he growled low in his throat. He needed that connection to know that she was alive—that she was *his*.

She whispered his name, and he breathed in the warm, sweet scent of her body, knowing that he'd found his home. He pushed deeper, and she greedily accepted him, clutching him in a hot, silken grip, and in that moment of perfect, blinding grace, he broke open, and the words he'd locked up inside for so long came rushing out, breathless and unstoppable. "I love you," he told her, moving inside her, the tight, clench-ing hold of her body making him shudder with jaw-grinding pleasure. He pulled back his hips, then thrust back in, working himself into her deeper…and deeper, the pleasure so intense it damn near killed him. "Christ," he growled, struggling to hold himself together. "I love you so much, Saige."

Her eyes went wide, and he shook his head, realiz-ing that she'd truly never expected to hear him say those words, which made the moment all the more meaningful.

"I love you, too," she whispered, cupping the hot side of his face in her small, cool hand. Her back arched as he increased his rhythm, moving in her harder…faster, the lush, slick friction the most erotic thing he'd ever felt in his entire life, so perfect it was as if she'd been made for him. "I love you, and I want to make you happy. Whatever you want, Quinn. It's yours."

"All I want is you. *Forever*," he groaned, losing himself in the taste of her mouth. It was like sunshine. Like promises and hope, and Quinn kissed her harder…deeper, while he gathered her beneath him, driving into her so powerfully that they moved up the bed. Bracing one arm against the headboard, he growled a feral, primitive sound of hunger as she lifted her long legs around his waist, allowing him to thrust all the way inside, until she'd taken every thick, demanding inch of him. Her love poured into him through the touch of her body against his, the blinding, breathtaking emotion filling all the cold, angry wounds that had been scored into the fabric of his soul. And as the mind-shattering pleasure crashed through them, binding them together, Quinn lowered his body over hers, trapping the small, silver compass he'd placed around her neck between them…knowing they'd finally found where their hearts belonged.

* * * * *

*Be sure to read the exciting conclusion
to the Primal Instinct trilogy,*
EDGE OF DESIRE,
*in which Riley Buchanan reunites with
the one woman he's never forgotten.
And now, for a sneak preview of*
EDGE OF DESIRE,
please turn the page.

CHAPTER ONE

Some desires can be deadly....

Saturday morning

HE NEEDED A WOMAN. In the worst, possible, gut-wrenching way. And yet, none of the women Riley Buchanan passed on his way through the quaint seaside town of Purity, Washington, fit the bill. None were quite what he wanted. What he craved.

Hunching his shoulders against the blisteringly cool breeze blowing in off the Pacific, he let the salt-scented air—so different from the dry mountain winds he called home in Henning, Colorado—fill his head, and for a moment he caught a flash of scent that stabbed at his insides, striking him like a physical blow. It was familiar and yet mouthwateringly different, and he stopped in the center of the sidewalk, his narrowed eyes scanning Purity's bustling Main Street, struggling to discern its source. He stood there gripped in a knot of panic, stunned, while his chest heaved from the force of his breaths. But there was no sweet, surprising face from his past. No big, luminous eyes blinking back at him in stunned recognition. No tender mouth curved in a shy, soft-focused smile. No one that he could pick out in the chaotic swarm of townspeople that nudged his memory, taking him back to a time he'd done his best to forget.

Blowing out a rough breath, he accepted that it was just his mind playing tricks on him, which seemed to be happening more and more these days. He thought he'd shoved that period of his life into an impenetrable mental vault, locking it away forever, but the damn awakening was screwing with his sanity, making him remember things, *and people,* that were best left forgotten.

And yet, isn't she the very thing that you crave?

Irritated that he'd let his imagination get the better of him, Riley forced a wave of unwanted memories from his mind, and set off again down the crowded sidewalk, while the edgy, restless need continued to slither beneath his skin. He knew its source—knew from exactly where it sprang—but there wasn't anything he could do about it. The ancient Merrick blood within his body was coming alive inside him, and that meant only one thing:

His days were numbered.

Darkness was knocking on his door, but it wasn't his life that hung in the balance. It was his soul.

Swearing softly under his breath, Riley shoved his hands into the pockets of his jeans, while the gusting bursts of sea wind whipped his hair around his face. Despite the violent weather, Purity, Washington, was a beautiful place, caught between the rugged, majestic beauty of a towering autumn forest and a sheer rock face that looked out over the thrashing fury of the Pacific Ocean. On any other day he'd have been captivated by the town, but then this wasn't any other day. He and Kellan Scott had just arrived in Purity that morning, their purpose to retrieve the Dark Marker they believed was buried here in the sleepy little seaside community. His sister, Saige, had only just finished deciphering the coded map that gave directions to the Marker's location the day before, and Riley had immediately insisted that he be the one to go after the powerful cross. His brother and sister had argued like crazy, but in the end Riley had won with the sheer stubborn force of his will.

Spotting Kellan coming from the opposite direction, he sidestepped a group of mothers chattering around a circle of strollers and waited for the Watchman to reach him. They'd split up not long after arriving in town, Riley heading to find out what he could about the land where they believed the cross was buried, and Kellan to check the local news database to see if any strange happenings or disappearances had been reported. They were almost positive that the Casus, who had briefly held possession of the mysterious maps a few weeks before, hadn't been able to decode them. But they weren't taking any chances.

"Find anything?" he asked the Watchman as he neared.

The younger man shook his head, the sunlight glinting like copper off the deep, auburn strands of his hair, his blue-green eyes glittering with an ever-present spark of mischief. Kellan Scott was a brawny, muscular bastard, which was why he'd been sent along with Riley to find the Marker.

"What about you?" Kellan asked, while two early-twentysomethings strolled past, their bright gazes eyeing them with obvious appreciation. Kellan flashed the blonde a wicked, come-and-get-me smile before Riley glowered them both away.

"The land where Saige told us to search is owned by the same woman who owns that café we saw when we came into town, out by the cliffs. Her name's Millicent Summers," he said, when Kellan finally took his odd-colored gaze off the blonde's ass and looked back toward Riley's scowl.

"Millicent. Mmm…sounds sweet. Let's go meet her," the Watchman murmured, grinning as he waggled his brows.

"I think Millicent might be a little old for you," he groaned, trying to reroute the direction of Kellan's thoughts. The guy's mental compass seemed to be permanently pointed toward sex. Morning, noon and night.

Kellan's smile twitched at the corner as he lifted his shoulders. "Women are like wine, Ri. They only get better with age."

Shaking his head, Riley set off down the sidewalk once again, with Kellan following at his side. When a smiling brunette strolled across their path, flashing a lip-glossed smile in his direction, Riley looked away. Again. Same as he'd been doing for weeks now.

"Look, it's obvious you don't have trouble attracting women," Kellan murmured while they turned left at the next corner. "So just pick one and give the

Merrick what it needs, already. And I'm not the only one who's thinking it. Everyone back at Ravenswing is saying the same damn thing."

"It's not a case of just picking one," he ground out. "Believe it or not, Kell, some of us are actually more discerning than you."

The Watchman muttered something under his breath, raked one hand back through his hair, then sent him a look of frustrated confusion. "Honestly, man, I don't know what it is about you Buchanans. Why do you always have to make everything so bloody difficult?"

Riley grunted, knowing exactly what Kellan meant. Ian's awakening had been far from easy. But unlike his brother, who had been afraid of feeding from the woman who would soon be his wife, worried he'd take too much blood and accidentally kill her, it wasn't the feeding part of his awakening that terrified Riley. He knew, after seeing Ian and Saige go through the change, that he could take what he needed without harming the woman beneath him. But that didn't change the fact that he would still have to find a woman willing to let him sink his fangs into her throat, which was pretty damn unlikely. And then there was the issue of the Casus, who would no doubt hunt down anyone he singled out.

Not to mention, you still haven't found the one you want....

He knew that, damn it. And he also knew that he wasn't going to find her. Not when *she* was on the other side of the country, probably settled down with a brood of children and an adoring husband who worshipped her the way she'd deserved to be worshipped. Hell, even he if did find the balls to track her down, he knew damn well just how Hope Summers would react if she saw him again. He'd either get her hand across his face, or her fist in his eye, and that would be that. No more than he deserved, and no less than he expected.

Gritting his teeth, he jerked his chin toward the quaint two-story, wood-shingled café that sat up ahead, nestled between the breathtaking, fenced-off cliffs and the thick, towering forest. "That's the place up there."

Kellan read the wooden sign that swung on a post down by the road. "*Millie's.* Cute name."

Riley sent the grinning Watchman a warning scowl. "Just do me a favor and try to behave."

"I always do," Kellan drawled, scratching lazily at his sweatshirt-covered chest, where the faded remains of an AC/DC logo could just be made out.

"Like hell you do," Riley grunted, a jarring clap of thunder punctuating his words, heralding a coming storm.

Opening the door of the café, they stepped inside and whatever Kellan was saying was lost beneath the buzzing in Riley's ears as he drew in a deep breath…and damn near died. There it was again. *That scent.* Familiar, like something he'd known before…but different. Richer. Sweeter. Deeper than he remembered.

He looked, searching, trying to find the source, his

heart hammering like a freaking drum, and then the kitchen door swung open at the edge of his vision. "Hope?" he breathed out, unable to believe it could be true. It was…impossible.

As though she'd heard her name whispered on his lips, the woman now standing behind the gleaming wooden counter slowly turned his way. She blinked a pair of big, luminous, topaz-colored eyes, her chin quivering as if she'd seen a ghost. As if she couldn't believe he was standing there, in the middle of the crowded café. She opened her soft, pink mouth, and he took a step forward, accidentally bumping into another customer. She swallowed, staring…her heavy breasts rising and falling beneath a long, baggy sweater.

And then she suddenly let out a bloodcurdling scream of rage.

"What the he—"

Before Kellan could finish his startled curse, Hope Summers took aim and hit Riley smack in the center of his forehead. But it wasn't a punch she'd thrown at him. No bare-knuckled wallop or openhanded slap. No, he thought, grimacing as the hot, melting mess she'd chucked with deadly accuracy dripped into his eyes, blurring her flushed, furious expression. The woman had slammed him with warm, homemade apple pie.

And fate, it seemed, had found one last way to screw him after all.